DARK UNDERTAKINGS

Fifty-five-year-old Jim Lapsford makes an unusually healthy-looking corpse. Although a life-long devotee of vitamin pills and herbal remedies, his GP diagnoses a heart attack. Trainee undertaker Drew Slocombe isn't so sure. An ex-nurse, Drew is convinced there is enough medical evidence to merit an inquest at least. Then there's Jim's personal life: in addition to his wife, sons and a grieving terrier, Jim has left behind a series of scorned mistresses. Drew knows he's lucky to have a job, but can he really turn his back on murder? He has plenty of suspects but no proof – and Jim's cremation is just days away...

DARK UNDERTAKINGS

DARK UNDERTAKINGS

by

Rebecca Tope

Magna Large Print Books
Long Preston, North Yorkshire,
BD23 4ND, England.

British Library Cataloguing in Publication Data.

Tope, Rebecca
Dark undertakings.

A catalogue record of this book is
available from the British Library

ISBN 0-7505-1624-0

First published in Great Britain by
Judy Piatkus (Publishers) Ltd., 1999

Published in Large Print 2001 by arrangement with
Piatkus Books Ltd.

Magna Large Print is an imprint of Library Magna Books Ltd.

Printed and bound in Great Britain by
T.J. (International) Ltd., Cornwall, PL28 8RW

For my husband, Ian
My sister, Jo
And my mother

CHAPTER ONE
TUESDAY

I

Jim Lapsford made an unusually healthy-looking corpse. His hair was springy, his skin lightly tanned and unblemished, and his open eyes were clear, despite the terrible emptiness of death. Vince and Drew, undertaker's men, said nothing, but their faces made comment enough.

'He's always been so *well,*' confirmed Jim's wife, pale enough to be taken for the deceased herself. 'Hasn't seen a doctor for years and years. He used to boast about it.' Her teeth chattered with the shock, and she held a small white wriggling dog tightly to her chest. Drew glanced at the older man doubtfully and waited for him to react. Vince paused in his deft wrappings and zippings.

'Not seen a doctor?' he queried. 'I thought you said–'

'Not until last Friday – four days ago – when he called in about his knee. There wasn't even anything the matter with that.'

'But he's – satisfied – the doctor, I mean?' The need for delicacy sometimes made meaning obscure; the question, however, was too crucial to evade.

'Oh yes.' Monica Lapsford nodded emphatically, grasping at one of very few certainties. 'He said it was a classic case. Died in his sleep, of a massive heart attack. It seems he was at a dangerous age.' She paused, wistful, the fine features blank. 'Massive heart attack,' she repeated. 'He was never a smoker, you know. Kept up his vitamins. Looked after himself. He was always so *well.*'

Drew watched her face, acutely aware of her shock and distress. He had yet to feel comfortable with his role at this moment of transition from life to death.

Monica stared intently at the body of her husband, the rosy cheeks and relaxed lips, as if searching for an explanation. 'I really can't believe it,' she summarised, with a helpless finality. 'This was never going to happen to us.' In her arms, the dog whined, and strained to get to its master; the widow clutched it closer, like a child with a doll. She had a nice face, Drew observed, even when pale and pouched with shock. They must have made a good-looking couple, her and Jim, surging cheerfully through life. Until now, when everything had collapsed. Later, he was to wince at his simplistic assumptions, based on no more than the tilt of a chin.

Normally, the relatives would wait downstairs while the men performed the awkward business of removing the body, but Monica had insisted on being there. Down in the living room her two sons behaved more conventionally, sheltered from any unsavoury mysteries. Drew had seen them for only a moment, but one of the faces remained with him. The younger son, he supposed, was in his early twenties. He had been shaking, teeth chattering and hands clutched tightly together, suggesting a struggle for control. His head was held on one side, and a shoulder was raised to meet it, in a frozen flinch of pain and apprehension. Drew had seen people in shock many times before, but never quite as dramatic a case as this. The house seemed to be full of a kind of stunned horror.

They had been greeted on arrival by the family GP, Dr Lloyd, who had hurriedly introduced them to Monica and her sons, and then muttered, 'Can't see any point in a post-mortem. Obvious heart attack. Tell Daphne I'll be along tomorrow to do the papers, if it's a cremation.' Together the three men smiled reassuringly at Mrs Lapsford, and then Dr Lloyd pointed the way to the bedroom, reminding Monica as he left that she could collect the Medical Certificate for Registration any time after about eleven. 'But I'd leave all that till tomorrow, if I were you,' he added, on the doorstep. 'You'll have your hands full without that, today,' and he glanced at the closed living room door.

From a natural curiosity Drew inspected the bedroom while Vince continued with his task. It was moderately tidy, though a disorderly pile of clothes lay on a chair next to the male side of the bed. Above the chair was a bookshelf, fixed into the corner. A row of paperbacks stretched from end to end, of a uniform size and colour. Drew examined the titles with a quickly suppressed smile. On the wife's side was a wardrobe and a small chest of drawers. The top drawer was not properly closed; something made of bright red satin had been hurriedly stuffed into it.

Vince cleared his throat, and tipped his head towards the job in hand. He was growing accustomed to Drew's vacant moments, when he'd be too busy watching and thinking to get on with his work. With a little jerk, Drew's attention returned. He grinned at Vince, apologetic. He knew Vince was unhappy about the widow being present – the next part of the process could be disconcerting.

'Now, then–' Vince gave the signal and they embraced the dead man around the shoulders and knees, making it look easy. With a body not yet in full rigor, there were more pitfalls than might be imagined. Clasped under the arms, for example, it would seem to come alive, elbows flinging up and out, torso slipping horribly to the floor. In the presence of family members, this could not be allowed to happen.

Vince turned to Monica, trying to smile reassuringly in the midst of the breathless manoeuvre as they deposited the body onto the waiting stretcher. 'Not long now,' he puffed. His gaze fell on the struggling terrier, and the widow glanced down at it.

'Poor old Cassie,' she sighed. 'I don't know how she'll survive without him. She went everywhere with him. Only had eyes for Jim.'

Vince pushed out his lips in judicious sympathy. 'They say it's best if you show them just what's happened,' he said.

'Oh, I did that,' she replied dismissively. 'Didn't really have any choice. As soon as I went downstairs to the phone, she ran up and jumped onto the bed. She seemed to know something was wrong. When the doctor arrived, she was lying on Jim's chest, licking his face. It was pathetic.' Abruptly, her voice cracked, and she struggled against a flurry of tears. Funny, thought Drew, why people fight so hard not to cry. The picture of the puzzled little dog, loyally trying to revive the dead man, brought a lump to his own throat.

Lapsford now safely on the stretcher, they performed the delicate negotiation of stairs, hallway and front door, before stowing him away invisibly in the specially modified Espace. Vince took the wheel, sedately driving away from the house, leaving the stunned widow watching from behind the front-room curtains. The white dog was still in her arms, its bright black eyes following every move. Beside Vince, Drew blew out a long noisy breath.

'Would you believe that?' he burst out. 'Saw the doc about his knee for the first time in years, and then died a few days later of a heart attack. Is that weird or what?'

'No big deal,' Vince corrected him calmly. 'Happens all the time. Did I tell you about the woman – an artist, she was – who'd gone to the doctor's to ask them if they'd display some of her pictures in the waiting room, and then dropped dead in the doorway? Classic symptoms of aortic aneurism, so they signed her up, believe it or not. Said the doctor had seen her before and after death, because he was chatting to a receptionist when the woman came in.'

'Makes you wonder, doesn't it.'

Vince's broad amiable face turned for a moment to examine Drew. 'Now what might you be meaning, lad?'

'Well – about fate, I suppose. As if he brought bad luck on himself by going to the doctor after such a long time. And that doctor – seemed in a rush to leave, didn't he?'

'More like random chance,' Vince responded, 'as our Daphne would say. One of her favourite phrases, that is. Great believer in random chance is our boss lady. Still, mustn't grumble if it saves the taxpayer. Nothing people hate more than a postmortem when there's no need. Keep it simple, I say. Sid'll tell you the same thing. Nobody likes the thought of that pathologist getting his hands on you if it's not necessary.'

'Mmmm.' Drew was thoughtful. 'Did you see those books he had?'

'Books?'

'Erotic stuff. A whole shelf of it. Looked pretty well thumbed to me. Needed help to get it up, I shouldn't wonder. The wife's got something saucy in red satin, too. Hanging out of the drawer, it was. Hey! D'you think that was what killed him? Up to something strenuous with his old lady?'

Vince guffawed. 'Wouldn't be the first time,' he agreed. 'Wouldn't blame her for trying to keep it quiet, if so.'

'But he's got his jim-jams on, all nicely buttoned. Could she have seen to that?'

'Maybe the doctor lent a hand.'

Drew lapsed into another spell of thoughtfulness, and then said, 'That son – didn't he look a wreck? Must be something wrong with him, don't you think? Not quite right in the head.'

Vince nodded absently: curiosity was not one of his strong features. *Just get the job done and don't ask too many questions* was his motto. To Drew this attitude was incomprehensible: finding out about people was what drove him through life.

'Wonder what the Coroner would make of this one, if he knew?' he mused.

'He'd tell us not to waste his time. Like he did the other week when Dr James refused to sign up the woman of ninety-six because he hadn't seen her for sixteen days. You have to use your common sense. After all, this one's been seen, in a proper consultation, only last week. And who are we to say he didn't complain of chest pains then, and didn't want the wife to know?'

Drew let the matter drop. He'd only been in the job a month or so, and was slowly learning when to keep his mouth shut. He took a pad of printed forms from the dashboard in front of him. 'I'll fill in the chitty, shall I? Number twenty-four, wasn't it? Primrose Close. Eight forty, near enough.' He was also still learning his way around Bradbourne, having moved in three months earlier. He and Karen, after three years of marriage, had left the nearby city for a quieter life in a smaller town. They were banking on 'New house, new baby' being true, after many months of disappointment on that front.

Vince nodded, and ducked his head to get a fuller view of the surrounding streets. 'Nice area, this,' he remarked. 'Alicia would give her right arm – well, left hand, at least – to live here.'

Around them the land sloped away southwards towards an impressive river, curving its way protectively around two sides of the town. A row of hills enhanced the distant view to the north. Between the river and the hills, the sprawl of more recent housing estates seemed intent on bridging the gap between Bradbourne and Woodingleigh, six miles away. On old maps, Bradbourne was substantially bigger than its neighbour; now Woodingleigh had grown to city status, thanks to government intervention and the combined employment opportunities of a huge hospital and a good railway link to Bristol, while Bradbourne rested on whatever meagre laurels it may once have had.

'Watch out!' Drew gave an alarmed cry as a young couple, oblivious to everything but the fierce argument they were clearly having, stepped off the pavement without looking. The youth had spiky bleached hair; the girl was small with a look of suppressed energy. Vince swerved with a hiss of annoyance; in the back, the body shifted on its stretcher. Drew caught a clear view of both faces as the startled pair pulled back.

'Idiots,' he said.

'The girl looked familiar,' Vince commented.

'That'd look good in the papers, wouldn't it,' Drew chuckled. 'Couple killed by undertaker's vehicle. They'd think we'd done it on purpose, to get the business.'

'Shhh,' advised Vince. 'Don't even suggest it.' He drove carefully for the next few minutes, shaken by the near miss. 'I know!' he announced suddenly. 'That was Susie. Sid's girl.'

'What? His daughter? Are you sure?'

'Yeah. She comes to the Christmas party most years – as well as dropping in to see Sid now and then. Seen her loads of times. Must be having boyfriend trouble. Wonder who he is. Can't see Sid approving of someone with hair like that.'

Drew turned to catch another glimpse of the couple. The girl had started walking away, leaving the boy standing alone, a picture of desolation. 'Looks as if she's dumped him,' he remarked, with a pang of sympathy.

Sid met them in the mortuary. 'Jim Lapsford!' he said, his pale eyes bulging a little. 'My God. He's not a day over fifty-five.' He hovered watchfully as Vince motioned Drew to take the feet end of the tray. They placed it on the hydraulic lift, then slid it smoothly into the refrigerator, on a top slot. 'Stiffening up now,' observed Vince. 'Must've happened this side of midnight, by the looks of him.'

Sid felt-tipped the name on the door and rubbed his cold hands. 'Played darts with Jim many a time, in the King's Head,' he told the others, shaking his head. 'Handsome bugger – women all over him. What did for him?'

'Heart.' Vince shrugged. 'Lucky it's not Coroner's.'

Drew stood back, waiting, thinking. 'I still think it's a bit iffy,' he said. 'Signing him up without any proper proof. How does he *know?*'

'Experience,' Vince offered carelessly. 'I told you already, it'd be daft to send him for a postmortem when he can see at a glance what's happened. *And* he'd lose his cash for the papers, if it's a cremation. Man dies in his sleep – or while having it off with the missis – this sort of age, what *else* is it going to be?'

'Plus,' added Sid heavily, 'it doesn't do to question a doctor. That medical certificate is Holy Writ, and don't you forget it. That side of things is none of our business.'

'But–' Drew couldn't just let it drop. 'It's so *sloppy*. It makes nonsense of the rules.'

Sid's face darkened, and he rolled his eyes up to the ceiling. 'Now listen to me, Drew Slocombe,' he began, stabbing the air an inch from Drew's chest. 'You're new here, and you've come from a medical background, where for all I know you did postmortems for your own amusement. But this is the real world. Look at Lapsford – a drinker, womaniser, stressed out at work, I shouldn't wonder, and carrying some extra weight, on top of all that. It's a textbook case. Now leave me in peace – I've got some embalming to do.'

When he'd answered the ad for a job in an undertaker's workshop, and been selected from seven applicants, Drew had felt little emotion other than relief. Four months on income support, after leaving his last job in uncomfortable circumstances, had been a time of limbo verging on panic. Only gradually did some of the implications associated with the funeral business sink in. Karen had gone carefully at first.

'Dead bodies?' she said neutrally. He nodded his head, slightly sheepish. 'I'm not sure how I'm going to feel about that,' she went on, looking at his hands. He read her thoughts with ease. 'We'll get used to it,' he assured her. 'It's just a disposal job, when you think about it. A service. I'll be driving the hearse, carrying the coffins into church. Smart clothes. Grateful families. It's–' he paused, lost for the right word.

'Different,' she supplied bravely.

'A challenge,' he corrected.

The challenge had been there all right, but not from the corpses. He quickly came to appreciate the passivity, the sheer uncaring malleability of dead bodies. Treated with a ludicrous reverence in the presence of their families, once in the mortuary corpses became almost embarrassingly insignificant. It was an effort, sometimes, to remember that they had been living breathing people only hours before. No, Drew had no difficulty with the bodies: it was the other men who made him watch himself constantly, and resist any temptation to drop his guard.

'Drew's a funny name,' said Big George, on his second day. 'Where's that from, then?'

Drew made the mistake of a small sneer of contempt. '*An*drew, of course,' he said. From that moment on, Big George had called him *Andy*, with an air of innocent sincerity.

'Lost your last job?' Vince had queried. 'What'd you been doing?'

'Nursing,' Drew replied readily, his story well prepared. 'They cut the budget. Offered me permanent nights, but I knew I couldn't take that. Worked for an agency for a bit, but it was too insecure. Never liked it much, anyway. Thought I'd find something new right away, but it took a bit longer than that.'

'Nurse Drew,' carolled Pat, a handsome Irishman who was normally the Conductor of the funerals: the widow's darling. Too late, Drew realised that despite *Casualty*'s cast of hunky male nurses, the job had not yet achieved full credibility amongst coffin makers and pall-bearers.

Four weeks into the new job, he was slowly and painfully establishing himself as a good sport, a willing butt of jokes and teasing. He earned credit by cheerfully assisting Sid with mortuary work, putting in dentures, stitching up lips and removing pacemakers with a deftness never before witnessed by his new colleagues.

'It's going to be okay,' he told Karen. 'It's obvious that the newest and youngest one is going to get some stick.'

'Well, don't let them bully you,' she said, running her fingers lightly the wrong way along the hairs of his arm. She had found to her surprise that living with a man who worked with the dead was seriously erotic. 'As if I have to prove we're both alive,' she'd laughed. Every time she did that to his arm, he felt raw and naked: nerve endings sprang to attention in all kinds of places.

'That baby's going to be here in no time at this rate,' he'd said, pulling her to him. She was almost as tall as him, and slightly heavier. Her forebears had been Polish, and she had the shoulders and cheekbones to prove it. She made him feel safe and important and lucky.

I must have a thing about shoulders, Drew said to himself now, as he followed Vince out of the mortuary. The other man was working his muscular upper arms in dramatic circles, a habit that Drew had noticed in his first week. Vince was due to carry a coffin later that morning, and had long ago established a routine in preparation. His shoulders were naturally built for the job, although he regularly remarked that pall-bearing had further flattened them into neat shelves – 'undertaker's ledges', he'd dubbed them.

'Hey, Sid,' Vince remembered, turning back for a moment. 'We saw your Susie just now, having a right old ding-dong with some boy.'

Drew felt a moment of anxiety. Maybe the girl didn't want her father to know her business. Wasn't Vince being thoughtless? It was a generation thing, he realised. He automatically identified with the girl; Vince with her father.

'Must have been that Craig she's seeing,' shrugged Sid. 'She says she's fed up with him. Who'd be young, eh?'

Vince glanced at Drew with a smirk. 'It has its compensations, I reckon. You don't get so stiff, for a start, after doing an early removal.'

II

In Primrose Close, the news of Jim Lapsford's death was rippling outwards by fits and starts. Over half the houses were empty on a workday morning, and few of the neighbours had been alerted by the arrival of, first Dr Lloyd, then the Lapsford sons, and finally Vince and Drew. Neither had anyone witnessed the discreet and hurried removal of the body, swathed in black and smoothly rolled into the back of the undertaker's vehicle in seconds.

There had, however, been a witness to the arrival of Philip, the elder son, when he drove urgently up to the house. His mother had met him on the doorstep, flinging her arms around him as if finally rescued from some unendurable torment. This witness was Sarah Simpson from next door, who had hurried upstairs to tell Dottie, with whom she lived, that something very odd was going on in number twenty-four. The two women – respectable widows both – wondered what emergency could have assembled no fewer than four vehicles outside one house between seven and eight o'clock on a Tuesday morning. They soon came to the conclusion that something really serious had happened.

'You don't think Jim might have *died*, do you?' Dottie whispered, eyes wide. 'That did look awfully like an undertaker's vehicle, now I come to think of it.'

Sarah opened her mouth to dismiss the idea, but closed it again, the words unspoken. 'We'll have to wait till the sons have gone. Then we could pop round. If something terrible has happened, we should do what we can to help.' Small and determined, Sarah usually made the decisions for them both.

'But wouldn't there have been an ambulance? Police cars?' Dottie pursued. She peered out of the window again, over Sarah's head. Dottie was tall and tending to vagueness: she had a long face, and eyes which had somehow stretched with age, like a bloodhound's. 'When Arthur died,' she went on, 'we had the whole *panoply* of emergency services.'

'But he did fall downstairs, dear,' Sarah reminded her. 'It's different when it's natural causes.'

'How do you know?'

Sarah shrugged. 'I just pay attention, I suppose. I never understand how it is you *don't* know.'

'Well, but Jim wasn't ill. I saw him on Sunday, in the garden. Laughing and putting up that new trellis thing. The picture of health. And I saw him last night, when I was putting the milk bottle out. He waved to me, cheerful as can be. No, no. He can't possibly be dead.'

'It was probably a heart attack,' pursued Sarah, as if Dottie had never spoken. 'Isn't that what they say? Never a day's illness, and then dead in seconds.' Sarah seemed to relish the idea. 'Lovely way to go.'

Dottie shuddered. 'Not to my mind. Too much of a shock for everyone. Think of poor Monica.'

Sarah frowned repressively. 'Poor Monica has plenty of friends to see her through.'

'Like us, you mean?'

'I was thinking more of a certain gentleman friend. A certain *very attentive* gentleman friend.'

'Oh, Sarah, how could you? That's just gossip. And anyway, she works for him, if you're talking about who I think you're talking about. He probably comes round about business things.'

Sarah swept across the living room to the kitchen, where she had a large bowl of blackberries waiting to be turned into jam. 'I know what I know,' she said meaningfully.

Dottie considered letting the matter drop, then decided against it. 'Sarah, the woman's at least forty-five, not some silly young thing. I really don't think–'

'That's nonsense and you know it. She might be forty-five – more, I'd say, judging by the age of those sons of hers – but that means nothing. Goodness, Dottie, you seem to live in quite a different world from the rest of us.'

'Well, it's no business of ours. And if something's happened to Jim, then we have to be good neighbours. Offer to help. We could take the little dog for a walk – I'm fond of that little dog.'

'All right, all right. We'll go when the moment is right, as I said. Now let me get on with this jam.'

Philip and David had each entered the house in his own characteristic way. Philip, older by three years, had stood tall and stiff in the hallway, before taking a deep breath and charging up the stairs. 'Leave me with him for a few minutes,' he said, closing the bedroom door behind him. When he came out, his hand covered his mouth, and his eyes were pink. Ushered into the living room by his mother, he glanced nervously at his father's chair, and then seated himself with his back to it. 'Oh, Mum,' he said grimly.

David hadn't even waited for his mother to open the door. He had used his own key and flung through the hall and into the living room as if pursued by demons. Finding his brother ahead of him, he glared angrily, visibly suspicious. 'I came as fast as I could,' he said defensively. 'The car wouldn't start.'

Then the last vestiges of control had left him, and he began to shake. He had not been to look at his father when the undertaker's men arrived. The sight of them only increased his shivering, and he threw himself into a jerky circuit of the room. Monica watched him helplessly for a moment before following the men up to the bedroom; Philip stayed behind, attempting to ignore his brother. When the muffled thumps on the stairs announced the imminent departure of the men, David put his hands over his ears.

Monica came quickly into the room, carrying Cassie under her arm. 'I still can't believe it,' she said. 'It just isn't possible.' She dropped the dog onto the floor as if it had become suddenly offensive.

'Sit down, David,' she commanded. 'Stop pacing. I'll make us all some coffee in a minute.' David flung himself onto a black pouffe close to the television, and she had a sudden sweet vision of him seated there, aged ten, twelve, fifteen. The corners were still ragged where he'd picked at them, one edge misshapen where he'd curled a leg under himself, as he did again now, though too tall and heavy to fit properly into the old contours. Philip remained in the armchair he'd chosen; Monica sat alone, queenly on the sofa, marooned.

Her gaze rested on her husband's chair. An

expensive recliner, it seemed to be waiting for him, inviting his ghost to return and use it. A bright blue coffee mug, left from the previous evening, still sat on the table beside it, next to the pen he'd been using to do the crossword in the *Sunday Express.*

'I didn't hear him come to bed,' she said quietly. 'He must have stayed up late.'

'Finishing the crossword, I see,' observed Phil, his voice refusing to match the forced casualness of the words. He took up the paper and rested it on his lap.

'Made himself a nice hot drink, too,' said Monica, looking at the mug. 'In his favourite mug.' Without warning, a brief storm of weeping overcame her. She smeared her eyes and nose with both hands, and forced a self-mocking smile. 'Fancy crying about a cup!'

'They say it's the little things,' Philip muttered. 'Haven't you got a hanky, Mum?'

She rummaged in the pockets of her slacks, but produced nothing. 'No,' she said in a small voice. 'I think there's a box of tissues upstairs.'

'I'll get them,' said David curtly, and levered himself up. Although his voice was harsh, Monica knew he was becoming calmer. She smiled hesitantly at him as he thrust the box at her and folded himself back onto the pouffe.

'Do you think he felt ill? Had any pain? How will we ever know whether he suffered?' She poured out the unanswerable questions.

Philip shook his head slowly. 'I don't understand any of it. How the hell did he come to die?'

Monica felt something loosen inside her, in the

region of her chest. She drew an easier breath. 'I feel like one of those Russian dolls, but without any of the little ones inside,' she said.

'What?' snapped David. 'What the hell are you talking about, Mum?'

She turned her head to look at him. Her second son had the same dishevelled hair and long-fingered hands as Jim, though his other features were altogether different: eyes narrow and close together, the outer corners downward-sloping, giving him an appearance of permanent anxiety. Where Jim had been renowned for his reliable good cheer, David was never perceptibly happy. Trouble with David had been a perpetual current in the Lapsford family. He had been retrospectively diagnosed, after years of worry and hard work, as suffering from a condition labelled Attention Deficit Disorder. Jim had found it more amusing than worrying. 'Stating the obvious, if you ask me,' he'd laughed. Monica had silently wished they'd at least been able to put a name to the trouble in those early years when the boy had been so impossible. It would have stopped her feeling guilty.

More recently, David had caused a major trauma in their lives by disappearing for almost a year. Since his reappearance, he had been keen to make amends, with partial success. Monica and Philip had been pleased to see him; an angry Jim less so.

Monica sighed now and turned to her other son. 'Phil, we'll have to start phoning people. The printworks, for a start. They'll be wondering where he is by now. I think he was supposed to be paying some outside calls this morning, which explains why nobody's phoned. And one of the biddies from next door will be around in a minute. They're sure to have noticed something. Do you think you could go and tell them?'

Philip groaned. 'Don't the police usually do all this for people? It's too much, leaving everything to us. Weren't the police called, when you found him this morning?'

Monica shook her head.

'But why not?' he pursued. 'Isn't it the law, when there's a sudden death?' He looked from face to face, bewildered. Monica felt sorry for him, at the same time needing him to be strong. She never doubted she could trust him; she knew the bond between them could withstand even this catastrophe. David, on the further edge of the triangle, clasped his quivering hands into fists, the bony knuckles standing out pathetically. She closed her eyes for a moment before explaining.

'I phoned Dr Lloyd. He came right away.'

David gave a grating laugh. 'Typical! If Dad had been alive, the doctor would've taken hours.'

'If he'd been alive, I would have called an ambulance.'

'So you knew he was dead?' David said the word flatly, deliberately, refusing to skirt around it. He heard his brother inhale a small gasp of pain, and felt a mixture of impatience and satisfaction.

'Yes,' said Monica weightily, knowing it was important to emphasise this point. 'It was obvious. His mouth was hanging open, with this nasty sort of froth on his lips, and there was no breath or pulse.' The odd loosening in her chest increased. Almost forgetting her sons, she relived those moments. 'He was cold – or not so much cold as – as if he was made of clay. Sort of *dense.* It's difficult to describe.' She grimaced. 'It makes me feel so awful to think I was lying in bed with him dead beside me, and I never knew. Not until the radio turned itself on, and he never got up to bring the tea. That's when I knew something was wrong with him.' A tear gathered itself, but never fell. 'All I could think about was how Jim never got ill. He didn't have one day in bed all our married life. I was the one to get flu and backache and sprained ankles. Jim was *invincible* – that's what we used to say. But there he was, all sunk and flat somehow – not him at all any more.'

Philip shifted in the chair, his face white. 'Mum – don't–'

'It's all right, darling. I don't mind talking about it.' Philip bit his lip.

She went on, compulsively, 'And then I suppose I must have shaken him, said something. Yes, I did. I said, "Jim, are you all right?" Isn't that stupid! But you don't believe it, when it happens like that, out of the blue. I still don't. At least,' she corrected herself with an air of wonderment, 'I suppose I do, now.' She turned from one to the other, eyes wide, brows raised. 'Where was I? Have I told you what the doctor said?'

'Look, Mum–' Philip tried again. 'You really don't have to go into every detail.'

It was as if she hadn't heard him. 'In the end, I went to get a flannel, and washed his face – after I'd pushed Cassie off him and shut her in the kitchen. Poor little thing. Look at her.' She nodded towards the dog, curled in the opposite corner of the sofa, ears limp and nose on both paws, the picture of misery. 'She knows he's not coming back.'

'Rubbish,' said David. 'She's always like that when Dad goes out without her.'

'No she isn't. Not on an ordinary work day. She knows something different has happened. She watched those men carry him out, and she knew they were taking him away forever. Dogs understand more than we think.'

'Rubbish,' repeated David rudely. 'And since when have you cared about her, anyway?'

She hugged her arms around herself, and pressed back into the sofa. 'I wouldn't want her to be miserable,' she protested.

'She'll get over it.' David hadn't much liked the succession of West Highland terriers himself, and never played with the puppies when Jim periodically decided to have a go at breeding from one of the bitches.

Philip got up then from his chair, as if to confirm the end of his mother's reminiscing. He rambled aimlessly round the room, finishing at the table under the window, idly flipping through a small sheaf of letters which had come in the morning's post and been ignored.

David, however, kept his eyes on his mother's face, knowing there was more to come. Echoes of the morning's phone call thrummed between them – David's impatience at being woken up, his refusal to believe what she was saying, something hurtful lying on both of them like a heavy weight.

'You still haven't told us what the doctor said,' he reminded her.

She resumed talking, the words strung together steadily, without pause. 'He listened for a heartbeat, looked down his throat, made me roll him over so he could examine his back. He was quite thorough. Said it could only be a heart attack, very severe, probably without much pain. Asked me if I'd felt him moving about in the night.'

'And had you?' Philip looked over his shoulder at her.

Monica shook her head. 'You know how deeply I sleep. As I said, I didn't even hear him come to bed.' She looked down at her legs, curious to see them shaking. Phil came back to her and took her hands between his own.

'Please, Mum. That's enough. It must have been terrible for you.'

'Let me finish, Phil. There isn't much more, and I – well, it makes me feel better, somehow.' He dropped her hands, and returned to his chair, perching on the edge, his forearms on his legs, wearily patient.

Monica pressed on with the story she had to tell. 'He said something about a note all the local doctors had been sent from the Coroner's Office, saying to try to cut down on postmortems. There have been a few done needlessly, and it costs some enormous amount of money every time.

He was very honest with me. Said there was scarcely so much as a tiny doubt in his mind, and we could safely assume it was his heart. I'm sure he was right. What else could it be? Even if it was a stroke, that's still natural causes. What difference would it make to know for sure?' She frowned, hearing herself, and glanced quickly at David. 'It wouldn't change anything, would it? Dead is dead, whatever causes it. That's it. You know it all now.'

Philip raised his head. 'Poor Mum,' he murmured. 'It's going to take a time to get over it. You can come and stay with us for a bit. Nerina won't mind.'

'No, no, I'm all right here. For today, anyway. There's lots to do.'

David uncurled his leg, and stretched his arms over his head. 'You've certainly put us in the picture,' he said, with a jarring grin. 'Told us a lot more than we wanted to hear, to be honest. Now do I get a go?'

His mother and brother gave identical wary nods, but he needed no encouragement. 'I just thought you might wonder how it was for me, things being as they are. In case you've forgotten, the last time I saw Dad was on Friday. I'm sure he told you about it?' he demanded of Monica. She shook her head wordlessly.

'Then I'd better tell you, before Jodie does. I went to the printworks, to ask him one last time if he'd give me a job there. I'm sick of greasy car engines and their stupid owners. I told him he owed it to me. I *pleaded* with him. And you know what he did? He laughed at me. Told me, in front of everybody, that I'd make a useless printer. Told me to stick with cars and think myself lucky.'

'Oh, Davy,' said Monica sadly, 'he didn't mean it. He couldn't have given you a job, not just like that, anyway. He doesn't own the place.'

'Don't give me that,' he snarled. 'They'd have taken me on, on his recommendation. That's not the point, though, is it? The point is, how do you think I feel after *that?*'

'But you didn't kill him, did you?' said Philip, calmly. 'You've got nothing to feel guilty about.'

David stared wildly at his brother, running his fingers through his tangled hair. 'You're a fool, aren't you,' he said, in some surprise. 'You don't understand anything. Well, stick around, brother, because there's a lot more of this to come.'

'Stop it, David,' Monica said sharply. 'That's enough.'

A silence fell, broken only by the rustling of David's jerky fidgetings. Finally Monica spoke. 'I have to collect the medical certificate from the doctor, and go to the Town Hall tomorrow morning to register the death. It was a heart attack. It couldn't have been anything else. That's what the death certificate will say, and that's what we'll tell everyone.'

Philip was suddenly unsure. 'You sound as if we're keeping something secret.'

Monica banged the flat of her hand down firmly on the seat beside her. 'It's the *truth*.'

Philip sat forward again. 'I should come with you. Only–'

'Oh, that's all right,' she reassured him, 'I know how busy you are. I might ask Pauline to come, if

I feel like taking someone. There'll be plenty of other things for you two to do.'

Philip stood up again. 'I was only talking to him on Sunday,' he said wonderingly. 'He had all sorts of plans for the garden, once he'd got the new trellis the way he wanted it.'

'He was always the same in September,' said Monica. 'He had to have something to look forward to in the spring. Every year we've been here, he's started some new project in the autumn.'

David snorted, and Monica watched him carefully as he stumbled to his feet. Knowing already that the coming days would be shot through with David's tangled needs and emotions, she wondered how she would manage. But she forced herself to reassure them both as best she could, addressing the space between them from age-old habit.

'Darlings, these things happen. You know they do. And nobody ever thinks it's going to be them. I like to think he enjoyed his last day. Things were going well at work, and he saw his friends last night – at least, I suppose he did. I can't be completely sure where he went – you know how it was with us–' Delicately, she stopped. It had been an iron rule with her and Jim not to allow any of their marital idiosyncrasies to impinge on their sons. 'I think he went to see Jack – you know, from the works. He's got some new computer game, and Jim's got hooked on it. Mist-something, I think it was called. They play it together. Sounds childish to me, but then men often are.' She was prattling, trying to obliterate

David's obvious suffering, trying to make the whole event everyday, ordinary.

Philip was more than happy to take her lead. 'There is a game called Myst – with a Y. I can just see Dad getting into something like that.'

'They surf the Internet, too. He comes home with all sorts of things printed out. Houses for sale in Italy, the diseases that West Highland terriers are most prone to, obscure American politics. He loved all that.'

'I suppose it shows an enquiring mind,' Philip acknowledged. 'No harm in that.'

'Don't say that!' David stood up, and went to the door. 'Dad's dead and we sit round talking platitudes. Pretending we're a normal family. At least now some of the secrets can come out. At least with him dead, we might get to some of the *truth* at last.'

Monica's pale face turned almost green; Philip's jaw sagged in bewilderment. When the doorbell rang, all three were relieved.

III

Drew had gradually worked out the hierarchy, the jostling for position, the jobs that nobody liked, the jobs that *everybody* liked: driving the lims was popular. 'You get to hear amazing stuff,' Vince told him. 'Like a taxi driver. There's always some joker trying to keep things cheerful. The times I've wished I had a tape recorder! And they say terrible things about the person that's died. Sometimes I think God'll send a thunderbolt down, right onto the back seat. Serve them right if he did.'

Pat, as Conductor, had special status. He struck Drew as something of a prima donna, forever brushing imaginary specks from his black coat, and obsessed with timings. Many a morning he would arrive, saying, 'Traffic's bad on the dual carriage this morning. They've closed a lane to lay the new gaspipes. Better leave a good five minutes early.' Or, 'The twelve-thirty's going to be a big one – they'll hang about afterwards. That means Little George'll be late getting back with the lim, and it'll be a rush to get down to St Joseph's for the Catholic one this afternoon. Vince – you'll have to help me get them moving. Don't let them spend forever admiring the flowers.' Behind his back, Vince and the two Georges would raise their eyes to the ceiling and grin silently. For Daphne, the boss, arranged the timings with extreme care, knowing exactly what was possible; to be late was virtually unheard of.

'You know the Lapsford chap?' Drew said to Vince, over the sandwiches and coffee which comprised their lunch. They were treating themselves to a full hour's break for once, in preparation for a busy afternoon. Vince nodded, and Drew went on. 'Well, I know what Sid said, and he's probably right – but do you think anybody'd mind if I had a shufty at the body? Just as a sort of exercise? A bit of practice for when I'm covering for Sid's holidays, if you like.'

Vince shrugged. 'Can't do any harm. Just be sure not to find any knives sticking out of his back. That would cause embarrassment all round. And – well, maybe leave it until tomorrow, when Sid's out doing that ashes interment. You know what he's like about his precious mortuary. He'd think you were interfering. You're not going to leave any marks on him, are you? Not going to do your own amateur postmortem?'

Drew forced a grin. 'I was only a nurse, you know. I've never used a scalpel in my life. I know it sounds weird,' he held his hands up in surrender. 'It's just curiosity, I suppose. I've never seen anyone after dying as suddenly as this. I thought maybe it affects muscle tone and coagulation – something like that.' He hoped he sounded convincing.

Vince grimaced. 'Morbid bugger. Never had any interest in that side of it, myself. Still, takes all sorts, as I have to keep telling people when they want to know why I do this job.'

'Right,' agreed Drew vaguely. He was struggling to conceal his feelings, which were causing considerable inner turmoil. The chance to examine Lapsford's body for himself was suddenly of immense importance. Never again would he let pass something that his gut told him was wrong. Never again in his life, if he could help it, would that be allowed to happen.

IV

Dr Julian Lloyd had finished his lunch – a scotch egg, Mars bar and apple – while idly flicking through the *Independent* and ignoring the telephone which rang several times in the adjacent office. Despite its late start, his morning surgery was long since over. He had gone home again after confirming that Jim Lapsford was indeed dead, and treated himself to a breakfast of cereal and toast; he hadn't turned up at the surgery until twenty past nine, although his first appointment had been at nine o'clock. The patients had waited for him restlessly, but without overt complaint. Now he had little to do until the afternoon stint at five, apart from a handful of home visits and a brief attendance at a nursing home to administer flu vaccine.

Susie, his young receptionist, was taking phone calls and dealing with anyone who came in for prescriptions or to make appointments. She seemed to be in the grips of some sort of crisis, which he had been trying not to notice. Her eyes were red and she kept dropping things. But there was to be a baby clinic shortly and Dr Lloyd planned to be out of the way before that. Strictly an all-female affair, it made him feel decidedly surplus to requirements.

'Many takers for this evening?' he asked Susie, having folded away his paper and disposed of his apple core. 'Doesn't seem to be much going around at the moment – praise the Lord.'

'Let's see.' She ran her eye quickly down the computer screen. 'Five, so far.' She spoke in a flat tone, completely unlike her usual chirpy self.

'That's good,' he said lightly. 'I like it quiet.'

'Don't speak too soon,' she said grimly. 'Things happen.'

'Now what might *that* mean?' he twinkled at her, in a desperate effort to lift her mood. If he'd had the energy or the courage, he might have been tempted to start something with Susie: in the gloomy dash towards forty, the appeal of a girl in her early twenties was increasingly powerful, and he suspected that there would have been some serious satisfaction in a sexual liaison. Time enough yet, he told himself. That spotty boyfriend of hers could surely be readily ousted. And Susie's normal smiling manner was very appealing. Today, though, he wasn't so sure. Moodiness was unattractive, and if she couldn't leave her messy personal life at home, he was much less interested.

'It's something my dad says,' she answered him, clearly making an effort to be chatty. 'Like poor Jim Lapsford this morning – that was a thing that happened, sure enough.'

'Ah yes. Poor fellow.' The doctor's collar began to tighten and he could feel the label on his shirt chafing the back of his neck; he wriggled his shoulders uneasily.

'Poor wife, more like,' Susie corrected him. 'What a shock for her. And how funny, you seeing him only last week, about his knee. After all those years!'

'Pardon?'

'I told you at the time, don't you remember? He hadn't seen a doctor since nineteen eighty-six, when he had his vasectomy. Must be close to a record – at least amongst our patients.'

'Well, I hope nobody thinks it had anything to do with me. I didn't prescribe anything for him, did I? You know what chaos my prescriptions get into. I seem to have mislaid yet another pad, God help me.'

Susie hesitated long enough to cause him to

glance up at her. She was sitting very still, apparently debating with herself. 'Did I?' he repeated.

She shook herself, and flicked at the computer keyboard, lips pursed. 'Ummm – no. Not according to this.' Still watching her, he observed a flush on her cheeks. An inner voice reminded him that he should at least ask her if she was all right. He was her employer – her friend – and she was quite obviously in distress. But he spent all day being kind and sympathetic against his real nature: doing the same for his receptionist was just too much.

He turned away, with a fleeting laugh. 'As it happens,' he said, 'it's rather lucky. From the paperwork point of view, at least. His wife'll probably be in tomorrow for the certificate. Can you ask her if it's a cremation, and if so, I'll do the papers.'

'Lucky for you, if it is,' Susie added sharply. 'You'll get your forty-one quid. A few more like this and you'll be getting that ride-on lawnmower in time for next summer after all.'

Dr Lloyd frowned. 'Susie, you know I'm as embarrassed as anyone at the way we get that money for doing virtually nothing. But the rules are the rules, and who am I to complain?'

V

Roxanne Gibson heard the news about Jim from her sister, Pauline, who'd been one of the irritable patients at Dr Lloyd's morning surgery that morning. Pauline had overheard Susie discussing events with the District Nurse; she phoned Roxanne as soon as she got home.

'Are you sitting down, pet?' she asked.

'No,' Roxanne was instantly suspicious of the *pet.* That wasn't how Pauline usually addressed her. 'Why?'

'Because this'll come as a bit of a shock. Unless you've heard already.'

'Heard what?'

'Jim. He's had a heart attack. In the night – out like a light, apparently.'

'You're kidding me. Jim wouldn't go like that.' She spoke with confidence; her sister's words hadn't even scratched the surface of her consciousness yet. They bounced off her and floated around the caravan for a moment or two before hitting her a second time.

'You mean, he never said goodbye?' Pauline winced at her own flippancy. 'Sorry. It's true, I'm afraid. Jim Lapsford's dead. Everyone'll be talking about it by this evening. I'll have to phone Monica – she is my friend, after all. It's a wonder she hasn't been onto me already.'

Roxanne's heart was doing something strange: trying to climb out of her mouth, perhaps. 'Christ,' she said slowly. 'How do *you* know? Doesn't sound as if you had it from your *friend.*'

Pauline explained.

'But – he was here only yesterday. We – er–' She glanced at the bed, which occupied a good quarter of the available caravan space; a rumpled quilt still carried the smell and memory of Jim. 'Shit, Pauline, I don't want to hear this.'

'Yeah, well, that's life, I guess. Kicks you when you're down.'

'I'm *not* down. Or I wasn't. I'd got everything exactly as I wanted it for once. Look, I don't want to talk any more, okay? Come and see me tomorrow.'

She heard Pauline sigh. 'I'll see. I'll probably have to go and sit with Monica. It's going to be awkward, Rox. You know how things always come out when somebody dies. Why am I always caught up in the middle? My sister sleeping with my best friend's husband! She's going to kill me when she finds out.'

'Try and come, okay?' Roxanne said through gritted teeth. 'Who else am I going to talk to?'

'I will if I can. Sorry it had to be me that told you.'

'Better you than reading it in the paper.'

Roxanne pressed the 'off' button on the phone and threw it onto the padded bench running down one side of her caravan. Then she went to the open door and looked out across the fields. Dusty September hedges ringed them round, protective and concealing. Blackberries grew luscious on the brambles; hazelnuts ripened and red haws clustered. Roxanne, latterday gypsy, had turned to the rural lifestyle with enthusiasm. The soup she'd been stirring on the stove before her sister rang comprised wild mushroom and common sorrel, an experimental mixture which she'd grown to enjoy inordinately.

She stretched her bare arms out in front of her and gazed down at her skin. Jim had loved her dark colouring, the all-over swarthiness of her. Her black hair was always glossy, like an Arab's but curly, with threads of white in it. Making love with Jim had been quite something; his unconcealed enjoyment had been a real turn-on. She believed herself to be like most women – happier to arouse passion than to have it aroused in herself. For three years, she had taken delight in Jim Lapsford's uncontrolled appetite for her. Three years ago, she had walked out on Martin, her insurance salesman husband, and decamped to the caravan. On that day, her life had changed from monochrome to technicolour.

'I knew it couldn't last,' she said to herself now, as the view blurred and her nose began to run. Then a thought hit her, and she pushed a knuckle between her teeth in sudden horror. 'No,' she insisted to herself. 'No – it can't have been.' She got up and went back into the caravan, bending to a low shelf beside the little stove. A jam-jar of brownish fluid met her hand and she lifted it out. 'Best to be on the safe side,' she muttered, and took it outside, unscrewing the lid as she went. At a point in the hedge, some yards away, she poured the contents over a patch of thistles. 'Enjoy!' she murmured.

VI

Drew wheeled his bike from behind the hearse, and called a good-night to Sid and Big George, who were walking around the corner to the car park. Five o'clock, on the dot, they all downed tools for home, unless there was a rare late-afternoon cremation, which could delay them by fifteen minutes or so, though the office staff were more dilatory. This made Drew uneasy: he didn't see himself as a clock-watcher, a mere time-server. Once, he'd stayed to finish a coffin, but the unanimously critical reaction from the other men had convinced him that this was not a good idea.

He glanced in through the window of the Reception area as he mounted his bike, seeing Olga standing over the computer, apparently in the act of switching it off. Presumably she'd be going home in another few minutes. Daphne, however, could be seen stationed firmly at her desk, telephone to her ear, papers spread out in front of her. Daphne was an enigma to Drew, and he always made a point of looking for her when he passed the office, hoping to catch her in an unguarded moment. Somewhere around forty, she was obviously struggling against her body's inclination to gain weight. Her legs were short and substantial, especially below the knee, where her calves ballooned unbecomingly. Dressed in classic navy suits and white blouses, the elegance she was obviously aiming for just eluded her. Thick brown hair, beginning to acquire a frosting of silver, was cut short. The overall impression that Drew gained was of a woman in the wrong place, having to hold herself in, when the reality beneath was something much more extravagant and uncontrolled.

She'd taken on the business from her father, with no reluctance by all accounts. Her younger brother, Nigel, had made a complete escape and now lived in Vancouver with a wife and five children. Local gossip assumed the childless Daphne would eventually pass the baton to one of her Canadian nephews, and good luck to him.

As Drew had half hoped, Daphne noticed him, and raised a hand to indicate that he wait where he was. She crossed quickly to the open window. 'Do you mind hanging on a minute? Come round to the door.'

Obediently, he presented himself, and she came to meet him, holding the removal chitty he'd completed that morning. 'I just wanted you to fill me in about Lapsford.'

'Did I leave something out?' he said.

'No, I don't think so. I just wondered how it was at the house. I mean – what sort of set-up. I knew him, of course vaguely. He was well-known locally. One of the King's Head crowd. How was the wife?'

Drew paused, wondering what, exactly, she was asking him. It felt like more than a trawl for idle gossip. 'She was very shocked,' he said inadequately.

'Shocked rather than upset?'

'Well – yes, I suppose. One of the sons was in a real state. Couldn't stop shaking.'

Daphne nodded. 'I've heard that the younger one's always been a bit – odd. They've had problems with him, I think.'

Drew waited for further questions. His unease over the morning's experience had not diminished in the course of the day; if anything, he was more agitated than ever, especially now that his boss was showing this unusual interest. He could still feel the peculiar atmosphere of the house, the intensity of the shock, which had something else mixed with it: a horror that somehow suggested more than mere surprise.

'Did you see the doctor?' Daphne continued. 'I gather he's going to sign him up.'

'He let us in, then scooted off about two minutes later. He saw the chap last week apparently, about a stiff knee. The wife said he was certain that it was a heart attack.'

Daphne smiled the smile of a conspirator, mischief and relief evident in equal measure. 'He's a rascal, isn't he. But nobody likes a post-mortem. Did she say when she'd go and register?'

Drew shook his head. 'She didn't seem up to it today.' He stopped wanting to say more, but wary of her reaction. There was a subtext here that he didn't understand. Even if it was only a habitual dislike of involving the Coroner and the police, he would have to tread carefully. Any hint of disapproval at the doctor's decision would be misguided, he realised. His job was to follow instructions and keep the customers happy, to look smart and behave tactfully, even when he was boiling with frustration inside.

'She'll be along tomorrow, I imagine. We're not sure it's a cremation, of course. George tells me we did another Lapsford funeral, about twenty years ago. He never forgets a name. He thinks it might have been this one's aunt. I'll get Olga to look it up tomorrow.'

Bradbourne was ill supplied with grave spaces. The swing to cremation had been both cause and effect of the shortage, to the point where it had become a general assumption that cremation was the preferred option. Some people had family graves in the small cemetery; others had firm objections to cremation and insisted on a burial space being found for them; but the proportion of cremations to burials currently stood at just under nine to one. The doctors rejoiced in this. It was a rare week that passed without the perk of the forty-one pounds' fee for the extra paperwork coming their way.

'I'll be getting off, then,' said Drew, awkwardly.

'Yes, off you go. Thanks, Drew.' She released him with a nod. He mounted his bike, and headed for home.

'Good day?' Karen asked him, when she got in at six. He had one of his home-made pizzas ready to go under the grill, and the breakfast plates and mugs all washed up; normally Karen arrived home before him, but this was the first full week of the new autumn term and she'd stayed late to a staff meeting. She was in her first few weeks at a popular junior school on the edge of town, teaching year five. Previously she'd worked in a much more urban school, and the change was proving very refreshing.

'Confusing,' Drew said, in answer to her question.

Karen raised her eyebrows. 'Let me go and change,' she said. 'Then you can tell me.'

Since he'd found a job, they'd allowed themselves a larger alcohol budget. He got two bottles of French beer out of the fridge.

'Go on, then,' she prompted, perching on a kitchen stool. 'What was confusing?'

Drew began warily. Today was Day Twenty-Five in Karen's menstrual cycle, and tension was rising. As it happened, it was also Month Twenty-Five of their attempts to start a baby. The baby should have been at least a year old by now. They'd made a Plan, and its failure to achieve reality was a perpetual subtext to their lives.

'Well,' he said, drinking beer straight from the bottle, 'you know about doctors having to certify a death?'

'Sort of.'

'They have to put the cause of death, for the Death Certificate. That it's due to natural causes. If they're not sure, then there's a postmortem.'

'Obviously.'

'We had a chap this morning, Jim Lapsford, his name was. Vince and I went to remove him. His wife found him dead in bed beside her. She kept saying he'd been really well, but the doctor insisted it was a heart attack.'

'Sounds straightforward to me. Isn't that what happens with heart attacks? That they're out of the blue? What did Vince say?'

'Seemed to think it was all quite normal.'

'What else could it have been?'

'Nothing, I suppose. But–'

'You're not seriously suggesting it *wasn't* natural causes? Surely if it had been poison or something, he'd have been sick, or shown some other signs? And you'd have noticed if he'd been strangled or shot or stabbed.'

'The point is, it isn't meant to be our responsibility to look out for these things.'

'I know that.' He could see she was losing patience; she began to speak to him as if he were a child. 'But the doctor had been, hadn't he? He must have looked for anything suspicious. I don't understand your problem.' Not until he had been silent for a good two minutes did she remember. 'Oh, hell, Drew. Not that again.'

Drew sighed. 'It seems as if it might be.'

'I *told* you. I *said* this would happen, if you took this job. It was bound to. People die in all sorts of bizarre ways – you know that. You can't save them, or see that perfect justice is always done. You have to take the doctor's word for it. What else can you possibly do?'

'I can't explain it rationally. But I am sure there's something wrong here. Little things. He was too peaceful, as if he'd gone into some sort of coma first. Normally cardiac victims get some sort of prior warning. And – oh, it's nothing I can really describe. But the atmosphere at the house, one of the sons looking as if he was being eaten up with guilt – it might sound crazy, but I'm absolutely sure Jim Lapsford was murdered. And I want to do everything I can to prove it.' He stared at her, hearing his own words. He'd finally said it. *Jim Lapsford was murdered.* The thought settled something inside him. *Yes,* he decided. *That's the truth of the matter.*

'You'll lose your job,' she said flatly. 'They're not going to stand for this sort of nonsense.'

'I lost my job before for not doing anything. Funny old world.'

'You lost your last job because there were budget cuts.'

'But why was it *me?* Because there was always that cloud over me, that's why. If I'd been more careful, that child wouldn't have died. Everybody knew that. It suited them to get shot of me.'

'And nothing's ever going to convince you otherwise. Okay, I know. So what are you going to do about this heart-attack chap?'

'Well, first thing tomorrow, I'm going to examine the body. Sid'll be out, so I'll have free rein. After that, I'm going to think of a reason to go back to the house – or find somebody who knew him well. I'm going to need some help. Are you up for it?'

'Good God! What on earth did you have in mind? I've never envisaged myself as a private detective.'

'It's always handy to have a woman's angle.' He went to her, and pulled her to him in a long hug. 'I think we'll make a great team,' he mumbled into her hair. Karen was the best thing that had ever happened to him, and he told her so repeatedly. She was braver, stronger, more quick-witted than he was. He had no idea what she saw in him.

Finally he released her, and went back to the cooker. He slid the pizza under the grill. 'Do you want chips with this?'

'Is there any salad? Or anything for afters?'

'I can do a salad,' he offered, bending into the bottom of the fridge. 'Afters is an apple or a banana. What did you have for lunch?'

'Egg mayonnaise and a Danish. No chips then.' Karen sighed. 'Although I *am* hungry...'

'I'm not.' He cut up two tomatoes and a rump of cucumber and shredded a Little Gem lettuce, humming slightly all the while. He could feel her watching him.

'I haven't agreed to be your partner in crime,' she said. 'I don't see how we're going to find the time, anyway. It's term time, remember.'

'And I never asked you how *your* day went!' he remembered. 'Sorry.'

'It went as it always does. I'm getting to like my new class, but they haven't decided whether they like me yet. That's about it.'

'They'll like you,' he said confidently. 'Now, if I'm right, and Jim Lapsford was murdered, the person who did it will be thinking there's not a chance in the world of being caught now. And if I'm really casual, it should be easy to get them all talking. I might not need you, except to help me think things through.'

'I still think you're crazy–'

'You see – we'll have it cracked by the weekend.'

'I wonder.' She grinned suddenly. 'Drew. Let's have chips, just a few. Throw caution to the winds. There're some in the freezer. I'll put the fryer on. And you can tell me what else you did today.'

'That won't take long. I lined two coffins, took some papers over to the crem, delivered some ashes to an old woman in a house full of cats – and that's about it.'

'And fetched a dead body from – where did this chap live?'

'Primrose Close. It's off Churchill Avenue, on the edge of the new Ravens Hill estate.'

'Nice. What did he do?'

'Printer, apparently. Everybody knew him.'

'Everybody knows everybody in Bradbourne.

Do you know – four of the kids in my new class are first cousins, from four different families! Isn't that amazing, in this day and age?'

'Amazing,' agreed Drew. 'Right – chips in, salad's ready. Another beer?'

VII

Sid and Big George drove home together, as usual: Sid's wife, Brenda, took the family car for her job as a switchboard operator at the hospital, ten miles away. When Big George had realised that Sid waited forlornly each evening for the unreliable bus, he offered him a regular lift. 'What say you give me half what the bus fare would have been?' he proposed, and Sid had no choice but to accept, knowing that he was more than paying the cost of George's petrol.

'Quiet spell's going on a bit,' George remarked. 'Only three for this week, and nothing at all booked in for next.'

'Lapsford'll go Monday or Tuesday,' Sid predicted. 'Might even be Friday.'

'Doubt it. Big do, that'll be. They'll want time for people to sort themselves out. Cremation, I expect.'

'Bound to be. I remember him saying, once, how he'd a horror of burial. All that guff about being buried alive. Been reading too much Stephen King, I told him.'

'You knew him well, then?'

'Only from the King's Head. He was there most Fridays. Always making a noise about something.'

'Sounds as if you didn't think much of him.' George glanced at his passenger. 'Not your kind of bloke?'

Sid frowned. 'I never said that. I'd no quarrel with him. It's his wife that had most reason to fall out with him, the way I hear it.'

'How's that then?'

'Well, he wasn't the most faithful husband in town, let's put it that way.'

'Isn't she the woman at the dentist – Proctor's, I mean? The one who makes the appointments and everything? I was there a couple of weeks ago, and it seemed to me they were very cosy together.'

'What – Monica Lapsford and Gerald Proctor?' Sid blew out his cheeks at this news. 'I never heard anything about that.'

'Bet you it's true, though,' chuckled George. 'I've got a nose for that sort of thing.'

'Well, you ought to have sniffed out Jim, then. Half the women in town will be wanting to come along to that funeral, for old time's sake. Even that nice little Lorraine Dunlop – d'you know her?' George shook his head. 'Word has it she's his latest bit of fluff. Stupid girl ought to know better. Got a kiddie, and a decent chap for a husband – can't think what she's playing at.'

'Sounds to me as if he's broken a few hearts in his time. Could be some'll turn up to celebrate, rather than grieve for him,' George commented.

'You can say that again,' Sid confirmed emphatically. 'And if you're right about Monica, they were both as bad as each other. What a world! Makes you sick, doesn't it?'

George grunted non-committally, and turned the corner into the road he shared with Sid. 'Here we are then, sir,' he said. 'Same time tomorrow.'

'See you, and thanks,' said Sid, as he always did. His house stood close to the road, a minimal patch of weedy lawn the only buffer between pavement and front door. Brenda wouldn't be home yet. Just the cat there to welcome him, and that was only because it knew he'd feed it.

With a sigh, he let himself in, and went through to the kitchen. They'd come here to live three years ago, when Susie, their only child, left home and got herself a little flat. Middle age seemed to last a long time, with retirement still nearly four years away, and every day the same jumble of bodies and mourners and self-important vicars. In an automatic routine, he switched on the television and the electric kettle, went upstairs to change his clothes, came down again to make tea, and picked up the telephone.

It rang six times – considerably more than was comfortable. 'Where were you?' he said, anxiously. The answer was evidently enough to soothe him. 'How are you, lovey?' he continued. 'Two of the chaps said they saw you fighting with Craig in the street. That isn't on, sweetheart, now is it? I don't want to hear stories like that about you... No, I'm not nagging you. Just worried, that's all. Will I come and see you this evening? Cheer you up?... You know it isn't any trouble. It's always good to see you. You know how bleak it is here without you... Well, if you're sure. You will come to me if there's anything bothering you, won't you? That's what your dear ol' dad's for, you know. All right... Yes... Night, night, then, lovey.'

Brenda's return from work went almost unnoticed. 'Good day?' they asked each other dutifully, without listening for an answer. She set a ready meal circling in the microwave, then changed into a shapeless 'house-dress' before bringing in their plates and flopping in front of the television. 'You going out?' she asked him.

'Not tonight.'

'Pity. There's nothing much on telly this evening.'

'I could do that light fitting in the roof,' he said, after a pause. 'Won't take long, though. Have to be an early night.'

Brenda sighed. 'Yeah,' she said.

VIII

At six, Daphne was still at work. Olga had left forty minutes ago, and the place was in silence. Daphne's desk was littered with papers connected with her work life and personal life in equal measure: as time went on, she found she made less and less distinction between home and work. Since Kevin had left her, and her Cairn terrier had died, there was little to lure her home at night. She'd been to the dog rescue, hoping to find a replacement for Sammy, but came away empty-handed.

There were, in any case, jobs to be done, which needed the peace of an empty office. During the day, there were constant phone calls, usually requiring instant action or decision. It was often difficult to speak to ministers – and even customers – in office hours, and Tuesday evening was a favourite time for her to phone people to tell them the ashes of their departed relative were now ready for collection. It was a growing tendency for people to retrieve the cremated remains, in the brown plastic jars provided, and take them to a favoured spot for scattering. Personally, Daphne found it unappealing, but she took care to avoid making any comment.

These phone calls could last nearly an hour, as she encouraged the bereaved person to give feedback on the funeral, and go on to talk about how the death had happened, what they felt about it. She had a natural skill, perhaps bred from the generations of undertakers before her, of listening quietly, and drawing people out. Aware of her strange status in the small town, she knew that people liked her, trusted her, but would seldom seek her out for companionship. Daphne Plant was recognised everywhere she went, but she had very few close friends.

This was proving to be a quiet September so far. Although in these days of overheated nursing homes and medical technology there were no reliable seasonal fluctuations in the death rate, the autumn was still a time when, traditionally, thoughts turned to endings. All around, the leaves wither and drop; grass turns brown and rank; dead wood is gathered in for fuel. With the dying summer, old people could lose hope, or the will to live. With the cleansing bonfires and pruning of November, the chance of increased activity at the undertaker's was high.

In preparation for this, Daphne was arranging for new stationery to be printed, a new consignment of coffins to be ordered in, and repairs to the flower racks to be put in motion. In the mortuary, the triple-tiered fridges, with space for six corpses, would have to last at least another year, probably two. Somehow Sid always managed to avoid any excessive overflow.

There was space for another three bodies in the viewing chapel, and two or three in the side room where finished coffins were kept. Bradbourne had a population of 25,000, which meant that more than six deaths in a week was unusual. But Daphne, with her ear constantly alert for trends, knew that a third fridge, with three more spaces, would be an asset. There were two new blocks of sheltered housing going up to the north of the town, as well as a sizeable housing development under construction, with a mix of starter homes, flats and medium-sized houses. The demographic reality was that a number of them would be bought by retired couples, in the declining years of their lives.

Finally, as the sky grew dark outside, Daphne made her last tour of inspection before going home. She went into the chapel, checking that the flowers would do for another day or two, turning off any lights, flicking at a newly-formed cobweb in a high corner. Then into the mortuary, always kept neat and clean, the floor scrubbed and the embalming equipment stored tidily next to the sink. Glancing at the labels on the doors, she remembered Jim Lapsford, and supposed that the wife would be in the next day.

Daphne knew Jim, of course. They had been at Chamber of Commerce meetings together, had rubbed shoulders at various parties and lunches, passed each other in pubs and car parks. She knew something about him, too: his reputation as a womaniser, the jokes that no wife or daughter was safe with him. The insatiable Lapsford had even flirted with her; she had wondered, only a few weeks ago, what made him do it. Although an apparently cheerful man, always ready with a joke, the look in his eye that evening, when she had found herself the object of his predation, had not been a contented one. There had been a need, a pleading, which had made her instinctively wary. When it came to relationships, Daphne was the needy one.

The body was on the top rack, at eye level, and the tray would not roll out easily for a casual look. Daphne was not a tall woman, and she had to stand on tiptoe to get any kind of view of his face. She almost gave up the idea, but something prompted her to persist. She reached in, pulled the white plastic from around his head and craned her neck to look at him. His cheeks were full, mottling slightly as the blood collected around his jawbone and ears. The hair was strong, slightly wavy, giving him a look of vigour, even in death. He wore bright blue pyjamas, old-fashioned and rather endearing. Eyes half-closed, lips parted to show the inside of his mouth, he was exactly as she remembered him. Funny how heart-attack victims so often seemed to glow with health.

In her early years in the job, Daphne had fantasised about Fate, about how there seemed sometimes to be a sort of cosmic mistake. She imagined the great loom of destiny, endlessly woven and patterned, disrupted by a sudden breaking of thread from some accident or carelessness in the weaving. The person who was controlled by that thread would abruptly die, perhaps while crossing the street, or making love. Heart failure, aneurism, stroke. In the old days, they'd called it a 'seizure'. It always came out of the blue, leaving shockwaves that could last for years.

The inside of Jim Lapsford's gaping mouth looked an unusually bright pink, but Daphne did not inspect it any closer. Her job did not involve any medical investigation; besides, a second doctor would have to come along in a day or so, to endorse Julian Lloyd's findings. In the process, the only really important fact had already been established – that Lapsford was dead, and could be safely cremated.

And so she locked all the doors, turned out all the lights, went out to the back yard where her neat new Ford Fiesta waited for her, and finally went home, secure in the knowledge that another day had passed without incident.

IX

In Primrose Close, lights were on behind closed curtains, and front driveways were filled with cars. Monica Lapsford had eaten a small supper of scrambled egg, and was now sipping coffee in the living room. She had come a long way since waking that morning. She was now firmly in the realm of widowhood, her feet on a new path, the past and future all mixed up and merged together on this momentous day when everything had changed.

The scrambled egg had been a mistake, though she had chosen it with a powerful instinct. It had given rise to a sweet recollection: twenty-seven years ago, when her contractions had begun, proclaiming the imminent birth of Philip, Jim had sat with her in the kitchen, making her eat scrambled eggs for strength. He had been calm and wonderfully kind. They'd lived in a village not too far away, with a now long-vanished maternity hospital only a mile distant. They had walked and talked, laughed and groaned, anticipating the baby but refusing to be rushed into the clinical clatter of routine hospital procedures. They had even debated whether to stay put, and demand that a midwife come to them. The scrambled-egg story had been told many times subsequently.

How brave we were, marvelled Monica now. *And what good parents we made to those boys when they were small.* David had caused them sleepless nights and a lot of agonising, but they had stuck with it, supporting him faithfully, fighting his corner against teachers and doctors. They had been united in their determination to bring the boy through whatever tribulations might assault him. In that respect, they'd done a fair job.

Once started, the memories of Jim at his best were impossible to suppress. Jim it was who got up and made tea every morning, collecting the early post and bringing it to Monica, dozing lazily. At the same time as he performed small uxorious kindnesses, he had hinted that there was plenty of space in the marriage once the boys had moved out. They ought not to cling too tightly to each other. They would go out separately, as well as together, and not restrict each other's movements. What Monica thought about this had been irrelevant – Jim had increasingly followed his own prescription, to the point when he was out four or five evenings a week, and a large part of the weekend as well. Monica had learned with time not to ask any questions about where he had been.

She had gradually come to the conclusion that Jim had a tottie – a floozie – a bit on the side, either already in existence or very much in mind. But she had not voiced her assumption. Carefully, she had smiled and nodded, and talked vaguely about evening classes and jaunts with women friends. Then she had signed up for electrolysis to zap the wiry new hairs on her chin, for Weightwatchers, for a year's subscription at a local gym. Within six months, she was so in love with her trim new self that Jim's activities caused her no more than fleeting worries.

Jim had been lavish in his admiration, stressing how young and lovely she looked. For a while he had come home a bit earlier from the King's Head and introduced her to one or two new bed-time intimacies, gleaned, she assumed, from his growing collection of erotic novels. He bought glamorous underwear and scented candles:

'Takes me back to when I first married you,' he said. 'You'll have all the blokes after you, at this rate.' Monica had merely smiled, non-committal, and kept her own counsel. When he began to read passages from the paperbacks out to her, she had taken a deep breath and endured it. If he needed that sort of thing in order to sustain his virility, she supposed she would have to indulge him.

At our age, Monica had thought, *it's pretty good that we do it at all.* She had friends who hadn't had sex with their husbands for a decade or more, but she and Jim both seemed to become anxious if they went for more than a week between encounters. Monica supposed that, as there was so little else that they did together, this was all they had to keep the marriage even partially alive. The first time that Jim had failed to perform had been a year ago, and Monica had unthinkingly accused him of spending so much time with his girlfriend that he hadn't anything left for her. He had laughed it off, blamed the beer he'd been drinking, but Monica had cursed herself, noting the panic in his eyes.

Now, holding the coffee mug between her hands, she tried to imagine the solitary bed, night after lonely night. Never again to feel Jim's warm skin, generously coated with dark hair; never to share all those silly little private moments. She had heard widows speak of 'amputation', losing half of themselves, never recovering from the dreadful loss. Well, it wasn't going to be like that for her. Jim had given shape to her life; he had been a kind of mirror, reflecting her wifely persona back at herself – but he hadn't been *part* of her. She still felt whole without him. And having the bed to herself might be pleasant, in a way. She could get cosy brushed cotton sheets, which Jim hated. Maybe even have a duvet, which Jim had always vetoed as newfangled and insubstantial.

But meanwhile, there was all the paraphernalia of death to be endured. Today there had only been a trickle of visitors – by the end of the week it would probably be a deluge. She should tidy up, buy extra coffee and biscuits and milk, prepare polite platitudes. When Jodie from the printworks had come to the door, while the boys were still here, Monica had been at a total loss as to how to tell her the news. Even responding to Pauline's avalanche of concern had been an ordeal. She had cut her friend short, and told her quite mendaciously that she had both her sons with her, throwing her the consolation prize of coming along to help arrange the funeral the next morning.

Tomorrow she had to knuckle down to business. Collect the certificate from Dr Lloyd; then to the Registrar; then to the undertaker. She ought to call in at the printworks, too, and commiserate properly with Jim's workmates – his second family. Try to be generous in allowing them to miss him at least as much as she herself did.

When the doorbell rang, Monica jumped a little, and then sighed, putting down the empty mug and getting tiredly to her feet. She had a good idea who it would be, an idea which proved correct when she opened the door. Dottie and Sarah from next door stood side by side, shoulder to ribcage, beaming sympathetic smiles on her. 'Come in,' she invited limply. They were both widows, after all. They must have some inkling of how chaotic it was.

'It was very good of your Philip to come and tell us the news this morning,' Sarah began. 'He said he thought you wouldn't mind us popping round this evening. We'll only stay a minute, of course.'

Both women were agog, darting little glances around the room, as if searching for signs of disturbance. Perhaps death somehow left its trace, not just in the air, but visibly. Or perhaps, thought Monica, they were looking for evidence that she had already begun to dispose of Jim's possessions.

'How are you managing?' asked Sarah. 'We'll be happy, of course, to do anything we can to help. We thought on the day of the funeral, we could keep an eye on the house for you. You do hear terrible stories about burglaries...'

'That's very kind. I haven't really given much thought to the funeral yet. It seems an awful hurdle to have to face at the moment.'

'Oh, but it can help *tremendously,*' said Dottie. 'I found it was the funeral that kept me going. Everybody was so kind, and it was exactly as Arthur said he wanted. A really good send-off.'

'I don't think Jim set much store by funerals,' said Monica, thoughtfully. 'I can't remember a single instance where we talked about it, except that he wanted to be cremated. It's just a disposal matter, really, isn't it? Seems to me rather a lot of fuss and bother.'

'Oh, *no,* dear,' Dottie corrected. 'It's so important to have a ceremony of some kind, to mark the passing. I've always thought so. I hate these modern cremations – so quick and bare. You mustn't let them hurry you.'

'I'm afraid it'll be very simple.' Monica refused to sound apologetic.

'But Jim had so many friends,' Sarah reminded her. 'They'll all want to pay their respects, see him on his way.'

Funny, thought Monica, *how we use the language of travel – of going on a journey from one place to another.* Though, in a sense, that was exactly what had happened. Even if the other realm was non-existence, total annihilation (as she strongly suspected was the case), the dead did make a kind of transit. The idea expanded, took on meaning, as she considered it. The Ferryman with his penny fee; the Styx and the great dog guarding it; the long tunnel that people claimed to go down when they momentarily died on operating tables, the one with the bright light at the end of it. What was happening to Jim? Where had he gone? Was he in some freezer, or lying on a cold slab? She had no idea what might go on in the murky mysterious backrooms of an undertaker's premises.

'But before the funeral,' Sarah pursued, 'there must be something we can do. All those jobs – I remember it clearly. Flowers, newspaper notices, telling everybody ... it just goes on and on.'

Monica sighed, feeling overburdened. 'I think

it'll all go smoothly,' she said. 'And the boys will be a great support, of course.'

'Of course,' agreed Dottie, directing a look at Sarah. 'You're very lucky in your boys.'

'And you've got a lot of friends, I know,' added Sarah. 'At times like this, friends are so precious.'

'Well, thank you very much for popping in,' said Monica. 'It was really kind of you.' She was saved from further insincerities by the warbling of the telephone. She smiled and raised her hand in farewell before moving to the phone. 'Hello,' was all her neighbours heard her say, before they were forced to retreat and close the door behind them.

'You've heard then?' Monica pursued, after they'd gone. 'Yes, it's been a long day... No, don't come round tonight. It wouldn't be right... Tomorrow – I'll phone you tomorrow... I know you do, but you shouldn't be saying it now. Night-night.'

She went upstairs, although it was still too early to try to sleep. The bed hadn't been made since Jim had been lifted professionally from amongst the tangled sheets; she'd have to change it. Funny how she hadn't thought of that before now. How could she possibly sleep on sheets that had housed a dead body? And yet they held the last impression of Jim. The last traces. Once those sheets were washed and put away, there'd be nothing left of his final hours.

Slowly, Monica lay down in Jim's place, on his side of the bed, and tried to capture a sense of him. His smell was faintly there, the pillow indented by his head. Something slightly abrasive rubbed her cheek, and she sat up to look. There was a dried stain, greenish-brown, a few inches long, on the pillow. It must have dribbled from Jim's dead mouth; she rubbed her cheek fiercely, disgusted at the thought. She picked up the pillow and quickly stripped the case from it, trying not to look at the stain. But as she threw it into the washing basket, it stared up at her. There were flecks of something brownish sticking to the cotton, amongst the dried crust. Had he actually been sick, she wondered?

Taking a deep breath, she went back and pulled the sheets off the bed. No place for sentiment now. Clean sheets; blankets tucked well in. If she was to sleep at all tonight, she would need to be comfortable. After all, tomorrow would be a busy day.

CHAPTER TWO
WEDNESDAY

I

In the morning, Monica woke to a disturbing noise. Downstairs, shut in the kitchen, the dog was squeaking, as if it wanted to go out. Before she could gather her wits, she was stumbling downstairs to see to it. She had no real feelings of affection towards Cassie; soon, she would have to make a decision about the animal's future. For now, she just prayed it would keep quiet and out of her way.

'What's the matter?' she demanded, blearily searching out the little white body. The dog was under the table, shivering, a pool of vomit a little way away. 'Oh, no.' She opened the back door and scooted the dog out with one bare foot. 'Get out, will you!' she said.

Averting her face, she fetched the mop bucket, and clumsily removed the offending sick. *Darn dog,* she thought. Whatever next? She shook out a double-page of last week's local paper and trod it down delicately, to soak up any residual dampness. By the time she'd got dressed, it could be thrown away.

By half past nine, she had pulled herself together enough to go along to the Registrar, via the doctor's surgery, where she collected Dr Lloyd's certificate from Susie on Reception. Susie smiled at her kindly, meeting her gaze full on. 'I am so sorry, Mrs Lapsford, at your sad loss.' She had been on a one-day training course about Patient Relations, and had been advised to confront death and terminal illness calmly but honestly. *Avoidance helps no one,* they had said.

Monica was surprised. She hadn't expected any recognition or acknowledgement, and the near-intimacy of Susie's words felt warm and consoling. 'Thank you,' she said. 'That's really nice of you.' The girl struck her as pale; her smile contained pain, which surely couldn't all be for Monica's plight.

'Doctor Lloyd asked me to say that he'd be very happy to talk to you if you feel you need him,' Susie continued. 'You know – if you have trouble sleeping or anything. It must have been an awful shock for you.' She paused, and swallowed. 'And – he wondered whether it's to be a cremation?'

'Yes, it was a shock,' Monica agreed. 'And yes, it will be a cremation. Tell him I'll be fine once all this business is over with.' She held up the squarish brown envelope.

Susie nodded wearily. 'I know. There's so much to do when somebody dies. But they say it's good for you. Helps to keep you going.'

Monica gave an impatient shrug. 'Just a lot of bureaucratic nonsense, more like. But thank you for being kind. It does make a difference.' And she left.

The Registrar was a woman with a severe hairstyle, heavy spectacles and a brisk manner. Monica had been first in the queue, waiting outside for the door to open at ten, but despite this, she had been kept waiting in an anteroom for almost ten minutes, while a disorganised minion tried to ascertain her business. By that time, three more people had appeared, glowing with pride and happiness, intent on registering their babies' births. They made Monica feel uncomfortable.

'Let me see now,' said Ms Registrar, opening the brown envelope. 'Oh, dear – so young. Do you know, this is the fourth man in his middle years to go like this since Easter?'

She shook her head, more disapproving than sorrowful. Monica guessed that she was about Jim's age herself. Anyway, the fact that Jim was not unusual was faintly reassuring. 'Were they all heart attacks?' she asked.

'I think so. Yes,' mumbled the woman, reading the certificate carefully. For a long minute, she scrutinised the document in silence, much to Monica's irritation. Then she sucked her teeth, and tapped her fountain pen on the edge of the desk. Outside the door, the wail of a baby came loud and clear: Monica wanted to point out the existence of the queue, but suspected that this would only have a delaying effect.

'Did your husband have any history of heart trouble?' the woman asked. 'Or did this come right out of the blue?'

'It was very unexpected. But then heart attacks are, aren't they.'

'You have no reason at all to doubt this diagnosis?'

'None at all. Jim was lying in bed beside me. His heart just failed. A nice way to go, some might say.'

'But not you?'

'I don't know. I suppose there isn't really any good way to die – not at that age.'

'Well, I'm not sure I can accept this at face value.'

'What do you mean?'

'We can't know for certain what the cause of death was. Not without a postmortem.'

Monica sat back in her chair, stunned. 'But – but isn't it too late for that?'

'Not at all. Why do you say that?'

'Oh – embalming, that sort of thing...'

'They're not allowed to touch him until I issue my certificate. It wouldn't even cause a delay to the funeral. No need for you to worry at all.'

'So, what are you going to do?'

'Firstly, I'll ring the doctor. I'll do it now, while you're here, and then take it from there.' The woman smiled, for the first time, and Monica tried to relax as the baby's howls grew louder outside.

Mercifully, Dr Lloyd was still at the surgery. 'This Mr Lapsford,' the Registrar said, 'you've put "myocardial infarction". How certain are you about that?' She listened, jotted a few words on a pad. 'Right ... right. Yes, I know. But that's not my problem. Well, I suppose that's true.' She laughed briefly. 'All right then. Sorry to disturb you. Goodbye.'

'Well, he's convinced me,' she told Monica. 'It *is* my job, you know, to be sure.'

'Of course.' *Sure of what?* Monica wondered. That she hadn't somehow murdered the man in his bed? For a moment, she half-wished there could be a postmortem, to settle the whole business once and for all.

But she had no time for doubts. Questions about dates, names, National Insurance numbers, were fired at her; the keyboard rattled; and finally a printer across the room disgorged a modest green document entitled 'Disposal Certificate'. This, apparently, was every bit as important as the much more impressive Death Certificate. 'Give this to the funeral director,' the Registrar instructed. 'It means you can proceed with the arrangements without any hitches.'

'Thank you.' Monica made her escape, squeezing past the prams and buggies now overflowing into the corridor, smiling apologetically at the waiting crowd. *What a system,* she thought. *And how spinelessly we all queue up to do its bidding.*

II

It was about ten when Drew found himself alone in the mortuary, with at least fifteen minutes to spare before Sid returned. Lapsford's body lay undisturbed in the fridge. It occurred to him that Mrs Lapsford could show up to arrange the funeral as soon as she'd registered the death – and there was a chance that she would want to view the body. If that happened, Sid would have to glue or stitch the lips together, and Drew's task would be impossible. The dual pressure of time made his insides shaky.

Nervously, he opened the fridge door, and slid out the tray bearing the body. In order to see it properly, he would have to bring it out altogether and lower it on the hydraulic trolley; he hoped earnestly that his precautionary word with Vince would be enough to explain his behaviour if anybody walked in and caught him. He had no genuine justification for what he was doing. It was well beyond the scope of his job description, and potentially an invasion of Lapsford's privacy. Anxiously, he ran through his plan of action.

The only logical cause of death, apart from a heart attack, a stroke or aneurism, must surely be poisoning. Although it was conceivable that someone had injected him with a toxic substance, the likelier method was oral administration, through food or drink. Therefore his stomach had to be the source of any evidence. And getting at the contents of a dead body's stomach was not a straightforward business.

At the sink there were the usual jars of pink embalming fluid, with their rubber and plastic tubing and assorted attachments. Trembling, Drew went to the sink and grabbed a piece of tubing – the most rigid he could find. There was no other way to get what he wanted without leaving obvious wounds on the body. This would also be quicker. But he would have to be extremely careful.

The body was stiff now, and very cold – too cold to work with easily. Forcing the tube down its throat was an act of real violence, and Drew was afraid that he was tearing the gullet as he went. If so, and if the case did come to the

Coroner's attention for some reason, the evidence of his intervention would be impossible to conceal from a pathologist. He was burning bridges in a major way.

Gritting his teeth and closing his mind against the implications, he worked on. Outside the door, footsteps came closer, and his heart swelled and then stopped. He hadn't known it was possible to be so afraid. Under his breath he cursed himself for a complete fool. Not only was he about to lose his job, but there would doubtless be a police investigation. Violating a dead body was a criminal offence. But the steps continued past the door, and he managed a wobbly breath before his heart resumed something like its normal rhythm.

Returning to his task, he gazed into the dead man's face. Lapsford was still looking healthy. Any lines on his face had been lines of laughter, and the thick hair gave him a youthful appearance. Only the gaping mouth looked wrong. The protruding plastic pipe gave a grotesque aspect to the picture, turning the man into a thing, inert and helpless. Drew felt sorry for what he was doing, and muttered an apology. 'But it's for your own good,' he added. 'You wouldn't want them to get away with it, would you?' Convincing himself that this was an unacknowledged murder victim was the only way he could bring himself to proceed with the next stage in the process.

He was sure that the tube had reached the stomach. Now came the worst part. He had to suck the other end, just enough to draw up some of the contents, but not hard enough to bring them into his own mouth. Like syphoning petrol out of a car's tank – the most terrible consequences would follow if you got it wrong. He could hardly bear to do it, but there was less sense in giving up now than in getting the job done properly. Two or three jerky little sucks, and he felt enough resistance at the end of the tube to know that something had been taken up. Keeping his thumb firmly over his end, and quelling his heaving stomach with extreme difficulty, he pulled roughly until the whole thing was clear. There was an inch of greyish matter lodged in the end of the tube.

Stepping away from the trolley, he carried his sample back to the sink, and grabbed a small plastic bag from a shelf above it. Inserting the tube into it, he blew hard, and dislodged the morsel of stomach contents safely into the bag. The feeling of nausea worsened; he clamped his jaws tightly against it. Never in his life had he done anything so disgusting. He tried to focus on the positive: at least now he would be able to produce some sort of evidence, feeble though it was, if there were to be a forensic enquiry into the death of Jim Lapsford.

He was washing the tube when Sid came in. 'Oh, there you are,' said Drew, falsely hearty. 'I was just familiarising myself with the instruments.'

'So why're you washing them?' demanded Sid suspiciously.

'Well ... I'd been handling them. Habit, I suppose.'

'We don't have to be sterile here, you know,' Sid

said. 'Dead people don't catch infections.'

'No, but they might give them to us, if we're not careful.'

'Not much danger of that.' Sid's light blue eyes conveyed no emotion, but he made a big show of rearranging his equipment around the sink. Drew decided to act casual and drifted away.

'Do you think we'll have to embalm Lapsford?'

Sid shrugged. 'Bound to. Not much chance of the funeral this week, and somebody's sure to want to view him. I'll get onto it soon as the second doctor's been.'

'Right.' Drew quickly made his escape, the tightly sealed plastic bag in his pocket making him feel both guilty and queasy. It went against all his training to remove unauthorised parts of human tissue and smuggle them away in such a surreptitious fashion. He would have to find somewhere safe to keep it until he decided on his next step. Although some awareness of what that might be was already pushing its way to the front of his mind. *No sense in giving up now. Got to carry on to the bitter end – and that means getting this stuff analysed as soon as you can.*

III

Monica was thankful that she'd arranged to meet Pauline for coffee before going on to Plant's only two streets away. She felt hot and thirsty, and in no mood for another gruelling interview without some sort of break first. Anyway, she thought defiantly, why was there such a rush to get on and tidy poor Jim away? Ever since yesterday morning, everyone had been in such a hurry. Those men, coming out so quickly, once the doctor had phoned them. And the instructions they'd given her. Register as soon as you can, they'd said, then come and sort out the day for the funeral. Choose a coffin. Sign the papers.

No, she'd move at her own pace. At least coffee never failed to brighten her up, however weary she might be. She could wait quietly for Pauline, and think about nothing for a while.

It was obvious that none of the staff in the coffee shop had heard about Jim. Everything was so normal that Monica was able to forget for a few minutes that she was a widow. She sat by the window, and watched the street outside. It was relatively quiet, although a short cut from the car park to the main shops ensured a trickle of pedestrians past the window. Opposite was a carpet showroom; on a Wednesday morning it might as well not have bothered to open. She could glimpse salesmen standing beside the counter, waiting in vain for customers. In dark suits, with neat haircuts, they seemed like undertaker's men to Monica. Standing like mutes, or birds of prey, waiting for victims. She had to force herself to drag her eyes away from them.

She jumped when someone put a hand on her shoulder from behind. Turning, she smiled at the sight of Pauline. 'Oh, it's you,' she said, inspecting the face which was now on a level with hers across the small table. Pauline's colouring was a striking contrast to her own ash-blonde and milky-pale tones. They had established their friendship at the school gates, when Monica's

David and Pauline's Craig had been in the same class. Craig had been almost as troublesome as David in his own way; their mothers had had plenty in common.

'Have a coffee,' Monica said. 'There's no rush – I've done the registration part. It's kind of you to keep me company.'

'Didn't you ask Philip to come too?'

'He's got something important on at work. And David–'

Pauline smiled. 'David would be more of a hindrance than a help. Tell me about it! Honestly, they never get any better, do they? Craig's in a dreadful state at the moment – Susie's trying to dump him. At least, I think that's what's happening. They never *tell* you anything, do they? But you don't want to listen to me rabbiting on.' She ordered coffee, and they sat together companionably, as they'd done a thousand times before.

'You look as if you're coping, anyway,' Pauline commented. 'Not that I ever doubted you would. But it's hard to imagine life without him.' She shook her head. 'Jim was quite something.'

'It still doesn't feel as if he's really gone. Not forever. Death's so weird. I suppose people always feel they're the first ever to experience its effects. And yet it's so ordinary. It comes to us all. I'm sorry – I'm talking drivel. I can't put it into words at all. I tried yesterday, with the boys, and just annoyed them.'

'It must be nice to have a daughter,' said Pauline wistfully. 'They always seem so much more – I don't know – *rewarding*.'

'Philip's all right. He and I are pretty close. And David can't help it. I still think it goes back to his early years. It was all so unsettled. Compared to Philip, poor Davey had an awful time.'

'Craig was a forceps delivery. Great dents on his head. Then, when his Dad walked out, he got terribly disturbed. We really messed him up, between us.' They sighed in unison.

'Well, this won't do.' Monica regained her morning briskness, and gathered up her bag. 'Let's get it over with.'

'It's cremation, is it?' Pauline asked, as they walked side by side down the street. The undertaker's office was situated in a side street at the far end of the main shopping area.

'I think so,' Monica said. 'He used to say he hated the thought of burial. I forgot to ask the boys what they thought we should do. I don't suppose they care much, either way.' She spoke in jerky sentences, matching the rhythm of her step; Pauline found the pace uncomfortably fast.

'They'll ask you about stuff like hymns and flowers,' she remarked. 'There'll be all sorts of decisions. I remember when my dad died–'

'It's all right,' Monica spoke impatiently. 'You don't have to try and prepare me. I don't care what happens at the funeral, quite honestly. He's dead anyway – what difference will it make?'

'Right,' panted Pauline placatingly. 'Anything you say. It's just down here, isn't it?' Monica increased her pace, and pushed open the front door of the building without waiting to see if her friend was still at her shoulder.

After a short wait, the two women were sitting

opposite Daphne Plant, who got straight down to business with very few preliminaries. The first question was the 'burial or cremation' one. Monica closed her eyes for a moment before answering. 'Cremation's the norm these days, isn't it? We'll go for that.' She shook her head, fiddled unconsciously with an earlobe. 'We never thought that this would happen. That probably sounds pathetic to you – avoiding the inevitable. But he *was* only fifty-five, and he'd never been ill...'

Daphne had no comment to make. Everyone complained that it was some kind of mistake when death came suddenly. Only gradually would it emerge that Jim had been breathless recently; that his uncle was waiting for a triple bypass; that he'd been worrying about money, or adultery, or promotion. 'Cremation, then,' she said eventually. And Monica found the ensuing decisions came almost effortlessly as Daphne posed her questions. Until they reached the one about chapel visiting.

'I have no idea,' she said flatly, when asked if anyone would like to 'view' Jim. 'What do people usually do?'

Pauline made a diffident contribution. 'Oh, I'm sure there'll be people who would like to see him when he's all nice and tidy in his coffin.'

Monica shuddered: a wave of icy water seemed to be flowing through her system. She didn't think she'd ever seen an occupied coffin – surely she'd remember if she had? Various good excuses had kept her away from funerals all her life. Even her own father had managed to die when she was in hospital with appendicitis, and she'd insisted they carry on without her.

'It seems awful,' she said. 'I don't suppose it'll even look like him.'

Daphne raised her eyebrows, and tapped her lips with her pencil. 'Most people say they're glad they came,' she said. 'It's a chance to say a last goodbye.'

'It'd feel – I don't know – strange,' faltered Monica. She knew they wouldn't understand, that she couldn't express the strong feeling that had gripped her at the prospect of visiting Jim in a strange impersonal 'chapel of rest'.

'I could just leave it open,' Daphne offered. 'You don't have to decide now.'

But Monica was still wrestling with her emotions. 'I *should* see him again,' she went on. 'Everything happened so quickly yesterday... Do you think – could we have him home again? That's what used to happen, isn't it? I think it would be nicer if people could come to see him where he belonged. Yes,' she looked up from the desk, 'yes! That would be much better.'

Daphne suppressed a sigh, and nodded accommodatingly. 'Of course,' she said, 'if that's what you'd like. When would you want him brought home?'

'Monday afternoon,' said Monica decisively. 'Then he can have one last night with me.'

And so it was arranged. The funeral would be at eleven thirty on the following Tuesday. Daphne had suggested a vicar whose name was dimly familiar to Monica, but no more than that. It was Pauline who pointed out that Tuesday would be the seventeenth, and that the following day was Monica's fiftieth birthday.

'Oh, God,' gasped Monica, half-appalled, half-amused. 'We won't be having a party, then.'

'I'll take you out somewhere,' promised Pauline. 'You mustn't be alone. And the boys'll want to do something. Life goes on.'

'That's true,' echoed Daphne, looking from one to the other with some curiosity. Monica met her glance. She liked this odd businesslike undertaker, who didn't flinch from reality. She liked the neat way in which everything fitted onto the printed forms on the desk – names, dates, coffin style, newspaper announcement. There was a space for everything. She imagined a similar form waiting for herself, her name pencilled in already. *It happens to us all,* she thought once more. *High or low, young or old: we all have to fill in our particulars to get ourselves disposed of in one way or another.*

'I'd rather not think about my birthday,' she said. 'Jim would have been so upset to miss it. He loved organising celebrations. He was good at that sort of thing. We were going to go, all of us, to the King's Head.' *I should cry now,* she thought, objectively. *It's at moments like this that you're supposed to be overcome.* But she didn't feel like crying.

'Just for a change,' joked Pauline, before she could stop herself. She turned pink. 'I mean,' she explained, 'Jim was there so much anyway – it wouldn't have been that different from being at home.' She forced a laugh.

Daphne waited, dispassionately; Monica could

feel the other woman's creeping indifference beginning to intrude on her initial sympathy and patience. She must have seen all this so many times before; she must know by heart the whole range of irrational reactions to the death of a spouse.

'Is that everything then?' she asked.

'Just about,' Daphne confirmed. 'Only one more form to fill in.' She produced a second sheet with a column of questions and spaces for the replies. She asked Monica if everyone in the family knew there was to be a cremation, whether anyone was likely to object. Then she asked whether Monica had any reason to suspect that the death was due, directly or indirectly, to 'violence, poison, privation or neglect' – a dramatic suggestion which she quickly diluted by tapping a finger on the green document supplied by the Registrar. 'We assume everything's above board, once we've got this,' she reassured. 'I'll just put a "No" for that one.' *Violence, poison, privation or neglect,* Monica repeated to herself. The sinister mantra made her mouth go dry. Those, then, were the official ways in which a person could be unlawfully killed. Another neatness in this whole untidy business that was dying. 'That's right,' she muttered. 'The answer to that is no.'

She signed the form. After some repetition of the principal details, she and Pauline departed.

'Well, that wasn't so bad, was it,' Pauline said, on an exhalation of relief. 'Could've been worse, anyway. She's a bit odd, but nice enough.'

Violence, poison, privation or neglect. The words

kept on and on, running through Monica's head.

IV

Jim Lapsford's printworks was in a state of suppressed panic. In effect, Jim had run the place: he organised the schedule; monitored the quality of the output; kept track of paper, ink, toner, film. Three people had worked under him; nominally there was a Chief Executive, owner of this business and several others, who put in occasional whirlwind appearances, but nobody had paid much attention to him. Jim had been the driving force. Without him, they floundered.

'Perhaps we should close for the day as a mark of respect,' said Jodie, designer and clerical officer. She wrote all the letters; filed orders, invoices, catalogues, plates; and advised customers on the appearance of their business cards or menus. Jodie was sensible, competent. Thin, tall and beaky-nosed, she kept herself firmly detached from her all-male colleagues. Her favourite pursuit was walking, alone on the hills or along the riverbank. Jodie used her legs as her means of transport, which was enough in itself to mark her out as different. Her lofty self-sufficiency only added to people's wariness of her.

'We can do that on the day of the funeral,' argued Jack, his eyes glittering behind his heavy spectacles. 'No sense in closing today, when we're in the middle of this big calendar job.'

'Right,' chimed in Ajash, the gnomish type-setter. 'I've got to press on with these party invitations regardless. Can't say to the customer, "Sorry, we missed your deadline because the boss died".'

'Well, I think you *can,*' said Jodie. 'I mean, what better reason could there be?'

'Makes no sense.' Ajash looked at her with resolution. 'It's a bad show about Jim – don't get me wrong. But this work won't wait. You know that. If we get on with it this week, work late maybe, then we can make a proper gesture next week. We'll all go to the funeral together.'

'I still can't believe it,' Jodie said, for the tenth time. 'Remember how cheerful he was on Monday afternoon? Laughing and joking? I thought he must have been high on something, he was in such a good mood.'

'Probably been off with one of his lady friends,' commented Jack, looking hard at her. 'Better not go round saying he took drugs. Not even as a joke. Not now he's dead.' Jack had a desperate, hungry look about him, which Jodie had long ago realised meant nothing. He was habitually unsmiling; any shreds of humour he might possess were invariably couched in satire or personal jibes. Even when he tried to be kind, the most he could manage was a crooked sort of sympathy. Yet Jim and he had been good friends.

Jodie shrugged. 'I'm not likely to, am I?' She returned his hard stare, challenging him to say more.

'Come on,' urged Ajash. 'There's work to be done.' Jodie jabbed him with a bony forefinger and he skipped backwards with a muffled squeal.

'Come on, you two!' Jack growled. 'This is no

time for horseplay. You're behaving like kids.'

'When's Justin going to honour us with his company?' Ajash asked. 'Doesn't he know when he's needed?'

'Don't know what use you think he's going to be,' grumbled Jack. 'All public relations and high-powered marketing – can't tell DocuTech from litho, half the time. This place'll soon fall apart without Jim unless the management pull their finger out.'

Jodie looked down her nose at him. 'Don't give us that,' she scorned. 'They'll put you in the hot seat, and take someone else on. Though we all know who it *won't* be.'

Ajash gave a snorting laugh. 'Young David, you mean,' he said, nodding knowingly. 'Jim put the kybosh on that idea, sure enough.'

Jack turned away. Jodie looked from him to Ajash, and back again. 'More fool him,' she said softly.

For a while, they worked on uncomfortably, the whirring of Ajash's printing press a familiar presence. But Jodie couldn't keep quiet for long. 'I can't just go on as if nothing's happened,' she burst out. 'Jim's *dead.*' She stared wide-eyed at Jack.

'Come on, Jode,' he reproached her. 'It's not like you to lose your bottle.'

'I haven't lost my bottle. It's just – oh, I can't get it out of my mind. I mean, Jim's the *last* person you'd expect to go like that–'

'That's rubbish,' said Jack fiercely. 'Death isn't something you ever *expect*. It happens.'

'Oh, you men,' Jodie huffed. 'You'll never allow

yourselves to feel any emotion. Never talk about what really matters.'

'Get away with you,' Jack's anger was barely under control. 'Don't give us that. There's things about nice Mr Lapsford you'd be shocked to discover, if some of us men chose to start talking.'

'Shut up!' Ajash shouted, from where he'd returned to watch over his whirling press. 'Just you shut up, Jack Merryfield. You'll be sorry if I hear you speaking ill of the dead like that again.'

'Silly old fool,' muttered Jack, and threw himself down in front of one of the monitors, hammering murderously at the keyboard.

V

Dr Lloyd's last patient left morning surgery at ten thirty. He spent a few minutes completing the notes on his computer, and sifting through accumulated papers on his desk. Susie would have coffee ready for him promptly at ten forty-five, and then he'd have to go out on the home visits. Wednesdays were generally relaxed, though less so than Thursdays: people didn't fall ill on Thursday, for some reason. Probably because the weekend was in sight, and to waste it being ill would be very bad planning. One or two accidents; children with mysterious fevers; but mainly midweek was a time for catching up with paperwork. *Which reminds me,* he said to himself: *I'd better get those crem papers for Jim Lapsford over to Daphne. She'll be chasing me, otherwise.*

Susie hovered over him while he filled in the

medical papers in the general office, sipping his coffee. 'Myocardial infarction, eh?' she said, reading over his shoulder. 'Last seen four days before death.' She sucked in a sceptical breath.

Doctor Lloyd sighed. 'Don't start that again, Susie. I'll be glad when the blasted man is safely cremated. Why doesn't anybody believe me?'

'Who doesn't believe you? I only said–'

'The Registrar phoned me just now. Said she didn't feel too happy about it. Stupid woman. The whole thing is bureaucracy gone mad, if you ask me.'

She tutted sympathetically. 'Well, you'd better ask Ginnie Parton to do Part Two then.'

'Why?' He looked up at her, pretending innocence. 'What's special about her?'

'Come on.' She widened her eyes at him, and he noticed that she was no less pale today than she had been yesterday. If she hadn't been speaking so accusingly to him, he'd have asked her whether anything was the matter. As it was, she elaborated her point before he could fully acknowledge his concern. 'She'll sign anything, sight unseen. It's a disgrace, if you ask me.'

'Not my problem, is it? She wouldn't thank me for telling her how to do her job. Actually, I was going to ask her anyway. I don't think I can face any more hassle over this chap. Anyone would think somebody had murdered him. Since I'm entirely satisfied that they didn't, I'm sure I did the right thing.'

'I like *entirely satisfied.* That has a very convincing ring to it. Now, here's your list for home visits. You could drop in and look at Mrs

Sinclair's foot as well.'

'I only saw her on Monday.'

'I know. But you've got loads of time, and she's so miserable. It would be your good deed for the day. And who knows – she might drop dead in the night like Lapsford, and then you can do her papers without any qualms as well.'

'Susie! That's going too far. If you've got something you want to say, then spit it out, without all this sniping. Are you saying Lapsford should have gone for a postmortem? Do you want me to throw everything into reverse, and call in the Coroner? Do you?' He leaned towards her, intimidating, his face close to hers. She backed away from him.

'You don't have to shout at me,' she sniffed. Without warning, she burst into tears. 'I've got enough trouble without you bawling me out,' she wept. 'I was only joking about the papers. I didn't mean anything.'

Briefly, he closed his eyes. 'I'm sorry. Sorry I shouted. Do you want to tell me about this – trouble? I've got plenty of time.'

She shook her head, and grabbed a tissue from the box that sat permanently on the windowsill. 'Just the usual–' she mumbled. 'Bother with the boyfriend.'

'Well, he ought to know better,' said Dr Lloyd firmly. 'He doesn't know when he's well off.'

She shook her head again, with despairing emphasis. 'You don't *understand,*' she said. 'It's totally the other way round.'

'Ah,' he nodded, with complete incomprehension.

She flapped a hand at him, and applied the tissue again. 'Go and do your good turn,' she told him. 'Mrs Sinclair's foot – remember?'

With some relief, he went to collect his bag and car keys. Whatever problems she was having with her boyfriend, he didn't really want to delve into them. He knew very little about her private life, except that her Dad worked at the undertakers; it seemed somehow fitting that there was that connection. Sid was always efficient and polite in the mortuary when Dr Lloyd had to go and view a body; it somehow gave Susie an air of respectability by association. He hoped she wasn't going to present him with some emotional crisis. Susie was an asset in more ways than one. The patients often commented on her friendly demeanour and the improvements she'd brought to the surgery.

'Don't forget to phone Ginnie,' she called after him, causing him to turn back with a sigh. Ginnie Parton was everyone's favourite backup for cremation papers: asking no questions, and gratefully pocketing the payment.

The conversation took barely two minutes. 'Ginnie? Julian Lloyd here. Can you do a Part Two for me? The body's at Plant's. Jim Lapsford. Heart... Oh, did you? Well, I saw him last week, providentially, so there's no Coroner involvement. I've written him up for MI... Well, the signs were all there. Have a look if you like... That's up to you. I'm taking the papers round now, so any time after lunch, he's all yours. Great. Thanks. Everything all right, is it? Good. Bye, then.'

Susie watched him stride out to his car, the

battered doctor's bag firmly gripped in his left hand. *I wonder if he'll remember Mrs Sinclair,* she mused.

VI

In the workshop, the men were hurrying over their mid-morning coffee, before getting ready for an eleven thirty funeral. Pat, the handsome Irishman, was brushing invisible specks from the shoulders of his black coat prior to putting it on, standing at his locker in boxer shorts and black socks. Changing clothes was a regular part of the job. Each man had at least three different outfits: formal funeral wear; smart but less formal for collecting bodies from private houses or nursing homes; and very casual for carpentry or mortuary work. Poor Olga had never quite grown easy with the way semi-naked men greeted her almost every time she came out to their part of the building with a message or instruction. Drew knew that none of the men was entirely comfortable with it, either. They made very sure that their underpants were all-concealing, and listened intently for the sound of women's heels on the corridor outside. Gaynor, the local florist, was another regular visitor; a coarse woman, she seemed to make a point of catching them half-clothed and making some withering comment. Daphne, always needing to be in control, took care to limit her appearances to times when she knew they would not be changing. She carried in her head a precise schedule of their movements, absorbed from a careful analysis of the day's commitments every morning.

'Drink up,' Pat encouraged the others. 'Six minutes to go, that's all, and you're none of you's changed yet.'

Vince, Sid, Drew and Little George completed Pat's team. It was to be a simple funeral, an old woman with few relatives or friends. Drew had 'made' the coffin without any assistance – stapled a plain piece of white satinised nylon all around the inside of the already-prepared shell, with a frill of the same material along the upper edge, and engraved a name plate which was tacked onto the lid. Nobody was coming to see the old dear, so it didn't much matter if the stapling went a little squiffy. But Drew had done his best and was pleased with the result.

He still felt a shiver of excitement when he climbed into the great shining hearse to sit alongside the coffin, with its flowers on top. 'It's just a disposal job,' he'd said to Karen, in the early days, but he knew it was more than that. He was present at an event of extreme significance: the end of someone's life, the start of a new phase for the survivors.

He sat behind Sid, with Vince driving. Little George made the fourth, and Pat had to get himself to the Crematorium independently. They chatted inconsequentially, the presence of the dead body in the car a matter of little import to the more experienced men.

'Saw Mrs Lapsford coming out of the office a while ago,' said Vince. 'Had a friend with her. Must've been to make the arrangements. Bet you it'll be Monday.'

‘Tuesday,’ said Sid, heavily. ‘The best times are taken on Monday, and Daphne’ll steer her onto Tuesday.’

‘Long time to wait,’ said Drew. ‘A whole week.’

‘It’ll soon pass. Plenty to do, you know. Specially when it’s so unexpected. All those people to tell, for a start-off.’ Vince adopted his tutorly tone, instructing Drew, the new boy.

‘Registrar must have taken the doctor’s word for it,’ Vince continued. ‘You’ll be surprised at that, Drew, my lad?’

Drew ducked his head, anticipating scorn, but couldn’t refrain from comment. ‘It’s a scandal, I reckon. Nothing’s going to change my mind on this. There is no way that doctor could be sure what the man died of. No way at all, without a postmortem.’

Vince smiled. ‘Anyone with a grain of nouse could see what the story was. Like I keep telling you.’

‘I know. But it niggles me. What’s the point of having regulations, if nobody takes any notice of them?’

‘Nobody broke any regulations,’ Sid interposed. ‘What’re you talking about?’

‘That doctor ought never to have written up a death certificate,’ Drew insisted doggedly. Even to himself, he was beginning to sound like a cracked record.

‘Just give it a rest, boy, or you’ll have us all down on you,’ advised Vince. ‘Enough’s enough. The funeral’s arranged by this time, and you’d only upset everyone if they heard you going on this way. If you’re going to be like this every time there's a dodgy doctor's paper, you'll be in the doghouse with a whole lot of people, just see if you're not.'

Drew gave this some thought. 'You make it sound like a – like some sort of mafia.'

He looked round at the others, wondering whether they'd laugh; he rather hoped they would. But all the faces were serious.

'Don't be a fool,' said Vince. 'It's not like that at all. Nobody's out to break the law. They just want an easy life – save some time. I don't know what's got into you, but whatever it is, you'd best get rid of it, quick. Right?'

Drew scowled, but said no more. Vince had a point. He could see there was sense in it. And yet – nobody could be one hundred percent certain that Jim Lapsford had died of a heart attack. And that was not right. Especially when he was to be cremated; there'd never be any hope of putting things straight once that was over and done with. He was both glad and scared at the thought of the little bag of stomach contents tucked into his jacket pocket, back in the changing room. The prospect of finding it full of some unmistakable toxin, which he could flourish with a triumphant 'I told you so!' was appealing, despite the implications.

It seemed a good idea to change the subject. 'Hey, Sid,' he threw over his shoulder, twisting to glimpse the other man's face, 'what happened about your Susie? Did you hear what the problem was yesterday?'

Sid stared antagonistically at him. 'You know,' Drew insisted. 'The boyfriend trouble.' He watched the other man's frown, and gradual comprehension. 'Oh, that,' he said dismissively. 'She hasn't said anything about it.'

Drew pressed on. 'But you don't like the boyfriend, do you?'

'She could do better.' The tight lips made it clear that there was nothing more to say.

VII

Pauline finally left Monica on her own halfway through the afternoon. 'I'll be all right,' the new widow assured her friend. 'I'll give Phil a call and tell him what we've decided. He can help me choose a hymn.'

Pauline hugged her, in a long squeeze that stopped Monica's breath. 'Anything I can do – just shout,' she said. 'That's what friends are for. If you're *sure* you'll be okay, then there are a few things I'm supposed to be doing. Always somebody to see...' She stopped herself.

'Thanks again for coming with me. You're being a real friend.'

'I was glad to do it,' Pauline reassured her. 'I'll see you soon.'

When she'd gone, Monica sat for a few minutes in the lounge, thinking about her friend. It was a lopsided relationship, she knew: Pauline was always the one giving time, attention, a listening ear. Monica had always been the taker. The one who needed help, the one who was flawed. There was something demeaning in the way her friend always went straight for the weak points in her life: the trouble with David, the hollowness of her marriage, the sheer awfulness of being fifty. All year she had moaned to Pauline about the oncoming birthday and all its ghastly implications. In vain had Pauline pointed out the multitude of glamorous fifty-year-old women at every turn, the sixties' generation matured but not grown dull. Pauline – at forty-six – had done her very best to insist that fifty was nothing. *Sixty* was young these days, she said.

It wasn't as if Pauline had no troubles of her own. Her son Craig was almost as difficult in his way as Monica's David had been. Sometimes it seemed that the two boys had been a decidedly bad influence on each other, plunging together into adolescent gloom and nihilism, no doubt making use of illegal substances to further confuse their muddled minds. It was a relief to both mothers that they'd survived to twenty-four without serious medical problems. David now had a job as a car mechanic; Craig was, half-heartedly, training to be a computer operator. Slowly, and with many setbacks, they seemed to be dragging themselves into some semblance of adulthood.

But Pauline had been kind today, a friend in a time of need. What had she said about having someone else to see? That was Pauline all over – only happy if she was ministering to as many people as possible. So I'm *really doing* her *the favour,* thought Monica, with a little smile.

A whining sound brought her back to reality. Looking round, she remembered with a shock that she had shut the dog outside early that morning and never let the wretched thing back in again. With a stab of guilt, she rushed through the kitchen to the back door, and flung it open. The animal was quivering on the mat, the picture of misery. Its coat was flat; its head drooped. 'Oh, Cassie, I'm sorry,' Monica apologised. 'Come in and have some dinner.'

She tipped a whole tinful of Butcher's Tripe into a dish, and offered it to the dog. But Cassie ignored it, turning her head away as if it offended her. 'Come on, you fool,' said Monica. 'You must be hungry.' But the dog would not be persuaded. Instead, it went to its basket, and flopped down on the cushion, looking unspeakably weary. 'You look a bit off colour to me,' Monica observed. 'I hope it's just that you're missing Jim. I can't cope with you being poorly, not right now.' Cassie moved her small stump of a tail a few millimetres to left and right, as acknowledgement that she'd heard herself addressed, but could manage no more than that. 'I'll give you a bath when you're better,' Monica promised. 'You don't look your best, do you?'

Then she went to phone Philip.

She could tell from his abrupt, overly business-like tone that he was in the middle of something important. He'd been in this job for nearly two years, and Monica had the impression that he was still struggling to keep up with its demands. She hadn't really tried to understand what it was he did, beyond knowing that success or failure rested on sales figures and product development, and that each month he dreaded the latest statistics. But he had never allowed her to share his worries. As a boy he had maintained a relentlessly cheerful demeanour with her and Jim, until they had come to believe in it. 'Philip's never been any trouble,' they would boast. She did her best to forget the occasions when a teacher or schoolfriend would let drop some story about Philip hurting himself, or crying over poor exam marks, or in black despair about a difficult girlfriend.

She had looked forward to depending more and more on her capable elder son, as their roles gradually reversed. His failure to accompany her to the undertaker's had caused a small pang of disappointment which slowly matured to a substantial lump of resentment lodged in her chest. If he dismissed her now in favour of some stupid office meeting, she might not be able to conceal her umbrage.

'I'm just back from Plant's,' she said with a deliberate lack of emphasis. 'We've got a date for the funeral.'

She could hear the quality of his attention improving, and sighed with relief. 'Oh, good,' he said. 'I mean–'

'It's on Tuesday next week, at eleven thirty. At the crematorium. Pauline came with me.'

She couldn't resist this slight prick to his conscience. 'Eleven thirty,' he murmured, and she knew he was writing it down in his diary.

'Oh, yes,' she added brightly, 'and I'm having him back here to the house on Monday evening. For the night. I thought you and David would want to come and say goodbye to him.'

A strangled cough came down the airwaves. 'Christ, Mum – what on earth do you want to do that for?'

'For Jim,' she said coldly. 'It's what he would have wanted.'

'Couldn't we just have gone to see him in the chapel of rest, or whatever they call it? Like other people?'

'I don't care about other people. I want what's right for Jim. I couldn't just let him be burnt without some sort of – I don't know – wake, I suppose. Jim's grandfather was a strong Catholic, after all. It was their family tradition for generations. It's a *nice* idea, Phil. Don't go and spoil it.' She could hear herself whining, and clamped her lips together.

'Well, I suppose I might just bear it. But you're never going to get David to something like that. He'll go ape at the very thought. Don't you think your first duty is to the living, Mum?'

Monica's anger told her that she was not yet ready for the role reversal which she thought she'd enjoy. How *dare* he refer to her duty? What did he know about her responsibilities to Jim? 'I think I'm the best judge of that,' she told him haughtily.

'Okay.' He retreated. 'It's up to you. Now, is there anything else?' His impatience had returned, and Monica's sense of being peripheral to his life added to the bleakness of the empty house.

'No, that's all. Except the dratted dog's not very well. I left her outside all morning by mistake, and now she's in a real state. She probably ought to see a vet.'

'Well, I'm sorry, Mum, but there's no chance that it'll be me who takes her. Try one of the old dears next door, why don't you?'

Monica felt herself rebuffed. 'Bye, then. I'll keep in touch.'

'Bye, Mum.'

Odd, she thought, what a crisis did to your relationships. Phil had only occasionally been impatient with her, embarrassed by her only when an adolescent. Since setting up home with Nerina, he'd been an infrequent visitor, making sporadic phone calls, but not inviting her into his life. The death of his father didn't seem to have made much difference. His manner was much more prickly than usual, yet she felt she could trust him. Underneath, she knew he was rock-solid reliable. Philip was a plodder; he spoke his mind, but he followed the rules. 'He's just like you,' Jim had often told her.

Monica had hated this assessment. Perhaps that was the main reason she had done what she did – to discover her own hidden depths. To kick over the traces.

Cassie seemed to be sleeping peacefully in her basket, and Monica decided to leave her to recover in her own way. Grief wasn't something a vet could cure. And after all, the animal was ten years old. That was seventy in dog years – she probably just needed a nice long rest. Monica knew how she felt.

VIII

Daphne greeted Dr Lloyd with a friendly smile. 'Jim Lapsford? His wife was here earlier on. I've typed out a form for you. Oh, you've done it already – I should have known. You won't need to see him again?'

'No. He got the thorough once-over yesterday, and I'm happy to stick to what I found. Ginnie Parton's coming in some time, and then it's all clear. When's the cremation?'

'Not until next Tuesday.'

'The wife seemed a nice woman, from what I saw of her. She's not one of my patients – I don't remember coming across her before. Nice little dog, too. All over the body, it was. Pathetic. Made me quite choked for a minute. Funny, the things that get to you. Shows we're human, I guess. I could have adopted that little dog. Specially as Lapsford's wife doesn't seem to know what to do with it. I like dogs.' He tailed off, staring into the road beyond Daphne's office window.

'Dogs are good company,' she replied, after a moment. 'So it's Dr Parton? Better have her fee ready. She usually doesn't stay more than about fifty seconds.'

'Don't tell me... Now, the burning question for me is, shall I go and visit Mrs Sinclair with the bad foot?' He looked at his watch. 'Oh, what the hell. It'll make me feel virtuous. Cheer the old bird up, too, if Susie can be believed.'

'And maybe she'll remember you in her will,' said Daphne, pertly.

'Maybe she will,' he laughed. 'Now wouldn't that be a turn-up for the book!'

IX

Pauline made the trek across Roxanne's field that

afternoon as promised, following the ribbonlike path which her sister had trodden out during the years of living there. A gate in the diagonally opposite corner from the caravan opened onto a small country lane, with a passing place just big enough to park a car. A few Hereford bullocks shared the field with Roxanne: big friendly beasts, with broad benign brows and rich mahogany coats. They followed Pauline curiously, but she ignored them. Only when she had to step off the path into a patch of thistles to avoid one of their circular deposits of manure did she turn to scowl at them. 'Damned nuisances,' she mumbled.

Roxanne was sitting on the caravan steps. She had seen her sister coming and sat and observed her walking across the field. It took perhaps four minutes. Roxanne's thoughts ranged across a number of related topics: how the two of them had always been uneasy together, from early infancy; how strange it was that they still lived in the same locality; how much she knew about Pauline, things that Pauline didn't know she knew; how she and Jim had actually come together through Pauline; and how she might yet come out of this encounter with her dignity intact and some sisterly points scored in the eternal contest that raged between them.

'All right?' said Pauline, when she was still fifty yards away. 'Got nothing to do?'

'Plenty. Just don't feel like it. Day like today, Jim would likely have come by. Would have phoned me, anyway. It's going to be strange without him. Don't suppose I'll even be able to go to his funeral. Awkward questions if I did.' She lit a cigarette from a pack in her lap, and blew smoke upwards, her head tilted back. Pauline searched for somewhere to sit, and found an old wooden box, which looked none too welcoming. She brushed it several times with her hand before sitting down.

'Well, you won't be able to see him at the undertaker's. She's having the wake at home, Monday night, in the old-fashioned way. I shouldn't think even you'd have the nerve to turn up there.' Self-righteousness oiled her words and enraged her sister.

'I might,' she said, with narrowed eyes. 'I just bloody might. What have I got to lose, after all? And how come you know so much?'

'I went with her to organise it all. Those useless sons of hers didn't want to know. Wouldn't like to do it again in a hurry, though. Bit depressing, talking about hearses and coffins.'

'I imagine it is. I've no intention of ever doing it.'

'Who's going to do Mum, then?'

'Mum will outlive us all.' They laughed at one of the few things they shared – an impatient, amused reverence for their mother, who had suffered from a confusing array of ailments for fifty years or more and still possessed more energy at seventy-five than anyone else they knew.

'How is she, anyway? Monica, I mean?' Roxanne returned to the unavoidable; Pauline noticed her sister's hand was shaking as she put the cigarette to her mouth.

'She keeps on about Jim never being ill, and it all being a tremendous shock. She *is* shocked, obviously. But I get a funny feeling that she isn't actually terribly *surprised*. She's numb, like people usually are, but there's something else. This business of having him back to the house. It seemed to me as if she was trying to make up for something.'

'What – make up to Jim? Do you mean she feels guilty?'

'Sort of, yes. I thought you'd have a better idea than me about why that might be.'

'Well, I certainly never got the impression that she starved him of sex. He wasn't one of those husbands who bleat on about their wives being frigid and driving them away. Jim didn't play that sort of game. He was just into sex, and took it anywhere he could find it. With as many variations as he could get.'

'I don't want to know,' said Pauline primly.

'Listen, duckie, there *is* only one thing to know about Jim Lapsford, and that's his addiction to sex. Okay, he had his job, and he enjoyed his pint with the lads at the pub, and playing with that weirdo Jack on the computer, but basically, sex was his thing. If Monica's feeling guilty about something, you can bet your last fag it's got something to do with sex.'

'Okay, okay, I believe you,' Pauline conceded. 'And it's true, I presume, what I hear about that little bimbo – what's her name?'

'Lorraine. Poor little cow. He was out of order there. Turned her inside out, so she won't know how to cope without him. Used to talk about her to me.'

Pauline pulled a face. 'That's perverted. How could you let him?'

Roxanne shrugged. 'Didn't bother me. But don't you go saying anything about her. There'll be hell to pay if her Frank finds out what she was up to.'

'Just tell me this – weren't you ever jealous? Not of Monica – that's all part of the package if you take up with a married man. But surely you weren't best pleased about Lorraine? Apart from anything else, she's twenty years younger than you.'

'Sixteen, actually. I've no time for jealousy. I wasn't in love with Jim, you know. He was just satisfying my urges, same as I was for him. I'm going to miss the bugger, all the same.'

Roxanne drew deeply on the last inch of the cigarette. Her thick hair was in a tangle round her face, one or two grass seeds lodged in it; her big bare feet were muddy, resting on the bottom step. The only obvious similarity between the sisters was the shape of their faces and the hazel eyes under black brows. Pauline was slighter, neater in every way, although her hair was similarly difficult to control.

'He was the sort of chap you couldn't really ignore,' Pauline contributed weakly, feeling more than a little out of her depth. She'd come to offer Roxanne sympathy and information; she was unprepared for the confidences that were spilling out.

'You said yesterday that secrets always come out when a person dies,' Roxanne remembered.

'Are you sure Monica doesn't know about me and the bimbo – and the others over the years? Surely she can't be completely blind?'

'I think she took care not to know. The details, anyway. She gave him all the space he wanted, especially when she finally woke up to the fact that that gave *her* more freedom.'

'But she never had anyone else, did she? Jim was always quite certain she'd never in her life slept with anybody but him.'

'Then Jim was fooling himself,' said Pauline, with a triumphant laugh.

Roxanne shook her head disbelievingly. 'He'd have killed her if he'd known.'

Pauline laughed again, genuinely amused. 'Have you any idea how funny that sounds?' she spluttered. 'In the circumstances?'

'You don't understand,' Roxanne protested. 'He'd have felt – inadequate, if he'd thought he wasn't satisfying her. That was what nobody grasped about Jim. He wanted to be everything to everyone. If you ask me, that's what killed him. He just couldn't take the pace of it, in the end.'

'Well, from what Monica's saying, he thrived on it, to the end. Always so *well*, she keeps repeating. I remember him boasting about his fantastic health often enough. Anyway, enough of this. I've got to get on. When will I see you?'

Roxanne began to pick at a tuft of grass. 'I get the feeling I should stay out of the way for a bit. I've got no reason to come into town. I'll see you when I see you, okay?'

'I brought you these.' Pauline dropped two batteries into Roxanne's hand. 'For your phone.

Make sure it's working – I might need to speak to you again.'

'Why? Will you have to warn me that Monica's on the warpath, coming out here to call me names, when she finds out I was screwing her husband?'

'I just like to know I can get you if I want to. And I thought it was the man who did the screwing?'

'You always were the naïve one,' grinned Roxanne.

X

On his way home, Drew stopped at a phonebox outside the Post Office, checking a number in the small notebook he kept in his wallet. It was over a minute before anyone picked up the other end.

'Pathology, please,' he said. Another long pause, then, 'Is Lazarus still there, please? Thanks.'

Unconsciously, he placed his hand over the pocket containing the sample from Jim Lapsford's stomach. Several times during the day he had wished he could just throw it away, forget all about it, but he knew only too well that he'd gone past that point. The little bag had weighed heavy on his mind.

'Laz? How are you? Still dropping petri dishes all over the floor? Listen, I've got something on the go. I need something analysed. Can I come and see you? When you knock off, maybe? Okay? Six, then.'

He phoned Karen then. 'I'll be late back,' he

told her. 'Not before seven or half past. I'm fine – how about you?' He laughed at her reply. 'See you.' She hadn't asked him where he was going.

The hospital was five miles away; cycling against the flow of the rush-hour traffic, he easily reached it by six. Lazarus appeared from a squat brick building just as Drew was securing his bike in a rack close to the car park. The distinctive shaggy black hair was impossible to miss. He hadn't changed since Drew first met him five years earlier, when for a few months, they were adversaries in the squash court provided by the health authority. Week after week they'd played a slow, polite game, each wondering why he was wasting time in this way. Before long they'd confessed their lack of enthusiasm, and taken to drinking beer together instead, sharing horror stories about their work.

'Come for a coffee,' Drew instructed now, accompanying Laz down the hospital approach road. 'I assume Billy's is still there?' The café had been a favourite bolthole, away from the institutional canteen where the majority of the hospital staff took their breaks. Lazarus trotted alongside him, the long legs appearing to be barely under control. He'd been born in Tunisia, to Christian parents, who'd made their faith clear by naming their children after New Testament characters: his sisters had been christened Magdalene and Dorcas.

Drew led the way to a table at the back. 'What's all the secrecy, man?' demanded Laz. 'This ain't like you.'

Drew produced his plastic bag. 'Stomach contents,' he said, with no preamble. 'I think they might contain some sort of poison. Would you be able to run some tests, without making it official?'

Laz blew out his cheeks. 'Jesus, Drew. I'm not Chief Pathologist yet, you know. They don't let me just do what I like. And what kind of poison did you have in mind? A lot of them aren't detectable.'

'I know it's a long shot, but do what you can. Something painless, so it isn't strychnine. The chap just died in his sleep. Something that wouldn't taste too obvious, as well.'

'Wait.' Laz held up one hand. 'I'm not sure I'm getting this. Some bloke's passed quietly away in his bed, and you don't really know why, but you think he ingested something toxic. Right?'

'I'm pretty certain he didn't die of natural causes, and poison's the only thing I can think of that fits the facts. But his wife says she was lying next to him all night, and he didn't cry out or move about.'

Laz shook his head. 'Needle in a haystack, my friend. Take an army of tests to sort that one out. Isn't the Coroner seeing to it anyway?'

'The doctor signed him up. It never went to the Coroner. Look, I know you can't do miracles, but if you get a chance, just run it through one or two procedures. Have a look down the microscope, at least.'

Laz reluctantly allowed Drew to press the bag into his hand, giving a distasteful glance at the contents before tucking it into his pocket. 'What do I do if I find something?'

'Phone me. Not at work, though.' He thought for a minute. 'Call me in the evening – or you could try Karen at school, in her lunch break. She knows all about it.' He wrote down the number. 'Don't lose it. And the deadline's Tuesday. After that, we can just forget the whole thing.'

Laz giggled. 'Deadline – ha ha. I can tell you now I'm not likely to find anything. Have you any idea what a song and dance it is to find something like aconitine or ricin? And they're the most likely ones, given how he died. Or some sort of hedgerow herb. Hemlock's common round here, like most of the nightshades. The others are harder to get hold of.'

'But not impossible, right?'

Laz shrugged. 'The recipes are probably on the Internet these days. Along with how to make a bomb, and where to buy a Kalashnikov.'

'Well, whatever. Thanks, Laz. I owe you one. Don't get yourself into trouble over it. I know it's a long shot.'

'Don't worry – I won't. I'll call the minute I've got anything. You off then?'

Drew was pushing back his chair. 'Yeah. Sorry to be in a rush. Glad to see you again, boy. You're the one thing about this place I miss.'

'Thanks. I miss you, too. Keep in touch, now.' They knocked fists lightly for a moment, the way they'd always done. A boyish parody of the orthodox handshake.

Karen wrinkled her nose when he told her what

he'd done. 'Sounds gross,' she said. 'Sooner you than me. So, the investigation continues, does it?'

'That's right,' he confirmed. 'Except that I haven't the least idea where we go from here.'

XI

David Lapsford phoned his mother at ten thirty that evening; she answered it on the second ring. 'I knew you wouldn't be in bed,' he said.

'I was just going to have a bath.' Why did she sound so defensive? 'Are you all right?'

'I'm alive,' he said, 'if that's what you mean.'

'I should have told you what we've arranged about the funeral,' she apologised. 'But I thought it could wait till the morning.'

'Thanks very much.' The sarcasm was impossible to ignore. So was the slurring in his speech.

'David, have you been drinking?' she couldn't stop herself from asking. 'You sound very peculiar.'

'Never mind that. I just need to ask you one thing. Mother–' He said the word with a profound irony which sent alarm tingling through her system. 'I want to ask you whether you don't think the time has come, what with my father dying and everything – whether you don't think the time has come, at last, to tell me who my real parents were. I just think I should know exactly how I'm related, if at all, to the man whose funeral I'm supposed to go to.'

The bombshell almost rendered Monica speechless. She swallowed painfully. 'David!' she said sharply. 'Listen to me! Are you on your own?'

'Angus is here, but he's gone to bed.'

'Well, I want you to put the phone down now, and go straight to bed as well. I'll see you tomorrow. We'll talk about it then.'

'Promise?' he whined, as he had done all his life.

'Yes, David, I promise to tell you what you need to know. And – Jim's funeral is next Tuesday morning. Can you remember that?'

But he hadn't heard her. The phone was unresponsive in her hand.

CHAPTER THREE
THURSDAY

I

Monica woke at eight o'clock next morning with the remnants of a dream still flitting through her mind. Something to do with Jim and David and Cassie, with Sarah and Dottie as a sort of Greek chorus, peering in through the house windows and commenting on what they saw. With a groan, she heaved herself out of bed. As had happened every morning for months now, the words *nearly fifty* flashed through her mind as she faced the day. A stab of fear accompanied them. Fifty was much more than halfway through most people's lives – her own mother had died at sixty-eight. And still she hadn't *done* anything! Was this all there was ever going to be? She remembered how Jim had been at fifty, desperate to sample everything that life could offer before it was too late. She had watched him with a mixture of admiration and amusement, and wondered how it was that her own efforts seemed so feeble by comparison.

David: that was the first challenge of the day. She had promised she'd meet him for a talk. The prospect was unnerving. She had no idea what she would tell him, or how he would react to hearing the truth. David was unpredictable at the best of times. There was a real possibility that he would reject her completely.

Her anxiety increased as she dressed and went downstairs. She looked for Cassie, expecting to see her curled up in her basket. But the dog had jumped up onto Jim's reclining chair, where he had often sat with her on his lap. She was lying on her side, stretched out, but her pose was unnatural.

'Oh, God,' Monica moaned. 'I don't believe it.'

Hesitantly, she prodded the animal, and was hardly surprised when her finger encountered cold unresponsive flesh beneath the dull hair. At least it looked as if she'd died fairly peacefully, although the stretched posture was worrying. Who could say what pain an animal might suffer, uncomplaining or merely unnoticed? Guilt washed through her, followed by helplessness: what should she do with the body? You didn't call the undertaker's men for a dog – more's the pity. Though perhaps, in the circumstances–? The idea took root and she toyed with it as she quickly fetched an old towel and threw it over the body. So long as she couldn't see Cassie, she might manage to forget about her for a while.

She made herself a mug of coffee and put bread in the toaster. A scatter of letters lay on the doormat, most of them the distinctive thick white or cream envelopes denoting cards of sympathy. She opened them as she drank the coffee, finding the commonplace messages disappointing. Only one sympathiser had hand-written something more personal, and this was Jodie at the printworks. *Please phone me if there's anything I can do,* she had said. *I knew Jim for eight years, and will miss him terribly.*

Monica knew Jodie quite well, not just because she had been working so long with Jim, but also because she had been David's girlfriend for a year, when he had been eighteen and Jodie was twenty-one. They had made a strange couple, but Monica had trusted Jodie to help the boy, in the midst of one of his worst phases of emotional turmoil. Whether or not she did had been a topic of debate ever since. A week after his nineteenth birthday, he had gone missing, and they'd heard nothing from him for eleven months. Monica tried not to think about that dreadful time. She had never come close to understanding what it had been about, and how she might have prevented it. Jim had been frantic enough for both of them. She had seen no option but to keep calm and welcome the boy when he came back, as she had trusted all along that he would.

Perhaps Jodie should go with her to see David that morning. A third person, who presumably had a working knowledge of David's past and his vulnerable spots, would be immensely useful. After all, she had offered her help, in the card. Forgetting the dog, Monica went to the phone.

II

Another quiet day for funerals, with Drew, Vince, Pat and Sid dawdling over their morning coffee for longer than usual. 'Got Lapsford's coffin to do this morning,' said Sid, nodding slightly to himself. 'Soon as the second doctor's been, we can get him embalmed. You can help if you like,' he added to Drew. 'Daphne's going to want someone to take over that when I retire.'

'Does he really need to be embalmed?' queried Drew, already inured to Sid's frequent, but premature, references to his retirement. 'It isn't particularly warm.'

'Funeral Tuesday – going home Monday, so I understand. Too long, son. Can't risk it. And it'll make him look good for the family.'

'He looked okay to me,' muttered Drew.

Sid gave an exaggerated sigh. 'How you do argue, my boy,' he said, half-joking, half-exasperated. 'Dead since Tuesday, and you never know what might happen once he's out of the fridge. I'm hoping we'll be able to get to it this afternoon.'

'Right,' shrugged Drew, sensing that he'd gone far enough. 'What are we doing before that – apart from getting the coffin ready?'

'Might get a removal – you never know. Tidy up the workshop. Check we've got a good stock of handles, lining sets, name plates. Polish the hearse.' Vince ticked the jobs off on his fingers. 'Always plenty to do. It can get a lot quieter than this, and we've still got to look busy. Never let the boss think we're overstaffed. Golden rule, that.'

'And we can always fill the time with a spot of embalming,' Drew added, unable to stop himself. Rinsing his mug in the little sink, he went through to the workshop with Vince and Pat. His exchange with Sid had merely reinforced his continuing unease about Jim Lapsford: time was inexorably working against him. His friend

Lazarus at the laboratory would probably take several days at best to come back with any kind of report on the sample of stomach contents; after all, he had to fit the job around his official work. Now that Lapsford was to be embalmed, any hope of examining further evidence was receding, and the lack of activity in the workshop just highlighted the problem. Frustration fizzled inside him, making him jittery.

Karen's willingness to help almost made it worse. How do you delegate when you don't know what you should be doing yourself? There was so much he didn't understand about the Lapsfords; so little inspiration as to how he might learn more. He looked suspiciously at Sid, who had followed him out of the kitchen, wondering whether he had incurred the man's wrath; but Sid was merely straightening tools on his bench, trying to keep his hands occupied, seemingly lost in his own thoughts.

'It must be a bit weird, embalming a mate,' Drew ventured tentatively.

Sid looked up and shrugged. 'Done it enough times. Small town, this – between us we know most people. He's not going to know anything about it, is he?'

'No, but *you*–' Drew knew better than to start talking about feelings: about the brush of death's dark wings on your shoulder when someone younger than you died suddenly. 'He seems to have been a popular chap. Be plenty of people wanting to see him off at the cremation.'

'Popular!' Sid was abruptly transformed. 'Where did you get that idea? The man was a menace.'

Drew recoiled at the violence of the words; the air crackled with Sid's intense outburst. Then Pat chuckled. 'Come on, Sid – you're just jealous that he was having such a good time. A local legend, old Jim. Good luck to him, I say. A short life but a happy one.'

'I thought you were a friend of his.' Drew was confused. 'You said you knew him from the King's Head, that you played darts with him. You've changed your tune a bit, haven't you?'

Sid was once more fiddling with his tools. 'We played darts, yeah. We were on the same team. And he never did anything to put my back up. Not personally. It's only that he–'

'Admit it, Sid,' interrupted Vince, 'he broke your old-fashioned rules. If you went round bad-mouthing everybody who's strayed off the straight and narrow, you'd be pretty lonely. You've got to live and let live.'

'Jim wasn't so bad,' confirmed Pat. 'I knew him a few years back. Handsome bloke – in a bit of a flap about hitting fifty. And that Roxanne – she's quite something, by any standards. Earthy. Uninhibited.'

Drew remembered the books and the satin garment in the Lapsford bedroom. 'Roxanne?' he queried. 'Who's she?'

All three men stared at him. Vince spoke first. 'You don't know Roxanne? Sure you do. She's the woman in that caravan, out on the road to the Crem. You've passed it dozens of times. She lives like a gypsy, making potions and jam and all kinds of stuff from what she finds in the fields. Left her husband and set up on her own. She's always in the paper, every time the council try to evict her and the town people rally to her support. She's mad, in a way, but you can't help admire her.'

Drew blinked. The description was ringing the faintest of bells. 'So she and Lapsford–'

'That's right. At least, that's the gossip.'

'Does the wife know?'

'Aha! There you have it. Does she or doesn't she? Nobody's sure on that one. The funny thing is, Roxanne's sister is Pauline Rawlinson, and she's a close friend of Mrs L. One day soon there will be a bucketful of shit hitting a very big fan.'

'You're forgetting Proctor,' growled Sid, who had turned his back on the spate of delighted gossip that he himself had unleashed. 'Reckon maybe Mrs Lapsford was glad to have her husband off her hands.'

Drew's eyes widened. 'You don't mean *Gerald* Proctor? The dentist?'

'The very same,' nodded Sid. 'She works for him. Receptionist.'

Drew could scarcely absorb it. He watched Sid for a minute, irritated by the obsessive ordering of tools. It was the same in the mortuary – everything precise. Daphne had made a joke about it when first showing Drew around.

'Sid's very particular,' she'd said, with a little laugh. 'The others say he's like a magician – or a sorcerer. His embalming's so good, people almost come back to life under his hands.'

Drew hadn't forgotten the remark. It told him as much about Daphne as it did about Sid; he got the clear message that Sid could do no wrong in her eyes.

But what should he *do?* he wondered again. Even with all this talking and gossiping, there still didn't seem to be any real evidence that Jim had been deliberately poisoned. Not yet, anyway, with the toxicology results an unknown quantity. He considered contacting Dr Lloyd, but realised that would amount to accusing the man of incompetence. He could go directly to the Coroner's Officer – perhaps anonymously – but that was far too risky. Questioning a doctor's judgment was akin to blasphemy, and nobody was likely to listen to him. The only course open to him seemed to be to follow up some of this new information about Lapsford's life and background. And he was aware of a sudden powerful urge to go and see the famous Roxanne.

Meanwhile, his researches were progressed indirectly by the arrival of young Dr Parton – who was blessed with the obvious nickname. 'Dolly's here,' hissed Vince, noticing the sporty purple car drive in. 'Looking knackered.'

Dr Parton was twenty-eight, heavily pregnant and now worked only one afternoon a week in a well woman clinic. The rules for cremation papers ordained that the two doctors who signed up a body must not work for the same practice, which sometimes gave rise to complications in a town with only two small GP groups. Dr Parton came in very useful; she was qualified, but not working in a local practice. Her husband was one of Bradbourne's best loved doctors.

'I'll take her through,' said Sid. He went down to meet the young doctor. Drew followed as casually as he could; fortunately, nobody paid him any attention.

Sid had put Lapsford back on the top tray in the fridge. He pulled the body out, and the doctor stood on tiptoe, her nose just level with the tray. 'I can't see much,' she said, and glanced at the paper Olga had given her. 'Coronary,' she muttered to herself, and peered again at the dead face level with her own. 'Hmmm. Better check his name tag.' She stood helplessly, waiting for Sid to assist her. He slid the tray out a little further, until it threatened to tilt like a seesaw and deposit the body onto the floor.

'Hold it, will you?' He motioned to Drew, who was tinkering with one of the coffin trolleys, pretending to have discovered a problem with one of the wheels. Drew came over to the fridge to support the head end of the tray.

'Why don't we get it right out?' he said helpfully. 'Then the doctor could have a proper look.'

'No, no,' said the woman quickly, 'that's ok. I can see him well enough. I just thought I should check his name – since I don't think I knew him.'

Sid roughly tugged at the cold right arm, until the red wristband was visible. He swivelled it slightly, and pulled again. 'There,' he said. 'Lapsford.' The doctor squinted up at it, and nodded. Drew wasn't sure whether she'd even been able to read it. *What a fiasco,* he thought. *She wouldn't notice if there was a knife sticking out of the guy's back.*

'That's that, then,' said Sid, when she'd gone. 'We can get on with embalming him now.'

Drew glanced reluctantly at the jars of bright

pink fluid, the rubber tubes and little pump. He knew the theory, but wasn't in any rush to witness the practice. The deception offended him; making a dead body look pink and healthy seemed a violation of nature.

'I'll just–' he began, trying to think of some excuse not to be present on this particular occasion. He was mercifully interrupted by Daphne coming into the mortuary.

'Drew,' she said, frowning slightly, 'I've just had a rather strange request. It's a bit unorthodox, but... Mrs Lapsford just phoned. Apparently her dog died during the night, and she's asked if we could possibly cremate it along with her husband. I said I thought we could probably do that. It's not as if anyone's going to know. So – would you go round there after lunch and fetch it?'

Drew could hardly speak for excitement. 'No problem,' he choked. 'No problem at all.'

III

David Lapsford was drunk – at eleven in the morning. It had been a deliberate process, pouring whisky into a tumbler, filling it half-full at regular intervals, and taking big mouthfuls. It tasted marvellous. He concentrated on the taste, and the friendly burn that followed every swallow. *Firewater is right,* he thought. *The perfect name for it.* He ought to be at work, of course, but he hadn't even bothered to phone in. If he lost the job, then too bad. It didn't strike him as worth bothering about.

The muzziness of the alcohol in his bloodstream brought relief, self-pity and frustration. At ten, he'd phoned the only person in the world he thought might understand him. 'Sorry, she's not here,' an impatient voice told him. 'She's gone off somewhere for the morning.'

David put the phone down without responding. An hour later, he was too skewed by the drink to remember he'd made the call.

The door opened without warning, and his mother came in: she had a key to his flat, just as he had one to the Primrose Close house. He could see her sniffing the air like a questing dog; it made him laugh. He stopped abruptly when a second person followed Monica into the room. 'Hi, Davey,' said Jodie. 'Haven't seen you for a while.'

'Brought reinforcements, did you, Ma?' he slurred, trying to remember why he'd already spoken Jodie's name that day.

'David, you've been drinking!' Monica was rigid with outrage. 'You stink of it!'

'Just drowning my sorrows,' he said extravagantly. 'Isn't that what you do when a person dies?'

Monica looked at Jodie for rescue. 'Have you seen him like this before?' she demanded.

Jodie didn't reply. David wondered whose side she was on, as she met his eyes with something of the old affection. He remembered then that his mother had come with a specific purpose, to talk to him about his real parents, and he took another swift gulp from the tumbler. Now she was here, he didn't think he wanted to know the truth after all.

'It's – nice of you to come and visit me,' he said slowly, trying to sound coherent. 'I appreciate it. Would you like a drink? Coffee, not whisky – I don't think there's much whisky left. Jodie, will you give me a hand, please? Ma, you sit down – I won't be long.' He led the way unsteadily down the narrow corridor to the kitchen, which was no more or less messy than usual. David had a flatmate, Angus; a divorced man with sorrows of his own to drown. He was a shadowy figure, even to David, saying little and keeping to his room for most of the time. Angus never washed up, never cleaned the floor or the sink or the cooker. David himself did the bare minimum, unless expecting visitors, when he could be capable of an impressive effort. To that extent, his early training at Monica's hands had stuck. But clearly the effort hadn't been made for some time.

Monica remained obediently in the living room, which had been furnished and decorated barely a year ago. The carpet had some unpleasant-looking stains on it, and there was a splintery gash in the wall, which looked as if it had been rammed with something sharp. Jim had lent David his deposit: not much chance of getting that back, thought Monica wryly.

The fact of David's drunkenness loomed over her like a heavy rock, teetering and threatening to land on her head. If she made a wrong move, there could be a disaster. She was far from sure that she had the strength or the skill to push it upright again, get it onto a firmer foundation. One thing she had realised in the first few moments was that today David was in no state to hear the truth about his origins. She simply couldn't trust him to grasp the facts, to react to them in anything like an adult fashion. Having endured the four-mile drive with Jodie, trying to rehearse what she would say, the sense of anti-climax was acute.

Jodie carried three large mugs of coffee back into the living room, on a tray.

David followed close behind. 'Here we are!' he trilled, the perfect host. Although he seemed steadier on his feet, his eyes were bleary and unfocused. Monica felt sick; she knew she couldn't drink the coffee. Sick and self-pitying and disgusted. Hurtful accusations crowded the tip of her tongue. As if aware of this, Jodie began to speak.

'David, your father died only two days ago, and this morning your mother found poor Cassie dead too. The last thing she needs is for you to start behaving like a complete idiot. You don't get many chances in this life. If you can't get yourself sorted out, stick with your job, tidy this place up, figure out what you want to do with yourself – then you'll always be a loser.' She spoke levelly, looking straight at him. Monica winced at some of the words, but was reassured by David's reaction. Despite the familiar sideways tilt of the head and jerky raising of his shoulder, he seemed to be calmer.

One phrase had hooked his attention. 'Sort myself out,' he echoed. 'Yeah. That's what I'm trying to do. I've been trying for years. And I was going to ask him – I was. I was going to tackle him – and her – this week. They don't know that I know. But I do, and I want them to explain.'

Jodie's blank expression almost made Monica laugh. It was obvious, as she had assumed, that David had never shared his suspicions about his parenthood with his former girlfriend. She herself had told Jodie no more than that she had something very difficult to discuss with her son, and would appreciate the girl's company. She hadn't used the word 'protection' – but the implication had been there.

Monica said nothing for a long minute, as the other two looked on. It was a flicker of an image from four or five years ago: a scene in which David and Jodie had defied Monica or Jim or anybody else to try and separate them. Monica had never made the attempt; she knew David was lucky to have Jodie. Jim's response had been a lot more complicated. He had obviously felt uncomfortable about the relationship, but Monica had never understood why.

'It's all right, Mama,' he said, with a startlingly sober smile. 'You can be excused for now. You've told me all I need to know, just by coming here. I know I'm not your natural son.'

Jodie's chin jerked up with shock. She stared wildly at David.

'What are you talking about?' she demanded.

'Didn't she tell you?' he frowned suspiciously.

Jodie shook her head. 'I never doubted you were her son. And Jim's.'

'Then you're in for a surprise,' he said, brandishing the mug like a beacon.

IV

The local weekly paper that day carried a brief report in the STOP PRESS column:

Popular local printer, Jim Lapsford, has been found dead. His doctor diagnosed a massive heart attack. Funeral details have yet to be announced. Jim, 55, was a member of the King's Head darts team and a breeder of pedigree West Highland terriers. He leaves a widow, Monica, and two grown-up sons.

For one person at least, this insignificant report was the first she knew of the death. Lorraine Dunlop had been on holiday in Cyprus for three weeks with her husband and young daughter; they had arrived home at eleven that morning. She felt the shock as a liquidising of her internal organs, puddling in her lower belly, fixing her to the sofa, where she had flung herself for a moment's flip through the news. She felt cold and terribly, horribly lonely. There seemed to be a vicious wind blowing from somewhere, forcing her into a dark void, where nobody would love her ever again.

She clamped her lips together, and quickly turned the page. Frank hadn't noticed anything; he was too busy inspecting his fishtank, checking for casualties of their absence. The urge to say, 'Jim's dead! Can you believe that? He's *dead!*' was almost beyond bearing. And why not say it? Frank knew Jim; *everybody* knew Jim. It was a piece of real news, which she could read out without betraying herself. Except she knew she wouldn't be able to say it. To say the actual words. Not without screaming, crying, running out of the room like a teenager. Swallowing hard, she realised that she would never be able to talk about Jim as she wanted to, not to anyone. Like that woman in Madison County, she would go to her grave with her love unspoken. The dramatic romance of it made her feel slightly better.

Putting the paper down, Lorraine allowed herself a few moments' reverie. Jim's strong arms, thick with black hairs, had always hugged her so warmly, so protectively, after they made love: Jim had been so different from Frank, who merely kissed her briefly and rolled away as soon as the sex was over. Jim had held her tightly to him, savouring the afterglow. Jim had always thanked her, as if she had given him the greatest gift imaginable; making him so happy had been the best part of the whole thing. Jim had understood how to take pleasure, gracefully and wholeheartedly.

Jim had let her talk about disappointment and frustration, and then laughed her into a new state of being. 'Enjoy life!' he had told her. 'Take it by the throat and squeeze every drop of fun out of it. That's what I've decided to do. This is just the start.' He'd been wicked and boyish and she could scarcely believe afterwards the things they'd done together.

The shock hit her again, harder than ever. It wasn't *possible* that he was dead. Jim had been too vital, too overflowing with life, to die. What would he look like, pale and cold in his coffin? Those lovely arms, stiff and folded. No, it was impossible to imagine.

She couldn't face the rest of the day, unpacking and washing the sandy holiday clothes, persuading Cindy to stay awake so she'd sleep properly at bedtime. The flight had left Cyprus at six thirty, which meant they'd had to get up at four. It seemed a million miles away already, the sun and the smiling brown people, everything so easy and uncomplicated. Frank had been a different man, swimming in the ocean each day, eating the foreign food with relish, and rampantly sexy into the bargain. With a mixture of fear and excitement, Lorraine suspected that they'd started a second baby during the first days out there. The sweaty afternoons – clothes had been sheer insanity – and the rhythms of the tides just outside the hotel had combined with something visceral and urgent to bring them together time after time. She hadn't given Jim more than a fleeting thought; she'd taken her pleasure with Frank, feeling a sense of wifely virtue in the process.

'I'd better go and get some shopping in,' she said, heaving herself up, praying that she sounded normal. 'There's nothing for lunch.'

'We could go to the pub,' he offered. 'We're still on holiday, after all.'

Lorraine shook her head, a shade too vehemently. 'There's lots we need. I'd best get it over with. I might be too tired later on.'

'It'll be tomorrow that it hits us,' he said, with his usual irritating certainty. 'Just when I've got to go back to work.'

'Well, time enough to worry about that. It's daft

going back on a Friday, anyway. Are the fish okay?'

'Seem to be. That self-feeder gadget worked, by the looks of it.'

'That's good. Keep an eye on Cindy, will you? She's up in her room. Don't let her go to sleep.'

'Might be a bit late for that. She's very quiet.'

'Oh, hell. Well, I can't be bothered with it now. I need to get out.'

Frank lifted his head. 'What's up with you?'

'Just tired.' She shrugged. 'Nothing. See you later, okay?'

'Okay.' He turned back to his fish. 'I'm sure the koolie eels have grown.'

V

In the mortuary, Sid was pulling an over-tight dress onto a woman of seventy whose daughter thought she should go to her Maker looking as if she were off to a cocktail party. There was no real knack to it, apart from being firm with the uncooperative limbs. It was a point of honour not to simply cut the garment down the back, put it on like a hospital gown and then crudely pin or stitch it up again. Never once had he done that, though many a time he'd been tempted. Perhaps it was less a matter of principle than an anxiety that somehow the family would find out and be outraged: Sid was highly sensitive to criticism.

Daphne's system worked smoothly: a shiny whiteboard was mounted on one wall, and on it she wrote details of jewellery to be left with the body; chapel viewing; whether the cremation papers were completed. Not until this last was accomplished could Sid proceed with any significant tampering with the body. He kept glancing at the board, half-expecting some unseen hand to have ticked the column for Lapsford. Dr Parton's visit should have constituted permission – but Sid remembered the day he'd jumped the gun, only to have Daphne's wrath descend on his head. 'You have to wait until I've put it on the *board*,' she'd raged. 'You can't just carry on regardless. For all you know, the second doctor might not be satisfied. It might seem stupid to you, just a formality, but I promise you it isn't.' Sid had apologised, and agreed to stick to the rules in future. He fully approved of the discipline, in any case: word of mouth and personal observation were not reliable, especially when things were busy.

Vince clattered in, swinging a tin bucket containing a spray of bright flowers. 'These are for the Chapel,' he said. 'Fancy arranging them for me?'

Sid looked unenthusiastic. None of the men were much good with the flowers, but Daphne never seemed to notice. Now and then she sent Olga to do it, but the result was no better than when Vince or Pat simply plonked them into a vase and fluffed them out roughly. Sid felt obliged to make a little more effort, with a mixture of resentment and conscientiousness.

'Where did Drew go?' queried Vince. 'He's taken the Espace.'

'Daphne sent him to fetch a dog,' Sid reported, with a straight face.

'A *dog?* Are you taking the piss?'

'Not just any dog. Apparently Lapsford's died. Must have had a broken heart.'

Vince groaned. 'Not that nice little white thing?' He was genuinely saddened. 'What a shame. But why–?'

'She thought we might put it in his coffin with him. Believe it or not. Better than burying it in the garden, I suppose. It's out of order, so we're not to say anything to the Crem. Better not tell the others, either.'

Vince thought carefully. 'Will it be going to the house, then? For the wake – if that's what she's calling it. Won't that look peculiar? Him and his dog all nestled in together?'

Sid shook his head. 'Don't ask me – I'm just telling you what Daphne told Drew. Anyway, that's where he is.'

'Well, I hope he isn't putting any poison down about doctor's papers,' Vince remarked, as he turned to go. 'That's the last thing we need.'

'He'd better not!' The absence of any expletives in Sid's vocabulary served only to add force to what he said. Vince looked back in surprise.

'Calm down, mate. I was joking. What's he going to say? He's an undertaker's assistant, not a doctor – or a policeman. I don't reckon even Drew is daft enough to stick his nose in.'

Sid rubbed his forehead with a fist. 'I'm going to embalm him. Get it over with. Once that's done, there's not much point in a PM. I don't want any trouble.'

'There isn't going to be any trouble. Unless they ask you to embalm the dog as well!' With a shout of laughter, Vince withdrew from the mortuary, leaving Sid rubbing stiff fingers back and forth along his hairline, in a gesture of thoughtful relief.

He returned to his smartly-dressed lady. He folded the white covers over the body, zigzagging a thin cord tightly across the top and stapling it at intervals to the inside of the coffin, to hold everything in place. Like a sculptor, he positioned the head symmetrically on its neck, tweaked the mouth, lightly brushed the hair with his fingers. When he was satisfied, he reached for the coffin lid, and laid it on top of the coffin; deliberately crooked, since he didn't want it closed yet. He began to trundle the coffin on its wheeled base into the chapel.

Although unspoken, there was a feeling that the chapel was almost as much Sid's domain as was the mortuary. He alone prepared the bodies for viewing, closing their mouths with small stitches hidden inside their lips, or a dab of Superglue, moulding faces into appropriate shapes and positions. There was a tendency for dead faces to droop, and look unduly grim, which had to be rectified; almost invariably, the relatives made approving comments on his handiwork. The flowers were an essential finishing touch, as was the fine net covering which went over the whole coffin, folded back only when visitors appeared.

Working with his silent corpses, Sid was contented. The only one of the men with any professed religious belief, he was the most conscientious in his dealings with the dead. 'Do you think they're watching you?' Vince had remarked one day.

'It doesn't hurt to think so,' Sid had replied.

VI

Monica got home from David's at twelve. She had delivered Jodie back at the printworks, apologising for making the girl wait in vain to hear the secrets of David's parentage. 'I can't tell you anything until I've explained it all to him,' she had said. 'You must see that.' Jodie nodded minimally, and Monica went on, 'It was really nice of you to come with me this morning. David can be so – unpredictable. I just didn't think I'd be able to cope if he started shrieking at me. I think we did the right thing, don't you?'

It was never easy to read Jodie's mood. With an air of intense consideration she would often pause for more than a minute before replying to the simplest remark. She seemed constantly on guard. Monica had learned to give her the benefit of the doubt, influenced by Jim's stalwart defence of her in the face of any criticisms. 'Jodie's pure gold,' he used to say when she first started working for him. 'True as a die. I don't know where we'd be without her. Never mind her manner – we can't help the way we are.' And Monica had believed him. Which made it all the more surprising that he'd been so uneasy about Jodie taking up with David. During that brief year of relative stability, Monica had found herself looking forward to accepting Jodie as the daughter she'd always hoped for.

'He's upset,' came Jodie's eventual reply now.

'I've never known him drink in the morning before. He's obviously got a lot on his mind. I wish I hadn't seen him like that. I thought he'd learned more sense.'

'Oh, Jodie, I'm sorry. I never thought how it might be for you. Especially with Jim – I know how fond you were of him. Oh, it's all such a mess, isn't it.'

'I was more than just fond of him,' said the girl with dignity, before climbing out of the car to stand upright in the layby outside the printworks. Before Monica could reply, she stalked away, her long thin legs and narrow shoulders marking her out as distinctive even when she'd crossed the car park and mingled with a knot of people gathered beside the outer door.

Monica drove home quickly, trying not to think about those last words. Surely *Jodie* hadn't been one of Jim's sexual partners? It was unthinkable – he'd regarded her as a daughter, hadn't he? That, presumably, was all she'd meant. After working with him so long, they'd have established an easy familiarity which transcended fondness. With a sigh, she realised that it hardly mattered anyway.

The young chap from the undertaker's rang the doorbell at one fifteen, standing on the doorstep exactly as he had done on Tuesday morning. It made her feel almost alarmed to have the whole scene re-enacted so soon. 'I hope you don't think this is very peculiar of me?' she said, nervously. 'It just seemed an obvious solution. Jim was very fond of Cassie. I think she must have died of grief for him. Does that happen, do you know? Have you come across it before, at all?'

Drew shook his head. 'But I've only been working here for a few weeks,' he said. 'Although–' He took a deep breath. 'It did come as a surprise. The dog hadn't been ill. And she's not that old. I'm not sure that grief would kill her so quickly. After all, it must only have been about forty-eight hours.' He eyed her earnestly, trying to convey his suspicions without having to spell them out.

Unfortunately, Monica was being obtuse. 'She's ten. That's fairly old for a little dog.'

He took the plunge. 'I remember you said she'd been licking his face – after you found him on Tuesday. I was just wondering–'

Monica stared at him, puzzled. 'I don't follow,' she said.

The full import of what he was trying to say hit him as he met her eyes, and paralysed his tongue. How *did you* suggest to a woman that her husband had actually been murdered? That he didn't die of a heart attack after all? That he had in fact been poisoned by substances unknown? Especially when she'd spent all night beside him, and would be anybody's first choice as prime suspect. He glanced around the room in a wild search for inspiration. The death of the dog had clinched it once and for all in his own mind. It was almost enough to justify calling in the police. Almost – but not quite, unless the widow co-operated much more than she was currently doing.

'I know the doctor said it was Mr Lapsford's

heart,' Drew pressed on valiantly. 'But I was just thinking – what if he'd eaten something the night before? Something that didn't agree with him? Then, if the dog had somehow taken some of it in as well, when she licked his face, that would explain– Was he here all evening on Monday?'

She gave him an antagonistic look. 'As it happens, he wasn't,' she said.

He contented himself with a raised eyebrow. Monica went on, 'He seemed perfectly all right when he got in. Although I suppose I didn't really look at him. You know how it is – well, you probably don't – but after so many years together, you don't really look at each other any more. Besides, I was only in the room with him for a minute or two, before going up to my bath. But he seemed cheerful enough. Made some silly joke about how macho he was – would he have done that, if he'd been feeling ill? Then he went into the kitchen to make a drink, and that's the last I saw of him. Alive, I mean.'

'And do you know where he'd been?'

'It's absolutely none of your business,' she flared up. 'You sound like a policeman – asking all these questions.'

He held up both hands, placatingly. 'I know,' he said. 'And I'm really sorry. I was just curious. It's such a sudden way to die.'

'He was with Jack Merryfield, if you must know,' she said. 'They've been friends for twenty-five years or more. Jack's absolutely devastated by what's happened.'

'I'm sorry,' said Drew again.

Monica indicated the dog, which she'd carried

into the hallway. 'Now, if you could just take her for me, I won't delay you any further.'

He seized on the only remaining postponing tactic he could think of. 'I know it's a terrible cheek of me, but I've been driving most of the morning and really need to use a loo. Do you think I could–'

Monica sighed, exasperated, and said, 'It's the first door you come to at the top of the stairs.'

In the bathroom, he made a hurried search of the medicine cabinet, in true detective style. He knew he'd have no chance to explore elsewhere. The mirrored door made a loud click as it opened, and he froze, thinking she might hear it. When nothing happened, he made a rapid survey of the contents. Headache pills; Deep Heat for muscular pain; sticking plasters; two half-empty bottles of cough medicine; and a plain white plastic container, large enough to hold a hundred or more tablets. He took this out and pulled off the lid. Inside were perhaps thirty bright blue lozenge-shaped tablets which, being bigger than most pills, filled the pot just over halfway. He had seen pictures of tablets like these, and knew what they were. He also knew they were not freely available on prescription, and were generally obtained only on a thriving black market. He slipped one out of the container and into his jacket pocket. Carefully he replaced the lid, and put the container back where he found it. He flushed the loo, ran taps, then he hurried downstairs again, where Monica was waiting for him with an air of impatience.

'I'm sorry about that,' he smiled, gathering up

the dog in its wrapping. 'Now I'll get out of your way. Will you be wanting the towel back?'

She shook her head, in some disgust. 'Perhaps you could dispose of it,' she said, screwing up her nose.

He remembered the arrangements for the coming week. 'Er–' he began, 'when we bring the coffin back to the house – well, will you be wanting it open?'

'Yes. Yes, I'm sure we will. There doesn't seem much point otherwise.'

'So the dog–' he prompted.

'Ah! I see what you mean. I suppose it might look a bit peculiar. And your Miss Plant did imply that it was rather against the rules. You think someone might report me to the authorities?'

'Something like that,' he nodded weakly: in fact, it had been the mere idea of displaying a corpse with a dead dog on its chest that had given him pause for thought. 'Don't worry about it. We'll just look after her for you until the funeral.'

'Thank you,' she said gravely. 'Since Jim was so fond of her, it just seemed a good idea to keep them together. I'm sure I can trust you to do what's best.'

Drew made for the door. As he reached it, the bell rang, making him jump. He looked helplessly over his shoulder at Monica; she reached around him and unlatched the door. A short bearded man in heavy bifocals stood there, scratching the back of his neck with one hand and holding a large sheaf of flowers in the other.

'Jack!' she exclaimed. 'Are those for me? How nice!'

With some deft footwork, she managed to eject Drew and replace him with the new visitor in seconds. Drew found himself on the garden path with the door firmly closed behind him, and no explanations given. 'Come on then, dog,' he muttered. 'Let's see what we can make of you.'

VII

Not for a moment did Drew believe it was a coincidence when Monica's two elderly neighbours emerged from their front door, side by side, wearing light autumn jackets and stout walking shoes. Heads down, they appeared to be deep in conversation all the way to their front gate.

'Oh, my goodness, what *have* you got there?' the smaller one asked innocently, as she almost bumped into him. He hefted the stiffly awkward bundle clumsily, causing one corner of the enfolding towel to fall away and flap against his knees. 'It looks awfully mysterious,' she added.

'Sarah!' the tall one remonstrated. 'It's nothing to do with you.' But she too fixed her eyes attentively on Drew's armload, her head slightly on one side.

'You must be Mrs Lapsford's neighbours,' he remarked, inanely.

'Obviously,' Sarah confirmed snappily. 'Unless you think we've just been burgling number twenty-two. Which is, of course, something we might accuse *you* of.'

'Except it would be number twenty-four in your case,' added Dottie helpfully. 'You know, I think I can see a little patch of hair just there. White hair. How intriguing!'

Could he claim it was a very small old person? He thought not. 'It's Mrs Lapsford's dog,' Drew confessed. 'She – died. I'm taking her away. It's a – service we do.'

Dottie gave a little moan of grief. 'Oh, no! Not dear little Cassie! But how? She was always such a fit little thing.' The echoes of two days before were loud in Drew's ears. How was it that these obtuse people couldn't see what was jumping up and down in front of their faces?

But perhaps he had under-estimated these ladies, for Sarah narrowed her eyes. 'Isn't this all rather odd?' she said slowly. 'First Jim – and now his dog? There isn't some sort of gas leak in the house, is there? Or has Monica been gathering mushrooms in the woods?'

Now it was Dottie's turn to speak sharply. 'Mind your tongue,' she warned. 'You'll be accused of slander, if you're not careful.'

'Tell me,' Sarah addressed Drew, 'how long have you known the Lapsford family?'

He smiled, and directed his gaze modestly at the pavement. 'Well, to be completely honest with you, I'm from the undertaker's – Plant's. I removed Mr Lapsford on Tuesday. The dog died this morning, and Mrs Lapsford asked us to keep them together. She thinks Cassie just pined away.'

'So she never called the vet?'

'I imagine she's been a bit too busy for that.'

Drew tried to sound neutral, fighting to hide his growing excitement at finally finding an ally in his conviction that all was not as it ought to be.

'Is it common practice for people to be buried with their dogs?' asked Dottie. 'It sounds rather nice to me. Though, of course, I don't suppose they often die at the same time. Not unless they were in some sort of accident.'

'It's not a burial, it's a cremation,' Sarah corrected her. 'Monica told us that yesterday.'

Dottie blinked. 'What difference does that make?'

Sarah looked full into Drew's face, and he could see an undimmed intelligence at work. 'I think this young man and I both know that it could make a very big difference,' she said. 'Oh, don't worry–' she reassured him, as he cast an anxious glance at number twenty-four, 'I already know that you have your own suspicions.'

He frowned, and tried vainly to rewrap the dog with the cumbersome towel, stalling for time. 'How?' he asked at last.

'Your complete lack of surprise at what I've been saying has given you away,' she said triumphantly, in an impressive parody of Miss Marple. 'Well, I wish you luck. Perhaps you'd like to come and talk to us again, when you've got more time? Tomorrow evening – or Saturday morning, perhaps. I think we might be able to point you in one or two helpful directions. But you'll have to move fast. The cremation–'

'We've got until next Tuesday,' nodded Drew. 'And I have to go now. But I'll be back as soon as I can. Thank you very much, Mrs–'

'Simpson,' supplied Sarah. 'Sarah Simpson. And this is Dottie. Now don't lose that dog! It might be just the evidence you need.'

VIII

'Visitor for you, Sid,' announced Pat, putting his head round the mortuary door. 'She says will you make sure there's nothing nasty in here, before she comes in.'

Sid looked up from the coffin he was working on in some alarm. 'Who is it?' he demanded crossly. 'There's nothing to see, anyway.' The coffin was empty, waiting for Jim Lapsford to occupy it in due course.

'Don't worry, Dad – it's only me,' came a familiar voice. 'I just didn't feel up to watching you embalming somebody.'

'Why? You're not pregnant, are you?' he asked suspiciously. He moved towards her, and laid a hand on her shoulder, examining her face earnestly.

'For heaven's sake! The number of times you ask me that I should get pregnant just to shut you up. It's obvious that that's what you really want, deep down.'

'Don't start that. What d'you want? Did Daphne see you?'

'Don't worry – I came straight round the back. I just wanted to have a little chat, away from Mum.'

'It's about that Craig, then, is it? Had another ding-dong with him?'

Susie leaned against the foot end of the coffin,

bumping against it slightly as she rocked restlessly on the balls of her feet. 'It's not my fault, Dad – he just won't take no for an answer. I don't know what else I can do. I thought maybe if you had a word with him–'

'*Me?* He's not going to listen to me, is he?'

'He might. He respects you. If you could just tell him you know for a certainty that I'm never going to change my mind about going back with him. Say anything you like about me, something really horrible, if it'll put him off. It's really getting to me now. He follows me about, phones me up, writes letters... It's like having a stalker.'

'You know what your mother would say, don't you?' Susie nodded. 'She'd say it was all your own fault.'

'I know she would. But I really did like him, to start with anyway. It's just – he's into stuff that'll get us both in trouble sooner or later. You won't say anything, will you – about what I told you the other week?'

'What are you talking about?'

'Come on – don't tell me you've forgotten.'

'I said then, I didn't want to hear.'

'It isn't that simple, Dad. I could get into real trouble, if you don't help me put a stop to it. It's getting too risky. To start with, he just made me pilfer a few things. Nothing too terrible, just prescription pads and–'

'*Just prescription pads!*' Sid hissed, in horror. 'Don't tell me any more. I will *not* have any daughter of mine mixed up in anything like that. The sooner you're shot of him the better. I'm out this evening, but I'll see if I can track him down tomorrow. Where d'you think he'll be?'

She shrugged. 'He drinks at the Blue Lion mostly. Can you lower yourself enough to go there?'

'Don't get sarky, my girl. A pub's a pub. I only go to the King's Head 'cause it's closer.'

'Thanks, Dad. I didn't think you'd do it. I should have had more faith.'

'Faith is just about what you need,' he agreed. 'If you went to church a bit more–'

She waved a silencing hand at him. 'Don't start that, either,' she pleaded. Then, she looked curiously at the coffin, which she had been using as a support. 'Is this for Jim Lapsford?' she asked.

'That's right,' he nodded curtly.

'People seem to be getting into quite a sweat over him,' she commented, deliberately casual. 'Your Daphne phoned Dr Lloyd again yesterday. Has someone been asking questions about the papers, or something?'

Sid frowned. 'Not that I know of,' he said. 'Why should they?'

'Come on, Dad. Dr Lloyd pushed it through when he never should have done. It was only because he's scared of annoying the Coroner again that he did it. You can't blame him – he's absolutely sure it was a heart attack.'

'That's what it looks like to me,' Sid nodded confidently. 'He's the fourth man of his sort of age we've had here this year. They weren't all Dr Lloyd's patients, were they?'

'Three of them were.' Susie was evidently anxious to chat. She leaned over the coffin earnestly. 'And don't you remember me telling you at the weekend about Mr Lapsford not seeing a doctor for twelve years?' she went on. 'No wonder people are talking.'

'People will talk about anything,' Sid told her. 'I'll be glad when he's well and truly burnt.'

She stood up straight, and walked the length of the coffin to where Sid remained at the head end. She kissed his cheek, and he put a brief arm around her, pulling her close. 'Thanks for listening, Dad. And if you can get Craig off my back, I'll be eternally grateful.'

'Anything for you, my darling,' he said.

IX

Drew had stowed the dead dog in the bottom of the chiller, and gone back to the workshop. Both Georges, Pat and Vince were there, engaged in minor tasks. Vince and Little George were itemising coffin handles, crucifixes and name plates, tidying up the boxes in the store cupboard as they went. Big George came up to Drew. 'Hey, Andy – there's a big memorial to come off a grave in the cemetery,' he said. 'Daphne thought you might like to come and help.' George was given most of the heavy jobs, including removing head-stones from graves preparatory to a second burial; his muscles stood out emphatically on his upper arms, and his neck would have done a bull proud.

'Fine,' Drew agreed. 'When do we go?'

'Now, if you're ready. Looks as if it might rain later on.'

Both the Georges were proving more resistant

than the others to Drew's attempts at friendship. Little George was a surly individual, inclined to detect insult or malice in the most innocent comments; at the same time, his sharp tongue made him readily offensive to others. Drew had quickly decided to give him the widest berth he could, and the decision appeared to be mutual. Big George, the oldest of all the men, was more affable, despite the provocative 'Andys'. Given to reminiscing about the old days, he had witnessed every kind of funeral from Hindu to Humanist. His memory was legendary; even Daphne consulted him on family histories. Drew was quick to grasp the opportunity of an hour alone with this fount of information.

'Daphne said we'd done another Lapsford funeral, ages ago,' he began, as they rode in the old van kept for such jobs as this.

'That's right,' George confirmed. 'Must have been the seventies. I'd say at a guess nineteen seventy-six. Yeah, it was that really hot summer. Remember?'

Drew laughed. 'I was only seven, but I do remember we had the paddling pool out in the garden, and my mum would get into it with us, because she was so hot.'

'Well, it was a bad time for funerals. Or good – depending on how you look at it. The heat finished them off like flies, and we couldn't keep them cool – the fridges weren't as good as they are now. We had this woman, quite young she was, as I recall. She died of MS, went off just like that. Anyway, her name was Lapsford. I remember her mother came to view, and we had to spray air freshener everywhere to cut the stink.'

'What relation was she to this chap?'

'Well, that I'm not too sure about. I didn't go to the funeral. I guess he's her nephew, maybe, or a cousin. Daphne said she'd look up the records, but she's probably forgotten.'

As they reached the cemetery and located the grave in question, it began to drizzle. 'Look, there's that woman – the one we were talking about the other morning,' George remarked. 'That Roxanne. What the hell's she doing here?' Drew followed his gaze and saw a wide-shouldered woman with a frizz of dark hair bending over a patch of long grass close to the boundary of the cemetery.

George answered his own question. 'Gathering herbs for one of her potions.'

'You mean, the woman they say was having it off with Lapsford?' Drew ventured. 'The one from the caravan?' He remembered the blue pill in his pocket, and fingered it delicately. Lapsford's use of Viagra didn't strike him as particularly unusual, in the circumstances: he simply needed to find out whether it could have somehow contributed to the man's death.

'That's the one. Roxanne Gibson. Her sister is Pauline Rawlinson, and *her* son is Craig, who goes out with Sid's Susie. Got it straight now?'

Drew shook his head in wonderment. 'It's amazing,' he said. 'Bradbourne's got a population of twenty-five thousand people, and somehow they're all related to each other.'

George rested on the large granite headstone. 'Twenty years ago, you know, this was a very small town. Say eight thousand, at the most. Then the developers moved in, and added all those new estates, one after the other. That made it seem like a much bigger place – but the *real* Bradbourne, which is the bit along the river, and up to the church, is much the same as it always was. Even if folks have moved into the new houses, and their kids get flats out on the city road, they're still all connected.'

'But there's loads of newcomers like me, surely?'

'Yeah, but a lot have got family here already.'

Drew picked at a tooth thoughtfully. 'It makes a big difference if people work locally, I suppose,' he concluded. 'That's where the hospital comes in. They employ a thousand or so, all told.'

'And the supermarket soaks up most of the rest,' added George.

Drew watched the dark-haired woman so intently, she turned towards him, as if she felt his eyes on her. She was thirty or forty yards away, so he couldn't see her face clearly, but he felt sure she was beautiful. He let out a long unconscious sigh. She wore a long blue cotton skirt and a skimpy purple singlet, apparently careless of the cold and damp; her arms were strong and brown, and as she bent down again, he could see heavy breasts swinging braless inside the top.

George echoed Drew's sigh. 'Lovely, ain't she,' he said softly. 'Every man's dream. Like some sort of goddess.'

Drew looked at him in surprise. He was unaccustomed to such poetry from George. But he nodded agreement, and his eyes returned to the woman. It was true – she had a kind of magical quality, something special about her. He remembered the rosy self-satisfied look on Lapsford's dead face. *Lucky bugger,* he thought.

They wrestled the hunk of granite into the back of the van, stuck a marker in the grave, and drove off. They had to pass the woman, where she stood tall against the hedge. Drew met her eyes for a second or two, aware of tawny depths. He could see now that she was older than he first thought, and less beautiful. She smiled at him, self-mocking, as she stood in the drizzle with bare shoulders and a large basket at her feet. Even as he felt a stab of attraction, he shivered a little, too. She was dangerous, he sensed. He very much hoped that he would see her again. Soon.

X

'What can I do for you, Jack?' Monica asked wearily. This was turning into a very long day, and it was still barely two o'clock: the thought of a nice rest with her feet up and something mindless on the telly made her impatient to get the visit over with.

'Well, we were wondering–' he began, in some confusion, 'whether you might want some sort of service sheet printed. For the funeral. Or some cards for people – thanking them for writing, or sending flowers. I – we thought it would save you some trouble, if we could do that. And Jim'd like it. Printed on his own machines. Don't you think?'

'Jack, that's a lovely idea,' Monica gushed,

while her heart sank at the prospect of composing all-purpose thank-you messages, or hymn sheets for a funeral she still couldn't begin to imagine. 'And how are you managing at the works, without Jim? It must be very strange for you. I know how much he put into it. You were his second family, in many ways.'

'We're managing,' he said shortly. 'I know you saw Jodie this morning. She said something about David. The lad's not ill, is he?'

'What?' The sudden change of subject caught her unawares. 'Oh, well, you know David. Always some drama.' Even as she spoke, she felt disloyal; the problem of David lay on her chest like undigested plum pudding, and she knew she'd have to make another attempt to have a serious talk with him, before long. Not that it was any of Jack's business, though.

'It must be a great loss to him – Jim going so suddenly.' The sympathetic words were halting. 'And to his brother, of course.'

'Yes, of course. But they're grown up now. They'll be all right. Once David gets over this latest crisis, and the funeral's done with, it'll all settle down again. Their lives won't change. Though I suppose there'll be a bit of money coming to them, from the life insurance. It's only fair that I should give them a share.'

Jack seemed ill at ease. She hadn't asked him to sit down, which now seemed rather rude; he rested his knuckles on the back of the sofa, and faced her over it. She could see the man from the undertaker's standing outside on the pavement, talking to Sarah and Dottie from next door.

Doubtless they were sticky-beaking again. She tried to keep her attention on her visitor. Almost idly, she remarked, 'Jim was with you on Monday night, wasn't he?'

Jack blinked. 'Well, yes. We had a game of Canasta, like we used to before I got the computer. He didn't fancy watching a flickering screen, he said.'

'Was that because he had a headache? Did he mention feeling unwell? You see, you were very possibly the last person to talk to him.'

'But, surely – he must have got home before ten. Didn't you see him?'

'Yes, sort of. Just briefly. Just enough to know he'd come home. But I didn't *look* at him. We didn't have a proper conversation. I've no idea how he was feeling. I thought you might have taken more notice.'

He paused, as if trying to remember. 'He was a bit quiet,' he offered. 'And he didn't really have his mind on the game. I won every hand – that's unusual. He seemed to lose interest.'

'Jack, you've known Jim for a long time. Longer than I have, even. You work with him all day, and see him at least one evening every week. Would you tell me, honestly – did you like him?' She spoke in an urgent rush, as if the question had been forced out of her against her will.

Jack cocked his head, first one way, then the other, examining the question. Then he sat down on one arm of the sofa, and gripped the edge of it tightly. 'We were like brothers,' he said. 'You don't ask yourself whether you like your brother. He's just – part of your life.'

'But there were people who didn't like him – isn't that right?'

He nodded. 'Loads,' he agreed. 'But I don't think you need worry about that. They won't take it out on you.'

She flapped a hand impatiently. 'That's not what I meant. It's just – well, I know it's stupid – only somebody suggested that possibly Jim didn't die of a heart attack after all. And if he didn't, then there's a chance that something else happened. I mean, there is just a faint chance that he was deliberately–' She couldn't say it. Especially not to the man who had been the last to see her husband.

'Garbage!' he said fiercely. 'The sort of thing people say just to stir up trouble. The doctor was happy enough, wasn't he? You forget that sort of talk.' His eyes, distorted by the glasses, bored into her: there was a sheen of sweat on his brow. He looked angry.

'I know,' she capitulated weakly. 'It's just – silly.' She cleared her throat. 'Why don't you and Jodie compose something for the front of the service sheet – name, place, date – and when I've sorted out the rest with the vicar, I'll let you have it. Tomorrow, probably. Or I'll get the undertaker's to fax it to you. Okay?'

He took the signal, and stood up slowly, saying nothing.

'Thanks very much for coming, when I'm sure you're busy,' she babbled.

Jack bristled. 'Jim and I were best mates,' he reproached her. 'Something wrong if I can't come to offer my condolences.'

She let him out with as much dignity as she could muster. The undertaker's vehicle had gone. With a belated pang, she realised that she would miss Cassie more than she'd admitted. The house was going to seem very empty that evening.

XI

Lorraine couldn't sit still. She'd done the shopping, put the holiday clothes in the wash, watched TV with Cindy and made supper for the three of them. Cindy was now in bed and there were two hours or more before Lorraine could decently follow suit. 'I'm going to get some cigs,' she said suddenly, not waiting for Frank to argue. 'I'll only be ten minutes.' And she was out into the darkening night, the late summer evenings closing in, still warm, but with a sense of conclusion in the air.

They lived just around the corner from the King's Head, where Jim had played darts. Unhesitatingly Lorraine walked in, knowing that half the people there would be her friends. And Jim's...

'Hi, Lorrie!' said a voice from the table inside the door. 'Where's Frank?'

'Babysitting. I just came to get some fags. How are you, Sid?'

'Can't grumble. Waiting for Brenda to finish in the Ladies, then we're off home. First time we've been out for ages.'

'That's nice.' *Did you hear about Jim?* she wanted to scream. She looked round, wondering who else might be there. No familiar faces caught her eye. Then she remembered. 'Sid? You work at the undertaker's, don't you? I was just catching up with the paper. We've only just got home from Cyprus. I saw–' Something in her throat, like a huge ball of cottonwool, prevented further words.

Sid looked at her closely, and said nothing. Was he suspicious?

'Hi, Lorrie!' came a second voice from behind her. Brenda stood there, smug and dumpy. 'I suppose you heard about Jim?'

'I was just saying,' she managed to stumble. 'Awful. So sudden.'

'Sid says he looks like he's asleep. Like they usually do after a heart attack. When they're youngish, like him. Poor Monica. It's her birthday next week, you know. Jim was planning a celebration. Not that we would have gone. Monica is my sister-in-law's cousin, actually.'

'Oh. Right.' Lorraine edged away. 'Well, must get back. Good to see you.' A throbbing headache began, switched on by an invisible hand. This was going to be unbearable. People were going to talk about him, and she'd have to pretend only a passing interest. A man twenty-five years older than her, supposedly beyond her reach. They had been so careful; Lorraine was sure nobody had suspected at all. Ever since that first afternoon in May when they'd met by accident on the footpath beside the river, got talking and fallen in love. They'd been able to devise times and places to meet which she was confident had gone completely unobserved. As manager at the printer's, Jim had been his own boss, popping out easily, claiming to be visiting suppliers, consulting with customers. Lorraine, with a five-year-old daughter, worked mornings in the supermarket. For three hours every afternoon, she was free to go where she liked. Even when Cindy was on holiday from school, there had been opportunities. The school ran Summer Activities; little friends invited her to spend the day.

How could she go home to her husband and her daughter, carry on as a normal wife and mother, after this? Without those secret afternoons, always spent outdoors in that long hot summer, life wouldn't be possible. It was as simple as that. She could feel her body drying up, flaking away, uncelebrated by the lovely man who had enjoyed it so unashamedly and always thanked her afterwards.

But she did go home, and Frank barely noticed that she'd been out. Why did she have to meet creepy Sid and Brenda, of all people? She hadn't wanted to know what Jim looked like dead. A healthy-looking corpse was no better than a mangled mess from a car crash. She couldn't bear to think about Jim on the undertaker's slab. She ran upstairs, but there was nothing for her to do. Popping her head round Cindy's door, she saw her child asleep, limbs flung out in the evening warmth, carefree and tanned. Would this brief secret summer form an unbreakable barrier between them for ever?

'Hey, did you see this?' said Frank, when she went downstairs again. He shook the paper at her. 'Old Jim Lapsford's dead. Can you believe it? Wasn't he in the King's Head, right as rain, the day before we went away?'

Lorraine closed her eyes briefly, then nodded. 'They were all talking about him in there just now. It's been a shock to everyone.'

'You know what I heard?' Frank went on, lowering his voice against invisible listeners.

'What?' She wasn't paying him much attention: the thudding ache inside her was too insistent. And she'd just noticed a telltale metallic taste on the back of her tongue. A certain sign of pregnancy, that. *Oh, God,* she thought.

'Well, someone mentioned to me, a while ago now, that old Jim was having it off with that Roxanne woman. You know – the one in the caravan, with the frizzy hair. He was always over there, apparently.'

Lorraine stared at him. She felt her stomach swelling, forcing itself upwards, filling her throat. Her head clouded over inside, so she could hardly see. 'What?' she repeated, foolishly. 'What did you say?'

'Steady on, love. You look really rough. Must be jetlag or something. Sit down before you fall down.'

'*Roxanne?* The one who's in the pub sometimes? The big woman? Who told you that? I don't believe it.'

'Can't remember now. Anyway, he died in his own bed, it says here. A blessing for his wife. Let's go up, shall we? It's been a long day.'

Lorraine allowed him to chivvy her up to bed. She pretended to fall asleep as soon as the light was off, but she lay there for hours, endlessly exploring ways in which she could learn the truth. Had Jim *really* been having sex with Roxanne as well as her? The sense of betrayal was as painful as it was irrational. *But he loved me,* she kept repeating to herself. *He said he loved me more than anybody he'd ever known.* And then, as she finally drifted off to sleep: *If he wasn't already dead – I think I'd kill him.*

XII

Monica's doorbell rang three more times that day, and the telephone hardly stopped. Apparently the traditional British habit of avoiding death and anyone touched by it was long departed. Now people came in droves, all wanting to commiserate, to help, to ask questions. She had known Jim was a prominent local figure, of course, but she had never fully realised how big a part he played in the lives of so many. Most of the people who called she scarcely knew. She felt invaded, loaded down with other people's emotions. One girl from a local shop had even started crying down the phone, saying how much she'd miss his cheerful face every morning when he'd called in for his papers and peppermints. 'I hope I haven't bothered you?' she said at the end, and Monica was very close to telling the truth.

'It sounds as if you and the rest of the world are going to miss him rather more than I will,' she could almost hear herself saying by the end of the day. 'Just let me get this damned funeral over with, and Jim can rest in peace as far as I'm concerned.' But she merely murmured platitudes.

It was eight o'clock when a fourth ring came at the door. Monica, at the end of her tether, opened it. Standing there, mouth slightly open, face slightly pink, was a huge man wearing a clerical collar and other accoutrements. 'Mrs Lapsford?' he enquired in sonorous tones, raising two thick grey eyebrows. 'It's not too late in the day for a visit, is it?'

She gave a little cry of exasperation. 'Vicar. They told me you'd want to see me. Oh – you'd better come in.'

'I know I should have telephoned first, but I was literally passing by, and decided to take a chance.' He moved gradually into the house. 'And I should have said, of course, how very sorry I am about your terrible loss.'

Monica tried to suppress the hysteria she felt gathering in her chest. The mere sight of this man was farcical enough, without his meaningless utterances. *He must weigh twenty-five stone,* she thought, mentally assessing his girth. *How is it I've never noticed him before?* 'Sit down,' she invited, indicating the couch. He waited for her to take an armchair and then sank quite gracefully into the cushions.

'I forget which church you're from,' she said. 'I'm sorry.'

'No matter,' he smiled. 'It's St James's, on the Hillbrow estate.'

'Oh, yes.' She summoned up a mental picture of a functional-looking church, built in the sixties, with a huge stained-glass front wall and a metallic crucifix standing outside. 'Of course.

I'm afraid Jim didn't go to church.'

He smiled again, forgivingly. 'I'm Father Barry, by the way. That's what everyone calls me. Now, perhaps we could just talk a little about the service on Tuesday, and what you'd like me to say about your husband? If it's convenient?'

Father Barry, Monica giggled to herself. What were his parents thinking of? Had they no inkling of their baby's vocation when they named him? Perhaps they had hoped it would effectively rule out any such calling.

The effort to concentrate was exhausting; she seemed unable to recall any suitable facts or anecdotes about Jim. She found herself idiotically telling a trivial little tale about the time he printed six hundred menus with 'Lobster' spelt as 'Lostber' and how lostber had become a family joke word for anything that went awry after that. 'But I don't expect you can use that,' she added lamely, at the end of the story.

'No,' he agreed regretfully, 'perhaps you're right.'

He stayed for an hour; she slowly warmed to him. They drank tea together, let a few comfortable silences develop. She knew he would do his best, and that it wasn't his fault Jim had never been inside his church, and didn't believe that there was any sure and certain hope of a resurrection to come. She ought never to have agreed to have a minister at the funeral. She should have been brave enough to do the whole thing herself. She should have been – but wasn't.

He left her an order of service for Jack and Jodie to print up, and patted her gently on the arm. 'I'll see you on Tuesday, my dear,' he said as he departed.

There was then a thirty-minute lull, during which she made herself a simple supper of soup and a sandwich. The day had felt somehow aimless; was she failing to do anything vital? People always talked about the great rush and bustle of paperwork and plans following a death. She supposed they meant things like the talk she'd just had with Father Barry, and the visit yesterday to the undertaker. And the letter to the life insurance people, enclosing a copy of the death certificate. If so, then she was clearly coping wonderfully, because here she was now with half an evening still ahead of her, and no idea how to fill it.

But she need not have worried. The final ring on the door-bell came just before nine. With a sense of being saved, she went quickly to answer it. Gerald Proctor was standing there, holding a great mass of yellow and gold chrysanthemums. His broad face with its horizontal crinkles at eye and mouth peered shyly at her from over the top of the flowers.

'Oh, Gerald,' she sighed.

He moved her gently aside and stepped into the house, closing the door quickly behind him. 'Nobody saw me,' he said in a whisper. 'Your reputation's safe.'

'It's a bit late to worry about that. And I'll bet you one of the old dears next door spotted you through the lace curtains.'

'Well, I'm here now, and I won't stay long.' His expression became serious, as she watched him.

His face was all curves: his eye sockets were deep, his nose rounded, his cheeks plump. Many times she had wished she was a sculptor and could make a model of his head. His hair was white, despite his being only slightly over forty. 'How are you, old girl?'

'Oh, Gerald, it *is* good to see you. I was feeling a bit sorry for myself, to be honest. Wishing I had someone to talk to. The dog died this morning, you know, so I haven't even got her for company.'

'What – little Cassie?' She was surprised he remembered the name.

'That's right. She was Jim's – I think she pined away. I was never that fond of her, but she would have been another life around the house.'

'You can get another one.'

'Perhaps,' she returned. 'Gerald, you shouldn't be here, you really shouldn't. I – people will think badly of me, if they see you.'

'Nobody could ever say you were a bad wife,' he assured her. 'Jesus, Monny, you'd been married for donkey's years. You'd earned a bit of fun. And Jim wasn't the type to be jealous–'

'Oh, yes he was!' Gerald shrank at the forcefulness of her words. 'He would have been devastated if he'd known about us. And don't start trying ever so coyly to remind me that he wasn't the most faithful husband in the world either. Everybody knows the rules are different for men. I've been terrified since Tuesday that somebody was going to take it upon themselves to whisper to me that Jim had *liaisons,* or some such rubbish. They think a dead man's fair game, and that there's no more need to keep his secrets.

They don't consider my dignity.'

She took hold of Gerald's arm as she spoke, to draw him further into the room, where he couldn't be seen from the street. Suddenly she became aware of the contact, and of the new freedom she had. There was at least no danger of Jim returning unexpectedly and catching them at it. Involuntarily, she gave a little laugh at the thought. 'What's funny?' he asked.

'Oh – life, I suppose. And death. Death is quite funny, I'm discovering. I never realised before.'

'Tell me,' he invited, frowning slightly.

'It's nothing I can spell out. Just the whole business, with doctors and undertakers and vicars. All sorts of meaningless rituals to go through. And most of it seems designed to make me forget what's actually happened. That Jim's in some fridge, cold and stiff and dead.' She poked Gerald's hand, pushing back his sleeve and taking his wrist. 'Not like you – warm and *glowing*, somehow. Dead people don't glow.'

'*Dead People Don't Glow* would make a terrific title for a crime novel,' he said absently, staring intently at a corner of the carpet as some embryonic plot began to form in his head. Gerald aspired to crime writing, which was the single thing about him that Monica found ridiculous.

'I woke up in the middle of last night, and I could see him, in that place, lying on some metal tray. Just meat. Worse than meat. Like a dollop of clay. Nothing. It gave me the horrors.'

'You should take a sleeping pill,' he advised.

'Oh, really, Gerald.' She looked at him again,

with a kind of curiosity. Gerald's wife had left him five years ago; he was very much available. She understood that this had already led to certain assumptions on his part, and the idea alarmed her. His clumsy lack of insight into how she was feeling similarly gave her pause. Despite his delicious eye sockets, she wasn't at all sure that she really liked him. Not as a person.

He was injured. 'Sorry,' he murmured. 'Do you want me to go?'

'I think so,' she said simply. 'You make things too complicated. We haven't even had the funeral yet.'

'Ah, yes. That was what I wanted to ask you. Do you think I should come to it?'

She looked at him again, this time in disbelief. 'Of *course* I don't,' she snapped. 'What possible reason could you have to do that? You scarcely even knew him.'

'But I know *you*,' he persisted. 'You work for me. It would be perfectly appropriate.'

'Well, thanks for the thought, but you'd better not. I wouldn't know how to behave with you around. I'll see you later – the middle of next week, when it's all finished with. All right?'

'It'll have to be, I suppose,' he pouted. 'You'll be back at work on Wednesday, will you?'

She gave a little cry. 'Wednesday's my birthday! The first day of the rest of my life...'

'I'll see you then,' he confirmed, and departed after a fleeting featherlight kiss.

CHAPTER FOUR
FRIDAY

I

Drew was making notes. He had lain awake much of the night, worrying. He now had only four days in which to gather sufficiently strong evidence that Jim Lapsford had been the victim of a clever murder: evidence strong enough to present to the police, or the Coroner. He had a whole mountain of facts and hints and possible leads, but still nothing tangible.

'You were restless,' Karen said, with more irritation than sympathy. 'I don't need to ask why, do I?'

'It's really getting to me,' he admitted. 'Only four days to go now, and I haven't got anything definite. If the cremation goes ahead, I don't know what I'll do.'

'Why do anything? What difference will it make?'

Something about her impatience, the faint whiff of accusation, tipped him back into the nightmare he'd forgotten until now. At some point in the small hours, he had dropped off to sleep, only to be haunted by the event that he could never quite escape.

In the busy short-staffed chaos of the Royal

Victoria Hospital, Drew had found himself on the Pediatric Ward the previous November, working the night shift. He'd been covering for sickness amongst the staff, and had not been properly briefed or trained in what was a specialised sort of nursing care. Nicholas had been brought down from Intensive Care, well on the road to recovery after a nasty attack of pneumonia. He was ten weeks old, and had not thrived as he should have done since birth.

The baby's mother had three other children at home, and no husband. She came to visit when she could, but never stayed the night, as most mothers did. The other babies on the ward were all off the danger list, and most also had parents popping in to feed or simply observe them during the night. Nicholas was Drew's main charge. He was a nice little baby, undersized, but with a placid manner, and Drew had played with him for a few minutes before he dropped off to sleep. His temperature and heart rate were monitored, but all other machinery had been removed. He was breathing well, without assistance.

The ward was quiet, as midnight came and went, and Drew relaxed. He even started to consider pediatrics as a speciality for the future. The babies seemed to respond well to a man, and many of the mothers remarked on how good it was to see him there. When he checked Baby Nicholas, at one AM, the child was showing no overt cause for concern, despite a slightly lowered temperature and a skin colour just a shade less pink than an hour earlier. Drew fleetingly wondered whether a few minutes of oxygen would help, but it seemed unnecessarily unkind to wake and disturb the baby. He would cry, which in turn couldn't fail to stir some of the others.

He tucked the blanket tighter, and resolved to make another check in twenty minutes. Caught up in conversation with a restless mother, it was half an hour before he went back. Nicholas was still sleeping peacefully, but his colour had darkened yet again. His heart rate was fractionally slower, too. But Drew believed this to be within normal limits, and something that often happened in the small hours. He ran through his options: administer oxygen; take the baby back to Intensive Care; call a houseman; pick the baby up and assess his condition when awake. He had never set up an oxygen chamber for such a small child, and knew it needed to be held in place and the dose carefully monitored. He doubted whether he was authorised to do it unsupervised. By rights there should be at least two other people within calling distance, but there were only nurses of the same standing as himself, each with their own ward to deal with. He could go and consult one of them, but pride prevented him. He leaned over Nicholas, listening to his breathing, and concluded that he was in no danger.

An hour later, a buzzer sounded above the baby's cot. His heart had stopped. Drew shook himself out of the semi-doze he'd fallen into, and hurried over. He lifted Nicholas free of his coverings, still not unduly worried; machines could give false alarms, and it barely occurred to him that there could be a serious problem. But the child was limp in his hands, the eyes half open. Drew gave a startled cry, which echoed around the corners and corridors, but brought no assistance. Even now, he was loathe to make a commotion, to bring the clattering cacophony of the resuscitation trolley.

But he had to, and it all got taken out of his hands, and Baby Nicholas officially died at four fifteen AM. Shakily, Drew gave his account of the events of the night; everyone agreed that the signs had not been sufficiently clear to justify any intervention. He was told, repeatedly, that he had done nothing wrong.

But doing nothing was wrong in itself, he concluded. Never again would Drew err on the side of inertia. His nightmares since then had all involved watching something or somebody die, hands loose and helpless at his sides, his mind repeating, *It's not your responsibility. It isn't up to you.* But he knew it was. If he didn't act, then nobody else was going to.

He had tried to explain it to Karen, knowing that she was deliberately refusing to understand his terror of history repeating itself. 'Lightning doesn't strike twice,' she told him. 'And anyway, they told you the baby would most probably have died, whatever you did. He had much more wrong with him than they realised. The post-mortem showed that.'

Words did nothing to change what he knew. He couldn't ever tell her how it had really been. How he had been afraid of waking the baby up in case it cried; afraid of being told off for making a fuss and calling in an exhausted houseman. How small fears could make you commit large sins.

And now the dilemma was visiting him again. It was as if he were being tested, given a chance to get it right this time. He could no more sit back and let Lapsford be cremated than he could watch another baby lose colour and warmth until it died before his very eyes.

Drew had, in the long night now over, come up with a plan. It might be risky, or even doomed to fail, but he was determined to follow it through.

He studied his notebook. *Gerald Proctor. David Lapsford. Roxanne Gibson. Other girlfriends? Jim's workmates? Means. Motive. Opportunity.* An arrow traced a path down the page, from *Means.* Under it he had written, *Poison.* After deep thought, he had added, *Lethal injection. Oral administration.* He couldn't see how else it could have been achieved, not without any signs of violence, or a struggle. Staring at the page, he realised helplessly that he had no idea of any motive, apart from the suggestion that Mrs Lapsford might have been carrying on with the dentist, and therefore possibly not too unhappy to have her husband out of the way.

It would be easiest to start with Proctor. Already Drew had phoned the surgery and pretended to have toothache. An appointment had been made for four thirty; he was going to lie to Daphne, saying he wanted to go with Karen to the doctor about a problem they'd been having. Let her assume it was a fertility matter, he thought; that was bound to gain him some space as well as sympathy.

There was, of course, a much more direct route he could take. He could telephone the Coroner's Officer, anonymously, and suggest to him that he should be taking an interest in the sudden death of Jim Lapsford. He promised himself that, if he had failed in his various investigations come Monday morning, then this was what he would do. The mere thought of it frightened him. His voice would be recognised; he would somehow give himself away; he would lose his job and be humiliated. At worst he could be arrested for wasting police time. And then, with no evidence, they might not even bother to pursue the matter at all. They might assume he was a crank, or someone with some sort of grudge.

There *had* to be evidence. He had to find someone who had wanted Jim Lapsford dead, and had means and opportunity to commit the deed. If only Lazarus could turn up something at the laboratory, everything would be so much easier. But Lazarus was a faint hope, given his limited access to all the materials necessary to test for a dozen different poisons. It would be folly to rely on him. Worse than that, he realised, with Lapsford now embalmed, there was much less hope of finding supporting evidence in his body tissue.

There was, of course, also the body of the dog. The knowledge that it might contain inside it the whole solution to the question of *Means* was acutely frustrating. He could not work out a way of getting it examined without landing himself in deep trouble. If he took it to a vet, they'd ask a lot of awkward questions, and probably take far too long to supply any results. If he took it to Lazarus, his friend would laugh in his face, assume he'd gone crazy. There might be some laboratory in Woodingleigh which would undertake a swift analysis, but short of slipping them a hefty sum of ready cash, he didn't know how he would persuade them to co-operate. Even private clinics would probably want some kind of authorisation before affording him their services.

He left for work in a gloomy mood.

II

A hand-delivered envelope lay on the mat inside Sarah and Dottie's front door. Sarah picked it up, bending easily at the waist, noting with pride how supple she still was, compared to Dottie.

'It's from Monica,' she said to the empty hall.

'Did you say something, dear?' Dottie's voice had a hint of impatience in it.

Sarah went back into the living room, where Dottie was on the couch with the local newspaper and the mug of coffee which comprised her breakfast. 'A note from Monica. Listen to this. *I've decided to have Jim brought back here on Monday, so he can spend his last night at home. If you'd like to come and see him, please just call in during the evening.* What do you make of that?'

Dottie considered. 'Well, it's what people always used to do. I remember my Gran in the front room, candles all round her, flowers everywhere. I was about fourteen, and thought it was lovely. She looked very contented, I remember. As if she'd finally got what she wanted. She was never a very easy person to please when she was alive.'

'But these days – well, it seems ghoulish, somehow. How will Monica sleep with a dead body in the house? I'm not sure I like the idea of being next door to one, either.'

'As for sleeping with a dead body, it seems she's already done that and survived. Funny about his last night... Anyway, I think it's a nice gesture. I'll certainly go round on Monday and pay my respects.'

Sarah made no reply. The letter in her hand had made her feel oddly agitated; such a reaction was unusual for her, which only compounded the disturbance. Should she go and speak to Monica now? Should she ask again if they could help with the funeral in some way? The problem was, they had had little social contact with the Lapsfords. She glared at the top of Dottie's head. This should be something they had discussed and agreed on. Instead, they seemed to be all at odds. Dottie had been most cross with her at the way she'd tackled that young funeral man yesterday, going on about slander and a lack of evidence. As if that mattered, in the circumstances!

A car drawing up outside with a violent squeal of brakes attracted her attention, and Dottie lowered the paper. Both peered out of the window and watched a young man jump out and stride up Monica Lapsford's front path.

'It's her David,' said Sarah.

'Early bird. Maybe she's just told him about the plan to bring his Dad home, and he doesn't like it. He doesn't look too happy.'

'Very likely,' agreed Sarah, more for the sake of harmony than genuine sentiment. She had exchanged barely five sentences with David since living next door to his mother, and would make no claims to predicting his reaction to anything. He had struck her as a somewhat spindly young man, with his bony limbs and floppy hair. The older one seemed to have more backbone.

'Well, there's nothing in the paper,' Dottie announced, dropping it onto the floor beside her. 'I don't know why we bother with it.'

Sarah gazed at her in surprise. 'It's not like you to be so tetchy, Dottie. What's brought it on?'

Dottie shook her head. 'I'm not quite myself this morning. This has always been a restless time of year for me, ever since I retired. September always meant a new term, new courses to study, fresh beginnings. And instead of that we drift along here. And then the man next door has to go and die like that. And we seem so helpless to act.'

Sarah raised her eyebrows. 'I must say it's good to hear you acknowledge that Jim's death might have more to it than meets the eye, at last.'

Dottie sagged suddenly. When she spoke it was with a mixture of apology and resignation. 'Oh, take no notice of me. I'm in a bad mood. I didn't sleep properly last night.'

'No wonder,' Sarah said with a burst of compassion. 'We'll go over on Monday, then, shall we?' She flourished Monica's note.

'I suppose we'll have to. We owe it to Monica. Poor woman.'

'I'm not sure that we should waste too much

sympathy on her,' said Sarah, slowly. 'That boyfriend was round again yesterday, just after supper. Carrying a huge bunch of chrysanths. Don't know how he's got the nerve.'

Dottie gave her a reproving look. 'Now don't go making any more hasty judgments. We don't know he's her boyfriend. That's just jumping to conclusions.'

'It isn't, Dottie. You know it isn't. When we've both got the evidence of our own eyes.'

III

Monica's pleasure at seeing her younger son lasted barely a minute: he began shouting at her before he was even inside the house. Dottie's guess had been accurate as to the nature of his complaint.

'Philip phoned me last night. He says you're having the coffin here on Monday. How *could* you, Mum? It's disgusting. You must have gone mad.'

Monica stood her ground, and waited for him to stop. Then she turned round and led the way into the kitchen. 'Coffee?' she asked, in a strong, cool voice.

'Oh, I don't care.' He was jigging up and down with tension, or rage. 'What does it matter?'

She put the kettle on, and sat down. 'It's at moments like this that I wish I smoked,' she said, with a tight smile. 'High emotion, I think they call it.'

David circled the room once, tapping the fingers of his left hand against all the surfaces, working his mouth as if trying to devour his own lips.

'It isn't really about the coffin coming home, is it?' she said. 'That's just an excuse.'

'I don't know what you mean,' he muttered, his head bent awkwardly away from her, one shoulder raised.

Monica was alarmed at his demeanour. 'David, calm down,' she ordered sharply. 'Sit there and talk to me properly. What did Philip say to you?'

'It wasn't Philip,' he corrected her. 'It wasn't anybody. I want to ask you about what I found.'

'Found? When? What are you talking about?' After the previous day's encounter with him, she had thought there would be a breathing space before he demanded any more of her. At least in his drunken state, he'd been easier to deflect from the subject.

'Adoption papers,' he said accusingly. 'My birth certificate.' He glared at her. 'How did you think I discovered that I'm adopted? I saw them in his desk, years ago.'

She sat back, stubbornly uncooperative, a deep frown grooving her brow. 'David, do you actually remember what happened yesterday? Were you so drunk that the whole thing's slipped your mind? You agreed to leave the whole thing until we've got the funeral over with. I'm perfectly happy to tell you everything, but not while you're in such a state. And not so soon after – what happened to Jim.'

His glare intensified. 'I haven't forgotten,' he said. 'But I can't wait any longer. You don't know what it's like. People always think they can keep secrets from their kids. They think it won't matter, and that living in the same house, growing up calling you Mum and Dad, is all that counts. But I'm grown up now, and I need to have it straight. You can see what it's doing to me.' He held out a shaking hand, exposing a painfully thin wrist.

Monica closed her eyes for a moment. 'I'm sorry, but this is too much for me. I can't just splurge the whole thing out, not like this. I need time to think. I'm sorry, Davey. I want to trust you, to come clean with you. But you're too wrought up right now. I'm not sure you could cope.'

He dropped into Jim's chair, throwing his head back. 'I take it Jim wasn't my father? At least tell me that much.'

'He *was* your father – officially. We legally adopted you when you were nearly two. We had you from a small baby–'

'*Adopted,*' he spat. 'You've *got* to tell me the truth, Mum. It's your duty.'

'I'm not playing games with you over this,' she said severely. 'I want to make sure the whole truth comes out properly, when we're not distracted by the funeral and people talking about poisoning–'

His eyes widened until she could see clear whites all round the iris. '*What* did you say?' he choked.

Wryly, she realised that she had successfully diverted him from his demands, only to plunge him into even murkier waters. She wished more than anything that she could tell him everything she knew about his origins – she'd wanted to for years, but Jim would never allow it. Now she didn't dare.

'Oh, it's silly,' she laughed unconvincingly. 'Cassie died yesterday. Did I tell you?'

He shook his head muzzily. 'I can't remember,' he said. 'But go on.'

'Well, I think she just pined away – or she might have been ill before, and we didn't notice. You know how animals hide their pain. Anyway, I asked the undertaker's to see to her. I thought she could be cremated with Jim.' David was trying to interrupt, but managing no articulate intervention, so Monica carried on. 'The young man who came to take Jim away came back, and he tried to suggest that Cassie had somehow been poisoned by licking Jim's face on Tuesday. It's stupid, of course–'

'But she did lick his face. You said so.'

'So what? That doesn't prove anything.'

'And now they think somebody poisoned Dad. Is that right?' He gripped his head tightly between both hands, and pressed inwards. 'This is ghastly,' he muttered. 'They'll think it was one of us. They'll think it was *me*. There'll be police, and questions and statements. Christ, Mum, you don't know what it's like when they get some idea into their heads. They don't leave you alone until they're satisfied.'

Monica went white. 'Then we must make sure they're not called in, mustn't we?' she said, faintly but firmly. 'And that means no more nonsense from you.'

He laughed harshly. 'You don't have to remind

me that I'm the unstable one around here. And can you blame me, when I don't even know who my real parents are? Don't you think that little fact explains rather a lot?'

'I don't know,' she said. 'I've always hoped that wasn't true.'

'You mean you hoped if nobody said anything, I would just *fit in* as if I was your own natural child. I assume that Philip wasn't adopted too? You really think you've ever behaved as if I was as good as him? As much a part of the family? Get real, Mum.'

'I think you'd better go home, now. Better still, see if you can salvage your job. How many days have you missed? This must be the fourth.' The steel in her voice shifted him, and he stood up obediently. 'And,' she added, 'let me just say this. Jim might not have been your natural father, but he was as close to it as a man can get. He loved you as much as any father could. When we first had you, he loved you more than Philip.'

David's lip curled. 'You'll never get me to believe that,' he sneered. 'That's not the way I remember him. Not the way he was later on.'

'He did his best,' she pleaded. 'You were such a difficult child. You would never show us any affection, pushing us away – especially Jim. Oh, I know–' She put her hands up to interrupt him as he drew breath. 'I know you couldn't help it. But at the time it just felt as if you hated us, after all we'd tried to do for you. It never occurred to us that you might have something physical, something organic, wrong with you. In those days nobody ever suggested anything like that. Now they'd probably diagnose you right away.'

He walked the length of the room restlessly, a scowl on his face. 'And that would have been better, would it?'

'I'm not sure that it would,' she admitted. 'We'd still have had to live with you and your tantrums and bad behaviour.'

'I tell you something,' he burst out, 'it might have been a whole lot better if you'd *told* me – and everybody else – that I was adopted. Given me some certainty. I always knew something wasn't right. I thought I was some sort of freak. Didn't it ever occur to you that that might have been at the back of it all?'

Monica stared at him, remembering the impossible little boy, possessed by some inner demon which forced him to scream and kick and sulk for hours in his room. She shook her head vehemently. 'We had you from just a few weeks old. Jim was there when you were born. You were as close to being ours as a child can be. And Jim loved you, very much–'

Tears gathered in David's eyes, and his mouth twisted. 'Don't say he loved me *now*,' he choked. 'For God's sake – that's the last thing I want to hear. Not now he's dead.' And shaking his head, he stumbled to the door.

'Mind how you drive!' she called after him, from long habit. A parental mantra, designed to keep him safe.

IV

Lorraine had waited with growing urgency for

Frank and Cindy to leave the house. She threw breakfast at them, hustled them into jackets and shoes, promised Cindy she'd be at the school gate to collect her at three o'clock prompt. She kissed them both absently, trying to ignore the persistent taste of metal at the back of her mouth.

She knew where Roxanne lived. Everybody did. There'd been a fuss when she set up home, with the Council objecting to her siting her caravan there without planning permission. She'd moved it around from one field to another until they got tired of her. She said she had her rights and wasn't hurting anybody. Lorraine had actually felt rather favourably disposed towards her: it was a stand against bureaucracy. Why shouldn't a person live independently, in their own caravan if they wanted to? It wasn't as if she was using services paid for by others – she had to collect water from someone's outside tap, and cope without any electricity. The farmer who owned the field didn't mind, so long as his cattle weren't upset.

Lorraine stood up. This had to be faced. She couldn't carry on without knowing the truth: it would eat away at her, and, being unable to ask Jim himself, the only option seemed to be to go directly to the woman in question. She'd know from the look in Roxanne's eyes whether or not the rumour was true.

Without the car, she had a thirty-minute walk, out of town and down towards the river. She didn't care who might see her. It didn't matter now, after all. But it was with a slight flush of embarrassment that she met Jodie, who had worked with Jim at the printworks. The girl was walking purposefully towards her on the pavement outside the last few shops. Lorraine didn't know where Jodie lived, but assumed she was walking to work; Jim had said something about her being mad keen on walking. They'd seen each other at the pub, and round about town, but had seldom spoken. There seemed no real reason to say anything, but Lorraine hesitated, just the same. Ought she to acknowledge Jodie's connection with the death?

But Jodie must have been late; she merely nodded, without breaking stride. Lorraine swallowed down her sense of offence and ploughed on, wishing she could be there instantly, by teleportation, without this tedious journey. Too many thoughts crowded into her head, encouraged by the rhythm of her stride: phrases formed themselves, unbidden. *What gives you the right to be jealous? You were just his bit on the side. It's his wife that should be doing this, not you.* Pictures of Jim making love with Roxanne tried to invade her mind, but she fought to keep them out. Which secrets had he told her? Had he really been just a lying bastard, who took his fun wherever it was offered?

At the field gate, she hesitated, staring at the caravan, wondering whether Roxanne was inside it. She was running low on determination, suddenly nervous. Was she being a complete fool? What was she going to say?

The Hereford bullocks didn't bother her; even if they had, she would not have given Roxanne the satisfaction of betraying any fear. *Everyone thinks I'm silly and empty-headed,* she thought crossly. *Just because I'm blonde and pretty.* Even Jim hadn't expected much in the way of intelligent conversation.

Roxanne opened the caravan door and stood at the top of the steps, waiting for her, as she covered the second half of the field. It was unusual to be observed so closely as you approached a person's home, Lorraine realised: nobody stood or sat at their doors any more, waiting for whoever might come by. The first thing you knew was a knock or a ring at the door, which sent you into a fluster of curiosity and apprehension. The patient scrutiny which Roxanne could give her visitors was almost witchlike, almost predatory: a female spider waiting for someone to walk into her web. Lorraine forced herself on, increasingly self-conscious and unprepared for the encounter to come.

The face that greeted her was smiling. Not in any kind of scorn or mockery, but with kindness, even sympathy. A sadness in the deep-set brown eyes gave the smile sincerity. And Lorraine felt a sudden urge to throw herself into this woman's arms.

'Hi!' said Roxanne, as if the meeting had been long arranged and anticipated.

'You know who I am?'

'Course I do. Lorraine. You drink at the King's Head. Married to Frank Dunlop. His auntie Mary was my mum's best friend.'

'I never knew that.'

'Small town, Bradbourne. Coffee?'

'Okay. Oh – perhaps not, actually.' The imagined taste of coffee was suddenly repugnant to her, reinforcing the conviction that she was pregnant. Barely three weeks, and already all the same old unpleasantnesses were returning. 'I'll just have water or squash or something, if you've got it.'

'You've come about Jim.' Roxanne was matter-of-fact.

'Yes.' Tears filled Lorraine's eyes. Was it possible that she would be able to cry with this woman, openly grieving for a relationship which was meant to be a secret?

'Unusual man, our Jim,' Roxanne added quietly. 'A lot of people are going to miss him.'

'Oh dear.' Lorraine sat down on a narrow seat under the caravan window and gave up the struggle against emotion. She sobbed noisily, tears trickling abundantly down her face. She rummaged for a hanky, finding only a small ladylike one in a pocket of her jeans. Roxanne poured something from a stoneware jug into a glass and handed it to her.

'Elderflower,' she said. 'My speciality.'

Lorraine took it, sipped awkwardly. 'Sorry,' she said, waving the damp hanky in explanation.

'No need to be. Nothing wrong with a good cry.'

'It's just–'

'Yeah. I know. Bloody rotten business. Leaves everything up in the air.'

'I came – actually – to ask you–'

'I know. Funny how the rumours get going

once a person dies. There we were, thinking our secrets were safe. Now I bet the whole town's talking about us.'

'Oh, no! Not me. I mean – we were terribly careful.'

'I knew,' said Roxanne flatly. 'And so did Pauline. Can't believe it'd just be us two. The thing is, lovey, most people don't care. They're having their own little carryings-on, and it makes them feel better knowing it's not just them.'

'Pauline?'

'My sister. Monica Lapsford's friend. *Best* friend, she likes to think. You'd know her by sight, probably. She's always out and about, collecting lame ducks.'

'But – well, if you and Jim were – you know, that makes me feel ... less important. As if I didn't matter to him. Not as much as I thought I did, anyway. And – wasn't it a bit odd, your sister being Jim's wife's friend? Wasn't it awfully *complicated?*'

Roxanne shrugged. 'Course it was. But that's life. And I know what you mean, about not mattering. Everybody wants to be special. But it doesn't work like that, not really. Even when a man has a wife and two lovers, the trick is to live for the moment and enjoy it while it lasts. Jim taught me that, bless him.'

'Do you think it was just us, or might there be others as well?'

'Not recently, no. But Jim was Jim. And the world's full of good-looking women.'

'He didn't ever say anything? About me, I mean?' She sipped again at the drink. It tasted wonderful. More than wonderful.

Roxanne smiled. 'He never said anything you wouldn't have liked to hear,' she said ambiguously. 'He had his own rules – it's just that they weren't the same as other people's.' Lorraine watched Roxanne's nose turn pink, and her eyes grow shiny. Never before had she felt such a sense of sharing. She put her glass down, and stood up, keeping her eyes on Roxanne's. It didn't matter what Jim had or hadn't said. Without a word, they hugged, tight and hard, the ghost of Jim Lapsford pushing them together, bonding them with a cosmic superglue.

Laughing and crying, they finally let go. Lorraine felt warm. Consoled. 'This is ridiculous,' she said weakly. 'I came to pick a fight with you.'

'What would've been the point of that? If Jim was still alive, maybe there'd be some sense in it – but not much, even then. He was never going to choose between us, or leave his missus for you or me. The way I see it, we were both bloody lucky. Jim was more than anybody deserved.'

Again a mutual sniffing and loss of control. Lorraine tried to speak, but couldn't get the breath. She sat down on the bench again and leaned her head back against the window. 'Why did he have to die?' she wept. 'I never dreamed that this might happen.'

Roxanne shook her head, her dark hair seeming to have a life of its own, suggesting Medusa. Lorraine watched her, feeling again the tight hug, strongly aware of the woman's physical presence. There was a magnetism to her, something earthy and knowing. Something Jim wouldn't have been able to resist. Lorraine waited for an answer to her question.

'I've been thinking about that,' said Roxanne. 'I don't think *why* is a sensible question. Not unless you think somebody murdered him. Otherwise, there isn't a reason. Though I always thought people's deaths were somehow bound up with the way they lived. Do you know what I mean?'

Lorraine shook her head slightly. 'Not really,' she said.

'It sounds daft, probably. But you see it all the time. Miserable, self-sacrificing women get breast cancer. Bad-tempered men, always shouting and in a rush, get heart attacks.'

'But – Jim wasn't like that.'

'No. That's what I'm saying. Or what I was going to say. It feels all wrong. Jim was going to do such a lot. I don't think people with plans die like he did. Something stops it happening.'

'But he did die.'

'Yeah. So they say. Fuck it.'

V

Monica phoned Philip at work. 'Phil, you'll have to do something about David. He's in a terrible state,' she said, with no preamble.

'What? What sort of state?'

'Well – I don't want to go into it now, but he's come out with a whole lot of nonsense, and I'm worried about what he might do.'

'I'm *at work*,' he hissed, and she realised that somebody else must be in the room with him. 'I can't do anything now. I'm going to be up to my eyes all afternoon.'

Sometimes, Monica thought this son, still in his twenties, sounded positively middle-aged. Jim would never have talked about being 'up to his eyes' in anything. Jim had understood how to keep everything in balance – work, play, family and friends.

'Phil,' she said, wearily, 'I don't often ask you for help. It's Friday and your brother needs you. Can't you take some time off for once?'

'Not really. Not unless you convince me that this is serious. David's a big boy now – he doesn't need me to hold his hand. What's he going to think if I turn up and start acting like Mother Teresa? Where is he, anyway?'

'I don't know for sure. But you didn't see him. He was very disturbed. Like he used to be.'

Philip sighed heavily. 'Well, if he's as bad as that, we should call an ambulance. Get some white-coats to take him in hand. I'm not confronting him. He might take a knife to me.'

Monica bit her tongue, holding back the angry remark. 'Okay,' she said, as calmly as she could, 'do what you can. *When* you can. I haven't got anybody else to ask, remember?'

Philip grinned sheepishly at Colin, who sat across the office from him. 'Trouble?' Colin enquired.

'Families,' Philip shrugged, and rolled his eyes for good measure. His colleagues knew his father had died, and were showing mild sympathy, but he was expected to continue working uninterruptedly. Philip was in Research and Development, on a trial basis: if he did well, he could stay and build an interesting and lucrative niche for himself. If he did not do well, he would be shunted back to Sales, which was a move he dreaded. He loathed the insincerity; the relentless good cheer required of him; the ill-concealed sneer on the faces of those he tried to persuade to become customers.

But he knew there was little prospect of giving the work his attention for the rest of the day, not after that phone call. Sifting quickly through the papers on his desk, and checking the scarcely-begun design on his computer screen, he chose two small tasks which could be easily finished. Philip prided himself on his skill at making a good impression. His folders were always neatly labelled, his reports and ideas perfectly presented. The substance might eventually be recognised as only slightly better than average, but he was gambling on establishing himself as the right man for the job before that happened.

His mother's request couldn't be ignored. Half an hour later, he made the papers neat on the desk, and saved the computer file to a floppy disk. 'Er, Colin,' he said, tentatively, 'I've done as much as I usefully can on this job. I need to check a few prices before I can go any further. And, well – you heard that phone call. My mother's in a tizzy about things. I think I should go and sort that out now, and then put in a bit more time on my computer at home. Okay?' He raised the disk and waggled it at Colin, who pursed his lips dubiously.

'Well, you shouldn't take it out of the office, you know. That's highly confidential, the stage it's at. If anyone gets hold of it now, there'll be hell to pay.'

'I know. I won't take it, if you think it's a problem. I just wanted to make up the time.'

'I wouldn't worry about that, mate. These things happen – and it is Friday.'

Philip had known this would be the response, and he obediently slid the disk back into a small box, and locked it into his desk drawer.

'Fine,' he said. 'I'll be in bright and early on Monday. But you haven't forgotten I'll be off all day Tuesday, have you?'

'No problem. Give your mother my condolences, won't you? Must have been a nasty shock for her.'

'Thanks. She's coping very well, considering.'

'Good,' said Colin absently, his attention already withdrawn. A brief shudder of rage went through Philip. *Where are my condolences?* he thought. *Wasn't it just as much of a shock for me?*

He drove to his brother's ground-floor flat, and ran up to the front door. Without ringing the bell, he turned the handle and found it was open, the yale lock clipped back. 'David?' he called. 'Are you there?'

A chinking noise came from the kitchen, and he went to investigate. His brother was standing by the sink, his feet surrounded by broken crockery, a blank look on his face.

'Christ, what *have* you been doing?' Philip scanned the scene, looking for blood – or a weapon. David had never been seriously violent, but Philip could remember times when he had come close. Since David's return from his long disappearance, his parents and brother had done their best to behave normally; all along Jim had argued for this strategy, refusing to consult doctors. 'Ruin his chances for life, that would,' he said. 'There's nothing wrong with the lad – just loses control of himself from time to time. He'll grow out of it, you see.' And Philip had reluctantly agreed with his father. Everything he had seen or heard about the mental health system led him to the same conclusion as Jim's. He'd heard about people labelled 'schizophrenic' after a single episode of aggressive or bizarre behaviour. But that didn't make him feel any more comfortable right now.

'Did you know about it?' said David lightly.

'Know about what?'

'Me not being his son. That Jim Lapsford was not my father.'

'Don't be stupid. I remember when they brought you home, after you were born. Of course you're his son.'

David stared at him, through narrowed eyes. His foot stirred some shards of china, making them tinkle musically on the stone tiles. 'Exactly what do you remember?' His voice was bright, taut.

Philip tried to think. 'Well, I was only three. I remember Mum holding you, all wrapped in a blue shawl. I remember your hands, tight little fists. And your hair was wispy – I could see your bare head underneath.'

'Well, the fact is, I was adopted. They never told you, then?'

'Not a word.' He sat down hard on an upright kitchen chair. 'Did all this come out today?'

'I saw my birth certificate years ago. When I was nineteen–'

'Shit, Dave – is that why you went away? Why didn't you tell me?'

'It wasn't that simple. I thought perhaps I'd just dreamt it. I was in a state about other stuff, as well. Drugs. Girls. It all happened at once. And they'd just figured out that I had that Whatsit Deficit thing – that made me feel like a freak.'

'I always did think that was daft,' said Philip. 'You were a little tearaway, I admit. But we took it in our stride. Some kids are like that. You were funny, as well. Kept me well entertained, you did. It wasn't all gloom and doom, Dave. You know it wasn't. Anyway, what's been happening today, to lead to all this?' He eyed the debris on the floor and wrinkled his nose disapprovingly.

'I went round there, and asked her for the whole story. She just said they adopted me when I was two. Wouldn't say any more than that until I was less "wrought up", whatever that means.'

'Two? But we had you from a baby. I know we did. I can remember holding you. At least – look, I was only a tiny kid myself. It's all blurred together. Somebody died, and Dad cried, I remember that. Cried for days. I was petrified. That was later, though, I think. I was going to school, so I must have been four, nearly five. You were walking. I remember you coming with Mum to collect me. Hell, Dave, you can't rely on

anything I tell you. It's all so hazy.'

David sighed, and Philip was relieved to note that he seemed calmer. The broken crockery, however, was a tangible reminder that nothing was ever sure where his brother was concerned. He tried to remember the early days, when they'd lived in a small village four or five miles away. They went back to look at the old house once in a while, marvelling at how poky and old-fashioned it was. Philip had been eight when they moved to Primrose Close. The house had been brand new, with a rough patch of sandy ground for a garden, and paintwork so clean it had seemed more like some big new toy than a home. Jim had been promoted at the printworks, and Monica had got herself a job as a school dinner lady when David started school full-time, so suddenly there had been money for a new house, a new car and a dishwasher. The perfect family.

'She'll have to tell you the whole story,' Philip said. 'I mean, it's your right. You could find it out anyway. When you're eighteen you're entitled to know who your real parents are.'

David nodded. 'I know. But I'm imagining all sorts of things. I mean – we always lived round here. There must be loads of people who know about me. I've been *betrayed*, that's what. It's a shitty feeling.'

Philip reassured him. 'I've never heard so much as a whisper. Mum didn't get friendly with Pauline till you and Craig were at school, so I bet she doesn't know anything. There might be one or two social workers or health visitors who'd remember, but that's probably all.'

David sighed again, and worked his hands, opening and closing them into tight fists. 'I feel – *shredded* by it all,' he said fiercely.

'Well,' Philip began, trying to sound in control, 'it should be easy enough to sort out. I mean, it isn't really so awful, is it? You had a good enough childhood. We got along pretty well–'

David looked at him for a long second. 'Did we?' he challenged. 'Aren't you forgetting the way Dad always came between us? One minute you'd be the blue-eyed boy, doing so well at school, playing in the school soccer team, with me just a menace he had to put up with. Then, overnight, he'd change, take me out on my own, buy me things, leaving you high and dry with Mum bleating uselessly in the background. Most of the time we hated each other, because we were fighting to be his favourite. And I never believed Mum really loved me as much as you.'

Philip pondered. 'Well, yeah,' he conceded, 'it was like that sometimes. But – I can't believe this adoption stuff. I mean – look at you. You're so like Dad. You've got his features, his shoulders, his hands–'

'Yeah. Mum said he always regarded me as his natural son – something like that.'

Philip was sidetracked for a moment thinking about Jim. 'I always thought of Dad as being like a bloody great tree. Keeping out the light a lot of the time, but basically good to have around.'

David gave a snorting laugh. 'And now it's fallen down, right on top of us. There's something else while you're here, by the way.'

Philip waited, knowing it wouldn't be anything pleasant.

'People are saying stuff about the way he died so suddenly. Someone's been talking to Mum.'

'Saying what, for Christ's sake?'

'Hinting at poison, apparently.' David glanced sideways at his brother, then quickly looked away again. The silence lasted a long time.

'Well, it's not surprising, when you think about it,' Philip said at last. 'He was always so healthy. The last person to die young. But Mum seemed so sure the doctor knew what he was talking about–'

'Yeah, well, it's down to him now, isn't it. I've no intention of rocking the boat in that department. Just roll on Tuesday, that's all I can say.'

Philip grimaced. 'I'm not sure about that,' he said. 'I'm not in any hurry at all for Tuesday to come.'

VI

At the printworks, Jodie was half-heartedly feeding pages into the folding and stapling machine, her mind on David and Jim. She didn't know what to make of the discovery that Jim hadn't been David's father. It was certainly news to her, and she'd thought she knew most of Jim's secrets. Working alongside someone for years brought a special intimacy where the need to hide and prevaricate was quickly lost. She knew about Roxanne, and Lorraine – and others. She knew Jim enjoyed women and felt free to indulge his pleasures. Jodie had worried slightly about

Lorraine; she was too young and too vulnerable to make a success of the affair. That kid of hers stood to lose out badly if Frank ever heard about what was going on. But there hadn't been much that Jodie could do to ensure that he didn't.

When she'd joined the business, at eighteen, Jim had been paternalistic towards her – a perfect gentleman. It had taken her a while to realise that she would have been off limits to him even if she'd had a better face and figure. She was too close to home. The relief of knowing this had made her very contented. She threw herself into the work, brought new ideas to it, mastered the computer valiantly, kept abreast of technological developments. 'You're a godsend, Jode,' Jim had said many a time.

The short-lived relationship with young David, a year or two into the job, had been unexpectedly complicated where Jim was concerned. He had seldom referred to it, but when he did he had looked resentful. When she had talked about this to David, he had grinned. 'He's jealous,' he said. 'Poor old geezer.'

She had refrained from correcting him. In some ways it might have been true. It hadn't taken her very long to realise that she herself was substituting the son for the father, getting as close as she could to Jim, who, she supposed, she loved as more than a fatherly boss. She had worried about how she was to extricate herself without hurting David, only to have the matter resolved for her. David's sudden disappearance had been as much of a shock to her as it had been to everyone else. The most hurtful part of all had been Jim's insistence that she must know where David had gone.

'But you're his *girlfriend,*' he had shouted at her. 'Didn't he tell you he was going?'

'No,' she repeated. 'Not a word.' And together they had waited and worried, even printed flyers asking if anyone had seen the boy. In the end it had brought her and Jim even closer.

Now she wanted to explain to someone how much Jim had cared about David; how it seemed impossible that they weren't father and son. The idea was almost offensive to her.

'Missing him, ain't you?' said Ajash, at her elbow. The little man was a good four inches shorter than her. She smiled down at him, putting on a brave face.

'Yeah,' she admitted. 'Does it show?'

He nodded at the machine. 'Is it meant to be folding them with the cover inwards?'

With a squawk, Jodie punched the Stop button, and grabbed at the remaining unfolded sheets. 'Oh, Christ,' she groaned. 'How many have I done like this?'

'A hundred or so,' he said. 'No problem. We can turn them right side out by hand.'

'Thanks.' The *we* was a consolation to her: for years, Ajash had been eclipsed by Jim, teased and patronised by the print manager; but endlessly good-humoured, he had laughed at himself and earned everyone's affection. Even Jack, who never laughed, could find little reason to dislike his workmate.

'Are we opening on Monday?' he asked her. 'Or what? We'll get behind if we don't, with taking

Tuesday off.'

Jodie shrugged. 'Not for me to say. We're meant to be doing Jim's Order of Service. Mrs L hasn't sent us the copy yet, though. You've finished the cards, have you?'

Eagerly he trotted back to his work table and gathered up a stack of printed cards. 'Here,' he said. 'Good, eh?'

He had used expensive vellum-look card, and printed a black border, with scallops to lighten the effect. All three of them had worked out the wording, from what Jack reported as Monica's suggestions:

Monica, Philip and David
would like to thank you
very sincerely
for all your kind wishes,
cards or flowers
at this sad time

'Bit vague,' said Jodie, doubtfully.

'Too late to change it now,' he said. 'And it's the thought that counts, don't you think?'

'I suppose so. Funny it doesn't mention Jim. Like he doesn't exist any more.'

'Well–' Ajash was groping for some reply when he noticed her tears. Without further words, he produced a large clean white hanky from his trouser pocket. Smiling at the incongruity, she took it and dabbed at her eyes.

'Sorry,' she said. 'Silly cow.'

'No, no. It's good to cry. At this sad time.' He quoted the words hollowly, flapping one of the cards at her.

'Nothing ever gets you down, does it,' she remarked, half-admiring, half-disapproving.

'Oh no, not me,' he agreed, wagging his head from side to side. 'I'm just the joker around here. Everybody knows that.'

VII

As if drawn by a magnet, Drew kept returning to the mortuary, where the two bodies lay. It was as if the lifeless flesh might speak to him, if he listened closely enough – give him a name, or a hint as to what had brought about their deaths. He pretended to Sid that he wanted to understand more about the process of embalming, asking searching questions about how much of the fluid reached the internal organs, what effects he thought it had when released as gas during cremation. 'Polluting sort of business,' he remarked, thoughtfully. 'Shouldn't wonder if it gets banned before long. Can't be very good for the environment.'

Sid stared at him. 'Never heard that one before,' he said. 'Come up with some daft ideas, you do, and no mistake.'

'Never heard of the natural death movement?' Drew was needled. 'Shallow burials in baskets – plant a tree at the head of the grave. That's how it's going to be in the next century.'

'Won't worry me if it is. I'll be long gone.' Sid paused to consider. 'Anyway, can't see it, somehow. There's too much money in funerals, specially with the Americans taking everything over. Strikes me you're more likely to have dirty great caskets and embalming for everyone. Only a few nutters'll go for the baskets, you see.'

'Meanwhile, Mrs L's taking a stand on having him home before the funeral. Just like in the olden days. You can really go to town on him – you'll have a proper audience this time. Stick his little pet dog snugly under one arm. That should jerk a few more tears from the mourners.' Drew's attempt at mischievous banter fell flat; Sid said nothing, but swallowed hard. Drew was amused at his nervousness, supposing it was a trifle daunting to have your handiwork under such scrutiny. The incisions necessary for the embalming were well hidden, and it wasn't as if there'd been a postmortem, with the top of the head removed and replaced, and the torso ripped through from throat to pelvis.

'Don't worry,' he reassured Sid. 'It'll be fine. In a way, it's rather a nice idea. Don't you think?'

'Lovely,' Sid responded glumly. 'All that loading the hearse and carrying the coffin into some poky front room with the fire on, and trying to keep track of the flowers. Ideal that is.'

There was more than the dead bodies occupying Drew's thoughts. He couldn't get the image of Roxanne out of his mind. He had never seen a woman like that before, so firmly-planted, so careless of how she looked to other people. And that smile she'd given him – how many women these days would do that where a stranger was concerned? Fearless and confident, it was as if she'd somehow possessed an extra dimension.

There was a hint of the same forthrightness about Karen – it was what had appealed to him from the outset – but Karen, unlike Roxanne, he suspected, wanted desperately to be liked.

It was a slow afternoon, as it had been a slow week. All he wanted to do was get home and go through the jottings in his notebook with Karen's help. They had to work out a plan of campaign for the weekend. Forty-eight hours in which to come up with some watertight findings. Maybe he could persuade his wife that the obvious first place to start was Roxanne Gibson's caravan. Except that he didn't want her to go with him. However sharp Karen might be at detecting clues and reading between the lines, he definitely intended to treat himself to some time alone with that woman. It would be innocent enough. Just a harmless bit of self-indulgence. Karen could be given the job of finding out exactly who Lapsford's other girlfriends had been, and perhaps try to line up some casual-seeming encounters. He knew that several of his fellow workers knew the whole story, but saw no reason to share it with Drew – one of his many frustrations. And he couldn't ask them outright, for fear of further castigation over raising suspicions about Lapsford's death. The best he could hope for was to overhear more useful snippets, as he'd been doing all week.

The snippet, when it came, was considerably in excess of his hopes. Vince and Big George had been given a mountain of old funeral records to put through the shredder, and they were doing it as slowly as they could, making the job last. Vince took the papers out of the big box Daphne had given him, and passed them to George, who carefully inserted them between the jaws of the machine. Every few minutes they stopped and emptied the hopper underneath. The results were used as pillows in the cheaper coffins, which didn't come provided with their own accoutrements.

The records comprised carbon copies of letters to ministers; information for the crematorium; notes jotted down during phone calls. Everything except for the actual record card, which was filled in as the arrangements were made with the relatives and kept in perpetuity in the large attic over the main building. The decision to shred the copies was a recent one, and the men had worked steadily through yellowing hand-written documents dating from 1932, when the current premises were established. They had now reached the seventies, and Daphne was becoming increasingly nervous. 'We'll stop at nineteen eighty,' she said. 'We ought to have twenty years' worth still to hand. Heavens!' she'd sighed, 'I'm glad my Dad can't see us now. He'd go berserk. Never threw *anything* away, my Dad.'

Vince was breaking the monotony by reading the surname off every sheet he gave George, and waiting to see whether the older man could provide a reminiscence.

'Satterthwaite.'

'Burial. It was raining, and the grave had a foot of water in it.'

'Cedriksen.'

'Norwegian chap. Nearly a hundred, he was.

Came over here at the turn of the century, as a youngster. Had thirty great-grandchildren, and they all came to the funeral.'

'Jones.'

'Never heard of him.'

'Lapsford.'

'What? Give me that. Hey, Andy! Remember me telling you I remembered a Lapsford? Let's see. Julia Catherine Lapsford, Miss. Age thirty-one. August nineteen seventy-six. Told you! They buried her in that little churchyard near Appleham – St Francis's. New single depth. It's closed now no more space. Hey, listen to this. *The funeral has been arranged by Mr James Eric Lapsford, brother of the deceased.* There you are! This is Jim's sister. Jim and Julia. Nice.' George beamed around the workshop proudly. 'I ought to be on *Brain of Britain* me, memory I've got.'

'You should,' agreed Drew, his heart pounding. 'Does it say what she died of?'

George laughed. 'Course not. These are just the copy letters. We don't have a record of what they die of – you know that.'

'If she was thirty-one then, she'd be–'

'Fifty-five now,' supplied Vince, renowned for his arithmetical powers. 'Same as Jim.'

'Twins!' Drew's excitement was out of all proportion. 'That was his twin sister!'

'So?' Vince frowned at him. 'Why the commotion?'

Drew made a big effort. 'No reason, really. I've just got a thing about twins. Always have had. They're – very interesting.'

'Not when they're dead they're not,' said Vince,

and pushed the Lapsford papers into the shredder's maw.

VIII

On his way home, Jack Merryfield called in at the Blue Lion, which was not a pub he often frequented. He didn't think he could face the King's Head: full of talk about Jim, and inevitable questions directed at Jack, as workmate and one of his closest friends.

It had been a hard week, and he was hoping for an hour of solitude, drinking slowly and steadily. It was an unpretentious place, with a wide fireplace filled with logs and seats in the bay windows. Jack chose the saloon bar, after a moment's indecision, on the assumption that it would be quieter.

It wasn't so quiet, though, after a few minutes. A young couple at a nearby table were engaged in a fierce disagreement, which had begun in low tones and grown louder as feelings warmed. He didn't recall seeing either of them before, although the girl rang a bell in his subconscious.

'I won't do it, Craig,' she said, in a ringing voice. 'Just stop asking me, will you?'

'I'm in deep shit if you don't,' he threw back at her, his voice shaking. 'What's your problem, anyway?'

'We're just getting deeper all the time. Look, I'd better warn you – I've spoken to my dad about it. I can't take any more, not after what's happened. It's making me ill. Look at me.'

Jack couldn't resist checking to see if the boy

did as instructed. It was true that the girl was pale, with dark smudges under her eyes.

'You look okay to me,' said the boy. 'You needn't make so much fuss. Nobody's going to bother about you. It's me that's going to get mullered.'

Jack's work and hobbies all centred on words. *Mullered,* he thought. *That's a good one. Wonder how you spell it?*

The couple seemed to have reached an impasse, and were quietening down again. But the boy seemed to be in genuine distress, and Jack decided he was on his side. The girl was a hard little bitch, reneging on something she'd agreed to do. Typical bloody woman. The boy had a note of desperation in his voice which Jack had heard before. Craig, she'd called him. Must be the Rawlinson lad, friend of Jim's David, he realised. Couldn't recognise anybody these days, the things they did to themselves. Both his hair and the clothes he wore seemed designed to conceal who he was. Buckles and chains adorned his outfit, from neck to feet – even his boots glinted with silver appendages. Jack sighed. It was a different world. He turned back to his drink, and tried to forget they were there.

A few minutes later, the youngsters got up to go. The girl paused beside Jack's table, and looked at him; she forced a little smile, as if desperate for a friendly gesture in the midst of her trouble. He had seen her before somewhere, definitely. He held her gaze.

The boy was barging ahead, and was almost at the door, when the girl leaned over. 'You know my Dad, don't you?' she whispered. 'Sid Hawkes, works at Plant's? Do me a favour – don't tell him about what you've just heard.'

Jack was puzzled. 'I know Sid, yeah. Vaguely. But I didn't know he was your dad. How'd you know me?'

'It's a small town,' she said. 'More's the pity.'

He watched her go, and decided he'd leave as soon as the beer was finished. He wouldn't hurry his drink, though.

IX

When Drew presented himself at the surgery of Gerald Proctor, the receptionist gave a crooked wide-eyed smile, indicating helpless apology. 'Oh, heavens,' she squeaked, 'I forgot all about you! We thought everything was clear for the afternoon. Mr Proctor's not here, I'm afraid. I was going to go home myself in a minute. You're a new patient, is that right?' She tapped a few keys on the computer in front of her.

Drew nodded. 'Only moved here a few months ago. Hadn't got around to finding a new dentist – until I got toothache.'

'Is it bad?' She peered at him worriedly.

'Let's say it isn't a real emergency. Is he going to be here tomorrow?'

'Well,' she hesitated. 'He isn't usually in on a Saturday. But he might be persuaded. What exactly is the problem?'

Drew hesitated. The ploy to meet the dentist and somehow turn the conversation to the Lapsfords now seemed half-baked and foolish. It would be obvious that there was nothing wrong with his teeth as soon as the man examined him. 'Actually,' he said, with a boyish grin, 'to be honest, it's been a lot better since I phoned. I think it might have settled down again. Maybe I'll just leave it for now, and get back to you if there's any more trouble.'

'If you like,' she shrugged. 'It isn't usually me here, anyway – I generally just do Mondays. But the usual receptionist is on compassionate leave. Everything's in a bit of a muddle because of that, you see.'

Drew seized his chance. 'That's Mrs Lapsford, I suppose?' he asked with a little frown of sympathetic concern.

'That's right. Poor Monica. She's such a nice lady – doesn't deserve such trouble, she really doesn't.'

'I gather it was very sudden.' He saw no reason to pretend ignorance; in fact, it had been his experience that people talk much more readily if they assume you already know as much as they do.

The girl sucked in a hissing breath of concurrence. 'Wasn't it!' she agreed. 'No warning at all, the way I heard it.'

Drew shook his head. 'None at all.'

'You know them then?' queried the girl, belatedly.

'Well, I didn't – but I'm working for Plant and Son now–' He paused. 'You know – the undertaker's.'

'Gosh! Are you! That must be a bit – I mean–'

He smiled. 'It's amazing what you can get used

to. Anyway, I mustn't keep you. If there's really no chance that the dentist will be able to see me?'

She lifted an apologetic shoulder. 'Sorry. Actually,' she leaned forward slightly, and lowered her voice, 'I think he might have gone to see Monica. They've always been very good friends.' She winked awkwardly. 'If you know what I mean.'

Drew pretended not to understand her. 'That's nice,' he smiled, inwardly rejoicing at this confirmation of the rumours. 'She'll need her friends now.'

He departed with a light step. Only when he was back in the car did he begin to wonder what use the information could be. It might constitute grounds for divorce, but it was a weak motive for murder in this day and age. On the other hand, he mused, a dentist presumably had access to various toxic substances – the anaesthetics they used could be fatally injected in large doses, for a start. If he was totally obsessed with Monica, he might decide to dispose of her husband. 'Hmmm,' he hummed to himself, deep in thought. At least it was something tangible to talk over with Karen.

Before that, he ought to find some constructive use for the hour he had gained. There must be all kinds of connections between the Lapsfords and people in the town, if he could only discover what they were. Always inclined to look for patterns, he urgently needed to make a more complete picture of where Jim had fitted in.

He tried to think of a pretext to call at Jim's printworks and have a look at the set-up, meet some of the other people who worked there. All the obvious ploys involved the funeral, and a pretended message from Daphne, and that would be extremely embarrassing if Daphne found out. Only if he learned something important about Lapsford's death would he be forgiven. A straight gamble.

He knew there was no real choice. He drove to the estate and scanned the big wide-fronted warehouses for the printworks. It took him some time to find Capital Press and recognise it for what it was.

He tried to walk with nonchalant confidence as he parked the car and headed for the small door beside a big corrugated roll-down barrier where he supposed that deliveries of paper and collections of finished work were made. Inside the small door, all was immediate chaos. The whirr of machinery was surprisingly loud, augmented by a ringing telephone and a loud radio playing pop music. A small man stood over one machine, entirely preoccupied. Stacks of paper stood solid and obstructive, forming crooked corridors. In a glass-partitioned room, a thin girl sat in front of a computer.

Carefully he threaded his way to the office and tapped on the door. The girl glanced up, and then stared blankly at him. He opened the door. 'Hello,' he said brightly. 'Can I come in?'

'Are you selling something?' she said, without a smile.

'Oh, no. I'm from Plant's. We – er–' Suddenly he realised he had not adequately prepared for this.

'Plant's?' she interrupted. 'You mean the funeral place? About the service sheets, is it?'

'Right,' he nodded, relieved. 'The service sheets.'

'We haven't done them yet. It'll be late Monday, probably. We'll deliver them, shall we? Makes sense for you to have them. I should have thought of that. Were you trying to phone? We've been letting it ring today. Sorry about that.'

'No problem,' he reassured her. 'It's just, well, we were wondering when–'

'Always a rush at times like this,' she finished for him briskly. 'Not that we've done any work for you before. It's always gone to the opposition till now.' She laughed grimly. 'It's an ill wind – isn't that what they say?' she went on.

'Terrible business,' he offered. 'You must be feeling the loss. I mean – it looks busy out there.'

'Oh, God,' she sighed, 'it's always busy. And Jack's gone missing again. Was there anybody out there at all?' She tried to peer around him into the main room; he half-turned to look with her.

'One chap,' he said.

'That'll be Ajash. I'm Jodie, by the way. And yes, we're missing Jim. Not so much workwise–' She stopped suddenly, and her nose became pink; he could hear her sniff over the printing noises.

'Knew him long, did you?'

'Yeah. Years. This should never have happened to him. Everyone's saying the same. What do you do at Plant's, then? You did my Granny's cremation, eighteen months ago. Not you personally – I don't recognise you.'

'No, I'm new. Drew Slocombe. Should we shake hands?' He held his hand out invitingly, deliberately comic. The girl was appealing in a funny sort of way: she reminded him of a stork, or a heron.

Jodie took his hand in a cool grip. 'Let me give you a quick tour,' she said unenthusiastically, as if courtesy demanded it. 'Maybe you'll persuade your boss to use us for the service sheets in future. Especially when you see what we've done for Jim. It'll be a masterpiece, I promise you.' He followed her through another crooked corridor, waiting for her to switch off the radio. A minute later, the chuntering printing press went silent too. The relief was tangible.

'That's better,' he said.

'That's Ajash,' she said nodding towards the small brown man. 'He's a bit busy, so we won't bother him.' Drew stared curiously at the figure; he was like something out of a woodland fairy-tale, an elf, or a gnome. 'He's brilliant with the machinery,' she added, waving kindly at Ajash. He clearly heard her, and gravely nodded back.

'What sort of things do you print?' Drew asked, inanely.

'Oh, newsletters, brochures, labels, tickets, calendars, invitations–'

'Not books, then?'

'Book*lets*, now and then. We're not really set up for full-sized books, though we could have a go if anyone really wanted us to.'

He picked up a small sheet of plastic from a stack beside him. It was bright orange, and carried a warning – *Poison* – at the top of other smaller text. 'What's this?' he said, eyebrows raised.

'Oh, a label for some pharmaceutical thing. We do a lot of work for the factory in Grensham. You know? They make medicines and stuff. We do labels in all different languages for them. No idea what they mean. We just scan it in from what they give us. See – it's self-adhesive. That was a job that Jim got for us.'

Drew could see wistfulness returning, and marched towards another big stack. Jodie followed, and gave brief explanations of the next few items they encountered. He began to wonder how long she would tolerate his presence.

'I removed Mr Lapsford from his house, you know,' he said suddenly. 'On Tuesday morning.'

'Did you?' She didn't seem to want to hear this. 'Must have been – unpleasant.'

'Not really. He seemed to have gone very peacefully. I just thought you might like to know that.'

'Peacefully? Funny the way people use that word. I don't think death is ever peaceful. Torn away from all your family and friends, without warning. How can that be *peaceful?*' She was almost shouting. Drew pushed his hands into his pockets and felt again the single Viagra tablet. The association between this and his last words struck him as incongruous. Maybe Jim hadn't died peacefully after all. Maybe he'd been dosed up on the drug and in the extreme stages of sexual pleasure. Pity he couldn't suggest this to Jodie.

As if attracted by the raised voice, another man

appeared from a side door. He seemed alarmed to see Drew there. Drew recognised him as Monica's visitor of the day before – the mysterious 'Jack'.

'Who's this?' he asked, coming closer and looking hard at Jodie. 'And what's all the noise about?'

'This is Drew Slocombe, from the undertaker's,' Jodie said, her voice still unsteady. 'He's come about the service sheets. This is Jack Merryfield,' she concluded. 'Jim was at his place, the night he died.'

Why did she tell me that? wondered Drew. 'Oh?' he said.

'We had a regular Monday thing. Usually played on my computer. Surfed the Internet – if you can believe two middle-aged blokes doing that. Sometimes did some fancy font work, trying out new designs for posters and stuff.' The man shrugged. 'Seemed right as rain, he did. I still can't believe what happened later that night.'

Right as rain? thought Drew. What was right about rain? 'The Internet?' he asked. 'That's something I haven't got into at all.'

'Oh, Jim was into all the new technology,' Jack said.

A connection wriggled itself into Drew's head. Didn't people buy Viagra through the Internet? Wasn't the Internet a crucial component in the black market in all kinds of things these days?

'It's a *crime,*' Jodie interrupted. The word lingered, as the three of them glanced at each other. 'I mean, a crime against nature. Nobody should die like that,' she added.

'You're making it sound almost violent,' Drew said, quietly.

Jodie paused a moment, looking at him in surprise. 'I am, aren't I,' she agreed.

X

Monica was enduring another restless evening; the days seemed to crawl by, and her emotions were all over the place. She had cooked and eaten a small supper for herself, and washed everything up in a sort of trance, but her thoughts were chaotic. Many a time she had eaten alone – when Jim was away with the boys, or late home from work, or out for some other reason. This was no different, except for the knowledge that, from now on, she would always eat alone. She mused on what a total change this would make. Knowing that Jim would never speak to her again; never sit down and start his meal, only to jump up for something she hadn't provided. A meal with Jim had seldom been a restful business. She had eventually realised that she could never hope to anticipate his every requirement – that was not the nature of the game. Some need in him ordained that he must forever be searching for Worcestershire sauce; or a slice of bread; or a twist of lemon. Over the years, she had made it easier for him by providing no peripherals at all. Even the salt and pepper now lived in a cupboard across the room from the dining table, and she automatically put them back there at the end of every meal.

She tried to visualise how it would be after the

weekend, when they brought Jim back to the house for his last night at home. She would sit beside him, talking to him, keeping candles burning, remembering their life together. Thinking about it now, she smiled to herself. The ritual felt brave and imaginative, and she congratulated herself. The coming weekend would be an irritating delay, an interlude in which she could do little but try to prepare herself for the funeral, and the new phase of her life which would follow on from there. People would keep visiting and writing and phoning, she supposed – although Sunday was a worry. She'd have to sort something out for Sunday, if she didn't want to sit here going mad, all on her own. It was still a day when people withdrew into their own homes, to mow lawns or watch old movies on TV.

Outside it was almost dark. The summer was ending, every fine day a bonus in the slow decline into autumn and dark evenings and dead leaves. When a car pulled up outside her gate, she could hardly see it in the twilight. The occupant was in shadow as she came through the front gate, but Monica knew who it was, and went to meet her.

'I didn't expect to see you today,' she told her friend, on the doorstep. 'Glutton for punishment, eh?'

Pauline shook her head dismissively. 'Thought you'd be all on your own, so I've just dropped in for a bit.'

'Nothing better to do, then. You should get yourself another husband,' Monica told her, with a twinge of irritation. Sometimes Pauline seemed to have too much time for others, and virtually no life of her own. *I'm not going to get like that,* vowed Monica.

Pauline flinched, and Monica could see the process of understanding and forgiveness taking place. *Poor Monica – she's not herself. She doesn't really mean it.* 'Aren't you pleased to see me?' she asked lightly. 'Wait till you see what I've brought you.' She rummaged in a flimsy Tesco carrier bag that seemed in danger of splitting, and produced a wine bottle. 'Rioja – that's your favourite, isn't it?'

Monica forced a smile. Pauline pronounced the word with the authentic hard throaty sound, thanks to regular Spanish holidays, but she'd had no real idea what she was buying. The irritation flared again. Two or three months ago, the two had gone for a meal together, and Monica had chosen the wine more or less at random. The fact that she had enjoyed it more than she'd expected to had obviously lodged in Pauline's memory. But the idea that it was somehow her 'favourite' wine was ridiculous. Wine didn't work like that – you matched it to the situation, the meal, the weather, the mood. The knowledge that Pauline had tried so hard to please her made her feel exasperated – perhaps guilty. *The mood I'm in,* she thought, *there's nothing poor old Pauline can do right just now.*

With poor grace she fetched glasses and corkscrew and sat down in the armchair. The wine was, after all, very palatable, and she belatedly expressed her thanks. 'I'm getting rid of that recliner,' she said, glaring at Jim's favourite seat.

'I can see him sitting there, every time I come into the room.'

'I'm surprised he ever had time to sit,' said Pauline, from the sofa. 'He seemed to be out such a lot.'

'Jim was good with time. Managed to fit everything in without any trouble. Including quite a few hours in that chair.'

'You'll have to drink most of this. I'm driving. There's another bottle in the bag – I thought I'd leave it for next week.' Pauline drained her glass, then immediately poured herself another, appearing not to notice the contradiction. Drinking and driving laws struck them both as something that applied more to husbands and sons than respectable middle-aged women.

'So – what happens next?' asked Pauline. 'And where's Cassie? She's usually on my lap by this time.'

'She's dead,' said Monica calmly. 'I found her yesterday morning, and we're putting her in with Jim. Don't tell anybody – it's probably against the regulations.'

'But – how can she be dead?' The wine increased Pauline's bewilderment. 'She was fine last week.'

'So was Jim. Maybe they made a secret suicide pact. Look, she just *is*, okay? I don't know what it was. Old age, probably. Or she pined away. She was miserable on Tuesday, worse on Wednesday and dead on Thursday.'

'Well, I think that's awful.' To Monica's annoyance, her friend began to cry quietly, making no effort to wipe her face or put the wineglass down.

'The final straw, that is. And you sitting there so unfeeling! I don't know about you sometimes, I really don't. No wonder Jim–'

'Don't say it! And don't make judgments. You might be my friend, but you don't understand me. And stop crying. It was only a dog.'

Pauline made an effort, but it took a while. 'Sometimes,' she sniffed, 'I don't know why I bother with you.' But she laughed feebly, to soften the words.

'You've got something to tell me, haven't you?' said Monica, suddenly. 'I don't want to hear it, but I suppose I'll have to sooner or later. I warn you – I doubt if I'll be surprised. I'm not a silly little wife, with my head stuck in the broom cupboard, you know.'

Pauline said nothing; Monica took a deep breath. 'Do you know what worries me most?' she said, almost casually. Pauline shook her head. 'Loss of dignity,' said Monica. 'People thinking I'm an object of pity, a victim of some kind. I've always needed to be in control. To not be dependent. But nobody ever seemed to realise what I was really like.'

'Not even Jim?'

'Oh, Jim must have done, though we didn't talk about that sort of thing. We were married for twenty-nine years, after all.'

Pauline looked at her thoughtfully. 'Then they're more likely to see Jim as the victim, aren't they? Whoever *they* might be?'

Monica laughed, a single shrill burst. 'You could look at it like that,' she agreed. 'So let me have it, then. Tell me the worst.'

'Ah.' Pauline looked as if she might have changed her mind. 'You're not going to thank me for this, are you? I don't even know, for sure, why I'm doing it. After what you said about dignity, I probably ought to keep my mouth shut.'

'Well, it's up to you. Quite honestly, I don't care much either way.'

Pauline wriggled restlessly. 'Well – it's just that, on Monday, when Jim's back here for the night, you are having open house, I take it?' Monica nodded. 'Well, I think you might find some unexpected people turning up. I mean – I'm not sure how much you knew about Jim's social life–'

'All his women around him at once, you mean?' Monica spoke lightly, but the words echoed around the room, dancing like demons in the fading light.

'Ah,' breathed Pauline. 'You knew all along then? I needn't have bothered to come.'

Monica smiled gently. 'I'm sorry I was such a bitch. It's nice to have someone to talk to,' she said. 'Those sons of mine can hardly bring themselves to show their faces. Got their heads pushed deep into the sand. Terrified of what I might say to them. No, love, I'm glad you're here. But I'm not really worried about cats coming out of bags. He never once even *thought* of leaving me. And I had the best of him.'

'I'm sure you did,' gushed Pauline, awash with relief. 'You're so *balanced.* The most sensible woman I know–'

'Steady on! But don't worry – I'm not going to scratch anybody's eyes out. Fair's fair. Jim wasn't doing anything that I hadn't done myself, but just the same–'

Pauline put a hand out, lightly patting Monica's forearm. 'I know. It's the dignity thing again, isn't it?'

'In a way.' Monica was dubious. 'But it's more that I think we ought to get him safely despatched first.'

'Right,' nodded Pauline. 'Right.'

CHAPTER FIVE
SATURDAY

I

Drew and Karen were discussing the full extent of his suspicions and discoveries to date, more for the sake of clarifying his own thoughts than eliciting any help from her. Indeed, it had been quite an effort to make her listen to him; he had followed her about sheep-like as she sorted washing and planned the weekend meals. She had been out at school meetings the previous two evenings, and had not wanted to know about Lapsford or Plant's or anything else when she'd finally got home.

'It's now or never,' he reminded her. 'There's a whole mass of leads. Once I started on this, it looked as if *everybody* wanted the man dead. Jealous husbands, unbalanced sons, unfaithful wife, dropout gypsies–'

'What?' Karen paused in the middle of putting a new pillowcase on Drew's pillow. *'Gypsies,* did you say? Do you mean travellers? Because there aren't any round here.'

'Well, no. It's just a woman living in a caravan, all on her own, in the middle of a field. Living off the land.'

'Oh, you mean Roxanne Gibson.' She resumed shaking the pillow into the case.

'You know her?'

'Not personally. One of the kids in my class is her nephew. Or her husband's nephew. Doesn't approve of her at all. Calls her an old witch. What makes you add her to your suspect list?'

'Lapsford was sleeping with her, according to Vince and the others.'

'And you think she could have bumped him off with one of her herbal potions.'

Drew shrugged. 'It's possible.'

'Fair enough. So what are we going to do to crack this mystery once and for all? I take it you haven't heard from Lazarus?'

'No, but we've got the dog now. Whatever happens, I'm not going to let that get cremated.'

'But why? Once Jim's turned to ashes, it won't matter what they find in the dog. There'd be nothing to connect them, not in the eyes of the law. You'll have to do a lot better than that. Look, love, it seems to me that the only chance you've got is for someone to be so confident that they've got away with it they start behaving carelessly. If the man was murdered for some sort of gain, the perpetrator – if that's the right word – will start to behave differently. Draw attention to themselves. And if it was for revenge, they'll probably be feeling quite pleased with themselves.'

'On the other hand,' said Drew, 'they might be noticeably agitated and on edge until the cremation's safely over. What this amounts to is watching everyone like a hawk. And since I don't know any of these people, and how they normally carry on, it's a bit of a fruitless exercise.'

'You have to ask people who *do* know them.'

She moved out of the bedroom, and went into the bathroom, where she started cleaning the bath. 'I'll do that,' offered Drew.

'No, you can do the loo. And water the plant. So – who's your prime suspect?'

'The son, David,' he replied without hesitation. 'Murder's usually committed by someone in the family, and he was certainly behaving very strangely indeed on Tuesday.'

'Do you know where he lives?'

'No idea. Why?'

'Well, maybe we ought to try and get to know him better. Let's see if he's in the phonebook.'

Karen fetched the book, while Drew tidied up the bathroom. She came upstairs with the open book in her hands. 'Lapsford, J, Lapsford, P. That's all. Perhaps David's sharing a flat, and the other person's responsible for the phone.'

'That'd figure,' Drew agreed. 'I tell you what, though – the two old dears from next door aren't stupid. One of them invited me to go back and have a little chat to them. That's what we'll do. Right after lunch. They'd be better placed than anyone to know of any goings-on at the Lapsfords.'

'*We?*'

'Of course. You wouldn't want to be left out, now would you?'

She grinned at him like a schoolgirl. 'Thanks, mister. Playing detective has always been my *biggest* ambition. But why wait till after lunch?'

'I thought I'd check out this – this Roxanne – this morning. If you don't want me for anything else. I can do any shopping on the way back.' He could feel himself blushing.

She narrowed her eyes. 'Hmmm. They say she's got a way with men. Animal magnetism seems to be the favourite phrase for it.'

'I'm a one-woman man, though, aren't I?'

'So what about these other suspects?' She changed the subject with a careless shake of her head. 'So far you've only told me about Roxanne and David.'

'The dentist is my second favourite. Gerald Proctor. She works for him, and the gossip is that they've been more than good friends for some time.'

Karen blew out a huff of surprised laughter. 'It gets better and better. He'd have access to poisonous substances, wouldn't he? He could have filled Jim's tooth with a slow-acting toxin of some sort. That would be brilliant. You could get his teeth analysed for evidence.'

'It strikes me that you're enjoying this a bit too much,' he said reprovingly. 'It's not a game, you know.'

'It's a puzzle, though, and you know how much I like puzzles. If you want me to help, then let me do it in my own way. That's only fair. Now, we can't just stand about chatting all morning. Tell me the rest while I get the old newspapers ready for the bin men. There's a mountain of them waiting to go. After that, you can go and see Roxanne – with my blessing.'

Drew told her about the previous Lapsford funeral, the one George had remembered, as well as more about his encounter with the old ladies next door to Monica, and the vague suggestion that Jim had had another girlfriend besidc Roxanne. As he spoke, some of the threads began to untangle in his mind. He described his visit to the printworks, and the effect Jodie had had on him. 'She's quite uncommunicative, but I suspect she knows the Lapsford family better than anyone. And Jim's company prints labels for a pharmaceutical factory – mostly for poisons, to judge by what I saw. I wonder if that's significant?'

'Pushing it, I'd say,' she concluded. 'Once you start looking for poisonous material, it's everywhere. Cleaning fluids, photographic developer, plants, medicines – you name it.'

'Hey!' Drew remembered. 'I never told you about the Viagra, did I?'

She frowned her bewilderment and shook her head.

'I managed to sneak a peep at Lapsford's medicine cabinet, and there was a jar of them. At least thirty tablets left, I'd say. Where do you suppose he got them?'

'No idea. You have to have a prescription, don't you? Maybe he went to a different doctor for them. A private clinic, perhaps.'

Drew shook his head. 'Doesn't sound right, somehow. The man I've been hearing about would never openly admit to impotence.'

'Well, he must have given somebody a reason for wanting it.'

'I reckon he must have bought it on the black market, from someone who'd ask no questions. I know you can get it via the Internet, and apparently Jim was a big fan of all that stuff.'

'If he'd been popping Viagra pills on a regular

basis, wouldn't that be enough to give him heart failure? That's what all the news reports said, wasn't it?'

'Not on its own, no,' Drew conceded. 'Not if you don't have a prior history of heart disease. But it isn't a good idea to use it without regular checkups – and we know Jim never went for anything like that. I wonder if I should try and have a chat with Sid's Susie? She might know more about it.' He tapped his teeth while he pondered.

'It's not going to be easy,' Karen pronounced, dumping three large stringed-up parcels of newspaper on the kitchen table. She sighed. 'Are you really sure you want to go on with it?'

'Yes,' he said firmly. 'I'm sure. First stop, Roxanne Gibson. I've a feeling she won't be all that surprised to see me.'

II

Karen had told him where Roxanne's caravan was, with some playful show of reluctance. 'I don't see why you want to go and talk to her,' she pouted. 'Not without me, anyway.'

He hadn't even tried to explain. Now, walking across the field, the grass damp from a rainy night, he had no idea what he would say. The door of the caravan was closed, and he could see no sign of life inside, yet he knew, somehow, that the woman was there. He knew, too, that she was watching his approach. When the door swung open before he could knock, he walked in as if hypnotised.

'You're the chap from Plant's,' she told him calmly. Close up, he could see creases in her neck, a lack of elasticity in the skin under her eyes, and white hairs growing above her ears. But she was also warmer, more normal than he had expected from his glimpse in the churchyard. Yet he still felt brave as he stepped into the steamed-up caravan and let her pull the door shut behind him.

'I can't really explain why I've come,' he started, looking around as he spoke. Swags of drying vegetables and herbs hung from the ceiling; jars and pots of all shapes and sizes stood on shelves. Hand-stitched covers protected the seats, and the floor had a long narrow mat woven from some sort of hairy fibre. It was the closest he'd ever come to experiencing the home of a New Age Traveller – except that Roxanne showed no sign of travelling anywhere. And she might not regard herself as especially New Age either, he suspected.

'I can safely assume it has to do with Jim Lapsford,' she said. 'Although I do get what you might call tourists coming to see me now and then. I know I'm fairly unusual, by Bradbourne standards. But then, that's probably because it's the dullest town in the western world. I get the feeling that you haven't lived here very long.'

'That's right.' He was still casting his eyes around the cluttered surfaces, and hadn't properly met her gaze. He wouldn't admit to himself that he was nervous of doing so.

'I hope it doesn't drive you mad,' she continued. 'That has happened in the past. It's a town without a soul.'

He did look at her then, his eyes wide and baffled. 'What do you mean?' he said, his voice loud in the enclosed space. 'The place seems fine to me.'

She sighed. 'Next time you're in the High Street, just look around you. Miserable squalling kids, couples bickering, aimless teenagers with nothing to do and nowhere to go. Shops selling garbage that nobody needs, money the only thing that counts. Nobody *makes* anything any more. They buy a thing, use it once and throw it away.' She pulled her arms tightly across her stomach, rounding her shoulders, sighing again, more deeply this time. 'Take no notice of me,' she added. 'I'm just a middle-aged hippy. If that isn't the way it seems to you, I don't suppose I'll be able to persuade you to see it my way. I don't usually start on like this the minute I meet someone. I just thought you seemed sort of – *sympatico.*'

He smiled at that. 'I'm not sure whether I am or not,' he admitted. 'I grew up closer to the moors, with not so many people around – I used to think I was missing something, a lot of the time.'

'So you never knew Jim Lapsford?' Drew shook his head. 'But you're curious about him. You've heard a lot of gossip and you're intrigued by his wife and sons.'

'Pretty well spot on,' he confirmed. 'They said you were a gypsy – you must have been using your crystal ball.' He grinned teasingly.

Roxanne gave no reaction, but continued. The

words poured out, as if rehearsed. 'Jim was a lost soul, it seemed to me. He was always making plans, never satisfied with the status quo, driven by fear of getting old without having lived life to the full. He was forever promising himself he'd leave Bradbourne, travel to South America, or some Pacific island – somewhere he could find a new world. But he could never get up the nerve to do it. I tried to encourage him. I might even have gone with him. He was worried about what people would think if he deserted Monica and the boys. He was conventional in some ways. Not to mention the printworks, and Jodie. He thought of her as a daughter – or sister. You probably don't know about his real sister, Julia? He never talked about her, but I remember when she died. I lived in the same street as her, before she went into a nursing home. He – and she – was only thirty-one, and it wasn't in any sense sudden, but Jim was wrecked by it. It must have been awful for Monica.'

She was speaking in a toneless outpouring, which Drew had difficulty in absorbing. Finally he put up a hand to stop her, at a loss to understand why he was being treated to so much unsolicited information. 'Wait,' he pleaded, 'you're losing me.'

She blinked. 'Sorry,' she muttered. 'You caught me in one of my moods. Don't you find that people generally talk very freely to undertakers? The shock of a death must loosen lots of tongues.'

'I'm new at the job,' he told her. 'And I don't see much of the families until the funeral itself.

But when I was nursing, people would often talk to me.'

'Nursing? What made you leave?'

And then it was Drew's turn to speak his mind. He screwed his eyes up against the impulse to tell her the whole story, and then gave in to it. What he had to say had been lurking in a dark corner for many months: even Karen had shied away from hearing the whole unhappy story.

'Officially because I was offered night shifts for an unlimited period, and I didn't fancy that. It wouldn't have done my marriage much good, for one thing.'

'But unofficially? Which I assume means the real reason?'

'I couldn't cope with it any more. A baby died under my care, and I just bottled out. The thought that something like that could happen again haunted me. I was getting completely neurotic about levels of medication, checking everything over and over – I couldn't really do the job properly any more. I wasn't openly blamed for the baby's death – it was just that I failed to notice warning signs, and – did nothing. Sat there and let it die. It's so easy to do nothing, you see. And so difficult to follow your gut feeling and *act*. I *knew* it wasn't right, but didn't have the balls to say anything. He turned out to be a lot sicker than we'd realised – we might not have saved him anyway. But none of that made me feel any better. So that's why–'

'Why you're not happy about the official cause of Jim's death,' she finished for him. 'Now I understand.'

'Do you? Do you really?' He was suddenly eager, even excited. 'And what do you think?'

She sighed again and hugged herself even tighter. 'If it's confession time, then I suppose I'd better come clean. I think he died of a heart attack, and I think it was probably my fault. But I didn't murder him. If I'm right, then it was an accident, and I don't think there's any need to call in the police.'

'An *accident?*' The word seemed false, unconvincing. How did a man die in his bed by accident? And what did Roxanne mean about it being her fault?

'An accidental overdose of a rather dodgy substance,' she elaborated, with a rueful grimace.

'You don't seem that upset about it,' Drew ventured. 'I mean–'

'I'm *extremely* upset to have lost him, believe me,' she corrected, with sudden animation; her eyes met his with a fierce look, making him quail. 'But what's done's done, and nothing's going to bring him back. After the first shock, I even thought it might be just as well that he didn't live to be old. He'd only have got more and more dissatisfied, looked for more and more idiotic magic cures for ageing. He was terrified of losing his sex drive, for one thing.'

'So it seems,' said Drew, without thinking.

'What do you mean?' She was sharper than ever, fixing him with her large dark eyes.

'Well, he had erotic books in his bedroom and Viagra in his bathroom–' Drew began.

'You're joking! He wouldn't be such a fool!'

Drew shrugged, silenced by her stormy

reaction. Slowly he retrieved the tablet from his pocket and held it up in front of her face. 'Viagra,' he said again. 'I know what a Viagra tablet looks like. And I don't think he got it from his doctor.'

'Well, that clinches it,' she said heavily. 'If he was mixing that with what I'd been giving him, he was a lot more stupid than I ever would have guessed.'

'Clinches it?' he repeated. 'You think this explains how he died?'

She sucked her upper lip unselfconsciously. 'I think it might,' she said.

'So what did you mean by "dodgy substances"?' he urged. 'What else was he taking?'

'Henbane,' she said flatly. 'I pick it from the hedges and infuse it. It's strong, but we never had much at a time, and it's not meant to have lasting effects. It hasn't done me any harm.'

Drew shook his head. 'I'm not sure I've even heard of it,' he admitted. 'But if Jim was okay when he left you, I'd say it was unlikely that he died of that.'

He contemplated Roxanne with a sense of bemusement. Talking to her – or rather, listening to her – had been an unusual experience. The directness, the dispensing with preliminary niceties, had been exhilarating, in its way. Like a roller-coaster ride. But there was something of an anticlimax in the air, too. If her henbane brew had by any remote chance killed Jim, perhaps by being mixed with Viagra and straining his heart beyond repair, there was no sense in pursuing the matter any further. The case was closed: there would be little to gain from disclosing the details. Drew could attend the cremation with an easy mind, and forget the whole unfortunate business. It might even explain the death of the dog.

But he simply couldn't leave it there. He couldn't be sure. 'I'll go now,' he said quietly. 'Thanks for talking to me. But – just to humour me – if somebody *had* deliberately poisoned Jim, who'd be your first choice of suspect?'

'You're asking me to slander somebody,' she pointed out, in a reasonable tone. 'And I don't think I could name just one person. There's a longish list of candidates. A lot of people disapproved of him.'

'Run some of them past me,' he coaxed. 'Just so I can get the picture. I'm new in town, remember?'

'*Nobody* murdered Jim,' she said emphatically. 'But if they had, I'd go for Frank Dunlop, Gerald Proctor, Sid Hawkes – and maybe the person who supplied him with the Viagra. I mean, if he got it under the counter, as it were – they might be no better than a drug dealer.' She shook her head angrily. 'If he really was taking that, as well as the stuff he had here with me, I certainly wouldn't vouch for the state of his heart.'

'Who's Frank Dunlop?'

'Husband of Lorraine. Look, this isn't to be spread around. It could do a lot of unnecessary damage, and I'm not one to gossip. Just let's say he'd be a jealous husband, if he knew what had been going on.'

'But if he didn't know, he shouldn't be on your list.'

'If,' she echoed, and shrugged.

'Nobody else?'

She pursed her lips. 'Not really. One or two who might have grudges from way back.'

'You did say Sid Hawkes, didn't you?' he queried. 'You mean Sid who works at Plant's? The mortuary man? Why, for heaven's sake?'

Roxanne grimaced. 'I shouldn't tell you, really. It's probably nothing. But there was a bit of trouble with his Susie, a while ago. You'd have to ask my sister for details – her Craig's going out with the girl now. Or was. I think Jim stepped over the mark there. Nobody ever talks about it, but I get the impression that Sid isn't the sort to forget that kind of thing. I shouldn't have mentioned it, with you and him working together.'

Drew shook his head doubtfully. 'Well, I'll be off now,' he said. 'It was really good to meet you.' And he meant it. As he walked briskly back across the field, her face remained vivid in his mind. His body tingled. Never in his life had he met a woman like Roxanne Gibson.

III

Jodie was walking fast, her head tipped forward, shoulders hunched, deep in thought. There had been something very odd about that funeral chap turning up yesterday at the printworks. For no real reason – she'd been a fool to assume he'd come about the service sheets. Thinking about it afterwards, she recalled his look of surprise and quick agreement when she'd mentioned them, making it obvious that he'd seized on it as a convenient pretext. The way he'd snooped about, examining the various stacks of work, was most suspicious in retrospect. Why would someone who worked for an undertaker's be so interested? The more she puzzled over it, the stranger the whole business seemed. But then, ever since Tuesday she'd had the feeling that there was something missing – some piece of information, some logic which would help to make sense of Jim's death. Every time she thought about it, the feeling became stronger, making her more restless and miserable with each day that passed.

She knew she would have to go and see David again. Amidst all that was going on – the anger and grief and confusion – David kept bobbing up to the top of her list of priorities.

Weekends had never been her favourite time. They reminded her how lonely she was, how empty her life. Sometimes she went to see an elderly uncle of whom she was very fond, a hundred miles away; occasionally she treated herself to a weekend in the Derbyshire Peaks or the Yorkshire Moors, staying in small B&Bs, and roaming the hills. But mostly she stuck to Bradbourne and its surrounding area. There were organised walks and rambles which could fill most of a day, but could also be frustrating: large groups walked too slowly, and tended to fragment into small cliques of friends, leaving Jodie marching out on her own more often than not. Pointless, really – she could do that for herself on a more interesting route.

She walked into town and bought a bagful of groceries. Then she made a wide detour to take in Primrose Close, in case David's car was outside his mother's house. It wasn't, and the extra two miles had brought her up to lunchtime. A quick bite to eat at home, and she'd be off again to visit David. For that, she'd have to take the car; he lived nearly five miles away, on the edge of Woodingleigh, and she hadn't time to walk there and back.

But the plan never materialised. Five minutes before she was intending to set out, someone knocked on her door. She lived in a big old house, using the basement for her main living area, with its own entrance down a flight of steps. Only someone who knew her would come to that door. Intrigued, she went to open it.

Philip Lapsford stood there, worry almost comically acute on his face. 'Oh, Jodie – thank goodness you're in,' he said, and pushed past her. 'I didn't know who would be able to help me, until I thought of you.'

She stood back to let him in, and waited for an explanation. She knew Philip least well of all the Lapsfords: he had never seemed to know what to say to her, and there had never been the slightest hint of a rapport between them. She was mystified.

'There is one hell of a mess brewing,' he burst out. 'Some bloke from the undertaker's came round to Mum's yesterday and took away the dog – it died, you know. Some young chap, it was – very sympathetic, nice manner and everything.'

Jodie nodded. 'I reckon it might be the same one I've met. Quite a little charmer, he is.'

'And he got her talking about Cassie, and led

her round to admitting she couldn't really believe it was a heart attack that killed Dad. You see, Cassie licked his face, after he died – and somehow that's led this bloke to think about poison. He left Mum all worked up, and suspecting terrible things. About David. She's talking about calling in the police, though I don't think she'll do it.'

He threw himself down on one of Jodie's dining chairs. She followed him slowly into the room, frowning deeply as she absorbed the import of his words.

'Cassie died?' she said blankly. 'That's awful. Jim loved that little dog. Had she been poorly?'

Philip shook his head impatiently. 'Apparently not. Though nobody but Dad is likely to have noticed.'

'What on earth makes him think of poison? I'd say he was treading on very dangerous ground. Putting the wind up people without any real evidence. I just bet it's the same one that came sniffing round the works yesterday. Sounds as if he's conducting some amateur detective exercise. Thinks he's Inspector Morse or something. Cheeky bastard. And now he's got your Mum all upset.' She sat down opposite him, and adopted a look of sympathy. It still wasn't clear why Philip had come to her.

Philip bit his lip in agitation. It was clear that he had more to say. 'The trouble is–' he began. 'Well, Mum's scared shitless that it might have something to do with David. As you can imagine. The more she thinks about it, the more sure she gets. She told me that you and she went to see him during the week, and he wasn't exactly calm and collected. She thinks now that he might have been suffering from a very guilty conscience.'

'Rubbish!' Jodie interrupted angrily. 'That's the most stupid thing I've ever heard! Wait till I get my hands on that bloke. What's he think he's up to? It's criminal. Look, you just tell your mum to forget all about it. She knows why David's upset. He's found out that he was adopted. Surely she's told you about that?'

Philip nodded. 'She only hinted at it on the phone, but David told me. He wanted to know if I could remember anything. He's still waiting for Mum to tell him the whole story. You can see her point – it isn't something you can just dump, especially not in the middle of coping with your husband dropping dead. You think that's all that's bothering David?'

'There was the row last Friday, of course,' she said, reluctantly. 'I've been trying not to think about that.'

'When he went to ask Dad for a job?'

'Right. He told you, then?'

Philip nodded. 'Actually, I assume that's what Mum's thinking about – wondering if Dave was so furious about it, he did something stupid. She's not thinking clearly, obviously.'

'No,' Jodie agreed solemnly, 'I should say she isn't. David wouldn't kill Jim. If he did, it wouldn't be with poison. He might fly at him with a knife, on the spur of the moment. But he's not the calculating type.' She spoke firmly, as if to a child, anxious for her words to take root. Philip looked at her dubiously. 'Honestly,' she insisted.

'You're right,' he said slowly. 'But the fact remains that he's in a pretty bad state. Somebody ought to go and see him. And quite frankly, I don't much fancy doing that on my own.'

'All right. I was going to see him, anyway. I know he's going through a bad patch. Monica is going to have to tell him the whole story, and she's going to have to do it soon. But this is a tough time for everyone – we ought to stick together, not run around accusing each other of murder.' Her temper was rising; once up she'd have difficulty in calming down again. The fury she felt with that Drew Slocombe from Plant's was overwhelming. How *dare* he! First thing Monday morning, she was personally going to make a complaint to his boss. Talk about exceeding his duties! It was bad enough that Jim had died at all, without this sort of mess being stirred up. A fierce desire to protect the Lapsford name increased her agitation: Jim had been a good man, a well-loved man, and nobody was ever going to say different – not in her hearing, anyway.

'Come on,' she chivvied him. 'There's no sense in sitting around here.'

They left together, and Jodie got into Philip's car without a second thought. They drove in silence for a mile or so, clearing the last houses in Bradbourne, and taking a small road through the brief stretch of countryside still remaining between the two conurbations.

Jodie spoke first. 'Do you think the undertaker chap's planning to go to the police?'

Philip shook his head. 'I doubt it. He doesn't

know that Mum thinks it might be David. If he had that much evidence, presumably he'd have done something before now. I get the impression he's just taking a bit of a shot in the dark.'

Jodie was thinking ahead. 'Only, it's getting so close to the cremation–'

'So maybe we should think about stopping him.'

'And how do you suggest we do that?'

Philip shrugged again. 'Any number of alternatives come to mind.'

'Philip Lapsford! Are you suggesting we kidnap him? Be reasonable, will you?'

'I'm not suggesting anything. But it's a tempting idea, all the same. Once the cremation's over and done with, nobody's ever going to prove anything, are they? And I for one would very much prefer it to be that way.'

'Me too,' she agreed forcefully. 'Me bloody too.'

IV

Sid and Vince often ran into each other on Saturday afternoons, usually in the company of their wives. Brenda liked Alicia, but the feeling was not reciprocated; Vince's wife would do her best to vary their shopping routines in an attempt to avoid the other woman, but somehow it nearly always failed to work. 'You plan it in advance,' she accused Vince. 'It's all a put-up job. Don't you see enough of him all week? It's not as if he's a particularly nice person.'

'He's all right. You have to get to know him.' Alicia didn't notice that he hadn't denied her accusation.

‘Well, *he* might be bearable, but Brenda is a monster. That woman has no humour, no charitable feelings towards anybody. She makes me want to wash after being with her.’

‘Come on,’ Vince demurred. ‘She works at the hospital. She’s Secretary of the League of Friends. You’ve got her completely wrong.’

‘I haven’t. She’s a horrible old busybody. And she’s foul to Sid. I don’t know why he sticks with her.’

Vince said nothing: the mystery of people’s marriages was forbidden territory to him.

‘Damn it, there they are,’ hissed Alicia, as they reached the end of the first aisle in Waitrose.

Vince shrugged. ‘We don’t have to speak to them. Where’s that list?’

‘She’s seen us. If this happens much more, I’m moving house. We’ll go and live in the Orkney Islands, and you can start your own funeral business.’

‘Shouldn’t think there’d be much custom,’ he remarked. ‘Sid, my old mate. Fancy meeting you here!’

The men nodded at each other, with a brotherly familiarity. Alicia watched them, trying for the twentieth time to understand the relationship between them. As always, she was distracted from her puzzlement by the overbearing Brenda, who habitually came too close and breathed too hard. She smelt of talcum powder, inadequately masking a sour body odour. She looked perfectly clean – Alicia believed it was the smell of Brenda’s unwholesome soul, overflowing into the physical world.

'We've had such a busy day,' Brenda began, in a complaining tone. 'I don't know where the time goes. Sid's supposed to be stripping the paint off the banisters today. I never did like that yellow he put on them, and now it's got to come off. Susie came over unannounced – bringing a streaming cold with her, the little pest. Never thinks, that girl. Wanted to see her Dad about something. Shut me out, they did. She doesn't realise how hurtful something like that can be, having secrets from her mother. Always was very thick with Sid, pushing me away.' She threw a spiteful look at her husband, who was studying the range of canned soups, with Vince beside him, maddeningly relaxed. He gave no sign of having heard what she said.

Alicia tried to edge away, keeping her gaze on the back of Vince's head, hoping to force him to choose an item and move on. But he had charge of their trolley, which left her feeling superfluous and vulnerable. She didn't even try to reply to Brenda's monologue. There was nothing she could say that would make the woman stop.

'I reckon she's thinking of throwing up her job, or something stupid like that. Though Sid says she's too fond of that Dr Lloyd to walk out on him. Mind you, if that's true, maybe she ought to make a change. Get herself a bad name if she's caught carrying on with her boss.'

Another of Alicia's objections to Brenda was her lack of logic. She seemed to throw remarks together at random, whether or not they had any meaningful connecting thread. It was far from anything that could be termed conversation, and

Alicia could think of no reason why she should be made to stand there and endure it. She took a deep breath.

'Sorry, Brenda, but we're running late ourselves. Vince wants to be home by three at the latest. Good luck with the banisters. Vince, I think we'll have to get on.' She was tense with the effort not to become shrill; her husband caught the edge in her voice and obediently turned towards her.

'Right then,' he said. 'See you, Sid.'

Sid raised a hand in a little wave. Brenda paused in mid-sentence, mouth slightly open; Alicia wanted to hit her, and cut those thin lips. The depth of her dislike disturbed her.

'Milk, yoghurt, cheese, spaghetti–' she read in a gabble from the list she was holding. 'Let's get on with it.' As they trundled the trolley away, she muttered, 'I could murder that woman. If this happens one more time, I won't be responsible. I'm warning you.'

'I can't help it if we bump into them.' Vince was all innocence.

'Well, you'd better help it. Find out where they're going, and be sure we go somewhere else. I mean it.'

'You're paranoid. Anyway, I like old Sid.'

'I know you do, though God knows why. I'll never understand men.'

'You try too hard. What you see is what you get.'

'That's rubbish. If that was true, there'd never be any adultery or embezzlement or–' She was shouting, and shoppers thronging the aisle were giving her hostile glances.

'Keep your voice down,' Vince interrupted, cuffing her lightly on the arm.

She flushed with embarrassment. 'Well, I just don't see the point of wasting time talking to somebody like Brenda, when all she does is moan and complain. And I don't see any point, either, in you going out of your way to meet Sid, when you're with him all week.'

'There isn't any *point*, Ally. It's just what people do. You see someone you know, and you stop for a few minutes to chat.'

'Well, it's really spoilt my day. I'm all jangled and cross now.'

'So it seems.' He was huffy himself. 'Shall we get on with the shopping?'

Alicia didn't want to let it go. Grabbing milk and cheese from the chiller, she reran the conversation with Brenda. Everything about the woman offended her, and she still blamed Vince for the encounter. She held her tongue until they'd loaded the shopping into the car and were driving home.

'I don't want to be rude to Sid – but I really don't think I can bear any more of Brenda. I'm serious. It might seem stupid, but it's true.'

'It's all right for you,' he said angrily.

'What? What do you mean?'

'It never seems to occur to you that ordinary casual conversation doesn't come easily to someone in my job. That anything that isn't about death or coffins or hearses is a breath of fresh air for me.'

She paused. He was right – it never did occur

to her. 'But–' she began, more gently, 'in that case, why *Sid?* Why not somebody who's got nothing to do with the funeral business?'

'Like who? When do I ever get the chance to meet ordinary folk?'

'Oh, Vince,' she sighed, 'I'm sorry. I hadn't realised it was like that. Maybe it's time you started looking for another job.'

'Yeah,' he agreed, much to her surprise. 'Maybe it is.'

V

Drew got home just as Karen was shredding red cabbage and slicing cucumber. 'Salad for lunch,' she told him superfluously.

'Am I late?' he ventured.

'You didn't say what time to expect you, so it wouldn't be reasonable to accuse you of that. It's fifteen minutes past our usual lunchtime, that's all.'

'Don't be cross. Wait till I tell you what I've found out.'

'You do know what today is, don't you?' She glared at him, her eyes full of reproach. He had no difficulty in following the apparent change of subject.

'Yes, my angel. I know what today is. And the best thing, as we both know, is to try not to think about it.'

'I don't feel like I normally feel.' The gleam of optimism was all too familiar.

'Darling, you know how irregular you are. Day twenty-nine really isn't so significant.'

'I know. But knowing what day it is, I'd advise you to do everything you can to humour me. Stay on the right side of me. That sort of thing. Now, sit down and eat. And tell me about this woman you've been talking to. She must be quite something – you're lit up like a Christmas tree.'

He crunched valiantly through the fibrous salad, trying to talk at the same time. He summarised everything he could remember of Roxanne's disclosures, but made no reference to his own confession about the dead baby, nor to Frank and Lorraine Dunlop.

'So, does that mean we pack it all in, and take her word for it that some unholy combination of stimulants finished him off?' Karen asked when he'd finished. 'Bit of an anticlimax.'

'What do you think?' he said.

'She might be protecting somebody. Or playing a game with you. Dropping Sid's name like that was mischief-making, if ever I saw it. It doesn't sound as if she's suffering from any real pangs of guilt over her part in all this. Surely she'd be absolutely distraught if she really thought she'd killed him with some herbal potion she'd made. No, I vote for at least one more try at working out what really happened.'

'I love you,' he told her. 'You always say exactly what I hope you'll say. Now, before you change your mind, we'd better plan what we're going to ask the neighbours.'

As they turned into Primrose Close, Karen was chattering nervously. 'Are you *sure* they invited you? What exactly did they say?'

'Calm down,' he begged her. 'We're just going to let them talk. We want to know as much as possible about the Lapsfords – that's all. It's normal practice – the police always interview the neighbours as a priority, don't they? They probably feel cheated because no one's been to interrogate them, give them a bit of excitement. We'll ask when they last saw Jim, whether they ever heard arguments going on – that sort of thing.'

'It feels like such an awful *cheek,*' she protested. 'We really don't have the right to nose about like this.'

'It was their suggestion,' he reminded her again. 'We're just responding to an invitation.' He glanced at her reproachfully. 'If you're really against the idea, you can stay in the car.'

She sighed. 'No, no. I'm right behind you.'

Once inside number twenty-two, welcomed in by a bustling Sarah, the couple stood patiently while Dottie cleared newspapers and knitting off the sofa. 'We weren't at all sure you'd come,' she burbled happily. 'We didn't think you'd even remember our little chat.'

'Of course I did,' said Drew, his natural charm rising effortlessly to the surface. 'I've been thinking about what you said ever since.'

'Well, now,' interposed Sarah, coming through the kitchen with a tray of tea and biscuits. 'We don't want to stir up anything unpleasant, of course. The whole business is obviously very – delicate. Have you been interviewing anybody else?'

'In a way. Just informally, you know,' Drew

smiled. 'After all, I've got no official standing whatsoever. It's just that–'

'Oh, yes, we quite understand,' Dottie picked up the thread again. 'We're quite relieved about it, aren't we, Sarah? I mean, if there *had* been something amiss, and we never had a chance to do our bit, we'd feel terrible. We'd be neglecting our public duty. Wouldn't we, Sarah?'

Sarah tossed her head impatiently. 'The whole thing seems clear-cut to me. A man dies suddenly, having been in excellent health, and the doctor issues a death certificate without a second thought. Nobody informs the police, the man's cremated, and his family carry on, possibly rather better off than before in several ways. As I see it, young man, you're doing society a service by trying to learn more. And I for one am more than happy to help you.'

Drew gave an appreciative laugh. 'Well, thank you,' he said, as Karen passed him a cup of tea from the tray.

Dottie spoke more hesitantly. 'He *did* seem very well on Monday. We – well, *I*, actually – saw him come home, at about ten. He trotted up the garden path like a man half his age. Waved to me as he went indoors. It's awful to think that he was dead just a few hours later.' She shook her head dolefully.

'He doesn't sound like the sort of man who'd have a heart attack?' prompted Karen.

'Oh, no! He didn't ever seem worried – *stressed*, as they call it these days. He'd go out with a cheerful whistle, often walking rather than using the car. And come back with a big smile, too, most of the time. Always light-hearted. As if life sat easily on his shoulders. I often said, "that man has a clear conscience" – didn't I, Sarah?'

Sarah nodded slightly. 'They never had rows,' she contributed. 'Nothing like that. In my opinion, it was one of those marriages where the partners have drifted apart and each gets on with their own life. The only real problems centred on the younger son, David. You've seen him, I presume?' Drew nodded. 'He isn't really – *right*, even now. Volatile might be the word for it.'

'So I understand,' Drew agreed. 'We are hoping to go and talk to him, but we don't know where he lives.'

'Oh, we can tell you that,' chirped Dottie. 'Monica left his address and phone number with us at Easter, when she and Jim went to Paris for a few days. In case anything went wrong with the house, you see. Philip was away, as well – on business, I think. Here it is–' She grabbed a large dog-eared address book from a small side-table. 'David Lapsford, Flat One, Number Five Froggett's Way, Garnstone. You know where that is?' she added helpfully. 'It's part of Woodingleigh really. You turn left at the main road, and then left again.'

Drew rummaged for a piece of paper, but was forestalled by Karen, who calmly took a notebook from her handbag. 'Five, Froggett's Way,' she repeated. 'That's very kind of you.'

'I don't feel we've told you anything very useful,' said Sarah, doubtfully. 'Somehow, it sounds so stark, listing possible motives for killing a man.'

'If it helps, we already know about the rumours concerning Mrs Lapsford and the dentist,' said Drew. 'And the even stronger rumours about Jim and, er – one or two lady friends.'

'Ah,' said Sarah, with evident relief.

They finished their tea, and chatted idly about the weather and the changing face of Bradbourne. They asked Karen about her job, and what she made of Drew's new career as an undertaker. 'I'm getting used to it,' she told them, with a rueful smile.

'It's an honourable trade,' said Dottie, reassuringly. The words hung in the air, echoing in Drew's ears. *Is it?* he wondered. *Is it really?*

Before they left, Sarah said, 'She's had quite a lot of visitors, of course. Her woman friend, the vicar, people bringing flowers. She seems to be well looked-after.'

'There was the man from the printworks, too. Jack somebody. He arrived as I was leaving, on Thursday,' Drew added.

'So there was,' she smiled. 'I'd forgotten him.'

'But you knew who he was?'

'Jim's best friend,' nodded Sarah carelessly. 'Funny little man. Something sad about him, with that awful beard and those glasses. He must be feeling wretched.'

Drew made no reply. The man had certainly seemed agitated at the printworks the previous afternoon: he was prepared to believe that could be a manifestation of wretchedness at losing his friend and colleague.

'We'll be off now,' said Drew, with finality. 'Thank you very much indeed.'

'It was nice to meet you,' said Dottie, 'we don't get a lot of visitors. It isn't a very friendly neighbourhood, you know. Everyone intent on their own business.'

Drew paused, remembering Roxanne's remark: A *town without a soul,* she'd said. Wasn't Dottie now saying very much the same sort of thing?

VI

Monica was feeling abandoned. Since phoning Philip earlier in the day, she'd had no contact from anybody. Dwelling in solitude, with no distractions, her anxieties mounted. If it was true that Jim had been murdered, the only person she could think of who was capable of doing it was David. Philip too had seemed capable of believing that his brother had poisoned his father: that was the thing which frightened Monica most. If Philip had laughed, dismissed the whole idea as hysteria, she would have felt much better.

Her mind was filled with images of David as he was when he last visited her – his behaviour bordering on madness, his emotions out of control – and she shuddered. If he *had* done it, then he must be protected. Nothing would bring Jim back, and to lose David as well was unthinkable. She loved him as if he had been born to her, and she reproached herself viciously for letting him find out part of the truth about himself without having first prepared him.

Perhaps it wasn't too late, even now. Having washed her face and brushed her hair, she left the house, ignoring the telephone which began to ring after she had pulled the front door securely behind her.

It took twenty minutes to drive to David's flat in Garnstone. Getting out onto the main road entailed a long wait. So preoccupied was she, that she didn't even ask herself why there was such a hold-up. Something ahead was slowing everyone down, so that they were backed up beyond her junction. *Hurry up*, she repeated to herself, as she edged forward. The time had come to tell him about his origins, and she couldn't bear to be frustrated in her intention, even temporarily.

Crawling behind slow-moving traffic, she finally understood that something must have happened. It was never like this on a Saturday, even in high summer. Bradbourne was not on a main route to anywhere, and did not go in for big public events which would attract this number of cars. *Must be an accident,* she said to herself, and the instinctive spasm in her gut gripped her, until she knew for sure that it was neither of her sons lying mangled in the road. A mother's curse, she'd long ago concluded: something you just had to live with.

The incident holding up the traffic had happened on a bend in the road, and did indeed involve a heavy police and ambulance presence. But it was not a car accident. There were flashing blue lights from two cars parked drunkenly on the grass verge, beside a field gate, and yellow-jacketed policemen trying in vain to wave the crawling traffic past. But nobody was in any hurry to proceed. They were craning their necks to glimpse the scene inside the gate. Monica was no different.

Another vehicle had been driven right into the field, and two men were kneeling over a body laid out on the ground. A big oak tree grew close to the gate, and a bright orange plastic rope dangled from a branch, incongruously vivid. It ended in a crudely hacked-off tuft of strands.

It was all astonishingly close to the road. Had somebody actually hanged themselves, here in full public gaze, in broad daylight? It seemed incredible. And yet, she thought, as she tried to see the face of the prostrate form, there was something grotesquely clever about it. How many cars would stop when they saw the jerking dangling body? The hedge would have partially concealed it, so anyone getting a brief glimpse while travelling past at speed would be inclined to persuade themselves that it wasn't what it seemed. Horror washed through her. They said that suicide was an act of anger, even hatred, against those around who had failed to observe a person's despair, didn't they? This was surely the case here. Young children; old ladies; even family members might have driven past and seen the hanging body. A cruel form of revenge. She turned her face away, belatedly obeying the policeman waving her past.

It hadn't been David – of course it hadn't. She'd glimpsed the person's feet, in black boots with silver studs and buckles. Nothing like anything that David would wear. But it could have been him. She remembered the anguish on her son's face the last morning she had seen him, and her hands began to shake. If David had indeed poisoned Jim, then suicide was a very real possibility, given his fragile mental state. Cursing herself, she began to accelerate, following the unblocked flow of cars, now moving at a more normal pace.

She had to save her boy. Whatever it took – however many lies or bribes she had to employ – she must return him to a semblance of his old self, sure of his father's love for him, and free from self-loathing. Frowning fiercely, she forced herself to prepare for the coming meeting. She would have to be very careful indeed.

VII

Roxanne could not get the image of the fresh-faced young undertaker's man out of her mind. He had arrived shortly after she'd treated herself to a stimulating mugful of one of her own herbal mixtures, designed to raise her spirits and remove a few inhibitions: she'd hoped she would feel less morose as a result. When her visitor had arrived, she had wanted to throw her arms around him. Instead, she knew she had talked too much.

When he left, she felt restless and anxious, bemoaning for perhaps the first time her isolation. The strangeness of Jim's death was giving rise in the town to gossip and surmising which she could not afford to miss. Her own part in it could not be ignored. Although nobody could ever prove anything, not now she'd disposed of the evidence, she'd said enough to the funeral chap to arouse unwelcome suspicions. What a fool she'd been! Her best hope now was to sniff out others who'd provided Jim with unwonted stimulation. Not least, the irresponsible idiot who'd given him Viagra.

That piece of information had come as a real shock. Jim was well known to be a health freak – he took vitamin supplements and experimented with a wide range of herbal teas. Since taking up with Roxanne, his horizons had broadened significantly, and he haunted the health food shop in town, seeking out new sources of essential minerals and life-enhancing substances. Ginseng, kelp and garlic had all been his favourites, one after the other. The idea that he would jump on the bandwagon that was Viagra diminished him in Roxanne's eyes. Somebody had exploited his vanity, his fear of growing old and less potent, and had sold him a powerful drug which, in the circumstances, could only have threatened his health.

It was Saturday afternoon, so Pauline would probably be at home. Without bothering to telephone, Roxanne set out across the fields to walk to her sister's house. The exercise would be therapeutic in any case. It was a little over two miles distant, avoiding the roads: a narrow bramble-choked footpath, scarcely ever used, opened onto the far end of Pauline's road. There had once been a railway line running there, closed over thirty years ago. It was not an official footpath, merely a forgotten route, crossing the closed-off ends of several of Bradbourne's older residential streets. Children played on the scrubby land, where nettles and brambles grew amidst rubble and abandoned rolls of barbed wire. The hilly terrain meant a scramble down into the streets, which few respectable adults would even consider. Roxanne scarcely hesitated before swinging her leg over a single-wire barrier, and letting herself half-slide, half-run down the steep embankment. It was the most direct way to Pauline's, and that was all there was to it.

The house was modest and inconspicuous. Pauline had lived there ever since she first married. When her husband had forgotten himself with a young housewife, during a longish building job in the woman's house, Pauline's reaction had led to his walking out and never coming back. With much less trouble than most people experience, he had moved in with his customer, enjoying the fruits of his own labour and ousting the bewildered civil servant who had paid him for his brickwork.

Nominally, Pauline's son Craig still lived at home, but he spent barely two nights a week there, staying with nameless friends or in Susie's flat. Roxanne privately considered that he was well past the age when he ought to be independent and finding his own accommodation; she took a cynical view of the excessively close relationship between him and his mother. His friendship with Susie Hawkes had been the only source of hope that he might one day leave home entirely.

Roxanne went round to the back of the house, down a narrow passageway. The kitchen door stood open, and the sound of a radio issued forth. 'Hello?' she called. 'Are you in?'

Pauline appeared, holding a mug in one hand and a cigarette in the other, her glasses perched crookedly on top of her head. She looked less than delighted to see Roxanne.

'Can I come in?'

'You don't want feeding, do you? I've nothing in. I ought to go and do some shopping, really, but I can't be bothered. I'm in a funny mood.'

'Me too,' said Roxanne, following her sister through into the living room. The house was packed with shabby furnishings dating back twenty years. Pauline's three cats left hairs and footprints on most surfaces, and her habit of knitting something for almost everyone she knew, as well as hoarding 'useful' items such as yoghurt pots and plastic bags, meant the house was as cluttered and messy in its way as was Roxanne's caravan.

'I don't need feeding,' Roxanne reassured her. 'This whole business with Jim is getting very complicated. I had a visit today. Very weird. I need to pass the time until the funeral as quickly as I can, and sitting alone thinking about Jim isn't the best way to do it.'

Pauline took the sagging sofa and stretched out her legs on it, leaving a threadbare chair for Roxanne. 'Who visited you?' she asked, with a singular lack of interest.

'A young chap from the undertaker's. I never did find out what he really wanted. I talked too much for that. He seemed quite bright – unusual for this dump. Seems to have got himself in a state over Jim – something to do with a baby that died when he was working at the hospital. Scared him so much that now, when anyone dies, he thinks it's down to him to make sure everything's above board.'

Pauline snorted. 'Sounds cracked to me.'

'I told him about the henbane,' Roxanne interrupted, with a tremor in her voice. 'That might have been a big mistake, mightn't it?'

Pauline's attention was abruptly hooked. '*What?* You told him what?'

'Oh, you know. Jim and I used henbane sometimes, for better sex. It's amazing – much better than pot or anything. But you have to be careful. It's poisonous if you use too much. I gave him some on Monday.'

'Shit, Rox. Did that kill him, d'you think?'

Roxanne shrugged. 'I only gave him a bit. He had to do a few hours' work, before going home, he didn't want to get too high. But this undertaker chap said he found Viagra in Jim's bathroom. Viagra! Would you believe it? I'd never have imagined he'd bother with something so – well, conventional, I suppose. Like any pathetic old failure. Jim wasn't like that. He didn't *need* that stuff. There wasn't anything wrong with him in that department.'

'Not when he was with you, anyway,' commented Pauline. 'Could the Viagra have killed him then? Is that what you think?'

Roxanne shook her head. 'They're saying it's safe enough, for men as healthy as Jim, anyway. But you can never be sure what things will do in combination. I very much doubt whether the drug people have tested it alongside henbane.

Which is a pretty powerful stimulant in itself. And he must have got it on the black market – ordered it off the Internet or something. In which case, he wouldn't have had any sort of check-up first. You know how he was always boasting about never having to see a doctor. After Julia died, he vowed off doctors – and stuck to it.'

Pauline laughed wryly. 'The perfect end to a life devoted to pleasure. Killed by too many sex aids. I can see the headlines now.'

Roxanne smiled grimly. 'I deserved that. But there won't *be* any headlines, not if I can help it. I owe it to Jim not to let him turn into a laughing stock.

'Lorraine Dunlop came to see me, too,' she added, crossing her long legs. 'We got on like a house on fire.'

Pauline refused to react. 'Really.'

'I was really nice to her. We agreed absolutely about Jim. The sort of person he was.'

'You were *nice?* Didn't she know she was risking being eaten alive?'

'I think she probably did – and decided to come anyway. She seemed to be beyond caring. She was very upset.'

'I'm completely gobsmacked.' Pauline was floundering, as was usual when with her sister: Roxanne seemed to twist all her normal feelings and assumptions into new, unpredictable shapes. Pauline had learned not to take anything for granted.

'I'm not that scary, am I?'

'You're the Witch of Bradbourne, as you know perfectly well. Everyone's frightened of you. They think you'll put the evil eye on them.'

Roxanne narrowed her eyes, and spread the fingers of both hands, examining the prominent knuckles and weathered skin. She cackled. 'Then that's what I'll be. Nothing simpler.'

'And then they'll think it was you who killed Jim Lapsford.' Pauline spoke softly, but with a sudden intensity. 'Won't they?'

'They can think what they damn well like – they're never going to prove anything.' A movement outside caught her attention. 'There's somebody coming to the door,' she pointed out. 'Looks like a policeman...'

'They're onto you already,' said Pauline. 'Better have your story ready. And don't think I'm giving you an alibi.' She waited for the knock before swinging her legs off the sofa and padding barefoot to the door.

Afterwards, they asked each other how they could possibly not have felt even a slight apprehension. No inkling at all of the devastating news that came to their lives that afternoon, as they lightly discussed murder and poison and the bizarre joke that was Jim Lapsford's death.

VIII

Monica felt cheated when she saw Philip's car outside David's flat: she didn't like the idea that her older son had stolen a march on her. But whatever she might find, nothing was going to frustrate her intentions now, and she marched to the front door. The door was locked, with the yale latch down. Pausing a moment, turning her ear to the glass panel, trying to catch conversation from inside, she gathered herself together. Then she banged the heavy knocker three times, having forgotten to bring her key.

'David, I have to talk to you,' she began as soon as he opened the door. 'I don't care what you're doing – this won't wait.'

'That's okay, Mum,' he said, pole-axing her with his calm response. 'Jodie's here, as well as Phil.'

Monica knew it was unreasonable, but she resented Jodie's presence. This was too much like a repeat of Thursday morning, with the added complication of Philip's presence. She had wanted a quiet talk alone with David, setting her own mind at rest, and possibly easing his at the same time. Now there would be interruptions and questions and sidetrackings, and the whole situation would carry on just as before.

'Somebody's hanged himself back there,' she blurted, before she knew what she was saying, but knowing she had to find an excuse for her agitation. 'Everyone's stopping by the road to stare. It's awful. I'm all shaken up by it. Except I was already shaken up.' She shook her head in a hopeless gesture. 'For a minute, I thought it might be you.'

David laughed incredulously. 'Hey, Mum – I'm not that crazy. I'd have to be a complete bastard to do that to you.' He paused, hearing himself. 'Though that's what I am, I guess. Isn't it?'

She gritted her teeth against the unkind stab. 'That's what I came to talk about,' she said. 'At least–' She stopped in confusion. There were too many words needing to be spoken, all at once.

'And about time, don't you think?' he said, more gently. There was something pathetic in his voice, and a pleading look on his face. But his voice was unwavering, and Monica knew that there was no going back now. She had to tell him everything. The build-up was reaching an intolerable level of tension; she began to tremble, blood rushing loudly in her head. She knew she wouldn't make a good job of this. She didn't think anybody could.

Jodie appeared from the kitchen, followed closely by Philip; David shook his head, instructing them not to say anything.

'Sit down, Mum, and get on with it.'

She clenched her narrow hands together, and glanced from one face to another uncertainly. 'Did you tell him what that man said?' she asked Philip. 'About Jim?'

Philip flushed, and glanced at Jodie. 'Not exactly,' he began. 'But David knows people are asking questions.'

Monica exhaled with relief, and sat down on David's greasy couch. She half-noted that there was a large recent stain on it, caused by something that included tomato ketchup, to all appearances. A closer look revealed two chips and several peas on the floor near her feet. 'Don't you ever clean this place?' she demanded. 'It's worse than a pigsty.'

'We were cleaning it up when you arrived,' Jodie said. 'David dropped his dinner.'

Monica wished she'd never allowed herself to criticise. Why start off on a bad footing? She could barely remember why she'd come: the image of the men wrapping up the hanged body recurred, clouding her inner eye, and filling her thoughts. There was probably another mother going through hell at this moment. The train of thought, and the echo of David's harsh remark, returned her to her senses.

'David, I've come to tell you who your mother was,' she said, with an effort. Her head was ringing strangely as if she were in an echo chamber. 'If you still want to know.'

'Of course I do,' he said, gazing at her earnestly.

'You're not Jim's son – but you are family. Jim's your uncle, not your father. And I'm not your natural mother.' The words came out in a monotone: she could hardly believe them herself after keeping the secret for so long.

'Uncle?' David echoed, in bewilderment. Jodie moved closer, her eyes fixed on Monica's face.

'But,' Jodie burst out, 'Jim didn't have any brothers. Did he? I mean – how can – you did say *uncle?*'

'No brothers. That's right. But he did have a sister. His twin, Julia. She died. Jim adored her. He was with her when she gave birth to David.'

David came to the sofa, and sat down awkwardly beside her, leaning over the sticky stain, resting a hand lightly on her arm. 'Now we're getting to it,' he said. 'At last. It's okay, Mum – I'm not going to freak out. Not any more. Just tell me the whole story. Please.'

Monica caught a whispered phrase passing between Jodie and Philip, even as she clutched David's hand and prepared to reveal the long-kept secret. She heard the word *incest,* its sibilance impossible to conceal.

'No! It wasn't incest,' she said firmly, catching Philip's embarrassed eye. 'But nobody but Jim ever knew who your father was. That part of the story will never be known now.'

IX

Drew and Karen were a good fifty cars behind Monica in the slow procession past the incident in the field. The traffic was still slowing down to have a look at what was going on, although the body had been removed by this time. 'My God!' yelped Drew. 'What the hell is that?' He was looking at the still-dangling orange rope.

Karen glanced cautiously beyond the gate. 'There's nothing to see,' she said, with relief. 'Keep driving.'

'But don't you want to know what's happened?'

'No. It's none of our business. Look, he's waving you on.' She nodded at the policeman, who was beginning to despair of the ghoulish inclinations of the human race.

'It's PC Gray. I know him. Hang on a minute.'

'Drew! For God's sake! What are you doing?'

He had pulled up beside the officer and wound down the car window. 'What's going on, mate?' he said, with a smile he tried to inject with a professional concern. The policeman showed no sign of recognition.

'Move on, please, sir,' he said stiffly. 'You're causing an obstruction.'

'Hang on. I'm from Plant's. Just thought I

ought to show an interest.'

The policeman looked closer, still seeming dubious as to Drew's identity. 'Well, you're not needed. Two of your chaps have been and gone already. Taken him to the Nat Vic. Bloody idiot hanged himself from the tree there. See the rope? Makes you sick, what people'll do – right beside the public road, too. No consideration for others.'

'Any ID?'

'Can't tell you that just yet. Got to be verified first. Local chap. Knew him vaguely – by sight – myself. You'll find out soon enough.'

Karen leaned forward on a sudden thought. 'It isn't David Lapsford, is it?' she asked anxiously.

'No, miss. That name hasn't been mentioned at all. Why – is this Lapsford chap someone who's likely to do something like this?'

'Oh, well, I don't really know about that. We're on our way to see him now, actually. I'm just being foolish.'

'Better move on now,' said the man again, glancing with a weary impatience at the long tailback of traffic. 'I'll never get this lot flowing freely at this rate.'

Drew obliged briskly. 'Sorry,' he said. 'Good luck.'

As soon as they had moved off, he turned to Karen. 'What made you think it might be David?'

She shrugged. 'Just a hunch – you said he seemed very unstable, that's all. Lucky I was wrong. Think of his poor mother, if he'd gone and done that.'

'God, yes.' They thought briefly about the awful

might-have-been, before turning into the smaller road at the end of which lay David Lapsford's home.

They found Froggett's Way after two circuits of the Garnstone housing estate. 'Looks as if we're not alone,' Karen commented, indicating the two cars parked outside the house.

'Might be for next door.'

'I think not,' she said. 'I can see people in there – look.' She nodded at the uncurtained window at the front of the house. 'Come on. Let's join the party.'

'Is this a good idea, I wonder?' muttered Drew. 'I'll feel a bit of an intruder if this is a family gathering. They might be discussing the funeral.'

'Don't lose your nerve now. We can always come back later, if it isn't convenient now.'

'But – how're we going to explain why we're here? What's our cover story?'

'Umm, how about – "We think your Dad was murdered, and we've come to check it out before his body is cremated and all evidence lost forever"?' She grinned at him mischievously.

Drew winced. 'I wish I hadn't raised the matter with the wife now. It'll look obvious that we're coming to nose around. Perhaps we should–'

'They've seen us.' There was a face at the window, and then someone was opening the door. David Lapsford stood staring at Drew with suspicion and hostility.

'What do you want?' he demanded, as they slowly got out of the car.

'Er – we were just hoping we could have a word

with you about your father.' Drew tried to sound as if this was a perfectly reasonable request; David's harsh laugh came as a shock.

'Oh, yeah?' he said unpleasantly. 'Then you're going to be right out of luck.'

As Drew stood on the path uncertainly, with Karen at his elbow, Monica and the girl from the printworks also came to the door. He saw them both recognise him; they immediately adopted a similar demeanour of hostility. Then the printing girl smiled, with a kind of triumph.

'Just the chap we wanted to see,' she said loudly. 'Bring them in, David.'

'Too late to escape now,' said Karen, with a little giggle. Her excitement only irritated Drew. If anybody was going to be damaged by this, it wouldn't be her. He hoped she'd have the grace to show some concern, at least, as he had his solar plexus battered.

Monica was pale; she looked exhausted. Once inside the house, she addressed Drew angrily. 'Could you possibly explain what you're doing here? Isn't it outside your job description to go hounding bereaved families like this?'

'Uh,' gasped Drew, helplessly. 'Well–'

'Leave this to me, Mum,' said Philip, nudging her aside. 'Now, look, you.' Drew could see in his eyes that it was out of character for him to be so forceful, that it wasn't coming easily. Somehow, that only made him more alarming. 'You've upset my mother very badly. You'd better know now that we intend to make sure you lose your job over this. It's an absolute outrage.'

Then it was Monica who took charge. 'Jodie,

look after his–'

'Wife,' supplied Karen flatly. 'I'm his wife. My name's Karen.'

'Thank you. Well, stay with Jodie, will you? This has nothing to do with you. Take her into the kitchen, Jodie.'

'It has if you intend to do anything to harm my husband.' Karen was fierce. 'I'm not going to make it any easier for you.'

'We won't *harm* him. Don't be silly. We just want to talk to him, find out what he's come here for.' David spoke placatingly, looking from face to face for support.

'Get on with it then,' said Drew, losing patience. 'And don't threaten me with getting me sacked. I've gone out on a limb here, following up a sudden death which never came close to looking like natural causes. When I spoke to your mother about it, she agreed with me. Whatever's happened since then, that much hasn't changed. So – whatever it is you want to explain to me, that's where I stand. And if you were any sort of a family, you'd want to help me, and not act so aggressive. This is your father – your husband – we're talking about.' It shook him to hear his own words lingering on the still air.

David was first to react. 'What on earth are you talking about? I don't understand what's been going on. I thought you'd just been upsetting Mum – that's what you just said, Phil–' He looked confused, suddenly vulnerable.

Jodie cleared her throat. 'We didn't have time to tell you, Davy – not with all this other stuff about your–' She stopped herself. 'This chap's from the funeral director's, in case you hadn't realised. He's the one who thinks somebody poisoned your Dad.' Monica, Philip and Jodie all stared intently at David as he registered these words.

'So – why is he here? I don't get it. Why *here?*' Nobody answered.

'Think about it, Dave,' Jodie muttered, into a long silence.

'Christ! He thinks it was me!' He turned in a slow circle, absorbing their tense attention. 'You *all* do. You all think I murdered my Dad. Or the man I *thought* was my Dad.' His face crumpled, and his shoulders began to jerk spasmodically.

'No, David.' Jodie gripped him tightly on the upper arm. 'No, we don't. Even if Jim was poisoned – we know that wouldn't be the sort of thing you'd do. These people are completely out of order. They know they haven't got a leg to stand on, or they'd have gone to the police.' She turned to face Drew. 'That's right, isn't it?'

Drew hesitated.

'Isn't it?' she demanded again.

'Try to see it from my point of view,' he began. 'If we cremated a man who'd been murdered, how do you think we'd feel afterwards?'

'It's absolutely none of your *business,*' Jodie shouted. 'You're just the people who dispose of the body. It's not for you to go poking your nose in. You don't know us – you don't know anything about us. All you're doing is causing trouble for people who are distressed enough as it is.'

She was still clutching David's arm, as if in desperation. Monica and Philip stood awkwardly, their eyes fixed on Drew's face.

'You're right,' said Drew, blinking hard. 'But–'

'Just go, will you. If you think you've got a case, then take it to the police. You should have done that at the start, if you thought there was anything suspicious about Jim's death. Otherwise, go home and forget all about us. Your conscience is *your* problem, not ours.'

'Hear, hear,' mumbled David, pulling his arm out of Jodie's grip. 'Well said, Jode.'

With scant dignity, Drew and Karen left the house. Behind them, the slammed door sent shockwaves down the short path to the street. A bird which had been on the roof sent up an alarmed squawk.

They drove away slowly, reluctantly. It didn't feel like an escape, but more like a slow withdrawal from the scene of the battle.

'Can we stop at a pub?' Karen asked, after a mile or so. 'I need a loo, for one thing.'

'It's only four o'clock. Most of them won't be open.'

'The King's Head will. They'll be watching football. And quite honestly, I don't care what time it is – I need a drink.'

'So do I, but it'll have to wait till we get home. A pub is the last place I want to be right now.'

'Humour me,' she begged. 'I just feel like having some nice cheerful ordinary people around me for a bit. I don't want to take these feelings home with me. Okay?'

'Well, I suppose I know what you mean. That wasn't very pleasant, was it.'

'We were completely out of order. We are never

ever going to do anything like that again. I don't know what we were thinking of.'

'Thanks for the *we*, anyway,' he said. They exchanged a wan smile.

The King's Head was open, as predicted, and they sat in a corner, where the loud volume from the wall-mounted television was at least bearable. Drew bought Karen a half-pint of Guinness, carefully making no reference to its reputation regarding pregnant women. They watched the congregation of football fans cheering and groaning in unison, eyes glued fixedly on the big screen.

The match was almost over. The final minutes seemed to be anticlimactic, and as soon as the whistle blew, the landlord turned the set off. The ensuing momentary silence was almost painful. Drew nodded to Karen, suggesting they leave.

As they stood up, a sudden burst of loud conversation came from the football fans. Karen and Drew both clearly heard the word *'Lapsford'*. Trying to appear casual, they lingered, in the hope of hearing more.

The barman was speaking. 'Oh, there'll be plenty of folks that'll miss old Jim in here,' he said. 'More long faces this past few days than when Bradbourne Rovers folded.' He winked, in unseemly fashion. 'Your Lorraine for one, Frank. Looks like a wet weekend, she does.'

One of the men became the object of attention. His features froze, and he seemed to have trouble taking the next breath. Then he gave a forced guffaw. 'Nothing to do with old Jim, that. That's because she's wishing herself back in Cyprus.

Fantastic time we had. Plus, well, it's a bit soon to say for sure, but she's maybe feeling a bit of morning sickness, as well. That'll be all it is.' He worked his shoulders, tried to look modest and proud all at once. One of his companions grasped the meaning of his words ahead of all the others.

'Hey! That's good news,' he said, too loudly. 'Time your little girl had some company.'

The barman perceived his mistake, and busied himself with collecting empty glasses. Drew and Karen made their exit thoughtfully. Outside he said, 'So that's Frank Dunlop.'

'Whose wife is pregnant, damn her. Am I missing something significant?'

'A bit of gossip, that's all,' he said uncomfortably, before changing the subject. 'Was I right in understanding David Lapsford to say that Jim wasn't his natural father?'

'That appeared to be the gist of it, yes.'

'Then maybe our afternoon hasn't been a total write-off, after all.'

'That's where I beg to differ. Drew, we've got to *stop* all this. Right now. Jodie was right – it's none of our business. Take me home, and don't talk to me about Jim Lapsford ever again.'

X

'I wonder where Monica is,' said Dottie, when she came in from the back garden late that evening. 'There aren't any lights on in the house.'

'With those sons of hers, most likely,' replied

Sarah. 'Or her friend. Maybe she got lonely.'

'Her phone's been ringing ever since early afternoon. Somebody's anxious to get hold of her.'

'Nothing we can do about it, is there?' Sarah was trying to finish her library book before going to bed. She had felt at a loose end on Saturday nights since her long-ago girlhood days had sown the habit of going out to a film or a dance – a habit which she had not been able to pursue for the past forty years or more. Even now, it felt as if she were missing something.

'I still think it's a bit odd. It's almost half past ten, and I'm sure she wasn't carrying an overnight bag when she went out.' Dottie's brow buckled with worry. 'I don't know, Sarah. Everything feels wrong, somehow. I feel all unsettled, ever since that young couple were here.'

Sarah raised her eyes to the ceiling, in a parody of prayer. 'I won't say it,' she sighed.

'That's a relief. I can do without your superior remarks. No, but really, shouldn't we *do* something? At least we might telephone one of her sons, just to check.'

'That would be gross interference. The woman's just lost her husband – doesn't she deserve some peace? She's probably safely tucked up in someone's spare room. It's the weekend. She doesn't have to be anywhere tomorrow, and I imagine the days are passing very slowly for the poor thing at the moment. She won't want you disturbing her.'

Dottie dithered, looking yet again out of the front window, onto the dimly-lit street. 'Oh, all right,' she conceded. 'I suppose I am getting worked up over nothing.'

A car outside drew her attention. 'Another caller!' she exclaimed.

A man jumped out and ran up Monica's garden path. 'Somebody else worrying about her, from the look of it,' Dottie commented, with some satisfaction. Sarah came to join her at the window. 'It's that boyfriend of hers,' she said, disbelief filling her voice. 'What a cheek! Talk about blatant.'

'Well, at least now we know she isn't with him,' said Dottie.

The man was banging on the door, standing back to look up at the front bedroom. 'Monica!' he called. It was some minutes before he gave up.

'Oh, this is ridiculous,' Dottie decided, and went to her own front door. She opened it, and stepped outside to call to the man on the next path.

'She's not there,' she told him. 'She's been out all day. Was it something urgent?'

'Oh ... ah...' he stammered. 'Well, not really. I just – I've been telephoning all afternoon. Then I tried again a little while ago, and was worried that she might be – ill, or something. Silly, really.'

'I don't think she's ill,' came Sarah's voice, from behind Dottie. 'I think she's out. She's a free agent, you know.'

Dottie tutted over her shoulder. 'Actually,' she confided to the man, 'we were a little worried ourselves. It is rather unlike her to be out so late.'

'Dottie!' Sarah hissed.

The man sucked his teeth in a moment of

embarrassed indecision. 'Well, never mind,' he said. 'I'm sure there's a perfectly ordinary explanation.'

'Good night, then,' said Sarah firmly. 'Come in, Dottie. There's nothing at all to worry about.'

CHAPTER SIX
SUNDAY

I

There was a definite tang of autumn in the air that morning, especially to Roxanne in her poorly-insulated caravan. On awaking, soon after seven, she looked out of the window, and glimpsed a bright red leaf on a straggle of bramble which had grown across the glass during the summer. There was little birdsong to be heard, and the sky was pink-tinged, a warning of rain to come.

'Bloody hell,' she groaned. 'Bloody Sunday already.'

A sense of foreboding hung over her; she huddled under the duvet, wishing she could go back to sleep and forget the whole day. Until this week, Sundays had often seen a visit from Jim, in the late morning, when Monica thought he was out walking the dog before lunch. Well, he *was* walking the dog – all the way to Roxanne's field and back. Mostly he would just stay for twenty minutes, the sex all the more exciting for being brief. She tingled now, just thinking about it.

The coming winter occupied a lot of Roxanne's thoughts: living outdoors became a serious matter once the autumn rains set in. It called for real determination to stick it out in the flimsy caravan, listening to water pouring off the roof, watching it drip through the invisible crevices around the windows. She was weaving a thick wool blanket on a frame loom, from fleece that she'd acquired last shearing time. It would need four separate pieces, stitched together; so far she had only completed two and a half of them. She had onions, carrots, winter cabbage, sprouts, all growing in the illegal garden she'd created behind the caravan. The plethora of official objections to her lifestyle had included pages of outrage at her 'change of land use' from arable farm to vegetables, which was domestic and therefore strictly forbidden. She had promised solemnly that she would not create a garden, and hoped this would satisfy them. Until the next official visit, all would be well.

All her life, she had instinctively lived for the day without worrying about the future. Meeting Jim Lapsford and finding he shared her philosophy had reinforced this approach considerably. But now she was forced to confront the coming months of cold and privation without Jim's comradeship. She knew she could do it, but the idealistic gloss had been wiped from it, and the prospect of loneliness loomed unpleasantly.

It was odd the way Sundays always found her depressed and lethargic. When every day of the week was scarcely different from any other, why, she wondered, did Sundays stand out so horribly? It wasn't just the absence of Jim – she'd hated Sunday for decades, before she even met him. She'd played tricks with herself, pretending it was a different day, but there were too many inescapable reminders. The church bells rang out all too audibly; the traffic passing the gate of her field followed a different timetable; something in the very air was heavy and quiet with Sabbath gloom.

Today would have been miserable anyway, of course. The news of Craig's suicide had appalled her. She and Pauline had driven to the hospital, where the discoloured body had been shown them in an anonymous room whose details were forever fixed in her memory. She would never forget the stained chromium pipe that disappeared into the floor in one corner. She had stared fixedly at that pipe, while Pauline cradled her dead son. Pauline's fingernails had left purple marks on the back of her hand from the unrelenting grip during the drive to the hospital; she still felt the throb of the horrified headache which had begun the moment the policeman on the doorstep had spilled out his message.

She hadn't wanted to leave last night, but Pauline had insisted, saying she just wanted to crawl into bed and let everything wait until morning. Roxanne had walked through the near-dark lanes, stumbling into the cold caravan and throwing herself onto the untidy bed, knowing there was little chance of sleep. The night had been full of anguished screams and croaks from unidentified creatures outside.

The warbling phone dragged her back to wakefulness. Wishing she'd switched it off – as she very often did – she groped irritably for the receiver. Before she had time to speak, a rush of distress filled her ear. She felt a horrible sense of *déjà vu – or déjà écouté,* to be more accurate. Her sister was babbling, half-hoping that Roxanne would assure her that Craig hadn't really died, that it had all been a grotesque dream. When she could do nothing but gently insist that it was still as true today as it had been last night, the resulting sobs were terrible to hear.

'Look, Paul,' she interrupted, 'the phone is no way to talk about it. I'll be with you in fifteen minutes. Okay?'

'No,' sobbed the voice. 'I've got to get out. I can't bear being here. How could he *do* it, Rox? What on earth was he thinking of? Right there, beside the road. Why didn't somebody *stop* him?'

'Has anybody told Susie?'

'Susie can wait,' came the snarling reply. 'Susie and her precious Dad are the cause of all this!'

Roxanne made wordless soothing noises. 'Well, don't do anything until I get there,' she said. 'If you're going out, then I'm coming with you.'

Pauline didn't seem to have heard. A fresh burst of weeping broke out, with barely discernible words interspersed between the sobs. 'It *hurts,* Rox. I can't tell you how much it hurts. Right through me – real pain. Physical pain. Nobody tells you that.'

'I know.'

Pauline's thick voice fell silent, and Roxanne shared with her a contemplation of the senselessness of what had happened.

'You're lucky – you know that – not having any kids. Fucking lucky.'

Roxanne closed her eyes, and breathed deep.

'Okay, Paul.' She spoke more gently than she felt. 'I'll see you in a while, whether you want me or not. Bye.' She hit the green button on the phone before her sister could say any more.

Roxanne knew something about suicide and its reasons. She knew that people did it mainly out of rage or a wish to punish another person. She remembered that pure childlike passion of fury which grips you so tight you'd do anything to work it out of you. When nobody will listen, when the world conspires against you, making you fail again and again, until you can see them all crossing the street to avoid the contagion of your despair – then the idea of killing yourself quickly gains in appeal. What had Pauline said about Craig doing it in full public view? Oh, yes, there was an obvious logic in that, now she gave it some thought. Defying the world to save him – making the point so powerfully that nobody could ignore it. *Here I am,* he'd said, *at the very end of my rope, and not one of you cares enough to press the brake on your car.* And there he'd dangled, for long enough to break his neck or crush his windpipe. And nobody had cut him down. Not until it was far too late.

She got dressed slowly, brushing away stinging tears with the back of her hand. It was too quiet, too conducive to destructive thoughts, in the lonely caravan. 'Jim!' she said aloud. 'Where are you now, when I need you?' Jim would have sat with her, holding her hand, smoothing away the misery. *You have to let people go,* he would have said. *If Craig was set on killing himself, nobody could have stopped him.* For all his sweet ways and willing kindness, Jim had had a sliver of ice in his heart. When it came down to it, Roxanne had known he lived for himself and nobody else. A man who could share himself out around three or more women at a time clearly had no real commitment to genuine intimacy. Roxanne knew – or thought she did – what had made him this way. It was oddly close to her own story, and the sense of their lives running on parallel lines was one of the things she had most valued in their affair. Jim, like her, had loved one person above all others. And had lost that person.

He had talked about her a lot – the way she had died, the last thing she'd said to him, the fact that nobody else understood him as she did. 'Nothing's been the same since Julia died,' he said once.

Roxanne had nodded. 'I know,' she said. 'There's probably only one person in any given lifetime who can do that for us. We spend the rest of our time trying to prove it otherwise, but we never quite manage it.'

'A bit more complicated when it's your sister,' he had grimaced. 'People don't understand that too well.'

She hadn't asked him any questions. She hadn't needed to. It was enough that Julia had become ill and died. Probably did Jim a favour, if he'd only admit it, Roxanne thought privately.

Having hacked herself a piece of bread, baked in the rickety caravan stove, and dashed a thick layer of that summer's strawberry jam over it, she went to open the door. It must be nearly ten by now, she calculated: any early mist had long since cleared and it was a sharply bright day, despite the warning pink sky. She'd told Pauline she would hurry to her side, but now she felt reluctant to do so. Once there, all would be despair and misery again; here, in the field, she could pretend there was nobody in the world but her and the bullocks, everything else an hallucination.

She followed the meandering path leading to the field gate and stood for a moment, looking back. The path became more clearly marked every day, trodden by Roxanne herself and her visitors: something told her there'd be more than one set of feet to tread down the encroaching grass, before the day was over.

II

Monica had the television on as she prepared breakfast: the silence in the house had been unbearable, and the raucous merriment coming from the box at least gave the illusion of company. The absence of Jim was a tangible thing. Not just the empty place in the bed, but the silence where his voice had been, the very pressure of his presence. Their marriage had been a minefield of mutual secrets carefully shielded, not so much for the damage they might do directly, but the uncomfortable shift in the delicate balance of power which any revelation would have caused. Nonetheless, she would have done a lot to have him back again.

She and Jodie had stayed all Saturday evening at David's, cleaning his flat, cooking supper, talking about Julia. Once the dam of secrecy had been breached, Monica had indulged in an ecstasy of reminiscence. She had described the onset of Julia's disease – multiple sclerosis being diagnosed when she was twenty-seven, forcing her to give up her much-loved job as an air stewardess. Monica, newly married to Jim, and unprepared for the emotional turmoil of Julia's illness, had chosen to concentrate on her new baby – Philip – and hope that Jim would eventually recover a sense of proportion. When Julia announced that she was pregnant, although by then becoming increasingly disabled and unable to support herself financially, Jim became even more distressed. 'We'll take the baby,' he insisted. 'You can see him as much as you like, but there's no way you'll be able to care for him yourself.' And Julia had been content with that.

At first Jim hadn't known the identity of Julia's lover. She had no obvious association with anybody, and flatly refused to explain herself. Only gradually did Monica realise that he had either guessed or been told, but he never shared the secret. 'It wouldn't be fair,' he'd said. 'David is ours now. Nobody is going to argue with that.'

Julia died, sooner than anyone expected, and after almost two years the baby was formally adopted. Jim's grief slowly abated, helped enormously by the presence of Julia's child – a piece of her, living on. 'But you were never an easy baby,' Monica told David. 'It was a difficult birth – they weren't sure that you'd live, at first. And I suppose the disruption of your first year must have had some effect. Julia insisted on having you with her some days, but by then she couldn't do much more than just hold you. You must have been very confused as to who your real mother was. It was a long time before I felt you were truly mine.'

And David had listened. Jodie had held his hand, her own reactions to the revelations causing tears to flow. 'I wish I'd known,' she said. 'Why did Jim make you keep it a secret?'

'He couldn't bear to have Julia's name mentioned,' Monica explained. 'He carried her around inside himself – nobody was ever allowed to talk about her. David would have asked questions, wanted to see pictures–'

'So he was protecting himself from pain,' supplied Jodie. 'Selfish, really.'

Monica had had no choice but to agree.

But this morning she felt calmer. She carried some toast and coffee into the living room, where the television was still on. A short local news summary was halfway through when she caught the name '*Craig Rawlinson*', uttered in the carefully subdued tones that accompanied bad news. 'What?' she said out loud. 'What about Craig?' But the scene had shifted to the local bowling club's current performance, and all that remained was an impression of calamity. She scanned her memory for whatever words might have lodged there. Had they said 'no suspicious circumstances?' She thought so. Choking with disbelief, fear, horror, she wondered what she would do. The simple thing was to phone Pauline and ask. Why was the simple thing always so impossible to do?

If Craig was dead, she realised, then Pauline would no longer be her chief support and mainstay. She, Monica, would have to look after Pauline, instead – the loss of a son was considered far worse than the loss of a husband. The idea was not appealing: her inclination was to run away, hide from this new wave of grief and confusion. If Craig was dead, then his timing could not have been worse. She found herself clutching her hands together, her fingers rigidly interlocked. The next unbidden thought did a little to loosen them. *It could have been David. You thought yesterday that it might have been David.* And then she made the link.

That body yesterday, just cut down from the tree, causing the traffic jam, that must have been Craig. She should have known it was him from the start. Those boots – hadn't she subconsciously recognised them? And even though Craig was the son of her friend – a boy she had watched grow up, who had been in her house a thousand times – she rejoiced that it was he who was dead, and not her own dear David.

Guilt followed fast on the heels of relief, but could not completely eradicate it. It was not, after all, any of her doing. Craig had always lived life on the edge, involved in a world which had sucked David in for a short time. His death had no meaning, no significance; it was just one of those ghastly tricks of fate, which brought troubles not singly but in battalions. *Poor Pauline,* she sighed. *Every mother's nightmare.*

She supposed that Pauline would be waiting for

her to get in touch. If Craig had died the previous afternoon, that would now seem a very long time ago, what with police and hospital and statements and all the things that happen after a violent death. Monica knew enough to be deeply relieved that Jim's death had avoided all that rigmarole. *But you might have got it all wrong,* a voice reminded her. *You might be leaping to conclusions about the body by the road being Craig.* Rationally, she knew this was true, but everything else told her she was right. Craig had died on that tree, by his own hand, with no suspicious circumstances. Beside that, the loss of her middle-aged husband, quietly in bed, was a tame catastrophe, a minor disaster. Uncharitably, she resented the loss of the limelight. *Now,* she thought, *everyone will be fussing round Pauline, instead of me. I'll be pushed aside. I'll have to take control of my life.*

She had to speak to someone, if only to prevent these unworthy thoughts from taking over completely. Someone prosaic and clear-headed, who was likely to have heard the local news. The choice was obvious.

'Phil – it's me,' she said, when the phone was quickly answered. 'I think I just heard something awful on the news.'

He responded cautiously. 'About Craig?' he said.

'It's true then, is it?'

'They say he was found hanging from a tree close to the Garnstone road. Well, you were there, weren't you?'

'Yes, I passed by. I *saw* him. But I had no idea it was him. At least–' The image of the silly studded boots returned to her. She hadn't seen the face; she couldn't have known who it was. She couldn't have done anything.

'David's going to be very upset,' remarked Philip.

'Maybe it'll take his mind off Jim,' said Monica, before she could stop herself.

'Possibly,' was the only reply, but she could hear a startled tang of disapproval in the voice. Was she really such a selfish bitch as she sounded to her own ears?

'I mean–' She tried again. 'It'll make him see that others are worse off than him.' It sounded pathetically trite.

'I think you've got that wrong,' Philip corrected her. 'As I see it, David's going to think the whole world's against him, if even his best friend is dead. You must admit it's quite a shock, losing two people in one week.'

'That's just the way it goes sometimes,' she said, trying to sound mature and wise, full of experience of life's ironies, but suspecting she just sounded hard. 'You just have to cope.'

'That's right, Mum,' he agreed, and the sarcasm was almost tangible.

III

Sunday passed miserably for Lorraine, too. After her visit to Roxanne, she had slumped into a state of inertia, unable to feel angry even with her rival for Jim's affections. Unable to feel angry with Jim himself. Frank had got his holiday photos back and was arranging them meticulously in a specially-bought looseleaf album. 'You're the only person in the world who does that any more,' she told him. 'Why can't you keep them in a drawer like a normal person?'

He ignored her. 'Now, *this* one will have to be enlarged. I can get one of those clip frames for it.' The picture showed Lorraine silhouetted against a dramatic flaming sunset, with a palm tree at one side of the frame.

'Nice,' she said shortly. 'You should enter it in a competition.'

'I might take up photography,' he said thoughtfully.

'What on earth do you mean? You do it already.'

'No, I mean the developing and printing. In a darkroom. I was chatting to an old lady down by the river, before we went away. She does all her own, apparently. Only black and white, though – colour's a lot more tricky.'

'And expensive.'

'Probably,' he agreed.

Cindy was cutting out pictures from a mail order catalogue and making a snowstorm of tiny scraps of paper on the floor: Lorraine waited for Frank to notice and complain. For all she cared, the child could fill the room with rubbish, so long as she didn't ask Lorraine to play with her. The prospect of a second baby was an alarming mixture of pleasure and dread. She hadn't said anything about it to Frank yet, but was aware that he knew exactly how overdue her period was, and was simply waiting for her to confirm it.

'Isn't it time the potatoes went on?' he said, glancing at her. 'I thought we'd go out for a drive this afternoon.'

'Where to?'

'Oh, blackberrying, up on Dunmore Hill. There might be some sloes, too. I thought I'd make some sloe gin.'

Lorraine contemplated this husband of hers, so domestic and easy-going. Frank hadn't a vice of any description; you couldn't even say that he was boring, when he was so enthusiastic about his fish and his photography, so generous with his attention and concern. If she'd mentioned a headache, or even tiredness, he'd have willingly left his album and trotted off to peel potatoes. As it was, she had nothing else to do, and levered herself out of the chair submissively.

'It'll be ready by one thirty. Plenty of time for an outing,' she said. 'That'll be nice – won't it, Cind?'

The child went on snipping, frowning fiercely.

'Fantastic. Thank you, Mummy,' supplied Frank, with a wink at Lorraine.

In the kitchen, she tried to feel cheerful: she believed that a person could control their own emotions, with a certain amount of perseverance. She ran through her usual bag of tricks for improving her mood. Plans were often helpful. Places to go; people to see; videos to hire; food to prepare. She liked to get the week ahead clear in her mind. It was also a good idea to have a reply ready for Frank when he asked about her intentions for the next few days. The fact that she brought no money into the house was an area of some uneasiness for them both – the new baby was good news from that point of view, giving her the best possible excuse to cruise through a few more years.

But plans were a bad idea this morning. They included Jim's wake, which Roxanne had told her about, and her desire to be there. She didn't think she'd have the nerve to show up. How could she ever explain her reasons for doing so? She had no public claim on him – they merely drank at the same pub. She wouldn't want Frank to know that she'd gone – it would look so peculiar – and there was every chance that somebody would mention it to him. She thought perhaps she would just drive to the crematorium on Tuesday and sit in the car park to see the hearse arrive. Say a final goodbye from the safe confines of her car. She knew she'd only cry helplessly, draw attention to herself, if she went into the chapel. Sniffing over the potatoes, she promised herself that this was what she would do. It would be much better than staying at home, knowing she was missing something important.

She tried again to distract her thoughts with something cheerful. The new baby was the obvious choice, and she gave it her best efforts. A boy, without doubt – Frank always got what he wanted, and he had said from the start that he wanted two kids: girl first, then boy. Girls coped better with being experimented on, and would be more useful for babysitting the younger one. A decent gap between them, too, make it easier to give them both plenty of attention. Lorraine sighed. If uxorious Frank ever found out about her affair with Jim, he'd probably die of the shock. It would never occur to him as being even remotely possible that a wife and mother like her should want to stray. For didn't she have everything she wanted?

Jim, Jim, Jim. Every time she tried to push him out of her mind, he crept back in some slippery new guise. She could feel his warm skin against hers, even now; the spring in his dark grey hair, which she had loved to hold and tug in moments of passion; the unselfconscious moans which marked his orgasms. She had loved being so much younger than him, revelling in her own lean body, not an ounce of surplus fat on her. There hadn't been any guilt. Jim had said such sensible things about taking pleasure where you can find it, about people not owning each other. She had felt proud and privileged to be singled out by him, made special by his attention.

But maybe he'd been wrong all along. Somehow his sudden death suggested that he must have been. His death felt like a punishment, a judgment – on him, and Lorraine, and Roxanne. It showed that you can't get away with breaking the rules, however right it might feel.

The potatoes peeled, she put them on to boil. As she turned away from the cooker, the fact of Jim's loss hit her like a physical blow. Now, she *knew,* in her blood and bones, that she would never see him again. Dizzy, she sat down at the kitchen table. Her mind felt like a captive bird, beating against glass, trying to find an escape from the awful truth. But the world had turned grey and unfriendly. Now she just had Frank and Cindy and a new baby and nothing at all to take her to the edge of ecstasy or risk. She trembled at the prospect. Words like *settled* and *ordinary housewife* hammered at her, until she wanted to run into the street stark naked, take a kitchen knife and stab the first person she met.

'Lorrie?' came Frank's voice, husky with concern. 'What's up?'

She shook her head.

'Are you ill?'

'No,' she replied, her voice harsh. 'Just pregnant. It must have happened on holiday. I'm only a week late, but I'm sure, just the same.'

He sat down facing her, and laid a hand very lightly on her wrist. 'I thought so. That's great. Isn't it?'

His predictable lack of surprise only increased her gloom. 'I suppose so. I feel sick – and I nearly fainted just then. That's all.'

'But you were fine last time. You'll be okay. Look, go and put your feet up on the sofa till lunch. I'll do everything in here. Okay? I'm going to think about being a Dad all over again, so if you hear a noise, it'll be me getting excited.'

'Oh, Frank.' She smiled weakly, looking up at him. 'You're very sweet.' His light brown hair was the same colour as his skin, after the Cyprus tanning: his blue eyes were vulnerably prominent, and his ears stuck out just a little too far. Frank was no beauty, but he was easy and kind and reliable. For Frank, life was simple, so long as you didn't expect too much. The world had always had a ballast of Franks, dutiful and unambitious. Other people exploited them, herded them like sheep, appealing to their sense of decency – and they never complained. Lorraine shivered. What madness had ever persuaded her to marry him? She was committed to him as irrevocably as if they'd been surgically stitched together. More so than ever now, with Jim gone, and a baby on the way. Even that escape hatch had been closed to her. Obediently she got up and went back to the living room. 'You could go and help Daddy with the lunch,' she suggested to Cindy, who thought about it for a while before deciding to give it a try.

The noise Lorraine heard from the kitchen a few minutes later did not sound like the excitement Frank had warned her about. Cindy's squeal made Lorraine sit up sharply. 'Oh, Daddy! You're bleeding all over the carrots!'

'Frank? What have you done?' He came to meet her in the doorway, his left forefinger bright red from top to bottom. His face was white.

'Quite a deep gash,' he said faintly. 'Chopped right into it with your best knife.'

She fetched warm water and lint, and wiped away the blood. It was immediately replaced. The gash was in the fleshy part of the finger, between the two lower knuckles: for some reason, she felt directly responsible. She smiled feebly at him, trying to reassure, to show she cared.

'It's too deep for a plaster,' she said helplessly. 'We'll have to get it stitched.'

'Will you drive me?' he asked, meekly.

'Of course. Cindy, go and get some shoes on. You'll have to come as well. With any luck they'll be quiet at Sunday lunchtime.'

IV

Drew's phone rang just before lunch. It was Daphne, much to his surprise.

'Drew? Sorry to phone you at the weekend, but there's been a change to the rota, and I was wondering whether you could take any call-outs this afternoon?'

'But–'

'I know you've never done it, but it's easy enough. I'd do it myself, but I've got a pretty watertight commitment. I can't take the mobile with me, either – I'm visiting my neighbour in the Nat Vic, and they won't let you use mobile phones in case you send the intensive care department into a spin.'

'Can't you get someone else to do that?' he queried.

'No, I can't. She depends on me for clean clothes and that sort of thing. We've been friends for fifteen years. She's got cancer.'

'Okay,' he conceded quickly, feeling ashamed. 'So, what do I have to do?'

'I'll transfer all calls to your number. If there is a call-out, you get onto Vince and he'll go with you. He's supposed to be taking his wife somewhere, but he'll have his mobile – he won't be going far. It's not ideal, but at least we'll be contactable. Otherwise we could lose funerals. Once we let a nursing home down, they'll be shopping round for someone else to do it, and that could have a serious knock-on effect.'

'So where's Sid? Isn't this his weekend?'

'Some crisis with his daughter. Well, more than

a crisis. Her boyfriend hanged himself yesterday. Sid and Vince had to collect the body from a field out Garnstone way and take it to the mortuary at the Nat Vic. Sid's pretty upset, by the sound of it. I don't know the details, but he says he can't face the phone today. I imagine he'll have his hands full anyway. I'll call you when I'm back, and do the transfer. It'll be about five, I should think – I'm not going for a little while yet. Is that all right?'

'Well–'

'I have to tell you, you're my last hope,' she added, a touch threateningly.

'All right then. Give me Vince's mobile number, and I'll try not to make too many mistakes.'

'Just get the address, and the person's name. It's simple enough. You also need to ask which doctor it is. Vince'll see to most of that – you just take the message, and do the removal. Anyway, you're not that likely to get anything. This is just insurance, basically.' She paused, and then read out Vince's number; Drew scribbled on a creased envelope lying beside the phone.

'Okay then,' he said. 'Have fun.' He winced, hearing himself.

'Thanks, Drew, but I'm not doing it for my own pleasure.'

Karen was listening in some puzzlement, mouthing questions at him which he ignored until the phone was safely replaced. He looked at her, eyes sparkling.

'That suicide we saw – the chap who hanged himself on the tree? It was Sid's daughter's boyfriend. I saw him on Tuesday, arguing with her. He nearly stepped out in front of the Espace. Hanging himself – who'd have thought it? Probably just to get back at her. Poor girl – what must she be going through!'

'And?' Karen prompted, gesturing at the phone.

'Oh, yes. Well, Sid's upset – he had to do the removal – and can't do the phones because he's coping with the girl. So I'm taking them while Daphne goes hospital visiting, I'm afraid that means we can't go out anywhere. Can't use the phone much, either, in case we block an incoming call. This is promotion, you know. Sort of.'

'And a bloody nuisance. I didn't want to spend all afternoon cooped up here.'

'Well, you don't have to. You can do what you like.'

'So long as I don't take the car, don't hog the phone, and do it on my own. Big deal.'

'Well, we just have to make the best of it. The job comes first, when all's said and done.' They were scowling at each other, the abrupt change to their anticipated afternoon an irritation neither felt capable of dealing with, especially in the light of other tensions.

'So what exactly are we going to do?' Karen's voice was loud, hectoring, and Drew shrank a little.

'We hadn't got much in mind anyway, that I can recall,' he snapped back. 'After yesterday's little adventure, I'm right out of ideas.'

Karen banged two plates onto the table, and

went to open the oven door. 'Lunch,' she snapped, losing patience with him. 'Then I'll go and get a video and we can watch it all afternoon. *Two* videos, even.'

Drew's face felt tight as he wrestled with conflicting feelings. He hated it when Karen shouted at him; besides, her sudden abandonment the previous afternoon of their investigations had been hurtful, though he fully understood her reasons. Underneath everything he felt an abiding excitement about the events of the past days, something he didn't expect her to share. Now there was a second death; could it be, somehow, connected? The fact that Sid was directly affected heightened the interest.

'I suppose I'll be glad of the chance to do nothing for once,' he told her peaceably. 'We could go and get a takeaway curry this evening, if you like.'

'I'm not fooled, you know,' she said quietly. 'I know you'll be thinking about death and murder and all that, whatever I say and do.'

'No, I won't,' he assured her. 'I promise. I'll watch the video with complete attention. You can test me on it afterwards.'

She let go of her anger so quickly he could almost see it escaping in the breath she exhaled. He picked up his fork, holding it upright in his fist, like a toddler. 'This looks good,' he said, eyeing the sizeable chop on his plate.

'It'd better be,' she said, with a quick forgiving smile.

A few minutes later, Karen paused, and frowned. 'Poor Sid,' she said. 'He thinks the world of that daughter of his.'

'So I gather,' he mumbled. 'I presume she dumped the boyfriend and he's hanged himself to get even.'

'Horrible thing to do. Mind you, she'll probably know more about why people do such things than most, with her job.'

Drew frowned. 'What job?'

'She's a doctor's receptionist. Dr Lloyd's practice. Surely you knew that?'

He shook his head. 'How did *you* know?'

'Let me think... I remember,' she said, waving her fork in the air triumphantly. 'That day, must have been the first week you were in the job – we bumped into Sid and his creepy wife in the High Street, and stopped for a chat. She told me all about Susie. Said Sid was always spoiling the girl, letting her have her own way, when he should be keeping her on the straight and narrow. Seemed to think she was about fourteen, still.'

'Everyone at Plant's must know except me. I can't believe I miss all these glaring facts that everybody else takes for granted. She even came in on Friday, you know. Slipped into the mortuary for a quick chat with Sid. Seems like a nice girl.'

'Well, I don't suppose she's got any connection with you-know-what. Unless she and the doctor and the boyfriend were all in cahoots to poison Jim Lapsford.' She clamped her lips together, remembering her veto. 'Except we're not going to talk about that any more,' she added.

'Okay.' He resumed eating. 'This isn't bad. Excellent fried onions.'

'We aim to please. Though onion gives me indigestion. I can practically feel it already.'

'The sacrifice does not go unnoticed,' he said carefully.

She grinned at him, seduced as always by his facility with words. 'I'll get videos, then? Is there anything you fancy?'

He shook his head. 'Whatever you like. There's plenty we haven't seen.'

'I'll go when we've done the washing up. It'll pass the time nicely.'

He knew this was what Karen most wanted during the next few days – for time to pass swiftly, without the onset of her period. Day thirty was half over, and he was allowing himself an early flicker of excitement; she'd never gone more than thirty-one since he'd known her. He could tell by looking at her that the usual gentle bloating hadn't happened this month, either. It was Sunday – he should pray. He should give himself up as a hostage to fortune, and promise to be everlastingly good, if only Karen was pregnant. He should make this baby happen by the sheer force of his will.

Then he remembered Baby Nicholas, and shuddered. Many times he had wondered whether some great Ledger had balanced out his credit and debit standing, and deemed that he should go forever childless, as the only fair outcome. He could have saved that baby, if he'd been wiser, sharper, a better person altogether.

There was no discernible sense in making this sort of connection. Even less in trying to earn some cosmic brownie points by ferreting out the truth about Jim Lapsford. His interference so far had done nothing but upset people. And yet – and yet – he simply *couldn't* let it rest. Having uncovered so much, with a developing pattern becoming clearer every day, he had to see it through to the end. He hoped Karen would choose some undemanding comedies which would leave his mind free to ponder. He hoped the phone would remain silent, and Daphne return quickly from her errand of mercy.

V

In fact David Lapsford knew about Craig well before his mother or brother. Very late on Saturday evening, after his mother and Jodie had left, he had been visited by Susie Hawkes, white-faced and shaking, holding a folded sheet of paper. 'I can't think of anybody else who'd understand,' she said. 'Craig's killed himself. He left this with the woman in the flat above mine. He told her to give it to me at seven.'
The paper was Craig's suicide note, addressed to Susie.

Let's face it, things are never going to get better, are they? I tried, you know I did, to get out of this drugs racket – but it's too easy, the money's too good. Sooner or later I'll be caught. Your Dad's even having a go at me now, threatening me with the law if I don't get my act together. Well, that's the hard part – I don't even know what it means any more. You're right to dump me, Susie – I'm never going to be any use to you. I'm not scared of dying. It's what I've wanted for a long time now. If I'm on some life support thing in hospital when you read this, tell them to turn it off, will you? Do that much for me. Tell my Mum it's not her fault. It's not anybody's fault but mine. Tell David to watch out for himself, and see if he can't learn from my mistakes. Be happy, all of you. Do it for me.

With my love,
Craig.

David closed his eyes when he finished, until the tears behind the lids stung so much he had to open them again. 'What a buggering thing to happen,' he whispered.

'I can't believe it,' she said, running her fingers viciously through her hair, scratching at her scalp as if she meant to draw blood. 'It's all so deliberately calculated.'

'When did it happen?' David asked.

Susie sighed. 'This afternoon. He hanged himself from a tree, not far down the road. They took him to the hospital for a postmortem. My Dad had to cut him down. He came round to tell me as soon as he could. I knew before Craig's Mum – isn't that awful? It was the police who told her. The postmortem won't tell us anything we don't know already.'

David sat down heavily. 'My Mum saw him,' he said. 'She thought it might be me.'

Susie had stayed with David for another hour. Slowly, they'd worked through the initial shock, remembering Craig at his best, acknowledging, even, that he might have been right to do what he did – though Susie refused to talk much about that, and David was happy not to press her.

When she left, Susie had been tearfully appreciative of David's attentions. 'You've made all the difference,' she told him.

He shrugged diffidently. 'It could have been me,' he said. 'Makes you think, doesn't it?'

'I haven't seen him,' she said quietly. 'Dad said he might be able to fix it tomorrow so I can.'

'You don't want to do that,' David assured her. 'He'll be all – bruised. Messed about.'

'I know, but I still want to. It can't be as bad as what I'm imagining. Will you come with me, Dave? Is that too much to ask?'

'Jesus,' he groaned. 'I'm not sure I'm up to that.'

'You don't have to look at him,' she hastened. 'Just take me there and bring me back again. Dad offered, but – he didn't even like Craig. It wouldn't be right, somehow. You were his friend.'

'Yes,' David acknowledged. 'I was. What time are you thinking of?'

'Eleven, twelve. Something like that.' They'd agreed on twelve, and David had done as she asked. He was now sitting miserably in a waiting area at the National Victoria Hospital with a scattering of other people, all of them looking as forlorn as he felt.

Susie had asked at the main desk for a name her father had given her, and after ten minutes a man had arrived to escort her. He had not looked happy, and as they walked, he addressed her in an earnest tone, bending close to her ear, obviously trying to talk her out of her intention. David watched with minimal curiosity, wondering how long she would be, and what sort of a state she'd be in when she came back. The idea of anyone voluntarily putting herself through such a grim exercise horrified him. The physical reality of Craig's death was something he wanted to banish as quickly as possible: he preferred not to think about how it had been achieved, what it felt like to have the weight of your body drag the rough rope around your neck tighter and tighter, until there was no hope of reversing the process. He knew he lacked the imagination to comprehend how it had really been, and was thankful for his own deficiency.

Fifteen minutes passed, and he was seized with the desire for a smoke. The only place he could do that was outside, so he got up and went out through the big automatic doors, positioning himself where he could see the corridor down which Susie had disappeared. There wasn't much danger of missing her; she knew where his car was, in any case.

Drawing deeply on the cigarette, he leaned against a low stone wall, and watched a white car drive up and park next to a large sign saying KEEP CLEAR – AMBULANCES PARK HERE. David laughed to himself. *Some people,* he thought. *Either arrogant or stupid.* When a young blonde woman jumped out of the driving seat, he concluded it was the latter.

Her passenger climbed out of the car more slowly, something white wrapped round his hand. David recognised him as a chap who'd been in Philip's form at school, but couldn't remember his name. Something to do with cars, or garages. He'd been a prefect when David was a runty little second year, and there'd been a bit of trouble over David smoking in the bogs. *Dunlop!* he remembered suddenly. Pity he wouldn't recall the incident – David would have enjoyed a defiant drag on his cigarette, right under the bloke's nose.

The woman bent down to speak to a child on the back seat, and then ushered Dunlop into the doorway that led to Accident and Emergency. *Doesn't look badly hurt,* David decided.

'Here I am,' announced a small voice at his elbow. Susie was tear-stained and unsteady, accompanied by the man who had taken her to the mortuary.

'Look, I've got to go now,' he said. 'But I think she could do with a cup of tea. The canteen's open. I suggest you go and get her something before going home.'

David shrugged accommodatingly. He wasn't in any hurry, and Susie certainly did look rough.

The canteen was serving lunch, and they ended up with a plateful of sausages and chips each. 'I can't possibly eat anything,' said Susie miserably. 'I don't know why I let you get this for me.' She picked up a chip in her fingers, sniffed it experimentally, then popped it into her mouth. 'Mmm,' she corrected herself ruefully. 'Maybe I can, after all. I can't believe I feel hungry, but still–' After a few minutes, she added, 'Good thing my Mum isn't working today. She's the last person I want to see just now.'

'She never was too keen on Craig,' David commented.

'Silly old cow. I bet you anything she'll say

something guaranteed to upset me, the minute I do see her. She'll be rehearsing it as we speak.'

'That's mothers for you,' he sympathised gloomily before tackling his own lunch with some relish. Organising meals had been the most difficult part of living away from home; he could go days without turning on the cooker or opening a tin. Packets of crisps, sandwiches from the corner shop, beer, chocolate, an occasional apple: this had been his basic diet since leaving Jim and Monica's care.

As Susie ate, she seemed to be returning to normal. Amazing, the capacity of some human beings to bounce back. 'I'm not sorry I came,' she said, after a while. 'He seemed so lonely there in that cold room. Abandoned. This time yesterday, he was still alive. I saw him on Friday. We had lunch in the pub and I bawled him out.' David expected tears, but none appeared. He made what he hoped was a sympathetic face.

'This must be dreadful for you,' Susie said suddenly. 'With your Dad, and everything. I completely forgot about that.'

David shook his head. 'It helps to have something to take my mind off it,' he said.

Once reminded, David's thoughts remained with his parents – or the people he had always regarded as his parents. He had originally seen the unbelievable truth as a betrayal, but now he merely felt weary and sad and defeated. There was nothing he could do to change the situation. Jim and Julia had clearly been unnaturally close, so bound up with each other that the people around them had scarcely mattered, the consequences of their actions had seemed irrelevant. David heard again the whispered word *incest*, which had passed between Jodie and Philip. That would be the obvious explanation to anybody, hearing what Monica had had to tell. A nameless invisible father, known only to Jim and Julia – a transparent lie, if ever he heard one.

The horror he felt at the possibility was tempered by a consideration of the alternatives. A sordid one-night stand, fathered by some stranger who used a sick woman for his own pleasures; a secret sad love affair with a married man, who perhaps never knew he'd got a son. If Jim had really been his father – as well as his uncle – then perhaps that was the best option, after all. David sighed, and dropped his chin into one cupped hand. And now his mate Craig. It was a crazy world, all right. In fact, he thought, compared to the world at large, he himself was really remarkably sane.

The meal finished, they stood up to go, and David saw the Dunlop family coming into the canteen. The man's hand now looked almost normal, a neat dressing around one finger. Fancy wasting hospital time over trivialities like a cut finger!

The wife saw him, and seemed to recognise him with some alarm, though David couldn't remember seeing her before. Her husband sensed her reaction, and followed her gaze. Contrary to David's expectation, he knew him instantly. 'David Lapsford!' he said. 'Haven't seen you for a while. Hey! Sorry to hear about your Dad. Saw it in the paper. Must have been a real shock.'

David had had enough: the last thing he wanted was sympathy from virtual strangers. 'Right,' he grunted dismissively, and turned away.

'David!' Susie's reproach rang clear. 'What's the matter with you?'

The Dunlop woman was trying to steer her husband and child across the room, away from the encounter. 'Come on, Frank,' she chivvied, 'they said you ought to have a sweet drink.' She cast an anxious glance at David, which he assumed arose from a fear that he was planning to pick a fight with Frank: the idea was not unappealing.

Susie too seemed disconcerted. With a familiar lurch of his gut, David understood how nervous he was making them. He knew he seemed peculiar at times, when his thoughts ran out of control. He shook his head, and made for the door. Hitting Frank Dunlop would be a very stupid thing to do.

But it seemed that a grim inevitability had taken charge of events. Just outside the door, they walked into Roxanne and Pauline, the sisters standing shoulder to shoulder, blocking the way.

Pauline's eyes were almost closed from weeping; the sight of Susie set her off again. Roxanne took a deep breath, and placed herself between the two other women. 'I won't ask what you're doing here,' she said. 'We're collecting Craig's things. Pauline needs to talk to you, but not yet. Not here.'

'Craig left a note,' said Susie breathlessly. 'I'll

show it to you, if you like.'

'Not here,' Roxanne repeated. They stood awkwardly in the doorway, the strangeness of the situation paralysing them all.

'Oh look,' said Roxanne, suddenly. 'There's Lorraine, and her family.' Lorraine, sitting at a nearby table with Frank and Cindy, heard her name and looked up. Roxanne moved towards her, and then noticed Frank's bandaged finger. She laughed. 'Don't tell me,' she said, 'David Lapsford did it. You two've been fighting over reputations.' She turned back to David. 'Though it seems to me you're the one who should have got the worst of it.'

Before she could say any more, David had grabbed Susie and marched her down the corridor. His head hummed painfully. Nobody, it seemed, liked him. They were all out to get him, for crimes he didn't understand. And here he was, doing Susie a favour, well beyond what most men would do.

'Strikes me Craig might be well off out of it,' he muttered, as he made his way to the car park.

VI

Jodie felt an urgent need to walk herself into a better mood. She often went for a long walk on a Sunday afternoon, usually beside the river. Sometimes she followed it all the way to the sea, ten miles distant. She strode out now, quickly, irritably overtaking strolling couples or families with young children. She crossed the bridge in the centre of town and headed upstream, where the ground was steep enough to deter most Sunday-afternoon ramblers. The river ran through the ever-dwindling gap between Bradbourne and its neighbouring big-city brother, its borders marshy in places. The sound of traffic was ever-present, but there were still places where no human habitation could be glimpsed, and a brief sense of timelessness could be enjoyed.

These walks were often prolonged meditations. She sorted through the jumble of the week past; the problems and difficulties of the working day; the tedium of her evenings. When her mother had remarried and gone to live with her oily new husband in Malta, she had signed over her Bradbourne house to Jodie, with no strings. So Jodie now lived in a three-bedroomed Victorian semi, in the older part of town, free from any mortgage payments, and with the simplest of tastes. Jodie had money to burn, and it worried her that it made not the slightest improvement to the quality of her life. If anything, it reduced it; once men discovered the truth of her financial situation, their resulting increased keenness was both offensive and alarming. There were very few men in the world whom Jodie trusted. Jim Lapsford had been one of those few.

David Lapsford was, in one sense, another. At least he wasn't capable of the cynical cupidity which had been her usual experience. But David was volatile in other ways, and she knew there was no way she could ever have married him, even if their relationship had survived his sudden disappearance. The news of his parentage had been a shock, but on reflection it explained a lot. The fleeting expression of pain that had crossed Jim's face every time his younger son was mentioned; the erratic behaviour from the boy's earliest years. Now, of course, everyone was going to be wondering who David's real father had been. Jodie had dismissed the incest theory before it got off the ground. So who had got Jim's sister Julia pregnant and then failed to own up to his responsibilities? Was it a total secret, unknown to everyone now alive? Or did Monica know, had she known right from the start, and incorporated that knowledge into the raising of the little boy who had grown up so troubled?

Jodie abandoned this train of thought. Trying to guess the identity of a man who had been to bed with Julia Lapsford twenty-four years ago was a mug's game. Except – except that she had the distinct feeling that the man in question might be still around. Still close by, watching his son grow up without ever making himself known. And, if that were the case, perhaps there was yet another mysterious link with Jim's death. Jim had written David off in recent times, leaving him to make his own life: Jodie herself had witnessed the scene at the printworks when David had come to ask for a job and Jim had angrily refused him. She had been careful not to take sides, to turn her back and let them get on with it. It had, after all, been none of her business.

Scarcely aware of her physical surroundings during these musings, she now found herself on a piece of high ground, looking down on the river. Pausing for breath, she cast an automatic glance at the view before her. As views went, it was quite a panorama. To her right, the haze and glints of the city, barely three miles away, spread to the horizon. The grey ribbons of major roads; the pale chunks of new office buildings, dotted with the greenery of conscientiously-positioned trees were all visible, as the ragged outskirts of the urban sprawl seemed to be edging towards her. As she turned in a slow arc, the plain that was yet to be developed and exploited gave the impression of a thickly-wooded piece of pure countryside. Yet it contained innumerable small villages, connected by roads, served by large shopping centres and the all-pervasive National Victoria Hospital. The Nat Vic was like a little town all of its own: Jodie sometimes felt it was like a magnet, drawing people in to be healed, or employed, or gratified in some other way. You could be a volunteer visitor or car driver; you could sell sweets or newspapers. You could be a non-medical clerk or telephone operator, or an on-site painter and decorator. It had a laundry, a vast kitchen, its own radio station and a number of charitable appeal funds. Jodie hated the hospital. For her it was a dark voracious monster, swallowing up the people she loved, making them promises it couldn't hope to fulfil. Her father had died there when she was eighteen, and nothing had really been right since then.

To her left lay humble Bradbourne, so jealous of its ancient identity despite the straggling new housing estates. A slow little town, famous for nothing more noteworthy than an eccentric medieval saint, rejoicing in the name of Penitent, who had suffered a particularly inventive and pointless succession of torments before dying nobly at the hands of an outraged feudal lord. The story was thin, even after all the subsequent embellishments; the only regular reminder was St Penitent's Wood, named for him from early times.

Jodie had lived all her life in Bradbourne, but had been removed from normal interaction with children her own age by being sent to a minor public school by her misguided parents. Her father had visited her and written to her so much that he had become an embarrassment to her. Her mother seemed to forget all about her. An only child, she had never learned the knack of ordinary society; and now, she supposed, she never would.

With a sigh, she turned her back on her home town and continued to walk. The haze over the city turned out to have been rain clouds, and there was now a thin drizzle falling. She didn't mind – her cagoule had a hood and her shoes were stout. She veered away from the river, following a path through fields and into a small country lane. Blackberries grew lush in the hedgerows, with no sign that anyone had been interested in gathering them. She pulled a few off as she passed, but they sat heavily in her stomach.

Thinking about living off the fruits of the land reminded her of Roxanne Gibson, who had defied the prevailing culture, which only understood food if it came in a small plastic tray from a supermarket, and was actively demonstrating that you could exist more than adequately on the contents of the hedges, spiced up with the meat of rabbits or pigeons – if you could catch them. No wonder Roxanne made people uneasy, living as she did. She was challenging everything society held dear. And no wonder Jim Lapsford had found her so exciting – she was doing what he had often dreamed of doing, but had not had the courage – or the selfishness – to achieve. Roxanne had found the sort of contentment that people like Jim and Monica and Jodie herself would never even glimpse.

But Jodie felt no sympathy or gratitude towards Roxanne. Oh, no. She blamed Roxanne for Jim's death.

VII

Craig's neck and jawline were dark red and purple, but the rest of his face had been surprisingly undamaged. Nobody had closed his eyes; they were still the same greeny-blue, but dreadfully, horribly empty. Like the glass eyes of toy teddy bears. There could be no doubt that whatever spark had been the real Craig had been firmly extinguished. In a strange way, that made Susie feel better. She need no longer worry about the fate of his body – it didn't know or feel anything any more.

Craig had in fact threatened to kill himself often enough for the idea to be almost familiar. He had talked frequently about different methods of suicide, making Susie angry, dismissive of his self-pity. Now he'd really gone and *done* it, for the reasons he'd put in his note. The part about Susie's Dad having a go at him made her wince every time she thought about it. Sid had, after all, only been acting on her prompting. And he'd already been on the phone, insisting on coming round later, desperate about his part in Craig's death. When he'd brought her the news yesterday, he'd looked ghastly, blaming himself for what he'd said to the boy that morning. Susie had tried to reassure him. Her Dad was all she had left now – the last thing she needed was for him to go to pieces.

In the hope of making him feel better, she had told him the whole story of the illicit business she and Craig had been conducting. She had been stealing prescription pads from the surgery for several months, and using them to obtain supplies of Viagra and other recreational drugs. The Viagra had been sold in carefully couched terms through small ads in local papers; Craig had dealt with the other stuff, careful not to let Susie become too closely involved. 'Even if we're caught, they're not going to come down too hard on you if we keep it like this,' he'd said. Even so, she'd been increasingly unhappy about it, and had first begged, then threatened, in her efforts to make him stop.

Sid, when he arrived, questioned her intently. 'How can I believe you?' he demanded, when she assured him that her only crime had been to steal the prescription pads and post out the tubs of Viagra to the men who replied to the advertisements.

'Just believe it, Dad,' she sighed. 'Why should I

lie to you now?'

She told him how, the day before Lapsford died, she'd tried to finish with Craig, once and for all. He'd clung to her, pleaded, menaced, until she'd been frightened and upset, but unshakable in her decision. Foolishly, she'd allowed him to spend all night with her from Monday evening to Tuesday morning, waking her up a hundred times to ask her again if she'd *please, please* change her mind. He'd followed her out of the house, making her late for work, pawing at her like a miserable abandoned dog.

In the end she'd shouted at him, turning on him, almost pushing him off the pavement. 'Just leave me *alone,* will you!' she'd screamed. And at last he'd got the message, and turned away, letting her trot quickly around the next corner without a backward glance. When they'd arranged to meet for lunch in the pub on Friday, it had seemed that he was beginning, finally, to accept her decision. The fact that Lapsford had died made it easier to convince him. 'He thought we might have killed him, you see,' Susie told Sid. 'Viagra can give people heart attacks, can't it, if they take too much of it? And we didn't really know how much to advise people to take. When Dr Lloyd diagnosed a heart attack, with no need for a postmortem, I couldn't believe our luck. Though I did feel guilty – half of me wanted the truth to come out. But Craig was terrified.'

'I *knew* there was a connection,' Sid said, smacking his right fist into his left palm. 'As soon as they brought him in, and I remembered he was Dr Lloyd's patient, I was scared stiff it was something to do with you. Especially after what happened with you and Jim.'

'Nobody's going to find out, are they?' she asked anxiously.

'Not if I can help it,' he promised her.

'Thanks, Dad,' she sniffed, burrowing into his chest like a little child.

After the scratchy encounter in the hospital, Susie knew she'd have to go and see Pauline – the sooner the better, before the numbness wore off and she got emotional. Craig's mother had always been the best thing about the whole business: 'You like her more than you like me,' he'd accused, more than once. And it was true. Pauline was funny and sparky and alive. She rushed round helping everyone in sight, cheerfully devoting her time to doing an old lady's shopping, or sitting down for a long leisurely chat to one of her many friends. Susie had always admired Pauline. If only she could be more like her.

Before she could find the energy to go out, there was a ring at her bell. She lived in a tiny flat, and had an entryphone which didn't work; she'd have to go down and open the door herself. She already had a good idea who it would be, and she was proved right.

'I was going to come and see you,' she said, feeling swollen with apprehension.

Pauline stepped inside, and began to climb the stairs without looking at Susie. From behind she seemed old, pulling herself up the steep staircase heavily, as if every joint hurt, as if she carried a burden. Misery was too light a word for it.

At last they faced each other, but they made no move to touch. 'I know you think it's my fault,' said Susie, marvelling at her own courage. 'I would too, in your place. Let me show you his letter. He'd have wanted you to see it.'

Pauline took the folded paper gingerly, and slowly opened it. 'Sit down,' Susie said. 'I'll go and make some coffee while you–'

'I can't read it,' said the woman, dropping the letter onto the table. 'The words are dancing about. It's like it's alive.'

Susie said nothing, but withdrew to her kitchen. Returning nearly ten minutes later, she found her visitor crouched on a battered chair with wooden arms, her elbows making sharp angles as she clenched her hands together. Susie waited. There was a hollow thumping inside her head, making it impossible to speak.

'The mother always blames herself,' Pauline said. 'Quite rightly, too. If I'd done it different, he'd never have got so obsessed with you.'

'I don't think that's true,' said Susie gently. 'He didn't want you to blame yourself – that's what he says. Craig just never really understood how to be happy. We all did our best for him – from his note, it sounds as if he knew that.'

Pauline looked up and gave a ghastly grin. 'Funny business, life,' she said bitterly. Susie closed her eyes and felt her whole body fill up with the sheer sadness of it all. A bottomless well of tears was suddenly there, where emptiness had been only moments before. Sadness was a relief after the fear and guilt there had been up to now.

'Yes,' she agreed. Mindlessly, she moved towards the chair, and sank onto the floor, pushing her head onto the older woman's lap, the smooth texture of Pauline's sweatshirt somehow familiar, friendly, ordinary. The tears soon soaked a sizeable area, while Pauline's hands rested heavily on her head.

'There, there,' the woman murmured. 'It'll be all right.'

Susie knew that it wouldn't, couldn't, ever be all right. But it sounded good, just at that particular moment.

VIII

Karen and Drew had dawdled over Sunday lunch and washing up, in an unspoken agreement to try to make time pass more quickly. Everything within reach had been washed and dried and put away. In the living room, Karen had plumped up cushions, run a duster over the television screen, and the front of the shelf unit on which it sat. The stage was set for an afternoon of video-viewing.

The phone hadn't rung so far, and Drew was already beginning to hope that it wasn't going to. 'I'm going in two minutes,' Karen announced. 'If I see two that we'd like, I'll get them. Otherwise, one long one, and then I'll make some biscuits for tea. I'm going to Alldays, right? I should be back in twenty minutes at the most.'

'Take your mac – it's raining,' he advised. 'And mind how you cross the road. I'm sorry about the car, but if there's an urgent call-out, I'll obviously have to use it.'

'No problem,' she smiled. 'It's only drizzle. I won't melt.'

'See you soon.' The door banged gently behind her, and he picked up the local paper for lack of anything else to do.

The streets were deserted: no pedestrians, and not many cars. The intermittent splashing of vehicles driving along wet roads was the only sound. Karen had a sensation of being at a great distance from the action. She had a sense of events taking place way beyond her perception, doors closed to her, nobody caring that she even existed. And she was glad to have it like that. There were more important things to think about than a shambolic murder investigation into a death that nobody really seemed to regret all that much.

She allowed her mind to return to the burning issue of the last few days. It swelled inside her, like a bright pink rosebud, secret and joyful. At the same time, she knew that this rising excitement would only make the eventual disappointment worse. The conflicting feelings were almost unbearable – all the more so for being repeated every two or three months. She preferred it when her period came early, before she'd even had a chance to start making assumptions. All she could do now was wait, try to keep busy and encourage the time to pass as swiftly as it possibly could.

She reached the shop in five minutes. Scarcely pausing to look, she stepped into the road, trusting her ears to tell her that it was all clear.

The Ford Fiesta came racing towards her at a rate far in excess of the speed limit, and Karen only saw it in the final second, just before it reached her. She did not recognise the woman behind the wheel, only saw the panic and horror on her face, as she tried to veer away from the spot where Karen stood.

She almost succeeded. The front of the car missed Karen by two or three inches, but the back was already skidding sideways, and the rear wheel arch gave Karen's pelvis a heavy blow as it careered across the road in a tight arc, the driver continuing to pull the steering wheel down to the right and slamming hard on the brake pedal. The wet street, the locked brakes, the excessive burden on the power-steering, combined to send the car smashing explosively into the front of the electronics shop next to Alldays. The presence of a protective metal grid, designed to prevent ram-raiding, ensured that the front of the car was comprehensively shredded. Half-sitting, half-lying on the wet pavement, Karen heard the noise through a comfortably detached mist. I'll *get up in a minute,* she said to herself. *Everything's going to be all right.*

And then, quite gradually, people appeared. A woman with ginger hair leaned over her with an expression of excited interest on her face. 'You don't look too bad,' she said, encouragingly. 'You don't seem to be bleeding anywhere.'

A man behind her said, 'You mustn't try to get up. There'll soon be an ambulance.' The first stabs of alarm began then. She looked across the street at the car.

'It was all my fault,' she remembered. 'Jesus – what have I done?'

Nobody answered. There was a much larger crowd gathering around the car now; a couple of men were pulling at the driver's door. She heard the words 'air bag' which filled her with relief. It was a new car, expensive-looking. Surely the driver would have been safeguarded by the latest technologies.

It was ridiculously comfortable on the hard wet ground, but also embarrassing. Shouldn't she make some effort to get up? In preparation, she began to pull her feet around, to act as leverage. Then, suddenly, a very decided pain happened, low down at the front, where the car had struck her. She put a cautious hand to the place. And, like a hot poker pushing into her brain, she remembered. How could it have taken so long? '*No,*' she sighed, giving in to the wave of misery and fear which bombarded her all at once. Tears began to pour down her face. 'Shock,' murmured the ginger-haired woman, who was loyally remaining at her post. The onlookers began to cast impatient glances up and down the road. If the ambulance didn't come soon, they might actually have to *do* something.

'Oh, look – they've got her out,' came a voice. 'She looks all right.' Karen grudgingly followed the general gaze, and saw a dark-haired stocky woman emerge from the shattered car. She stood surrounded by helpers, somehow larger than any of them, big with the aura of survival against the odds. Then she looked across the street and her gaze fell on Karen. Slowly, she walked towards her, people fluttering disapprovingly, but making no attempt to prevent her. 'This is all your fault, you know,' she said in a flat tone. 'You stepped out in front of me.'

Karen closed her eyes. You weren't supposed to admit responsibility for an accident. Something about insurance. And who had come off worst, anyway? Something hot broke through the despair.

'You were going much too fast,' she said loudly, accusingly. 'And now I'm going to lose my baby.'

Horrified intakes of breath all round and a full set of reproachful stares at the woman. After all, she was the aggressor, on every level. The mangled car was only a *thing* – it was replaceable, whereas a baby wasn't.

An ambulance siren sounded in the distance. And from the other direction, with no fanfare, came a police car. In no time there were uniforms, notebooks, questions. Gentle questions, which made Karen feel weak and childish. She cried again. Someone asked for her phone number and she remembered Drew for the first time. She gave her name, and asked them to phone him. The dark-haired woman driver heard her, and gave a shriek. 'You're Drew's wife?' she cried. 'My God!'

Karen looked at her. 'Who are you?' she said, with a frown.

'His boss. Daphne Plant.' She seemed to regret having given herself away; too late, she put a hand over her mouth.

'But – you're supposed to be at the hospital,' said Karen, thickly. 'He's at home on call because you said you were going visiting.'

'Change of plan,' Daphne muttered. 'So what's all this about a baby?'

'If you don't mind, Madam,' interposed an ambulance man, 'I think we should get this lady to hospital as soon as we can. I'm sure you can catch up with her news later.'

They wrapped Karen in a warm red blanket and lifted her onto a stretcher, then into the ambulance and away. Every now and then she pressed a hand to where it hurt, assessing the damage. There was no sensation of bleeding. As the paramedics took her blood pressure and pulse, the lack of concern on their faces was reassuring. They gently manipulated each leg, feeling the hip joints as they did so. Finally one said, 'I don't think anything's broken. It seems you've been very lucky.'

'But the baby?' she whispered.

'How many weeks are you?' he asked.

At this, she grew hot and embarrassed. How could she mention something which was still only a slowly forming hope? She shook her head. 'It hasn't been confirmed yet,' she admitted. 'It might be a false alarm.'

His face cleared even further. 'In that case, we'll just have to keep our fingers crossed, won't we.'

She lay back, and secretly crossed the fingers on both hands, under the red blanket.

IX

The police desk was quiet as the night shift came

off duty. The changeover needed no special briefing. The new officer glanced down the list of calls for the day, and paused at the brief account of Daphne Plant's car crash. 'That's the undertaker, isn't it? That'll make a good story for the *Chronicle.*' This was the only real excitement of the day. There had been one break-in; one missing child, found within twenty minutes; and three stray dogs reported, to complete the list. 'Just one mad hectic whirl,' he commented. 'Hotbed of crime, is Bradbourne.'

'Don't tempt fate,' advised his departing colleague. 'If you're not careful, you'll be dealing with serial rape, multiple pile-ups and the mysterious deaths of a whole houseful of people, all before midnight.'

'That'll be the day. This place is still living in the nineteen-fifties. I'll have finished this by morning, you see.' He held up a large paperback.

'Good luck to you, then,' was the parting comment.

The phone rang fifteen minutes later. 'Control room here,' came the broad-vowelled voice of the woman who fielded all police calls. 'We've got something for you. Alarm ringing at Plant's Funeral Director, in East Street, and the contact number isn't answering. Funny, that – they're supposed to be on call round the clock.'

'I know why that is. Miss Plant smashed her car up this afternoon. She's probably still in Casualty. We'll send somebody over.'

'Thanks. Sounds as if it isn't her day.'

When they arrived at Plant's, the police found

nothing suspicious, apart from a slightly open window, which appeared to have been carelessly left unfastened. They looked at each other warily.

'Should we open up and have a look round, do you think?' asked one of them.

The response was immediate. 'Nah! What's the point? Who's going to nick anything from an undertaker? The office looks okay – see.' He shone his torch through the office window, to reveal a tidy desk, a placid computer and not a hint of disturbance.

'That's what I hoped you'd say. You reckon we can go, then?'

'I do. We wouldn't know what to look for, anyway. Unless some nutter's decided to steal a dead body, and I somehow don't think that's very likely. One thing's sure – a corpse isn't going to care, so whatever's been going on can wait till morning. We'll get one of the cars to patrol for a bit – keep an eye out – and leave it at that. Right?'

'Right.'

CHAPTER SEVEN
MONDAY

I

Drew had stayed at the hospital on Sunday evening until they threw him out at ten. Karen had been sedated, examined cautiously, and not given any X-rays. There seemed to be no suspicion that her pelvis was broken, for which he was tearfully grateful. On her uncovered body, the still burgeoning bruise spread from hipbone to hipbone and navel to pubis, a terrible shade of purplish red which looked inhuman. The thought of a tiny cluster of new fetal cells surviving inside such damage was unthinkable, despite the assurances of the doctor.

'If she is pregnant,' the young woman said, 'there's every chance that it'll be okay. It's almost too small to be seen by the naked eye – it can hide in a safe little fold of flesh, deep inside, and never notice a knock or two.'

Karen and Drew looked at each other and gave wan smiles. The image conjured by the words was enticing. They considered their hypothetical little one, nestling invisibly somewhere safe behind the bruise.

'But she'll be very stiff for a week or two,' the doctor went on. 'The bruising is severe, by any standards. We'll find some arnica, and keep her in bed for a day or so.'

'Arnica!' Drew was surprised.

'It's safe, cheap and very effective,' nodded the doctor. 'We've become very progressive lately, and returned to the ways of the wise women. They used arnica in the Dark Ages. Before that, even. I think the Romans used it.'

Karen found the herbal treatment cool and soothing, and they watched some of the redness abating visibly. 'Very effective,' said Drew approvingly, and kissed her lingeringly. 'I'll see you tomorrow,' he promised.

Monday morning brought a number of dilemmas, as well as a severe shock. He had deserted his post at the telephone without a second thought, when the hospital called him about Karen. When he heard that it was his own boss who had crashed into his wife, he was simultaneously angry and embarrassed. Attempts to phone Daphne when he got home had been in vain: he supposed that all calls were still being directed to him, and would be until someone turned up in the morning to divert them back to the office.

He had no real excuse to miss a full day at work: Karen wouldn't need clothes or make-up until they discharged her. There was a funeral at midday which would require him as a bearer, as well as the delivery of the Lapsford coffin to Primrose Close late in the afternoon. If Daphne was off work, suffering delayed effects from her accident, then it would be chaotic enough without Drew going absent as well.

He knew there was a procedure for diverting calls – some push-buttoned code which Sid and Pat and the others understood, but which nobody had explained to him. With some trepidation, he drove as quickly as he could from home to work, and made immediately for the office. Olga was already there, the phone to her ear: this alone brought some relief. There was no sign of Daphne, for which he felt even more thankful.

'Are the phones okay?' he asked Olga, as soon as she finished her call. She frowned at him, her large brown eyes full of puzzlement.

'What's been happening?' she said. 'Daphne just phoned and told me she wouldn't be in until lunchtime. She sounded a bit – distracted. Said you'd taken the phones yesterday, but you weren't rostered to do that, were you? Sid isn't in yet, either. And, to top everything, the burglar alarm went off in the night, and the police were called.' The phone rang, interrupting her, and she answered it.

'Oh dear, I *am* sorry,' she said, after a few moments. 'I'm afraid we've had a few problems overnight... I'll make sure someone's there right away... Yes, I know. I really do apologise.' She turned back to Drew, looking accusing. 'That was Heathlands Nursing Home. They called us at nine last night and got no reply. Said they almost decided to use a Woodingleigh undertaker.' She shuddered dramatically. 'Perish the thought.'

'Karen's in hospital,' Drew burst out. 'She was hit by a car yesterday afternoon – and guess who was driving it.'

Olga shook her head reproachfully. 'How can I possibly guess?' she said, in her usual solemn manner.

'Daphne, that's who,' he told her, soberly. 'Karen's not badly hurt, but it's been a bad shock.'

'It must have been. How extraordinary! Is that why Daphne's not here this morning?'

Drew shrugged. 'I have no idea where Daphne is,' he said. 'But her car was a write-off. It smashed into a shop front which happened to have an anti-theft barrier across it. Very solid, by the sound of it.'

'Well, you and Vince'd better go and get this lady from Heathlands,' she dismissed him. 'Can't keep them waiting any longer.'

The removal was carried out efficiently, the body stiff by now and heavy, the other inmates of the nursing home distracted by a loud singsong in the dayroom, and the staff ushering them out of a side door as unobtrusively as possible. Drew wondered what the secrecy was for. Would poor old Mrs Dunmow simply drop out of everyone's awareness now, as if she'd never existed? He hadn't yet shaken off the sense of something Stalinist about this kind of institutional death – a person deleted overnight, no questions asked.

In the mortuary, there was still no sign of Sid. Vince opened the door of the chiller and pulled out a tray. Drew went to the foot end of the newcomer, and prepared to lift her onto the tray; as he did so, he automatically glanced downwards.

'Hey!' he yelped. 'Where's the dog?'

Vince almost dropped Mrs Dunmow's head as Drew failed to take his share of the weight. 'It was here,' Drew continued, bending to examine the whole length of the bottom tray.

'For Christ's sake,' Vince grunted. 'Get this one in first, will you?'

Impatiently, Drew thrust the new corpse onto its rack, and resumed his search for Cassie's body. It was gloomy inside the fridge, and the dog was, after all, small. Ignoring Vince's spluttered protests, he hoisted himself up, one foot on the lowest shelf, and peered into the recesses of the fridge. 'She's definitely not here,' he announced. 'Somebody's taken her!'

There was nowhere in the mortuary a dead dog could have been hidden. And who would have done such a thing, even as a joke? Drew stared frantically at Vince. 'Someone's stolen it!' he shouted, angrily. Then he remembered what Olga had told him. 'The alarm went off in the night. That must have been it. Someone broke in and took Cassie away!'

Vince grinned slowly, then hooted a deep guffaw. 'Just one bloody farce after another, this place,' he said cheerfully. 'And I always said there was nothing anyone'd ever want to steal at an undertaker's. Just shows how wrong you can be.'

'But–' Drew was desperate. Any idea that he was alone in his suspicions, investigating a crime that nobody else would acknowledge, had long evaporated. Now he was a puny meddler in something much bigger than he was, something dangerous. Nothing was what it seemed. He forced himself to think. The disappearance of the dog's body could mean a dozen different things, ranging from an objection on principle to an animal sharing a human coffin on the one hand to a cunning removal of vital evidence on the other.

Who knew it had been there? Everyone at Plant's, for a start, plus the whole Lapsford family and whoever they'd told. The two old women next door, who had seen him take Cassie away, possibly the people at Jim's printworks. Any number of people, in fact.

'You okay?' Vince asked curiously. 'Something I ought to know about?'

Drew regarded him narrowly. Vince had acted innocent from the start, bluffly dismissive of anything suspicious; Drew wondered now how much he'd been deceived. If he'd been forced to point a finger at any of his colleagues, it would have been Sid, with his startled reactions and solitary habits. But Vince had known Sid for years, and would probably protect him if the need arose. Drew felt as if he'd walked into a bog, and his feet were slowly sinking into clinging black mud.

The associations formed slowly. 'You know why Sid's not here, don't you?' he said.

'Course I do,' came the ready answer. 'His girl's bloke hanged himself – not so funny, that. Specially as Sid was one of the chaps called out to collect him. The kind of thing we all dread.'

'Did Sid like him? I got the impression it was otherwise from what he said the other day.'

'That's not the point, is it? It's the shock.

Bound to cause trouble in the family, a thing like that. But he'll be in soon, you see. He's not one to let us down when he's needed.'

Drew felt a strong desire to go somewhere quiet and have a good think. It couldn't be as complicated as it seemed. The answers must surely lie in working out what everyone's basic motives were, and that was something he'd always imagined himself to be good at – understanding people. 'Yeah,' he nodded at Vince. 'I expect you're right.'

II

Karen was stiff, as the doctor had predicted, but she was also deliriously happy. When there had been no overnight bleeding or undue pain, the ward sister had suggested they do a pregnancy test. 'You're late enough now to make it worthwhile,' she said. Together they had applied the drop of urine to the magic scrap of chemically-enhanced blotting paper, and within seconds a blue line was clearly visible. When Karen cried, the sister had given her a hug. 'Congratulations,' she said.

She had tried to phone Drew at work, only to be told that he was out. 'Please ask him to come to the hospital as soon as he can,' she begged Olga. 'You can do without him today, can't you?'

'Probably not until this afternoon,' Olga replied carefully. 'Things are a bit chaotic here. Daphne's having the morning off – oh, I suppose you know all about that – and there's a funeral midday. I don't think we can let anyone go until that's finished. That'll be about two thirty.'

'That'll have to do, then,' said Karen, lying back on her pillows. She found she didn't mind waiting. After all, she would have to do a lot of it over the coming months.

But the time was filled instead by an unexpected visit. Daphne Plant herself came hesitantly around the nurses' station, peering at the people in the beds, dodging trolleys and chairs. As far as Karen could tell, the woman was suffering no ill effects from the previous day's accident. Even so, she felt a mounting nervousness at the likely reason for the visit.

'Sit down,' she invited warily, nodding at the metal-framed chair beside the bed.

Daphne did so, leaning forward earnestly, speaking in a low urgent voice. 'You must be wondering what all that was about yesterday,' she began. 'I gather that you and Drew knew Sid's daughter's connection with yesterday's suicide? You might even be aware that Susie works for Dr Lloyd. Well, anyway, when I asked Drew to take the phones, I admit I made up a story about the reason. It's delicate, you see – professionally, I mean. Dr Lloyd phoned me and wanted to talk about the whole thing. He's worried about rumours involving him and Susie – which have absolutely no foundation in fact. He's got a few other problems as well, which I've known about for some time. To be frank, he's not always as careful as he might be with controlled drugs, and prescription pads. He's not the most organised person in the world, to put it mildly. Now poor old Sid's got himself involved, too. He came to see me first thing this morning. Look, don't take this the wrong way, but I really must ask you to have a word with Drew. He's more likely to listen to you. I know he's got some funny ideas. Just tell him to drop it, will you? He doesn't understand the full story. The Coroner has been getting at the doctors about sending too many bodies for postmortem. He told them to use their common sense, which is exactly what Julian did. It wouldn't be fair to involve him in any trouble, not at this stage. There's a world of difference between the procedure as laid down in the rule book, and real everyday life. Drew's going to have to understand that if he wants to go on working for me. Now, I've got to get back to the office. I hope you'll be better soon – and congratulations on the baby. Brilliant news.' And she was getting up to go.

Karen gazed at her. The dark hair had been carelessly brushed and the clothes were crumpled; the anxiety in Daphne's face was acute. 'Wait a minute,' she said. 'I hardly understood a word of that. I have no idea why you're telling me – or what you want me to say.'

Daphne drew back as if stung. She blinked several times, and glanced around the quiet ward. 'Don't play games with me,' she hissed. 'This is *serious*.'

'I'm sure it is,' Karen nodded. 'It's just that you seem to think I know something that I assure you I don't. If you and Dr Lloyd are operating some sort of racket, and you think Drew's onto you, well, I'm afraid you've come here needlessly. I'm sure he's got no suspicions of that sort at all.'

Daphne narrowed her eyes. 'Maybe I've jumped the gun a bit. But I've been watching your husband. He isn't such an innocent as he'd like everyone to think. Now, as far as the accident is concerned, I think we can agree that we were both careless, and there's no need to take it any further.'

Karen's head swam. Something was deeply awry in all this. Annoyed, she sat up straighter.

'I think we can leave all that until I'm home again,' she said. 'It seems very odd to me that you should come here making veiled threats, considering you don't even know me. The best interpretation I can put on it is that you're suffering from shock and aren't quite in your right mind.' She shivered at her own boldness, wondering whether there was any hope at all for Drew's new career after all this.

Daphne got up, and smiled tightly. 'I think we do understand each other,' she insisted. 'I can see that there's little harm done, except to my poor car. I'm sure we'll be able to put it all behind us once everything's – settled down.'

She left, with Karen staring after her. Nothing made any sense. Except that Karen couldn't help feeling that what they had actually been talking about, all along, was the sudden, unexpected death of Jim Lapsford.

III

Monica was feeling fraught. She had invited all and sundry to come and pay their last respects to Jim from five o'clock onwards, and belatedly realised that they'd expect tea and cakes. Or should it be wine and cheese? She ticked off on her fingers all the people who might show up. Philip and Nerina; Sarah and Dottie; Gerald; Jodie; Jack; and assorted mates from the King's Head. Monica had asked Daphne Plant to tell anyone who enquired that they would be welcome to come to the house. And as if that wasn't bad enough, there was now this awful business with Craig. Which meant that Pauline would not be fulfilling her promise to help with the wake. Not only that, but Monica knew she ought to be at Pauline's house, commiserating with her on her loss. That was far more important than organising what amounted to a sort of party.

But Pauline would have to wait. The only thing Monica could focus on now was getting Jim's funeral over with. After that, then maybe she'd find the strength to give her friend the support that Pauline had given her.

For now, the pressing tasks appeared to be to do some shopping and to run a vacuum cleaner round the house. Philip had promised to come over before the coffin was brought home; he could do the heavier job of shifting furniture to create a suitable space in the middle of the lounge. Trying to visualise it, she almost decided to cancel the whole idea. It seemed morbid and melodramatic, these days, to insist on such a performance. Yet something inside had prompted her – some sense that, given Jim's character, it was a fitting thing to do. Father Barry, with his hopeless lack of comprehension, had unwittingly confirmed her decision. If there was no chance of a meaningful ritual at the funeral, then she would have to do what she could here at home to mark the event. Jim would have understood. 'That's it,' he'd have said. 'Give the neighbours something to talk about.'

She walked to the little parade of shops two streets away, to buy tea and biscuits and cake. She added peanuts and crisps, and some frozen sausage rolls. 'Having a celebration?' smiled the shop assistant, with no idea who she was. Monica wondered whether she had the heart to explain.

'Sort of,' she said.

It was more difficult than she'd anticipated, trying to construct a presentable compromise between a full-scale party and an embarrassing 'viewing' exercise. How long would people stay? Would they nibble crisps in the lounge, with the coffin open beside them, or discreetly in the kitchen? She half-giggled to herself at the bizarre nature of these questions. Whatever she did, it was bound to go wrong – David alone would probably see to that. Despite the improvement in his mood since he'd been told about his parentage, she knew better than to take anything for granted. The death of Craig might well have temporarily put his own problems into perspective, shaken him into a more amenable mood, but experience suggested that he wouldn't stay like that for long. However hard she tried, she just couldn't imagine a mature and balanced David, accepting his lot in life, never causing any trouble.

She left the shop, with the plastic carrier bag pulling her slightly off balance. The presence of

Dr Lloyd on the pavement outside struck her as incongruous. His manner only fuelled the feeling: doctors were supposed to be hurrying, intent on the next call, the next appointment – Dr Lloyd was standing idly, with, apparently, nothing at all to do. 'I saw you go into the shop,' he explained, 'and decided to wait for you. I just wondered how you are? Is there anything I can do for you?'

She looked at him – the well-proportioned face with its light tan hinting at some expensive summer holiday, the small tight frown between the eyes. He was a typical doctor, carrying the weight of ordinary people's dependence with a straight back and a charismatic glance. The gloss of medical magic seldom failed. And yet Monica could hear anxiety in his words.

'I'm all right,' she said. 'I'll be better once tomorrow is over and done with. It's been a very difficult week.'

'It has indeed,' he agreed with feeling. 'One awful thing after another.'

'Oh?' Then, 'Oh, of course. You mean poor Craig Rawlinson. It's terrible, isn't it. Such an awful waste.'

'Susie's dreadfully upset, of course. The brave girl turned up for work this morning, but I sent her home again.' Something abstracted in his manner snagged Monica's curiosity; she still had the impression that he'd been waiting for her with a need to say more to her than simple platitudes.

'She was very kind to me last week,' she said, 'if that's the girl you mean. Suicide is always so difficult, isn't it? Everybody blames themselves for it.'

He nodded slowly. 'And you–' he said. 'How are you bearing up?'

'Oh, well,' she shrugged. 'I've got used to the idea of life without Jim. Last Tuesday seems a long time ago. There's been such a lot happening since then.'

'You certainly seem very different in yourself,' he commented. 'You couldn't believe it had happened, last time I saw you.'

At last she understood. 'That's true,' she agreed. 'It never once occurred to me that Jim would die of a heart attack. But these things happen, don't they. At least it's quick and straightforward, this way.'

Apparently reassured, he gave her a friendly smile. 'That's a very sensible way of looking at it,' he approved. 'And now I must be getting along. If you need me for anything – well, you know where I am.'

She watched him walk away, his steps short and jerky, as if holding himself together. Shaking her head, she went home, and unpacked the shopping.

The kitchen was a mess; she hadn't washed up properly for days. Since the scrambled eggs on Tuesday evening, she'd hardly cooked anything for herself, living instead on bread and cheese and apples and warmed-up tins of soup. She'd made several mugs of coffee and one or two of tea – tea had been Jim's drink more than hers. He had had his own little teapot, enough for two cups or one large mug, and she never touched it, preferring the bag-in-mug approach. It sat there now, its cheerful red tartan design a familiar splash of colour in the avocado-and-antique-lace decor.

She supposed she should fish out the inevitable leftover teabag and wash out the pot. She grimaced at the thought. She'd always disliked cold squashy teabags – it was one of the reasons why she preferred coffee. She pushed the little pot to a corner of the worktop, perhaps in a futile hope that someone else would eventually attend to it. An innate laziness in Monica's character had never quite gone away, despite the demands of modern domestic standards. Jim had done almost half the housework throughout their marriage, teaching her the value of keeping the edges clean where the floor met the walls, and putting things away to give at least the illusion of a well-kept house.

But Jim wasn't going to do it this time. The silly red stripes seemed to dance before her eyes, even when she turned away. *Damn it,* she inwardly cursed, and snatched up the pot, clattering off its lid as she did so.

There was almost no liquid in the pot, but a square-shaped bag clung to the inside, across the opening leading to the spout. It was like one of the teabags you got in hotels, with a little tag at the end of a string stapled to the teabag itself. Jim had had a habit of 'collecting' them, when he was on holiday or staying overnight away from home. It had a faint crust of white crystals rimming its lower edge. Awkwardly, Monica fished it out.

Jim had used all sorts of different teas. He

bought boxes of herbal mixes from the health food shop, tried exotic variations from all sorts of places. He had even been known to gather fennel or comfrey and make his own. He had tried to make her drink them too, saying they were good for the libido, or as a general stimulant. Once in a while she would indulge him, but seldom noticed any of the promised effects.

She put the teabag on top of a small collection of apple cores and other debris intended for the compost heap: anything biodegradable was saved for this purpose. She then went to wash her hands. Before she got there, however, a movement in the back garden caught her eye. A cat from further down the Close had caught a blackbird, and was struggling to subdue its flapping. The scene was unpleasant, and Monica automatically put her finger to her mouth as she watched. The resulting bitter taste didn't register for several seconds. She rapped on the window with her left hand, but the cat ignored her. The bird would be too badly hurt by now anyway, she decided. Better to let nature take its course.

In her mouth, something unusual was happening. The bitterness was expanding, rather pleasantly, reminding her of something medicinal. She sucked her finger again, thoughtfully. She looked at the teapot and remembered the empty mug beside Jim's chair on Tuesday morning. She looked at the cat outside, and remembered Cassie's last hours.

There was really only one person who would listen calmly to her resulting thoughts, and she knew she must go and speak to him quickly.

IV

Lorraine was terrified.

Frank sat on the sofa, his legs up on a footstool, watching her through unblinking eyes. They had been awake most of the night, both of them crying, Frank shouting, Lorraine begging him not to distress Cindy. Now the child had gone to school, and Frank was late for work.

It had taken him some time to reach his conclusion. There had been a couple of hours – as they drove home from the hospital and ate their long-delayed lunch – when she thought she'd got away with it. Roxanne's words hadn't been at all clear, after all. Something about 'reputations', and an assumption that Frank had reason to be angry with David Lapsford. She'd done everything she could to take his mind off it, prattling away throughout the drive home, joking about people they'd met in Cyprus, pulling out all the stops in her desperation. Finally, he'd said, 'Just shut up, will you. I'm trying to think.'

She knew then that it was hopeless. Once the suspicion was rooted in his head, he'd nag and nag, ask around, ferret out every little detail, until he'd got the whole story. She could kill Roxanne for what she'd said. And after they'd been so friendly together, too! It just wasn't fair. She wanted to walk away now, before things got any worse. Because, despite the terrible night they'd had, she felt sure that things could get *much* worse.

Frank sipped cautiously at the mug of coffee

she'd just given him, and then set it down beside him. 'What are we going to do?' he asked. His voice came out hollow, as if all feeling inside him had died.

Lorraine decided to fight it to the end. 'Why do we have to do anything? It's all finished now. You've nothing to worry about.'

He shook his head like a stunned bull. For the first time since she'd known him, Lorraine felt afraid of him. 'Sorry, darling, but you're completely wrong about that.'

The *darling* was a snarl of disgust that sent waves of fear through her. Frank couldn't have changed so much in a single night. 'Shall I tell you how I worked it out?' He gave a bitter little laugh. 'It wasn't just what that woman said in the canteen. I doubt I'd have worked it out from that. It was Saturday, in the pub. They were talking about Lapsford, and somebody mentioned you. Tried to backtrack, of course, and I didn't think much of it. Not at first, anyway.' He put his head in his hands, and yielded to one racking sob. 'How could you, Lorrie? I *trusted* you.'

She didn't even try to answer. A small voice was whispering in her head. *People don't own each other. Your body's yours, to do as you like with.* Jim had said that, and it had seemed so true at the time. Now she wasn't sure. It felt now as if her body had belonged to Frank all along, and she'd never fully realised.

Now he was saying things, using language she had never heard from him before. What had she done to him? Where had so much pain and rage come from? She clasped her face between her hands, wishing she could hurt herself as much as Frank was hurting now.

'I'm not stupid, whatever anybody might think,' he went on, repeating a line he'd used many times during the night. 'But everyone in town thinks I am. They'll be laughing at me for trusting my own wife. How *could* you, Lorrie? Wasn't I enough for you? Jim Lapsford was old enough to be your father. It's disgusting.'

'I know,' she whispered. 'I'm so sorry, Frank. It wasn't anything to do with you. It didn't mean I didn't love you. It was just–'

He cut her off, and she could see an even deeper spark of hurt flicker in his eyes. 'This new baby,' he said, for the first time. 'It's his, isn't it? You'll have to abort it. If you do that, then for Cindy's sake, maybe we can patch things up. The man's dead, after all.'

'No!' she screamed, the sound bouncing off the walls. 'It's *your* baby, Frank. Of course it is.' An overwhelming sense of her own powerlessness gripped her. What had she done? Put the innocent life of a baby at risk? Wide-eyed she stared at him, her body rigid with shock at what he'd said. She saw ahead of her the choices he would force her to make, each of them equally unthinkable.

'I'm going to work now,' he said slowly, and got to his feet, the coffee forgotten on the side table. He staggered slightly, and put a hand to his face. But Lorraine made no move.

Only after he'd gone, and she reran the conversation through her mind again, did she understand her position. And then she knew who, of all people, she had to go to for help.

V

Roxanne reached Pauline's flat before midday, and took upon herself the task of making some lunch. 'I bet you haven't eaten,' she accused. 'And for God's sake stop smoking like that. Your hair's going yellow. You look like some old vagrant.'

'Susie's coming round soon. She's been sweet,' Pauline said thickly. She'd only been up for an hour, having consumed an unwholesome mixture of alcoholic drinks the night before. 'And I've got to phone some Coroner chap in a bit. He's supposed to be telling me the cause of death. As if I didn't know. Then I can go along to friend Daphne and order up the coffin. Jesus, Rox.'

Roxanne turned away from the cooker and moved closer to her sister. 'Come on,' she said. 'Bear up. You're not holding it against Susie, then?'

Pauline shook her head. 'She's been sweet,' she repeated. 'And she showed me his note. His – his suicide note.'

'What did it say?'

'He tried to convince me – her – himself – that this was nobody's fault. He'd got himself into a mess of some sort, and couldn't see a way out.'

'What sort of mess?'

'Drugs, of course. Isn't it always? It wasn't very clear – Susie wouldn't go into any details. She's scared about something coming out at the inquest and making more trouble.'

'Oh, Christ,' Roxanne burst out, as she made the connection.

'What?' Pauline's curiosity was tepid.

'What if it was *Susie* supplying Jim with his Viagra? She could nick prescription pads from Dr Lloyd – he's too disorganised to notice. Presumably Craig was in it with her. That was what he was referring to. Possibly even thought it all up in the first place. It'd count as drug-dealing, where the law's concerned. And when Jim died–'

'No!' Pauline was suddenly animated. 'You're not telling me Craig thought he'd killed Lapsford? How do you know Jim didn't get the Viagra from some perfectly legal clinic?'

'Because that wasn't his style. Queueing up with a lot of impotent old wrecks, telling some doctor a lot of fibs about his sex life – never in a million years. I thought at first he must've got it from the Internet, but – we have to face facts. It all fits. You ask Susie if you don't believe me.'

'There'll have to be a postmortem done on Jim.' Pauline said angrily. 'To prove it one way or the other. I can't live with something like that.'

Roxanne did meet her eyes then. 'Hold on,' she said gently. 'If you do that, I'll be implicated as well. Don't forget the henbane.'

'Roxanne Gibson, I ought to kill you, here and now.'

'Can't blame Craig... Can't blame anybody, really. Jim should have known better. I was always very careful ... took it myself, with no problems. But then, he was always a greedy sod. Always wanting more. Trust him to go too far.'

Pauline thought for a long time, before saying bitterly, 'It must make you feel better, knowing you weren't the only one. You can pretend it was all right to cook up lethal poisons, just for the sake of a nice big shagging stick, because he was going for the same effect elsewhere. The way I see it, Craig would still be alive, if it hadn't been for you.'

Tears gathered and dropped down the grooves beside Roxanne's nose. 'I'm sorry,' was all she could say at first. Then she rallied, and gave a tentative smile. 'You didn't mean it about a postmortem, did you? We can just keep this between ourselves, can't we?' She could hear the pleading note in her voice, the wheedling that had previously been Pauline, the younger sister's prerogative.

Pauline shook her head, more in anger than denial. 'You're only scared for yourself,' she accused. 'You're not thinking about me.'

'You haven't anything to gain, and a lot to lose.' Roxanne's usual animation was returning; she waved her hands energetically, to emphasise her point. 'Nobody knows exactly what Craig did. You don't have to show anyone his note, unless Susie insists. If the truth comes out about Jim, a lot of people will be embarrassed. Worse than embarrassed. Viagra's a joke, for a start. And Monica's nose would be rubbed in Jim's infidelity. Think about it,' she repeated. 'You'll see I'm right. Jim Lapsford will be cremated tomorrow, as planned. It's the best thing for everyone.'

VI

Olga came running down to the workshop, looking for Drew. 'What's going on?' demanded Pat, surprised to see her moving so fast. 'Are we on fire, or what?'

'There's somebody here to see Drew,' she told him. 'And there's only me in the office, so I have to be there for the phone. Where is he?'

Pat looked around vaguely. Vince and Big George were both at their benches, one attaching handles to a coffin and the other making an oak casket for an ashes interment. 'Dunno,' said Pat. 'Can't be back from taking the family home off this morning's funeral yet. Or is he visiting his wife, maybe? Never know where that boy is, and that's the truth.' He twinkled maddeningly at Olga. 'Who's the visitor, anyway?'

'Mrs Lapsford,' she said, sounding baffled. 'I'll have to ask her to wait while I try and find out where he is.'

'Well, speak of the devil!' yelped Pat, as Drew came in, almost bumping into Olga. 'We were just looking for you.'

'I was in the mortuary,' said Drew. 'Looking for the dog.'

Pat shook his head wearily. 'It's crazy you are,' he said. 'Wait till Daphne comes in – she'll have taken it, you see. Put it somewhere safe. Nobody else wants a dead dog, now do they?'

Drew ignored him, distracted by Olga's urgent glances. 'Mrs Lapsford's here – she wants to talk to you,' she told him.

With as calm a demeanour as possible, he

followed her back to the office, where Monica sat on the edge of an upright chair in Daphne's sanctum. 'Better see her in there,' said Olga, doubtfully. 'Though it's all very odd–'

Drew, rather rudely, closed the door on her, and sat down on Daphne's chair. Monica needed no invitation to begin her story. 'I'm sorry about Saturday,' she began, her cheeks an embarrassed pink. 'You arrived at a rather emotional moment. Jodie was right, of course, in a way, but I never thought you had anything but the best of motives. I mean – there isn't anything in this for you, is there?'

Drew smiled bleakly, and shook his head. 'So,' she went on, 'I've come to say I think you were right all along.' She recounted the finding of the teabag; her renewed suspicions that Jim might have drunk something containing poison late on Monday evening, that Cassie had licked up some of the same substance from Jim's face. 'I didn't know who else I could talk to,' she finished. 'Everybody else seems to be a possible – well – *murderer*, I suppose.'

Drew thought carefully. Mentally, he ran through a list of names, starting with Gerald Proctor and finishing with his own boss. 'What do you think we should do about it?' he asked her gently. 'The cremation's tomorrow, after all.'

She frowned worriedly, and rubbed a finger between her eyes, as if to erase the groove she was making. 'I really don't know,' she said. 'It's all such a terrible muddle. I suppose I should have phoned the police that morning. They would have examined Jim and we'd know by now what'd killed him. After all, it did *look* like a heart attack, didn't it?' She was desperate for reassurance.

Drew nodded agreement. Then he met her eyes. 'I wondered whether – er – his taking Viagra might have been a contributing cause? It does put a strain on the heart, in some cases, apparently.'

'You found it in the bathroom, I suppose? Mr Amateur Detective.' Drew nodded sheepishly.

She flushed. 'Well, I told him he ought not to take it. It wasn't as if he really *needed* it. He was so keen to please, you see. He'd do anything to make sure everything kept working. Do you think that was what did it, and the teabag doesn't mean anything, after all?' She sounded hopeful.

'I don't know,' he said, wishing he could tell her about Roxanne and the henbane. 'But it's possible.'

Monica looked more cheerful. 'In that case, it wouldn't be anyone's fault, would it? We wouldn't have to make a fuss and call the police. I *really* don't want to do that. On the other hand–'

'By telling me what you have, you make it very difficult for me to go along with the cremation, you know. It's making me an accessory, in a way. Besides, why in the world would you come to me now if you didn't want me to do anything?'

She looked at him in confusion. 'I didn't come for that reason at all. I just felt you were owed the truth. And – well, there isn't anybody else I could share this with, not at the moment. I couldn't keep it all to myself – not with the cremation tomorrow.'

'So you think someone close to you might have poisoned your husband, and you wanted somebody neutral to set your mind at rest.' He maintained his gentle tone, but injected a new firmness into his words. 'Or even somebody to share the responsibility.'

'I suppose that's true,' she admitted. Then she straightened her shoulders, and groped for her handbag. 'Well, I've decided. I'm going to throw that teabag away and forget all about it. We're having the funeral as planned, and Jim can rest in peace. After all – who in the world would go to the trouble of tampering with a teabag, let alone persuade Jim to use it? The idea's ridiculous.'

Drew stood up. 'So you want me to forget everything you've just told me?' he summarised.

'If you would,' she said, with dignity. 'You can tell your secretary that I came to discuss the arrangements for this afternoon if she asks why I was here. Will you be one of the men bringing Jim home?'

'Probably. Oh – there is one small problem. Your dog's body has gone missing.' He hadn't intended to tell her, in the hope that the terrier would somehow reappear, but now he saw no reason to hide the truth. 'Either someone's trying to conceal evidence – or there's a chance that someone else has suspicions, and has taken her for a postmortem. A vet would do one on a dog's body–'

'Dogsbody,' she smiled, before the full import of his words hit her. 'But that could ruin everything! I thought your mortuary was the safest place for her. Do you often lose bodies?' Anger was rising visibly and she stared at him accusingly.

'I think this is the first time,' he said mildly. 'And I have no idea how it happened. Sid and Daphne are both away this morning – one of them might have an explanation. I'm just warning you. I doubt if there's any need to panic.'

'Just help me get through the next twenty-four hours. That's all I ask. After all, you do seem to have got yourself involved in my family's business. There'll be a bit of a bonus for you, if we can see it through to the end with no trouble.'

Blackmail! thought Drew, with a shiver of excitement. 'No need for that,' he said reprovingly. 'If I thought it was the right thing to do, I'd phone the police here and now.' Hearing himself, he felt a shock of surprise. Why *wasn't* it right, to report what was almost certainly a murder? What possible excuse could he have for remaining silent? His reasons seemed to have changed through the past week, as he encountered successive candidates for the role of poisoner. What had started out as a quest for truth and justice had now become much less well-defined. High moral standpoints were all well and good if you weren't acquainted with the individuals concerned. Once you'd met them, come to know them, it was a different matter entirely.

First the wretched David and his obvious instability, then the valiant team of colleagues at the printworks, all seeming so loyal; next the bewitching Roxanne; finally, the elusive dentist. If one of them had deliberately and maliciously poisoned Jim Lapsford, then so be it. Drew recoiled from the idea of causing any of them to be tried and convicted for murder. Who was he to judge them? Besides, from what he had learned of Jim, he had brought his death upon himself. Whatever the substance in the teabag may or may not have been, the chances were that the Viagra and henbane he'd also been taking had fatally weakened his heart already.

'I deserved that.' Monica rose. 'Let me just mention one more thing. My friend Pauline's son hanged himself at the weekend, as I expect you know. If there were to be a murder investigation into Jim's death, the truth about the Viagra would come out, and I think that would implicate Craig. Pauline wouldn't be able to take that.'

He nodded doubtfully. 'I'm really not at all sure that I can hide the truth. But, for now–'

'Yes, I know. I must go. I'll see you later on, then? And thank you. Thank you very much indeed. I really am sure you're doing the right thing.'

Drew sighed. He was sure that he wasn't 'doing the right thing' – for a start, he was once again doing nothing, and that did not feel *right* at all.

VII

Olga told Drew that Karen had phoned, as soon as Monica had gone. Although Sid had presented himself as Vince had predicted, looking tired and wan, Daphne still hadn't shown up, which came as quite a relief. 'I'm going to the hospital for an hour or two,' Drew told Vince. 'I'll be back about four, to carry Lapsford in.'

'We'll all be glad to see the back of that one,' said Vince.

Sid, tinkering as usual with something on his workbench, looked up. 'You can say that again,' he muttered. His usual moroseness had been compounded by the shock over Craig's death. Drew had tried to convey sympathy, but Sid had merely shrugged. 'Can't let it get to you, can you. It's not as if he was a blood relation. Susie doesn't need me to hold her hand these days, either. She's more interested in being with his mother.' This had been a long speech for Sid, and Drew had turned away with a sympathetic smile.

Karen was lying on the bed, with her eyes closed, when he reached her. He stood for a minute looking down at her, the light brown hair lank on the pillow and her skin a shade paler than usual, and he trembled to think what might have happened. His wife had transformed his life, brought him new dimensions he had never imagined possible. The idea of losing her was terrifying. Gently he took hold of her hand, and her eyes flew open.

'At last!' she said. 'I thought you'd never get here.'

He smiled and shrugged. 'I'm here now,' he said and bent to kiss her. She tasted different – something metallic and slightly sour lingered on his tongue.

'They did a pregnancy test,' she said, without preamble. 'Sit down – Daddy.'

He sat, and felt himself fill up with emotion.

More emotions than he thought could possibly occur all at once. Karen's face mirrored a number of them. A glaze of tears in her eyes, a crooked half-smile, raised eyebrows. 'Oh,' he said.

They held hands tightly, and laughed breathlessly at each other's expressions. 'The arnica's working,' she said, after a few minutes. 'I can go home tomorrow.'

'Tomorrow is Lapsford's funeral,' he said, without thinking. Hearing himself, he looked at her anxiously. Was he allowed to mention Lapsford now?

'I know it is. And we've got to keep trying to figure out what happened,' was her surprising response. Then she told him about Daphne's visit.

'The bloody cow!' Drew exploded. 'She can't do that. That's blackmail!' Twice in one day was too much.

'It still doesn't make much sense,' Karen mused. 'I've been lying here trying to work it out. She seemed to be telling me there was some sort of scam going on with the doctor, but I can't see what it's got to do with you or me. And I can't see how it ties in with Jim being murdered. Until this happened, I'd more or less settled for it being a sort of accident. The Viagra and Roxanne's stuff doing something in combination. Now I'm not too sure.'

'There's more to it, anyway,' Drew told her, without enthusiasm. 'Mrs L thinks somebody gave him a doctored teabag. He made himself a night-time drink – could be that's what finished him off. But she only told me in order to get me off her back. She said she wanted the cremation to go ahead as planned, for me to just back off, and forget the whole thing. Typical female logic.'

'And will you? Back off, I mean? Who does she think it was? Why isn't she more worried? Is she trying to protect somebody – presumably David?'

Drew shook his head. 'She didn't say. Somebody stole the dog, by the way.'

Karen leaned back carefully against her pillows, and put both hands flat across her lower belly. Then she laughed. It was a quiet laugh, but she soon lost control of it. Tears began to shake loose and she grabbed her lower lip between her teeth when her bruises complained. Drew watched with irritation and mild alarm.

'Don't worry,' she spluttered. 'I wouldn't be able to explain. It's just the look on your face, that's all.'

He tried to smile, but puzzlement made it difficult. Karen took his hand again. 'Drew,' she wheedled. 'Can't you take me home tonight? I don't want to be here with all these people.' She glanced round at the elderly women patients surrounding her. 'They're so *noisy*.'

'I'll ask,' he said. 'I don't suppose they'll object.'

'Thanks,' she sighed. 'And Drew, that visit from Daphne had more to it than meets the eye. She was trying to tell me something. She sounded jolly threatening but I wonder if she was actually trying to prompt us into keeping at it. Confirm our suspicions – lead us in the right direction. I wonder if she knows something – or suspects – and wants us to do the dirty work, because of her so-called professional reputation. She can't afford to upset anybody. I think you ought to try and talk to Dr Lloyd, or at least his receptionist.'

Already he could see the light of victory in her eye, and wondered whether he had it too. The fact of the pregnancy had shifted his focus on the world: anything was possible, now they'd finally achieved a conception. And in some obscure, half-embarrassed way, it made the quest for the truth about Jim Lapsford even more urgent. Some chaotic unconscious reasoning insisted that, if there were a murderer loose in the world, then, as a new parent, he had a duty to identify and remove him. He wanted life to be just that tiny bit safer for his child.

'Susie's got enough to worry about already,' he pointed out. 'But I'll watch out for any chance to get this whole business straight. Now I've got to go. We're taking Lapsford home for his last night. I'll come and get you after that, okay?'

She nodded. 'Thanks,' she said again.

'See you then,' he said, kissing her lingeringly. 'Don't do anything silly now, will you?'

'Don't you worry about me,' she told him.

On an impulse, he turned in the opposite direction from the car park, outside the main entrance, and headed for the hospital mortuary. Sam, the attendant, was eating a large chicken and tomato sandwich in the partially walled-off area that was his office. He nodded a casual greeting to Drew, his mouth full. He was thin and small, with nothing to betray his daily tasks apart from a greyness under the eyes which had little to do with weariness. It was as if all the noisome smells and evidence of pain and misery accumulated there, having passed through his retina and optic nerve. Sam saw all the suicides and the sudden devastating heart attacks and the car crash victims. Children and women in their prime; vagrants who'd lain for weeks in a ditch; young lads shattered by coming off their motorbikes at ninety miles an hour.

'All right?' Drew asked him, routinely.

'Rawlinson's not ready for you,' Sam said. 'Should have been by now, but it was a heavy morning. Typical Monday. They're not doing him till tomorrow now.'

'I'm not here officially. My wife's upstairs, so I just dropped in to say hi.'

'Nothing serious?' Sam cocked his head on one side, unsure how much to ask.

'Could have been. My boss's car tried to kill her.' Drew hadn't known how angry he felt with Daphne until this moment: Karen might have been killed.

'What?'

'One of those crazy coincidences. It was raining, and Karen started to cross the road without looking properly. Daphne was coming along, much too fast, and skidded sideways. No real harm done, thank goodness.'

'And the car?'

'Did a brilliant ram-raid attempt on a shop and is unlikely to recover. Daphne's okay, though.'

'Yeah, I know.'

'You what?'

'She was in here this morning. Had a look at young Rawlinson. Passed the time of day with His Majesty and Stanley. Never misses a trick, that boss of yours. They say the local Post Office is the place to get all the gossip in a small town – well, if you ask me, the local undertaker's even better.'

'I'm beginning to think you might be right about that,' Drew nodded thoughtfully. His Majesty was the epithet used to refer to the Pathologist, Mr Metherington, and Stanley was the Coroner's Officer, to whom all sudden deaths were to be reported. Drew had so far only met the latter.

'Does the name Jim Lapsford mean anything to you?' he asked on a sudden impulse.

Sam pursed his lips. 'Saw it in the paper. I gather the doctor signed him up and convinced the Registrar that there was no need to take it any further. There's been talk, of course, behind the scenes. Often is, with a sudden death like that. Officially, we're all relieved it didn't come to us. As I say, it's busy, and the taxpayer's bill is growing all the time.'

'That's about what I thought,' nodded Drew. 'But unofficially?'

'It's one that got away. There's a dozen or so every year, signed up when they shouldn't be. It's not worth worrying about. The odds must be a thousand to one that it was his heart. When does he go?'

'Tomorrow. It's been getting to me, just between you and me. Too many loose ends. The family's acting strangely. Even our Sid doesn't seem happy about it. Embalmed him right away.'

Sam shrugged. 'That'd make our job pretty hard, then, even if someone did throw a spanner in the works. You'll get used to it, mate. Just get the job done and don't rock the boat. Maybe I'll see you tomorrow, if you come for Rawlinson.'

'Maybe,' said Drew. He found that he wasn't ready to think about tomorrow, for a variety of reasons. Time was rapidly running out.

VIII

Philip and David let themselves into the Primrose Close house at three o'clock that afternoon. Monica was on the sofa, with a mug of coffee, her feet stretched along its length. She didn't budge when her sons came in.

'Mum? Are you okay?' asked Philip. 'Look – I've brought David to see you. Nerina sends her apologies. She couldn't face it after all.'

Alerted by the stilted care in his voice, she inspected her younger son comprehensively. He looked tired, but determined; he wore a clean sweatshirt and his hair was well brushed. He'd shaved recently and was making an effort to square his shoulders and be a reliable support to her. She gave him a grateful smile and patted both her sons on the arm. 'You look very smart, both of you,' she said. 'We've got an hour or so before they arrive. If you could just move a few things out of the way for me – take the coffee table up to the spare room, and probably Dad's big chair will have to go.' All three cast uneasy glances at the chair in which Jim had reclined, and which carried the marks of his body still. Taking it out of the room would be awkward both physically and emotionally.

'Are you really sure you want to do this, Mum?' Philip asked. 'There's still time to change your mind. It might be okay this afternoon – but what about tonight? How will you feel in the early hours, knowing he's down here? I must say, I wouldn't like it.'

'I'm not frightened of my husband's dead body,' she said gently. 'And don't forget, I've seen it already. I've slept in bed beside it. I've got to make my peace with him and I think this is one way to do it. Don't worry about me, darling – it's sweet of you, but there isn't any need.'

'Make your peace?' demanded David, a warning harshness in his voice betraying his alarm. 'Why? What have you done?'

'Nothing that need concern you. Jim and I were married for twenty-nine years. We haven't always played it by the rules – middle age isn't as quiet and boring as it used to be. But we understood each other, and I don't mean that I've anything to feel guilty about. I just want to tell him – to tell him–' Without warning, she broke into a storm of tears, taking herself by surprise. It felt as if the knowledge that Jim was really and permanently gone forever had been waiting behind a thin veil of calm, which had now torn and released a tidal wave of unexpressed misery and loss.

To tell him I loved him, was all she'd intended to say. Little words, but they amounted to something uncontrollably vast.

'Oh, Mum,' sighed Philip, with something close to satisfaction. 'Here.' He handed her a hanky and put his arm around her shoulder. David hovered, outside the circle they made, watching with a mixture of anger and grief.

She was still crying when Vince rang the doorbell, having parked the hearse outside. Pat, Drew and Sid were climbing out, and moving to the back of the vehicle. Monica recoiled at the sight of it. It seemed enormous, filling the whole street, signalling death in all its most Victorian splendour. Inappropriately, the sun was shining, glinting on the polished black surface and the brass handles of the coffin as they began to carry it in.

'We weren't sure about the lid,' said Vince. 'Whether you wanted it on or off.'

Monica closed her eyes. 'Off,' she said, much more firmly than she felt. It wasn't a difficult decision – what would be the sense of having Jim home if she couldn't look on his face?

She watched as they lowered the heavy box onto the trestles they had brought with them. The manoeuvre was deftly choreographed, but cumbersome nonetheless. *They must have very strong arms and shoulders,* she thought, remembering how Vince and Drew had carried Jim downstairs on the stretcher, sliding him around corners with genuine skill.

The coffin lid, held in place by large screws with decorative brass-effect tops, was removed and propped against the wall. Inside, Jim's body was covered with a neatly-folded sheet of white material, which made Monica think more of a pram than a bed: something to do with the care with which it had been laid over him, and his helpless acquiescence in what happened to him. The difference, horrible and intensely sad, was the square of thin but opaque white satin covering his face.

With a fingertip delicacy, Vince leaned over and took the cover away. He laid it on Jim's chest and stood back. Without thinking, Monica reached out both hands sideways, to grasp a son in each, and together the three took a few hesitant steps forward. Despite her earlier brave words, Monica was afraid.

Since waking up to find him dead beside her, Jim had undergone a mysterious absence which had removed a lot of his familiar identity. His face was pinker than she remembered it, his hair brushed at an angle which was very slightly wrong. His chin was tilted up just too much, making him look uncomfortable and oddly defiant. And yet the features were all too obviously those of her husband. Those lips had kissed her, talked to her, eaten the food she cooked. The face had been animated by the powerful force of Jim himself. The endlessly insoluble mystery of where that Jim had gone was terrible in this moment. 'Oh dear,' she said.

Watching her, Drew cast away any slight lingering doubts that she might have deliberately killed her husband. Although she was obviously agitated, even afraid, he felt sure that she was genuinely sorry that the man was dead. Slowly she advanced until her hands rested on the side of the coffin and her sons stood at either shoulder. She stared as if fascinated at the cold face, but made no attempt to touch it. Vince made a slight movement, trying to catch Drew's eye. Having succeeded, he tipped his head very slightly towards the door in a familiar signal. Pat and Sid were ready to leave, working their shoulders slightly and swinging their arms.

'Will you be all right, madam?' Vince asked, with impeccable formality.

'What? Oh, yes, of course. Thank you very much. I'll see you tomorrow. We'll be fine now, won't we, boys?'

Philip and David reacted in their different ways. Philip nodded briefly, with a vague smile, his head turned stiffly away from the sight of his dead father; David pulled a grimace of mocking agreement. 'Oh, yes,' he said, in a choked voice. 'Just fine.' Unlike his brother, he could hardly take his eyes off the body. He seemed greedy for the sight, avid to understand what his eyes were seeing.

Sid opened the door and Drew's attention was quickly drawn by a shocked intake of breath. Coming up the garden path were two people. Drew recognised them as Jodie, and one of the men from the printworks, the man who'd brought the flowers to Monica; he had forgotten his name. Sid had gone pale, his light blue eyes bulging, but he quickly recovered himself. 'You gave me a shock,' he said with a laugh, before turning back to Monica. 'You've got visitors, Mrs Lapsford,' he said.

'Jodie! Jack!' she said, with little discernible

pleasure in her voice. 'I didn't expect to see you two so early.'

Vince determinedly tried to shepherd his crew out of the house, before they could get trapped by the greeting of the visitors and their unpredictable reactions to the sight of their dead colleague in the middle of the living room.

Drew, however, was very curious to observe it. He had taken little notice of the man – Jack – during his visit to the printworks, but now he gave him more attention. Lean, in his early fifties, he seemed to wish himself somewhere else, somewhere far away. Jodie was clearly in charge of him, flapping a firm hand at him to direct him into the house ahead of her.

As Jack passed Sid, Drew noticed an odd look pass between the two men. He could see Jack's face more clearly, but the awkwardness of the clustering on the doorstep forced both men to turn slightly sideways, so Drew could also see Sid's profile. Each man ducked his head in a complex exchange, suggesting recognition; agreement; reassurance.

It was not, on the face of it, surprising that they knew each other: Bradbourne was a small town, and the men of roughly the same age. Doubtless Jack too drank in the King's Head. But the suggestion of complicity, Sid's shock at seeing Jack – or was it perhaps Jodie? – coming up the path, had been strange. The peculiar nod definitely gave grounds for misgivings. Once again Drew felt a surge of helplessness; how could he make use of his suspicion? His ignorance as to who these people really were, how they were connected, made him feel desperate. How did police detectives ever manage, going into a strange community, interviewing complicated families who were determined to hide a morass of dark secrets? It was impossible. Despondently, he followed Vince, Sid and Pat out to the hearse.

IX

Sarah and Dottie watched the hearse drive away. They looked at each other doubtfully. 'She did ask us to go over,' said Dottie. 'I think we'd better get on with it, before we lose our nerve.'

'But those other people are there. We can't barge in when she's got guests already.' Sarah was annoyed with herself for feeling fluttery and unsure; she was supposed to be the capable one, and here she was getting into a real state over paying her last respects to a neighbour. 'Let's leave it for half an hour.'

'But Monica won't mind us being there with other people,' Dottie argued. 'She made it sound rather like a little party, in her note. I expect there'll be more arriving soon.'

'Perhaps you're right. It all feels very awkward, somehow. I mean, what if that *man* turns up? I don't think I could look him in the face.'

Dottie stared at her incredulously. 'Isn't it a bit late for that? And wasn't it you who said we shouldn't jump to conclusions? Assuming you mean the dentist, that is. Sarah, I wonder at you, I really do.'

'Well, I'm sorry, but I feel uncomfortable about

going round there now. It all feels wrong to me.'

Dottie laid a stern hand on her friend's arm, and looked her full in the face. 'Now, Sarah, we really can't have this. I know you – you like everybody to think you're so strong and sensible, but all too easily you get yourself into a state. I heard you last night, pacing up and down – it isn't good for a woman of your age. I don't understand what you're worrying about. Whether or not Monica's been having a little fling doesn't change the fact that Jim's dead. Does it?'

'Well, it depends how you look at it,' said Sarah. 'It depends on your views about responsibility. I'm not sure I could control my tongue, if he were to turn up.'

'Sarah, this is nonsense. It isn't our *business.* We've done everything we can by speaking to that young man. We can leave it all up to him now. If there is anything that needs to be done, then he'll be the person to do it.'

'Perhaps you're right,' said Sarah, giving herself a little shake. 'Well, the sooner we go, the sooner we can come home again, as my mother always used to say.'

'That's right,' sighed Dottie. 'Though why anybody should be in such a hurry to get home, I can't imagine.'

X

Roxanne was weary by five o'clock. The emotional demands of dealing with Pauline's grief had been compounded by a visit from an hysterical Lorraine, flying over her field only five minutes after Roxanne had dragged herself home from Pauline's flat. The girl's story was predictable, but none the less affecting for that. In the course of spilling it out, Lorraine had scarcely paused from her own self-pity to acknowledge the disaster of Craig's death. The sense of the world collapsing all around them was increasing by the hour, and they sat in the caravan surveying the wreckage.

'I shouldn't have said what I did in the canteen,' Roxanne admitted, flatly. 'I jumped to completely the wrong conclusion. I wasn't thinking straight, after what happened to Craig. I should have kept my mouth shut.'

'It wasn't just you,' Lorraine consoled her. 'Somebody said something in front of Frank at the pub on Saturday. He'd have worked it out sooner or later.'

'I can help you,' Roxanne offered, as a thought struck her. 'We can *prove* the baby isn't Jim's.'

Lorraine blinked. 'Oh, yes – with blood tests, I suppose. But Frank won't wait for any of that. He says I've got to abort it right away.'

'No, no,' Roxanne interrupted. 'It can't be Jim's, because he had a vasectomy. Years ago. Funny he never told you. I mean – how did you go on for contraception?'

Lorraine blushed. 'I always put my cap in. After the first time, anyway. And we didn't ever talk about it – not in proper words. You know?'

Roxanne smiled, seeing how it must have been. She could well understand how Jim wouldn't have wanted to utter a word like *vasectomy*, with its clinical, mechanical overtones. Quite a romantic, was Jim.

'Look, why don't we both go to Jim's wake?' she suggested suddenly. 'We might as well. Don't you think we owe it to him, to say a last goodbye?' *And you could give me a lift,* she thought. *Otherwise I'll have to get the bus. Not a very stylish entrance.*

Lorraine wiped her hand childishly across her eyes and stared at the older woman. 'What?' she said.

'The Lapsfords' house. Monica has got Jim there for the evening – and all night, I suppose – until the funeral tomorrow. So people go and pay their final respects to him. I rather like the idea of you and me turning up together, don't you?'

It was a pivotal moment for Lorraine. The instinctive recoil from the idea of coming face to face with her dead lover lasted only a few seconds, as she looked at Roxanne. She remembered that she had very little left to lose. She was going to need a large dose of courage from now on, whatever happened. Maybe this would teach her something about how to be brave. 'Do we dare?' she wondered. 'Does Monica know about us? Everything's in such a mess, with Jim and Frank and now your sister's boy. Won't they refuse to let us in?'

'We won't know till we get there, will we?' shrugged Roxanne. 'But this is our last chance – I can't see either of us turning up at the cremation.'

'I was thinking about that,' Lorraine admitted.

'Well, now you won't need to. This is going to be much better.'

Lorraine began to smile. She visualised Jim's

two mistresses standing either side of the coffin, wishing him a tearful farewell. In the midst of her trouble with Frank, this felt like something she could do for herself, something to make things better. A statement she could make, regardless of the consequences. 'Yes!' she gasped. 'Why not?'

'Come on then. You can drive.' Roxanne pushed her feet into a pair of frayed leather sandals and reached for a packet of cigarettes.

They walked briskly across the field, saying nothing. But once in the car, conversation began to flow. 'You're divorced, aren't you?' Lorraine began, as soon as she'd turned the car round in the narrow lane. 'What happened?'

Roxanne blew smoke out of the open car window, and put her head back against the head-rest. 'He had too much money,' she said.

Lorraine turned to stare at her. 'You're joking,' she said. 'Aren't you?'

Roxanne shook her head lazily. 'Nope. Every time I needed anything – wanted a new pair of jeans, or to go away for a few days, or get my car fixed – he insisted on paying. I had a job which I put a lot of effort into. I earned about a tenth of what he did, despite putting about six times the effort in. But it was impossible for me to feel I was *getting* anywhere. He undermined everything I did. Do you understand?'

Lorraine frowned. 'Not really. I mean – what did it matter who paid for things?'

'Apparently it did.' Roxanne watched the town getting closer: the square church tower, the land sloping down to the river, the housing estate a bright red and grey scab on what she remembered as a grassy hillside. Even now she could feel the poisonous, creeping sense of futility which had washed over her every time Lennie had smilingly waved his credit card and removed all purpose from her daily grind at the garden centre.

Lorraine made another attempt. 'Well, I suppose it would be annoying. Like being a child. Never having proper responsibility. Is that what you mean?'

'*Exactly* that,' agreed Roxanne, exhaling another generous cloud of smoke. 'And by the time I hit forty-five, I figured I ought to be allowed to grow up a bit.'

'Didn't you love him, though?' Lorraine sensed the naivety of the question. But it seemed important to know.

'Oh, *love,*' Roxanne dismissed, 'that's something else entirely. Love doesn't last – not the way you mean. I was in love for six months when I was twenty. I'm lucky to have had that much. It was like being picked up and squeezed by a giant hand, until I thought I'd burst. After that, you don't use the word if you can help it.'

'I suppose not,' Lorraine said, wonderingly. 'But I know what you mean about money – sort of. Frank takes care of everything important. Except Cindy, of course. But he pays the bills and organises the holidays, and gets the car fixed. He's a fantastically good manager. I've always told myself I was lucky. I never really thought of it in any other way.' She shook her head. 'I'm going to remember this day, aren't I. Everything happens at once.'

'Would it make any difference if Jim was still alive?' Roxanne asked the question easily. 'I mean – would *he* help you decide what to do next?'

Lorraine was silent, slowing the car unconsciously, to give herself time to think. 'He wouldn't have offered to leave his wife for me, I know that much,' she finally replied. 'And probably he'd have been scared stiff at what Frank might do to rock the boat. Actually, it would all have stopped anyway, once he knew I was pregnant.'

'So in a way it isn't such a disaster that he's dead after all.'

Lorraine gave a strangled yelp, half-shocked, half-amused. 'You do say some awful things,' she choked.

'True, though. It's the same for all of us, when you think about it. Even Monica. You knew she had a chap on the side, didn't you? We're all in it together, one way or another.'

'A chap?' repeated Lorraine faintly. 'No, I never knew that.'

'Oh, yes. Jim didn't know though, and I only found out last week. Everything was for the best, as it turns out. Nobody really has any cause for complaint. Except maybe your Frank. But real life never does work out as neatly as people like Frank – or Jim – wish it would.'

'You sound as if you didn't really like him. Wasn't he–' She interrupted herself as they reached a T-Junction. 'It's left here, isn't it? I've never been to his house before.'

'Left, then second left again. Jim thought he could love everybody and be loved in return. He didn't see the point of confining himself to one exclusive relationship. It suited me, most of the time. But – I've been thinking since he died. I think he went too far, and now there's just a trail of trouble and misery behind him. And bugger-all to show for it.'

'So why are we going to see him now?' Again the car slowed, as Lorraine's courage began to fail.

'To tie up the loose ends. To be sure he's really dead. Curiosity. Sentiment. Because it's a chance to make a bit of mischief. Take your pick.' Lorraine's sigh brought Roxanne out of her bitter reverie. 'Sorry, love. But you did ask.'

'That's okay,' muttered Lorraine. 'What number is it? I think we're there.'

'Twenty-four. We're here all right. Now, have a good blow and keep your chin up. As you say, you're going to remember this day for quite some time to come.'

XI

It was impossible to discern from Monica's expression whether she knew the nature of Jim's relationship with either Roxanne or Lorraine. Jodie had let them in, and ushered them into the living room without a word. 'I hope you don't mind–' Lorraine began, but Roxanne interrupted her.

'Good of you to let Jim's old friends come along,' she said, with a jarring heartiness. 'I see we're not the only ones.' She looked hard at Jodie, and then at Jack. 'Hi,' she greeted him.

'Haven't seen you for a while.'

'You know each other?' queried Monica, scanning all the faces with a bemused expression. 'Are you all from the King's Head crowd?'

'More or less,' agreed Roxanne. 'Everyone knew Jim, and most of us know each other, at least by sight. I'm Roxanne, and this is Lorraine.'

Monica nodded. 'I know you by sight. You're the one in the caravan, aren't you? But I'm afraid–' She faltered, eyeing Lorraine doubtfully. Jodie came to the rescue. 'This is Mrs Dunlop,' she said, with no further explanation.

'Well, Jim's here, as you can see. If you'd like to have a quiet minute with him, I'll go into the kitchen. I was going to make some more tea, anyway.' Monica's energy was going into maintaining her dignity; Jodie put an arm round her shoulders. 'I'll come with you,' she said.

In the kitchen, Philip and David were sitting at the table, shoulders hunched, expressions fixed. 'You look as if you're in hiding,' Jodie joked. 'Probably wise. Stay out of the way, and let the women get on with it. There'll be more yet, you see. Women seem to like dead people better than men do. Or maybe they're just more accepting of death.'

'Sarah and Dottie aren't here yet,' said Monica, vaguely. 'And what about Ajash?'

'He's not coming,' said Jodie. 'I meant to tell you. He said it would upset him too much – he didn't want to blub in front of everyone. He's a real softie. That rather proves my point, I suppose.'

'I thought his people went in for public

weeping and wailing,' said Philip. 'He's missing his chance.'

Jodie gave him a piercing look. 'I think "his people" are from Solihull,' she said tartly.

'Who's that who just came?' asked David, with minimal curiosity.

Jodie glanced at Monica with a little frown. 'Just a couple of women from the pub. They probably drew the short straws, and are representing the whole gang. They seem pretty upset.'

'It's very kind of them,' insisted Monica. 'I wasn't sure anyone would show up.'

'Mum,' said Philip, conveying worry and irritation and impatience in the single word.

'Yes?' She confronted him. 'Mum, what?'

'I just wish everyone would go away and leave us in peace to get on with it.'

'They will,' said Jodie, with bracing firmness. 'The sooner we give them tea and cake, the sooner they'll go.' And she filled the kettle and set it boiling.

The picture of Lorraine and Roxanne leaning over the coffin – not on opposite sides, as Lorraine had imagined, but shoulder to shoulder, in silent contemplation – brought a red-hot anger to Jodie's lips. Glancing back at the kitchen, she hissed viciously at them. 'What do you think you two are *doing?*' she demanded. 'How do you have the *nerve* to do this?'

'She doesn't know, then?' said Roxanne, in a calm tone. 'Well, don't worry about it. We're not going to tell her.'

'And what about when she tells her friends that

you came? Everybody else in town knows. They'll assume she does too, and the whole thing'll be out, just at the worst possible moment.'

'Calm down,' Roxanne persisted. 'You always were one for making everything complicated, weren't you? Never just let things be, Miss Jodie Perfect. I've lost count of the times Jim's told me about the way you stir up trouble everywhere you go. Okay, he was fond of you – I'm not denying that. I don't want to hurt any feelings. But, Christ, just *relax* for once, will you? Stop looking for trouble. Lorraine and I just wanted to–'

'And that's another thing,' Jodie continued, as if nothing had been said, 'how come the two of you are so matey all of a sudden? That's really sick, if you ask me.' Again she glanced towards the kitchen, ignoring Jack, who sat in the single armchair, apparently sunk in his own morose thoughts. 'Jim's two women, turning up here practically arm-in-arm – it doesn't make sense. Something's going on.'

'Nothing's going on, love. Believe me. Tell her, Lorraine,' Roxanne invited.

Lorraine met Jodie's angry gaze warily. 'We're not here to make trouble,' she said, hesitantly. 'Mrs Lapsford said anyone could come. It looks to me as if she understands that a lot of people loved Jim. She seemed quite happy to see us, anyway.'

'Nobody loved Jim. Not really,' said Jack suddenly, from the armchair. His narrow face turned on them with a haunted look of sorrow. 'Not any of you. Not his sons, not his wife. Jim was all for himself, you see. All those friends –

you women panting after him like bitches on heat – he never cared about any of you. Jim Lapsford was all take and no give, if you want the truth of it. So long as he was all right, he didn't give a damn about anybody else.'

From the hall, a voice said, 'Now, that isn't very nice, is it? Speaking ill of the dead.'

When everybody had turned towards her, Dottie went on. 'The door wasn't properly shut. I hope you don't mind us letting ourselves in.'

By eight, the last of the visitors had gone, and Monica sat in the kitchen with her sons. Philip whistled his relief as the front door finally closed. 'Thank God for Jodie,' he said. 'We'd never have coped without her. I don't know what was going on, but there seemed to be quite an argument out there at one point.'

'Jim knew some funny people,' Monica remarked. 'I hope they all behave themselves tomorrow.'

Her sons looked at each other warily. The unsavoury details of their father's life were only just beginning to creep out from under the carpet, but already they felt an impending turmoil.

'Do you want anything to eat?' Monica asked them. 'We could have a takeaway.'

'Most of them are closed on a Monday,' Philip reminded her. 'I'm all right, anyway, after all that cake.'

'David?'

'It'd choke me,' he said with a scowl.

'Oh, here we go,' groaned Philip. He gave David a disgusted look, and pushed back his chair. 'I'm going to phone Nerina, and tell her I'll be home soon. Then I'll sit quietly with Dad for a while. If you two have things to say, keep the noise down, and come and tell me when it's over.'

Monica turned to David, her manner much calmer.

'We're not having any more dramatics, are we?' she said softly. 'That's all behind us, isn't it?'

David nodded. 'I didn't mean anything just now. Philip always assumes the worst. I'm okay, Mum. Just tired.' The twisted smile he gave her confirmed his words. If only his eyes didn't look so sunken and strange, she might have been able to relax. As it was, she knew she wouldn't be able to let him out of her sight tomorrow, for fear of what he might do.

She patted his shoulder gently. 'Go home, and get a good night's sleep. We'll all feel much better this time tomorrow.'

'I'll wait till Phil goes,' he said. 'He's not the only one to want a few minutes alone with Dad.' He gripped two handfuls of hair, in a sudden spasm. 'I'll always wonder how he felt about me,' he said bleakly. 'Whether I was only important because I was a piece of *her*.'

'I hope that isn't true,' she said gently. 'But I can understand that that might be how it would seem to you.'

'I *have* to know who my real father was. Can't you remember Julia having a boyfriend? Am I the result of a one-night stand? There can't be too many people to choose from.' He was pleading, and she put a firm hand on his wrist.

'It might be better not to know,' she said. 'He

isn't going to accept you now, any more than he would then. Jim told me just one thing: when Julia told the father she was pregnant, he threatened her, persuaded her to keep his identity secret. Perhaps he was married. That's really why she handed you over to us. She knew she'd have to give him away, or ask him for money at least, if she kept you. He can't have been a very nice person.'

'Did he go to her funeral, do you think?' David's train of thought was obvious, as he looked towards the living room and the coffin standing in the middle of it. There was no sound from Philip, and neither gave him a thought.

'I don't think so.' She shook her head. 'It was a very small affair. She'd been in a nursing home for nearly a year, and people here just seemed to forget her. Out of sight, out of mind, I suppose. It was very sad. I remember watching that little coffin sliding into the ground, and thinking that there really wasn't anything to show for her life except for you. Jim said the same. It made him more ambitious, in a way. After that, he got started at the printworks, and worked harder than I'd have believed possible for those first few years. I think he was doing it for her. And for you, David. And now he's gone as well.' She sighed.

'Taking the secret with him,' said David bitterly. 'If only I'd known–'

'It wouldn't have made any difference,' she consoled him. 'He'd never have told you. He promised Julia, you see. Now, we'll have to tell Philip he's safe to come back. We're still friends, aren't we, darling?'

Tears stood in her eyes, as she took his hand. The pathos in her voice filled his chest with a choking cloud of emotion, and he put his face close to hers.

'Course we are, Mum,' he said.

XII

Drew collected Karen from the hospital at seven. The nurses had tutted disapprovingly, and made irritated remarks about the bed going to waste for a whole night: people went home in the mornings, not the evenings. Karen was made to sign an alarming form, in which she promised to take all responsibility for her own welfare. But then she was free.

They went to bed early. He stroked her bruises with butterfly fingertips, and hummed her a lullaby. 'Stop it, you idiot,' she giggled. 'Don't be so sloppy.'

'I *feel* sloppy,' he said. 'I feel as if I'm being rewarded for good behaviour at last. Just when I was thinking it might never happen. Except it's all too good to be true. We'll wake up tomorrow and find it was all just a dream.'

'Stop talking about it,' she said. 'You're spoiling it.'

'Am I? How?'

'Tempting fate, for one thing. Two days ago you were telling me it was all my imagination. Now I suppose you're writing your speech for when she gets married.'

'She?'

Karen giggled again, and followed it with a long

sigh. 'All right – I admit I'm just as bad. I can see her now, with your nose and my hips. Aren't we stupid.'

'Yeah.'

The bedside phone roused them from a long contented cuddle. Drew reached out for it.

'Drew?' came Daphne's voice. 'You're not in bed, are you?'

'I am, actually,' he said, making no attempt to disguise his irritation.

'Ah. Sorry. But I thought you should know now – just in case you were still thinking stupid things about Lapsford–'

'What should I know?'

'I had the dog's body examined. You might have noticed it was missing. I went round late last night – accidentally setting off the alarm, as it happened; I wasn't quite firing on all cylinders – and took it to a friend of mine at the animal hospital lab. They did a postmortem this afternoon. She died of a large ovarian tumour. Nothing sinister at all. Must have had it for some time, but they don't always show symptoms until the vital organs are affected. There wasn't anything else.' She was speaking slowly, with considerable emphasis. 'I hope you understand what I'm saying. I don't want any more nonsense. Jim Lapsford died of a heart attack, in his own bed, and there's nothing more to be said on the matter. I'll see you tomorrow, okay?'

'Okay,' he replied, and put the receiver down.

So that was that, then.

CHAPTER EIGHT
TUESDAY

I

Waking early, with Karen warm and solid beside him, Drew felt a weight of worry and apprehension descend the moment he opened his eyes. Outside it was drizzling: summer was definitely finished. Even if there were weeks of sunshine to come, the long days and high temperatures were over with for another year. And for Jim Lapsford, they were over forever. Jim Lapsford would be cremated today, and Drew would have to let it happen. The dog had died of natural causes; wild tales about poisoned teabags and overdoses of herbal aphrodisiacs would only make him a laughing stock if he tried to convince the Coroner or the police now.

The pale tormented face of David Lapsford floated in front of him, and Drew wondered again what dark secrets lurked in that young man's background. Something more than ordinary grief and shock was certainly preying on his mind, and was proving alarming to his family and friends. For why had his mother insisted so vehemently that the funeral go ahead? Almost certainly because she wanted to protect someone. If not her son, then perhaps her lover. If Gerald Proctor had administered the final lethal blow, then Drew was on much shakier ground: that was not something that could be argued away on any dubious moral pretext. Society had taken an especially unsympathetic view of a man bumping off his lover's husband ever since King David took that doomed route in order to win Bathsheba.

The suicide of Craig Rawlinson was another factor. It had been devastating to Sid, which was a surprise: he'd evidently thought the boy was no good for his daughter. Guilt, Drew concluded, was the only explanation. Only guilt knocked a griefless person sideways.

Karen stirred beside him; he was immediately attentive. 'How are you?' he whispered. 'Did you sleep?'

'I'm stiff,' she said. 'And sore.'

'Let's have a look.' He peeled back her night-shirt and inspected the bruises. They were yellowing now, and much less angry. The skin looked tired and grubby, a greyish tinge marking the outline of the bruising. 'It's a miracle you weren't badly hurt,' he said. 'You could have broken your back.'

'I know. But this is bad enough. Do you really think – I mean, can there *really* be a baby in there?' She stared at him anxiously. 'It doesn't seem possible.'

'Time will tell,' he said. 'We should try not to get too excited. It's early days.' He leaned down and brushed his lips across her belly. 'But we'll do everything we can to see that it's all right. You're staying in bed today. And probably to-morrow as well.'

'Wouldn't it be wonderful if today was Wednesday, and the Lapsford funeral all over and done with? Everything would be back to normal, and you wouldn't be so preoccupied.'

He tried to smile, but made a poor job of it. 'Tell me, honestly,' he said. 'Do you think he was murdered?'

She shifted uncomfortably. 'I think he was helped on his way,' she prevaricated. 'He was living on the edge, and several things seem to have tipped him over all at once. But I'm not sure I believe that anybody deliberately killed him. No.'

It was a rush, making Karen a proper breakfast, getting himself ready for work, ensuring that there was something tasty for her to eat at lunchtime. The phone rang five minutes before he was due to leave.

'Drew? It's Laz here.' Drew's heart missed a beat. 'Bet you thought I'd never get back to you – it's been bedlam here. I ain't supposed to do jobs like this, you know. But just for you I came in early for one last look at your stomach contents sample. Just in the nick of time, eh? And guess what I found?' The excitement was crackling in Drew's ear.

'What?' he choked.

'Codeine! Good old-fashioned pain-relieving narcotic. Simple way to knock someone off his perch. Tastes a bit bitter, but works a treat. Plenty of it, I'd say, judging from the amount I found. Water-soluble and available over the counter. Probably the key to any number of unnoticed poisonings. Does that help you, old friend? Please tell me it does.'

'I think so,' said Drew slowly. 'It's rather a surprise – but yes. Thanks, Laz. Yes, it helps.'

As he put the phone down, there was a loud knocking at the front door. Still struggling to make sense of this latest revelation, he went to answer it, apprehension swelling inside him with every step.

The door was pushed back as soon as he unlocked it, and a tall brown figure strode in. 'I've got to talk to you,' she announced. 'If we're not careful, it's going to be too late. I can't give you any rational explanations, but I just bloody *know* Jim was murdered.'

Trotting alongside her, into the dining end of their main room, Drew ran a hand through his hair. 'How did you know where I live?' he asked inanely.

'I asked Olga,' she said, throwing herself down at the table. 'Can I smoke?'

He nodded automatically and stared at her. He wondered whether he was dreaming.

Roxanne observed his confusion, and gave his arm a cuff with the back of her hand. 'Now, come on,' she said, 'I need you to pull yourself together. You're the detective around here. Olga and I go way back. She was my bridesmaid. Don't worry about it.'

'Who says I am?' He felt the chilly anxiety that comes from the knowledge that people have been talking about you behind your back.

'Never mind that. Look, this is important to me, as you might realise. I don't want to spend the rest of my life wondering if my henbane killed him. And poor Susie's admitted that she supplied him with Viagra, so she's feeling just as bad. But knowing Jim, and how fit he was, I just don't believe that was enough to kill him. There *has* to have been something else.'

'There was,' Drew said. 'I've just found out about it. When he died, his system was full of codeine. In fact–' He stared at her, unseeingly; his head seemed full of electricity, as the connections were made. 'In fact, I think we might still be able to prove where it came from. Would you say it was possible to doctor a teabag without anyone noticing?'

'Codeine?' Roxanne was having trouble keeping up. 'What – the headache stuff? Jim would never take that. He didn't believe in painkillers, in pharmaceuticals.' She spoke emphatically, but Drew could see the doubt crossing her eyes. 'At least–' she amended.

'Viagra's a pharmaceutical,' he supplied.

She nodded reluctantly, obviously disturbed. 'You don't think he took it himself? Tell me the bit about the teabag again.'

Drew explained briefly, adding, 'I'd say someone gave him a teabag full of ground-up codeine, and told him it was best taken last thing at night. Probably added some story about it being good for his sex life.' He spoke with an irony not lost on Roxanne.

'Well, it wouldn't be difficult,' she confirmed. 'Obviously not those flimsy paper ones which are all sealed up – but you can get proper little muslin bags, with the top corners turned down and stapled shut – with a string and a paper tag. But who?' She shook her head impatiently. 'It must have been someone who knew his movements well. It seems such an odd way to poison somebody. I mean – there'd be the evidence of the teabag, for a start.'

'Teabags get thrown away. Teapots and mugs get washed up. If that *is* what happened, I think it's rather clever.'

'So how do you know about it?'

'Mrs Lapsford told me. She found it. It looked peculiar – had white crystals attached to it. They tasted bitter.'

'Then come *on*,' she urged. 'There's no time for messing about. We'll have to go and get it and take it to the police.'

He shook his head. 'Too late,' he said. 'She'll have got rid of it. She said she was going to. Besides, are you sure you want to call the police? Isn't it enough for you to know it wasn't you that killed him?'

She inhaled impatiently, and blew out smoke like a raging bull. 'I thought it was, but now I've changed my mind. I want revenge. I want to spit on the miserable swine who did this to Jim.'

'Christ! Look at the time!' Drew jumped up as if on fire. 'I should have been at work five minutes ago. You'll have to go. My wife's upstairs in bed, and I've got things to do.'

'Okay,' she said, stubbing out the cigarette on a convenient plate left over from supper the night before. 'Can I reach you this morning? I might need to speak to you again before the funeral.'

He frowned. 'Difficult – Daphne doesn't like us

getting personal phone calls. I think you'll have to get along without me. Sorry.'

'Well then – it cuts both ways. You're going to have to keep your wits about you and see if you can get the cremation stopped. This is murder, you know. Without question. I'm beginning to realise that just about the entire population of Bradbourne wanted Jim dead. Everybody *except* his son David, oddly enough.'

Drew shook his head wonderingly. 'He seemed the obvious one to me. Now – please go. Being late is a hanging crime at Plant's.'

Roxanne grinned at him, a sudden beam of fellowship and sympathy. 'Good luck, then,' she said, and let herself out.

In a whirl, Drew slammed out of the house at ten to nine.

He had his excuse ready when he parked his car in the small yard behind the office, and ran full tilt into Daphne as he hurried up the stairs to the workshop. 'Oh, God, I'm sorry,' he panted. 'Karen's home from hospital, but she's in bed, and sorting her out made me late.' He took some pleasure from pressing what had to be a sensitive nerve in his employer; he watched her with gratification as she winced.

'That's all right, Drew. How is she now?'

'Still very bruised,' he said, his face serious. 'I don't think she'll be going back to work this week.'

'It could have been very much worse for both of us,' Daphne said. 'As for my poor car–' She turned down the corners of her mouth in a parody of grief. Drew wondered at her manner;

she seemed a lot more light-hearted than he had expected. Remembering the phone call of the previous evening, he thought she ought at least to be embarrassed. Instead, she looked relaxed, in charge of the situation. Her dark hair, with its metallic flashes of grey, was smoothed down, and her make-up was immaculately applied.

'You've got twenty minutes before loading up for the nine forty-five funeral,' she reminded him. 'Pat's getting worried – he wants you to drive the lim. Vince and Little George have gone over to St Bridget's on a removal. Then there's Lapsford at eleven thirty. I don't suppose you've forgotten about that?'

She was looking hard at him: he had no idea how to respond. If he was going out on the first funeral of the day, that put the kybosh on any chance he might have had for some last-minute detective work. Was Daphne deliberately ensuring that this would be so? Or had she let fate decide? If Vince and Little George were out, that left only Pat, Sid, Drew and Big George to carry the coffin. 'You'll be conducting, then, will you?' he asked her. This was something that happened once or twice a month, if demands on the men were heavy.

Daphne nodded. 'Looks as if I'll have to,' she said.

Drew changed into the black suit, with its neat striped waistcoat, and gave his shoes a belated polish. Driving the limousine was a favoured job, and he would normally have been grateful to Pat for choosing him. As it was, he could hardly concentrate on the directions to the house where he was to collect an elderly widower and his bossy daughter. The two sat in the back of the car and bickered heatedly all the way to the crematorium. Drew's head felt full of flapping moths, stirring up his thoughts until they made no sense; he could barely remember how to drive. The drizzle had lightened, but not yet stopped completely; the swish of the windscreen wipers only added to the chaos in his mind.

As Daphne led the coffin into the chapel, and they deposited it neatly on the catafalque, he realised that, in not much more than an hour, he would be doing this very thing again with Jim Lapsford's coffin. The thought was enough to clear his head. Walking in step with Sid back to the waiting room, Drew murmured, 'Will you be on the next one? Or am I carrying with Vince?'

Sid shook his head slightly. 'We're all going. Pat's conducting. You, me, Vince and Big George'll carry. We'll be off now. See you later.'

Drew watched the other three bearers drive away in the hearse, no longer needed. Daphne had driven herself in her own car – or rather, the borrowed substitute for her own wrecked vehicle – and would return to the office once the mourners had all gone. Drew would wait, too, until they were ready to climb back into the limousine and be taken home again. Only then did he realise that he had even less time to himself before the Lapsford funeral than he thought. He would probably get back to the office at about ten to eleven, possibly even later. He'd be lucky to grab a cup of coffee before setting off again for Primrose Close.

And so it turned out. Before he knew it, he was sitting in the hearse with four other men, pulling up outside Monica's house. Working hurriedly in the front room, Pat screwed down the lid of the coffin, and then laid discreet pieces of nonslip webbing across it, to anchor the three large wreaths in place. The house seemed to be full of people. Drew lost all hope of trying to find any kind of clue as to Jim's death by codeine.

They only had four or five minutes in which to load the coffin and set off for the five-mile drive to the crematorium. Philip was driving his mother and brother, and a couple of other cars were drawn up further down the road, ready to follow the hearse. Vince would drive the hearse, while Pat walked in front of it to the top of the Close, in the time-honoured, time-consuming ritual which so often took families completely by surprise. Just as often, it seemed to embarrass them. Now and then, someone would call a halt to it after barely a dozen yards.

Today, they were about two minutes late when they turned out of the Close, and Pat was showing signs of anxiety. Drew turned to look at the cars behind them, wondering how their occupants were feeling. Was one of them a deliberate murderer? If so, was he now complacently assuming that the crime would go forever undetected?

Beside Drew, Sid coughed: a single barking sound, which attracted comment from Vince. 'Sounds rough,' he said.

Sid gave a shaky laugh, but said nothing. 'We're going to be for it,' grumbled Pat, driving slightly faster than was strictly dignified. 'There's another big funeral following this one. We're never going to be out in time. That Father Barry never knows when to stop–'

'Stop moaning,' said Vince. 'We're in plenty of time. So long as Sid doesn't let us down.'

Sid was coughing again, drawing whistling breaths between spasms. Drew looked at him; the man was shaking. 'What's wrong with you?' he asked.

Sid shook his head. 'Nothing,' he choked. 'Something went down the wrong way, that's all. I'll be fine in a minute.'

'You've got three minutes,' said Pat unfeelingly, from the driving seat. Sid took a deep careful breath, then another, and nodded.

'He's okay,' said Drew, catching Vince's eye. Vince scratched his head, and shrugged. 'Bit pale, though.'

'I don't care what colour he is,' said Pat grimly. 'Just so long as his legs are working.'

Drew sneaked another look out of the back window, his view partly obscured by the coffin and its surrounding flowers. 'Who's in that third car?' he wondered. 'The second one looks like people from the printworks.'

'Probably some of his lady friends,' muttered Sid, with a hint of bitterness. Drew remembered Sid's comment, almost exactly a week earlier, when he and Vince had carried Jim into the mortuary. *Women all over him.* His wits sharpened, now that the eleventh hour was upon him, Drew wondered whether perhaps Sid's wife had been one of Jim's ladies, hard to believe though it was. There was certainly some resentment in the man's tone.

'That could liven things up,' laughed Vince. 'I gather there were quite a few of them. I bet yesterday's wake was a barrel of laughs, if they all showed up.'

'They say he was careless about his dalliances,' remarked Drew, hoping to provoke further disclosures. He was well rewarded.

Sid turned, and smacked the coffin beside him, hard. 'Careless was his middle name,' he spat. 'And being careless can kill, as everybody knows. I wouldn't mind, except that my girl's got herself all tangled up in it, and she'll be lucky if she's not in real trouble when the truth gets out.'

The crematorium gates in sight, Drew rushed to prompt, 'What do you mean?'

Sid smacked the coffin a second time. 'Selling Viagra prescriptions to the randy old so-and-so, that's all,' he burst out. 'Her and that Craig. Criminal offence, that is. When I saw him on Saturday – doing as Susie asked me to, telling him to leave her alone – he went to pieces. Topped himself the same afternoon. How was I to know there was more to it than she told me? How'm I supposed to feel now – eh? And all because of this – bastard.' Coming from Sid's lips, the word carried enormous force. No wonder he was shaking, thought Drew, with sympathy. Calculations and conclusions were clicking together at the back of his mind. *That's one mystery cleared up, then,* a small voice said.

'We're here,' he said, gently. 'Buck up, now. It isn't your fault, Sid. None of it's down to you.'

The coughing fit seemed to have passed, but Drew noticed that Sid's hands were still unsteady as they slid to an immaculate halt outside the entrance to the crematorium chapel. Quickly, they climbed out of the hearse, and Pat tugged automatically at his sleeves as he stood waiting for Philip Lapsford's car to disgorge Monica and her sons. A second woman stood close to Philip, small and dark. *Must be his wife,* thought Drew dismissively. His own hands were unsteady now, and his guts were churning. *This is it,* he told himself. *The point of no return.*

As he'd assumed, the second car held Jodie, Jack and Ajash, who had been driving. They stood together, an ill-assorted trio, Jodie so tall, Jack so pale as to be almost green, Ajash groomed to such perfection he could easily have substituted for one of the bearers.

And as Drew had partly feared, the third car proved to contain not just Roxanne – standing broad and defiant, and clearly intent on meeting his eye – but also a bleary-eyed woman who looked like her sister and a younger blonde woman who all too obviously fitted the description of Lorraine Dunlop. She too looked so pale as to be green, with vivid eye make-up that only increased her tragic appearance.

With practised ease, Pat arranged everybody according to rank. The waiting room was already full of lesser mourners, who were chivvied into taking their places in the chapel. After a moment's consideration, he also sent Roxanne and her companions in ahead of the coffin. Strictly speaking, it should be family only who followed it in, but in a brief exchange with Monica, he was persuaded that the printwork colleagues could be permitted to share the honour. It was, after all, a very small family.

Drew and Vince took the foot end of the coffin, and waited for Sid and Little George to take the other as it rolled out of the hearse. With linked arms, they carried it down the short corridor, as they had done so often before; even in his limited time at Plant's, Drew had already done this perhaps twenty times. Pat went ahead. As they entered the chapel, it was clear that Jim had been known by a lot of people. About thirty were standing around the walls, an overspill from the seventy-five or so available seats. Towards the front, they passed Gerald Proctor the dentist, sitting with Dr Lloyd. The landlord of the King's Head was evident, with his large belly crammed into a dark suit. Shopkeepers; business people; one or two families; several men of Jim's age: all looking wary and uncomfortable.

The coffin successfully deposited on the catafalque, the bearers all withdrew. The organ surged to a climax and then fell silent. The monumental Father Barry stepped forward, and the funeral began.

With nothing else scheduled that day, the men were in no hurry to leave. They could wait for Pat, who, as Conductor, was obliged to supervise the funeral to its conclusion, and be available to the mourners – then they could all drive back to Bradbourne together in the empty hearse. Vince and the Georges wandered round to the office for their customary chat with Diana, in the Crematorium office; Drew hovered beside Sid. There was something he needed to ask. 'You knew Lapsford fairly well, didn't you?' he said casually.

Sid nodded reluctantly. 'But I don't really want to talk about him, all right? I should never have said what I did just now. It's a tough time for us.'

Drew had to persist. 'I mean – if you knew about his girlfriends and so forth – that's pretty personal information. He must have confided in you.'

Sid shrugged. 'Not specially. Common knowledge. Everybody knew what he was like. But I didn't know what Susie was doing – I only got the full story on Sunday. I didn't know then who she was supplying. Look, I just don't *need* this. I told you already. Give it a rest. Another hour, and he'll have gone up in smoke – and good riddance.'

'And yet the chapel's full,' Drew pressed on. 'That suggests that he was well liked.'

'Liked!' Sid squawked, loud enough for Drew to worry that people in the chapel might hear him. He flapped a subduing hand, and Sid dropped his voice from long habit. *'Nobody* liked the bastard. They're all in there now *celebrating.* There wasn't a wife in town safe from him. And precious few daughters. The man was an animal. All he ever thought about was sex. New ways of doing it. New women to add to his list. Humiliating for Monica. And his sons. They all had to go round with their eyes tight shut. His death has done this whole town a favour. Take my word for it.'

'But it wasn't a heart attack, was it? If you know

so much about him, you know that, as well as I do.' Drew braced himself for the response.

'Too late to worry about that now.' Sid forced a horrid grin. 'Nobody's ever going to prove anything now, are they? And don't try to tell me that a few Viagra tablets are going to kill him. My conscience is clear on that.' His expression contradicted his words. A sheen of sweat made his skin look sickly; his eyes flickered, without meeting Drew's, and he seemed to be having trouble breathing.

'*Your* conscience?' he echoed. 'I thought it was Susie's you were worried about.'

'Same thing,' muttered Sid.

A cold hand squeezed Drew's guts. The murky depths of Sid's private life were not something he wished to explore just now. Whatever Sid thought Susie had done, Drew didn't believe he had anything directly to do with Lapsford's death. As calmly as he could, he started to move away. 'I'll be in the vehicle,' he said. 'We'll be off soon.'

He then sought out Desmond, the Crematorium superintendent, and found him on the flower lawn, where tributes from the week's funerals were laid out, talking to a woman in black. Desmond noticed him hovering, and soon made his excuses. 'Can I have a quick word?' Drew muttered awkwardly. 'It's rather difficult–'

The superintendent raised his eyebrows and nodded, so Drew went on. 'How long have we got before you charge this coffin? I mean, the one going on now?'

Desmond considered. 'It'll be after lunch. Gavin's being very particular about getting his hour's break these days, so I'd say it'll be around two this afternoon before he gets to it. Why?'

Drew forced a laugh, and improvised desperately. 'You're not going to like this... But the chap's little dog died, and the wife thinks it'd be nice if they could go together. But she doesn't want the sons to know. They'd think she was crazy – and they might object to the idea. You know what people are like. So – if I can get back here with it by two, d'you think we might bend the rules a bit?'

Desmond worked his mouth thoughtfully. 'Can't you get it cremated at the vet's, and just put the ashes together later on? That's what most people do.'

Drew shrugged. 'Apparently that's not good enough. I know I shouldn't have, but I told her I'd have a go. She asked me on the quiet, so don't say anything to Pat or the others, will you? I don't even need to open the coffin – just sling the dog in with him when Gavin's charging it. Okay?'

Desmond sighed. 'I suppose it'll be okay. I'll have to see it first, though. I'm not having you dispose of your old granny pretending she's a German Shepherd.'

'Thanks, Des. I owe you one. I'll be back by two.'

'If you're not, then we're going ahead without you.'

Drew shivered at the rush of adrenalin caused by knowing he now had a mere two hours' grace. Two hours when he could hardly hope to speak to any of his suspects, since they'd be consuming the funeral baked meats. But suddenly anything seemed possible.

He joined Sid in the hearse. 'May as well wait for Pat. Don't suppose he'll be long,' Sid remarked. 'Not that I like hanging about here when I've got work to do in the mortuary.'

'He can't get back otherwise, can he?' queried Drew. 'There isn't another vehicle here.'

Sid frowned impatiently. 'All right, Mr Clever. So we'll wait. That's what I said.'

At five to twelve, the door at the back of the chapel opened, and Pat stepped out, holding the door like a flunkey for Monica and her sons to emerge. Mourners then streamed out, flowing to the end of the long strip of bowling-green lawn, where they stopped and began to talk mutedly amongst themselves. At the other end of the chapel, a new hearse arrived with another coffin, and the conveyor-belt system began to operate all over again. Drew visualised Lapsford's coffin being hauled out from the trapdoor behind the catafalque and trundled on a trolley to take its place in the queue for the furnace. He had consulted the day's schedule earlier, and knew that it was a full diary: five or six different funeral directors, most of them from the nearby city, used this crematorium, and it was rare for there to be fewer than ten funerals each day.

Monica was pale, her jaw clenched. She smiled vaguely at the people who approached her to offer their sympathy, but it was obvious that she did not want to linger.

Drew watched anxiously from the hearse. He saw Jodie walk over to Lorraine Dunlop, and say something to her: the beaky nose seemed to peck angrily downwards, and the smaller woman put a hand to her mouth in surprise. Suddenly, everyone else noticed, too. David Lapsford took a few long strides towards the women, followed by Monica, Jack and Roxanne. Drew had opened the big door of the hearse and jumped down before he could stop himself. Something important was unfolding, and there was no way he was going to miss it.

David got to Jodie first, and reached out to take her arm. Jack shadowed him. From the angle at which Drew stood, the two men looked like twins. Jack's hair might be shorter, his shoulders narrower, his heavy spectacles hiding the way his eyes sat in their sockets, but their profiles were identical. Astonished, he took a few steps closer, for a better look. The impression only grew stronger. David and Jack had the same mouth; the same nose; interchangeable ears. Was he seeing something that everyone else had always known and taken for granted – or had he made a momentous new discovery? Deep in thought, he retreated a little, aware that whatever disagreement was threatening had been diverted by David's timely intervention. Jodie spun on her heel and headed towards the car park, with Ajash trotting worriedly behind her, and Jack hovering uncertainly, close to Monica.

Jack Merryfield is David Lapsford's father, Drew said to himself. The encounter at David's home on Saturday afternoon, which now seemed so misguided and pointless, had involved some mention of David's parentage, he remembered. He needed to check out the relevance of this new information, but he had only two hours in which to do it. Which of these people would be most likely to provide him with the help he needed?

By five past twelve, the full team was back in the hearse and Pat was driving back towards Bradbourne. 'Went okay?' Drew asked him: as Conductor, Pat had been the only member of the crew to witness the actual funeral service.

Pat nodded. 'There were some tears,' he said. 'The blonde girl – the one that came in the following car. Was that the Dunlop wife? She cried the whole time. The gypsy woman had her arm round her.'

'She's not a gypsy,' muttered Drew.

'May as well be,' Pat corrected him. 'The way she lives.'

'What was that just now – with the girl from the printworks? Did you catch what she said to Mrs Dunlop?'

'Something about her having a nerve, showing up like that, pushing in where she wasn't wanted. All true. I was shocked myself.'

'The Mrs didn't seem to mind,' remarked Drew. 'Women can be funny like that. Unpredictable.'

'Yeah,' laughed Pat, and Vince and George echoed the laugh.

'You can say that again,' Vince added, with feeling. 'I've been having a right earful from Alicia lately. Worse than ever since she heard about young Rawlinson.' Drew barely listened. He was repeating, over and over, *Jack Merryfield is David Lapsford's father.* Almost bursting with the frustration of not knowing enough of the background, and the stress of the imminent cremation, he still had no idea what he should do next.

Everyone was presumably going back to Monica's house after the funeral. He glanced at the road ahead and behind, hoping to see one of the cars which had followed the hearse earlier. 'Where did they go?' he wondered aloud.

'Who?' asked Vince, confused by the interruption.

'The family. They left at the same time as us.'

'Most of them turned the other way. Going back to work, apparently.'

'Surely not!' Drew was shocked; the cold-bloodedness of it was almost offensive. Then he remembered. The wake had been the previous day. To gather everyone together for a second time for another round of tea and sandwiches would be excessive. How would Monica be feeling now, he wondered? Did he have the nerve to try and find her to ask?

The phrase 'back to work' stayed with him. Work was the printing place. Work was Jodie and Ajash and Jack Merryfield. And that little group included the people he might most fruitfully speak to. 'Drop me off here, will you,' he said suddenly, as they entered the outskirts of Bradbourne. The industrial estate was a quarter of a mile away. 'I want to, er – go and see someone. Tell Daphne I'm having a long lunch hour, because of Karen. She won't make a fuss about that.'

Walking into the industrial estate, Drew realised he ought to have gone back to Plant's first, to retrieve his car. He'd forgotten that he'd taken it that morning, since Karen had no need for it. It would take a precious twenty minutes now to get back to it – time that might make a crucial difference to what happened next.

And what happened next depended on the reaction of Jodie and Jack when he appeared in their workplace.

It was twelve twenty-five when he got there. The door, when he tried it, was locked: not surprising, he realised, when he paused to consider his next move. At the very least, the threesome would surely have gone for some kind of drink or meal after the funeral. He dithered for several minutes, torn between waiting for someone to turn up and needing to make the best possible use of the time.

While he stood there, a car drove up, with a woman at the wheel. He didn't recognise her, but she seemed to be heading directly for him. For a second he worried that she intended to drive right into him, but she braked in good time. She met his eyes, as she opened the car door. 'You're Drew, aren't you?' she said.

He nodded. 'I'm Alicia,' she introduced herself. 'Vince's wife.'

His mouth dropped open. 'It's all right,' she laughed, 'there's no mystery. I work in the Path Lab at the Nat Vic, and I know your friend Lazarus. I caught him doing some unofficial tests this morning, and he told me a bit about it. Well, obviously I'd heard about Jim, and I put two and two together. I was waiting for the hearse to get back to Plant's just now, to have a word with you or Vince. He told me where you were headed. And I just made an assumption – luckily I was right.'

'Right,' he said, still bewildered. 'But–'

'Look,' she said briskly, 'it's pretty obvious that Jim was deliberately given that codeine. Laz is in a state, because he thinks he'll be arrested for concealing important evidence. He wants your direct permission to discard that sample – but first he has to be sure that the cremation's actually taken place. We both know it can be quite a while after the funeral. So I said I'd come and find you, take you back to the hospital, and do the necessary together.'

'Right,' said Drew again. His mouth was dry. 'I'd better get my car. Otherwise I'll be stranded at the hospital.' It was the only way he could find to give himself some time to think.

'No problem,' she smiled. He noticed what a friendly open face she had, with intelligent eyes and a generous mouth. For the first time, in spite of his discussions with Karen, he wondered just what it would be like to be married to an undertaker for much of your adult life. Alicia made him think you probably had to be someone rather special.

She drove him back to Plant's, but waited discreetly out of sight while he went to fetch his car. He followed her the six miles to the hospital, impressed by her fast and competent driving. They pulled up side by side in the small car park next to the mortuary; only then did Drew become aware of a third car pulling up next to them. With some apprehension, he waited for a police constable to emerge and walk towards him. His thoughts were turning slowly, gradually, coalescing on the crematorium and a sense of stubbornly unfinished business there.

'Mr Slocombe?' asked the policeman.

'That's right,' nodded Drew, with a sense of impending doom.

'We have to ask you some questions, sir,' the officer continued. 'Would you please follow us back into town?'

'But–' Drew looked wildly at Alicia. 'I've got important things to do here.'

'It'll have to wait, I'm afraid. We've got an officer at your house, with your wife. Now, now, sir, there's nothing to worry about.' These last words spoken with a soothing motion of outspread palms, in response to Drew's anxiety-impelled forward jerk. 'Everything's quite all right. We know about her accident, and she's in no danger at all. We just wanted to settle a few little worries that have arisen. Would you follow us, please, sir? Now?'

Drew looked again at Alicia; she nodded sympathetically, and moved towards the mortuary. Drew could only hope that she would protect Laz from trouble, while at the same time preserving the stomach sample for a little while longer. It would be disastrous if it were destroyed at this juncture.

With a sigh of resignation, he turned his car round and followed the police car back to Bradbourne. It was five to one when they reached his house. Another police car was parked outside.

The next forty minutes passed grindingly slowly: Drew assumed the police had stopped the cremation, and therefore had all the time in the world. They allowed him five minutes upstairs alone with Karen, during which they exchanged puzzled guesses as to what was going on, and mutual reassurances. 'It's all terribly mysterious,' Karen said. 'It seems to be more to do with Craig Rawlinson than Jim Lapsford. Apparently they're here mainly because of what I said when we stopped on Saturday afternoon. Do you remember?' Drew shook his head. 'I said, "It's not David Lapsford is it?" I never thought they'd register it as remotely important.'

They all sat down in the living room: Drew and Karen, the policeman who'd stopped Drew at the roadside, and a policewoman. The police were very gentle and polite. And agonisingly slow. Unsure of the precise nature of the police officers' suspicions, Drew was careful not to give them too much information. It felt like walking on eggshells, where one false step could incriminate the wrong person. Images of Sid and Susie, Roxanne, Jodie, Monica and David flitted through his mind, each of them vulnerable to accusations of murder, or something very close to it. If he'd been certain, he would have freely informed the police. As it was, he felt all too aware of the trouble he might cause. And anyway, it soon became apparent that this was far from being an investigation into the death of Jim Lapsford.

Karen had been right – they were trying to satisfy themselves about Craig Rawlinson, in the light of a rumour they'd heard concerning the sale of drugs. Did they have any idea why he had hanged himself? None at all, Drew and Karen insisted. They had never seen him alive – apart from Drew's glimpse of him arguing with Susie on the pavement a week ago. Had they any knowledge of his criminal activity? Certainly not. What precisely did they have in mind, Drew demanded, losing his patience. The policeman rubbed his jaw, and indulged in a long thoughtful silence. 'Young Mr Rawlinson was not unknown to the police,' he said, repressively. 'Now, perhaps we could proceed?'

The questions continued. What exactly did they know of David Lapsford, who had evidently been a close friend of Rawlinson? Why had Karen believed the body in the field might be that of young David?

Glancing at the clock, Drew saw that it was now one forty-five. With a growing sense of disbelief, it occurred to him that they really had no suspicions about Jim's involvement at all. Was all his work going to be in vain? The following ten minutes, spent discussing the relationship between Craig and Susie, with Drew earnestly trying to convince them that he knew almost nothing about any of these people, confirmed this assumption.

Then something snapped. 'Tell me – *please* tell me – why you're here,' Drew begged them. 'We're getting nowhere, and I still haven't any idea what you're hoping I'll say. Is this an investigation into the death of Craig Rawlinson or the death of Jim Lapsford? Or is it just such a quiet day, you thought you'd pass it in a pleasant chat?'

The police officers exchanged a baffled glance. *'Lapsford?'* said the man. 'Why would we investigate Lapsford?'

'He's dead,' said Karen, with a little laugh. 'Doesn't that count for something?'

'Rawlinson's dead, too,' said the policeman. 'And not by natural causes. You seemed to think David Lapsford was involved. We just ran his name through the computer in the office, and found a file on young David. Unstable, missing from home for a year, been in odd bits of trouble. But he's not dead.'

'No, but his father is,' said Karen, with a sigh. 'We thought you knew that.'

Another glance was exchanged. 'Did we?' said the man.

The woman shrugged. 'Don't think so.'

'No, you wouldn't, because the doctor signed him up,' said Drew patiently. 'Put him down as a heart attack. And when you asked me so politely to accompany you back here for questioning, I assumed it was not unrelated to that fact. Because, just at that moment, I was going to instruct a lab technician to hand over some evidence that Jim Lapsford was poisoned. I was going to do that to save him from being implicated, because I thought I had time to go back to the crematorium, and insist they phone the police, and the Coroner, and declare it to be an unsafe certificate in the light of new findings. And then I thought they could do a postmortem and just possibly find enough tissue – despite his being embalmed – to prove he was poisoned.'

'Wait, wait,' pleaded the policeman. 'You lost me five sentences ago. All we've got is a suspicion of some link between Rawlinson and a break-in at Plant's, where you work, which might have something to do with David Lapsford. Quite honestly, we thought it was a fool's errand. Just somebody at the station trying to be clever. But when we cottoned on to the fact that Mrs Slocombe here was hit by Miss Plant's car, it seemed worth following up. Too many coincidences always make the police uncomfortable, you see. And now you've gone charging off with some story about poison. You'll have to start again, sir, if you don't mind.'

Drew had just opened his mouth to do so, when a bleeper went off in the policeman's pocket. He scanned the room for a telephone. 'Sounds as if I'm needed,' he said weightily. 'Could I use your phone, do you think?'

Drew nodded. 'It's in the hall.' Another glance at the clock: one minute to two. Whether or not Gavin was back from lunch, whether or not Lapsford was next in line for charging, he felt an overwhelming sense of lost opportunity. The great slough of mist and plodding procedure that was the average police mind was certain to defeat any efforts he might make to see justice done. He looked at Karen helplessly.

'I really think,' she began, addressing the policewoman, 'that you should listen to us–'

'Please don't worry, madam,' came the calmly patronising reply. 'We–' She never finished. Her colleague came into the room with rather more animation than he left it.

'We're needed,' he said shortly. He turned to Drew. 'Thank you, sir. We'll follow up what you've told us as quickly as we can. You realise that you might be required for a further interview at some stage?'

Drew began to laugh, at first quietly, but then with rising hysteria. 'Yes, officer. Forgive me. It's been a very long week.'

Left on their own, Drew and Karen sat together on the sofa, his arm across her shoulders. 'Are you all right?' he asked her, more than once. 'This can't be doing you any good, not in your condition.'

'I'll survive,' she said cheerfully. 'It's all rather exciting, isn't it?'

'I wish I could be there when they find they're too late and Jim's already ashes.'

'What about poor Monica?' she said suddenly. 'This isn't the end of it for her, is it? Shouldn't you try and see her, perhaps warn her? I can tell you aren't going to just settle down here to wait for whatever might happen next.'

He kissed her gratefully. 'If you're really all right, I think I might just do that,' he said. 'I knew the police were dim, but this is ridiculous. You show them an obvious murder, right under their noses, and they go running round in circles, like a dog chasing its tail, following up everything but what's important.'

'That's not really fair,' she objected. 'You were miles ahead of them. You've had a whole week. And you didn't really give them much to go on. I bet you they'll be wide awake once they've had a chance to think.' Drew pursed his lips doubtfully. 'Go to Primrose Close,' she said, giving him a little push. 'The story's not over yet. There's a fat lady waiting to sing somewhere, you just see if there isn't.'

In Primrose Close, something seemed to be happening. Cars were clustered along the road, as close as they could get to number twenty-four. The front-room curtains were closed, which seemed odd, and Dottie from next door was standing in her own garden, gazing in puzzlement at Monica's upstairs windows. When she saw Drew she urgently beckoned him to her. 'I heard some shouting,' she said. 'There seems to be some sort of disagreement going on.'

'Who's there, do you know?'

She shook her head, and indicated all the cars. 'We didn't think they'd come back here – not after yesterday. She hasn't got any food in, you know. Sarah and I said we'd keep an eye on it while they were all at the funeral. You know – in case of burglars.'

Drew nodded. 'I think I'll go and see if I can find out what's going on,' he said. 'Don't you worry.'

Drew began to walk up the short front path. Before approaching the door, he stepped sideways to peer in through the front window, through the slight gap between the lace curtains. He saw Monica and Jodie sitting together on the sofa, both heads turned towards him, as if they'd been expecting him. Jodie got up, and came to the window, pushing back the curtain.

Drew waved his hand in a circle, forefinger pointing at the front door, indicating his wish to be allowed in. Jodie disappeared out into the hall, and he moved expectantly to the doorstep, leaning his head towards it to catch the sound of her approaching.

Louder than expected, her voice came clearly, 'Can I let him in then? David? Can I?' A very muffled reply seemed to give her permission, and the door was unlocked and slowly pulled inwards.

'Didn't expect to see you again,' were her welcoming words. 'Hurry up. Things have got a bit – complicated in here.'

In the hallway, Drew automatically looked up the stairs, which had become almost familiar to him. 'What's going on?' he said.

Jodie's face was drawn, grooves running from nose to the corners of her lips, revealing fear, shock and a kind of horror. She moved stiffly, as if under someone else's will rather than her own. She spoke flatly. 'He wants you upstairs. Don't worry – I don't think he'll hurt you.'

'Who? Who are you talking about? Who's here?'

'Monica's with me. And Jack's upstairs with David. Philip went to get some food, a few minutes ago. That was when it happened. I think David was just waiting for him to go.'

Drew felt cold with apprehension. 'Something's wrong, isn't it? Something's going on up there.'

Jodie shook her head slowly. 'It's got to be straightened out, once and for all. I said I'd sit with Monica until they settled everything. But – well, you never know with David. He told us not to go up there. But I think he might let you in. He probably wants you to understand.' She gripped her hands tightly together.

As if in a dream, Drew began to climb the stairs. Something had happened in the short time since the funeral, something he couldn't guess at. His own part had shifted dramatically from a peripheral doubter, uneasy about the cause of Jim's death, to a position right at the heart of events. He wasn't at all sure he liked it.

David appeared in the doorway of the master bedroom, where Drew and Vince had come only a week before to collect Jim's body. 'What do you want?' he snarled. 'Bit late now, isn't it? We should have listened to you sooner, shouldn't we?' He held a large knife tightly in his hand, and spun round at a sound from the bedroom. 'Don't move!' he ordered. 'Just you stay where you are.'

Propelled by a grim curiosity, Drew followed David into the room. Jack Merryfield sat on the foot of the bed, hands gripping his own thighs. His glasses were huge on his face, hiding his expression.

'Why the knife?' asked Drew. He looked again at the implement, a serrated-edged carving knife, which would not make a clean wound if stabbed into someone. It would not slice through flesh cleanly like a razorblade. It would hack and saw. It would bite and sting. It would hurt to be attacked by such a knife, but it might not easily kill.

'He says he's my *father,*' David accused, staring at Jack, eyes bulging. 'He called me *son*, said I could go and live with him now. Don't you think that's *disgusting?* He was my Dad's best friend. All those years, without saying a word. And now–' He choked on the strength of his own feelings.

Drew said nothing, silenced by the shock of having his own observation so quickly confirmed. The sense of being in a dream persisted.

'Then why–?' he managed faintly, nodding at the knife.

David looked down at the knife in his hand with a momentary surprise. 'I just want to *kill* him,' he said. 'Look at him.'

'He looks harmless enough to me,' Drew ventured. 'Can't you just talk about it, without all this drama?'

'You don't understand,' David grated. 'You haven't *got* it yet, have you?'

'Please, Davy, calm down,' came a soft voice from the doorway. 'Do as Drew says, and let's talk about it properly. Like grown-ups.' Monica stood there, looking sadly at Jack sitting dumbly on her bed.

'Go away!' David screamed. 'I told you to stay out of it. You've done enough damage. Go downstairs and *stay* there. Don't let anybody else up, or I'll cut him. Not even Philip when he gets back. I'll cut his throat.' He sneered exaggeratedly at Jack, who turned his face away. But Monica held her ground.

Without warning, Jack stood up, his hands in tight fists at his sides. Automatically Drew looked from face to face, checking the similarities; they seemed to have faded somewhat since that morning, but they were still discernible.

'It's true,' said Jack, having drawn a deep

breath. 'Whether you like it or not. And I'm not putting up with any more of this. Do what you like with me – I *am* your father. I promised Jim and Julia not to tell you, so the adoption would work out. So I wouldn't be around to unsettle you. It was them, not me, who wanted to keep the secret. So I got the job at Capital, with Jim, so I could watch you grow up, and hear about what you were doing.' He kept his gaze on the floor, his shoulders still awkward with strain. 'I planned how I'd tell you, after the funeral. I thought you'd be pleased. I just couldn't go on any longer, you see.' The pathos of these final words affected each listener differently. Drew closed his eyes on the sudden wash of tears that filled them; Monica moaned briefly. But David was further enraged.

'Pleased!' he echoed, and lifted the knife in a swift underarm swing. As Drew opened his eyes, he judged the knife's trajectory, calculating that it would catch Jack in mid-chest. His medical training flashed signals of alarm – pneumothorax at the very least; at worst extensive lung damage, possibly the heart involved too. Yet the swing could not be stopped – both David and Jack were beyond Drew's immediate reach. He flung himself forward and pushed Jack back onto the bed just as the knife connected. Jack and Monica both cried out loudly. David made a hissing sound, and pulled back, still holding the knife, before blindly lunging a second time. Stumbling, Drew tried to keep his eyes on it. When the pain struck his right side, he flinched away, landing on top of Jack.

Jack began to talk, the words flooding out now. 'Yes – pleased,' he repeated. 'He was a lousy father. I couldn't stand to see it any more. That day you came and asked him for a job – the look in your eyes when he sent you packing. And he was going back on his promise.'

'Promise?' echoed Monica, torn between agonised concern over David and a need to understand exactly what Jack had done. Jack's words had emerged close to Drew's ear, the rush of sound merging with his panic at the continuing pain from his side.

But Jack didn't say any more. Slowly the three men were assessing the aftermath of David's attack.

Liver, Drew kept thinking. *He's stuck the knife in my liver.*

There were footsteps and voices on the stairs. A strange high-pitched twittering came from Jodie, threading through curt phrases from the policemen. Without ceremony, they strode into the room, flanking David and easily taking the knife away from him. Drew realised that he had been waiting for further blows to come stabbing down on himself and Jack. The relief was pathetically disabling, removing all vestige of dignity. 'He's hurt me,' he whimpered. 'Look.' Fearfully, he took his hand away from the hurt place and looked at it, pulling up his shirt warily. The amount of blood was much less than he'd expected, the wound disappointingly superficial.

One of the policemen also looked. 'We'll have that seen to, sir. There's an ambulance on its way. Is the other gentleman injured?'

Clumsily, Drew and Jack disentangled themselves and made a more careful assessment of the damage. Jack was found to be unhurt. 'He was going to kill me,' said Jack, wonderingly. 'He tried to kill his own father.' He stared up at David. 'You'd have been better off with me, you know. Jim Lapsford was a bastard, through and through. He never cared about you.' He glared round the room. 'He never cared about *any* of you.'

'What did Jim promise?' Monica persisted. 'You must tell me.'

'He conned me,' Jack spat. 'Took me for a right fool, he did. After I let him use my computer, wasting his time on his stupid dirty pictures, thinking about nothing but sex – he owed me something. Owed me for *him–'* he dipped his head at David – 'as well as all the rest.'

Monica's hand was flat against her upper chest. 'Dirty pictures?' she whispered, flushing crimson.

'Oh, that wasn't it. Not really. He promised to give me a good reference, when I went for *his* job.' This time he swivelled round to glare at Drew, who was still tremblingly exploring his injury.

A silence fell as everyone tried to absorb this bizarre new twist. '*His* job?' queried Jodie. 'You're mad. You wanted to be an undertaker?'

'I wanted to be close to Daphne,' Jack muttered. 'Jim knew I'd been carrying a torch for her for years, getting nowhere. But when her bloke moved out, I decided I was in with a chance. Jim said he'd do me a good reference –

but he conned me. Told Daphne I wasn't good with people, and would never make a good impression on a funeral. Sid Hawkes showed me what he'd written.'

David, now in the tight grip of the flanking policemen, seemed not to have heard anything since Jack's first remark. He struggled briefly, and then shouted, 'I didn't kill anybody. And *you're* not my father!'

'No, you didn't kill anybody, Davy,' came Jodie's voice from the knot of people on the landing. 'But *he* did. I've been stupid, haven't I, Jack? It was all there, from start to finish, and I never saw a thing.'

Jack looked steadily at her. Then he took off his glasses. 'He's like me, isn't he?' he said, with a little smile. 'Nobody ever noticed how like me he is. The glasses were Jim's idea. I don't need them, you know. Then he suggested a beard as well. I've worn this disguise for twenty-four years, just in case any clever dick thought young David looked like me. Jim made sure I never got the chance to betray the secret. Always kept me dangling with his promises and phony friendship. But he was just using me, the same as the rest of you.'

'So you poisoned him?' Jodie asked faintly. 'After all these years?'

Jack's smile grew more cunning. 'Don't know what you're talking about,' he said. 'And nobody's ever going to prove anything, now he's been cremated.'

In stunned silence, the whole party clattered downstairs. A paramedic appeared and inspected

Drew's wound. 'Nothing serious,' he concluded. 'Just a shallow cut.'

Drew struggled to recover some of his poise; he had, after all, saved Jack Merryfield from a probable nasty injury. Muzzily, he looked at the people in the room. 'I won't prefer any charges against Mr Lapsford,' he said, with an effort. 'I'm sure you can let him go now.'

'I'm afraid not, sir,' said the senior policeman he'd spoken to outside. 'Threatening behaviour. Holding a person hostage at knife-point. Disturbing the peace. Can't just let him go after all that, now can we?'

'But it isn't *David* you should be arresting,' said Jodie, her voice loud with frustration. 'It's *him*.' She pointed at Jack. 'He killed Jim!'

'All right, Miss – we'll look into that, all in due course. Although, if the body has indeed been cremated–' He shook his head.

Drew felt a sense of crashing disappointment. He had no doubt that Jodie was right: at last it was making sense. From the look on Jack Merryfield's face when she'd accused him, there had been little room for doubt. But an expression suggestive of guilt and some resentful words spoken in the heat of the moment would hardly qualify as evidence in court.

As preparations were being made to leave the house, Drew looked back and caught Monica's eye. She was crying; Jodie was holding her hand. Drew hesitated, wanting to console her. 'David's going to be okay,' he offered.

'I'm not crying for David,' she mumbled, almost too low for him to catch. 'I'm crying for

Jack.' The tears ran without stopping.

Disappointment was almost tangible in the room. Had it all come down to this? David reprimanded for threatening behaviour, and Drew going home with an Elastoplast on his side, before having to explain himself to Daphne? He felt like crying himself.

A beeper went off; at the same time, the telephone warbled. One of the policemen answered it, and then handed it to his superior. 'Coroner's Officer, sir,' he said, with evident surprise.

The man listened. 'Yes ... that's right,' he said. 'Not as far as I know... Good God!...' The conversation was abruptly cut short.

'They've held back the cremation,' he said. 'The Superintendent had a call which made him stop it. Perhaps you, Miss–' nodding to Jodie, 'and you, sir–' to Jack, 'would be kind enough to come with us and answer some questions. And if you, sir and madam–' encompassing Monica and Drew, 'would remain where we can find you for the next day or so, we might get to the bottom of all this. All right?'

Karen had gone back to bed when Drew reached home. She was pale, and he saw tearstains on her cheeks. 'What is it?' he demanded, already knowing.

'I'm bleeding,' she told him.

So am I, he wanted to say, still unsteady from the day's traumas. Instead, he sat down next to her, and pulled her to him. 'How much?' he asked.

'Not much. But there shouldn't be *any*. Oh,

Drew. Why is it so difficult? It isn't supposed to be like this?'

'Look,' he murmured, resting his cheek against hers, 'it doesn't necessarily mean anything. You've had the test, remember? Women often get spotting in the early stages. Would it help take your mind off it, if I tell you what's been happening to me?'

She nodded, like a little girl. 'I was worried about you. You've been gone for ages.'

He told her the whole story, embellishing it with imitations of the bewildered policemen, and comments on his own part in the action, but leaving out his reaction to his own minor injury. Then he leaned back with a deep sigh. 'It's out of our hands now, anyway,' he said. 'So much for Drew Slocombe, Ace Detective.'

'Mmm,' she murmured sleepily beside him. He wondered how much she'd really cared about who killed Jim Lapsford.

There was still plenty of unfinished business, Drew realised, as he carefully extracted his arm from behind Karen's shoulders, and tiptoed downstairs. He had to phone Daphne and explain his absence from work that afternoon. And he had to straighten out his story before the police summoned him for interview. A nervous fluttering in his stomach reminded him that he could yet find himself in trouble. He could be accused of withholding evidence of a crime, along with Lazarus, who had only wanted to help. He could even lose his job. And Karen could lose the baby – if there had ever been a baby there to lose. It might have been simply what they called a 'chemical pregnancy'. It could all have been wishful thinking from the start.

It had been a long week. Wearily, he picked up the phone to call Daphne. When Olga answered it, he heard an unusual level of animation in her voice; when he asked to speak to Daphne, she almost squealed. 'About time too! She's been hoping you'd call all afternoon. She's got loads to tell you.'

Daphne came on quickly, her voice loud with portentousness. 'Drew, we're in trouble. Not just us, but Julian Lloyd, Sid, Susie – I don't know who else. Why ever didn't you say something to me from the start? It's obvious now that Lapsford should have gone to the Coroner. It's all a serious mess – it is really.'

'You wouldn't have listened to me,' said Drew, too tired to watch his words. 'Nobody wanted to listen to me.'

She paused a moment. 'Well, I think you're wrong about that. But we won't argue. Too late now.'

'So what changed their minds?' asked Drew, with a vestige of curiosity.

'Pardon?'

'Why didn't they just go ahead with the cremation?'

'Oh, that was the dog,' she said shortly, as if it were obvious.

'The *dog?*' Drew echoed.

'Desmond phoned me at two, to ask if the dog was coming or not. I said I didn't know what he was talking about, there wasn't any dog. Or not any more, because it had been disposed of already. I said you knew that perfectly well.'

'We never squared that with Monica,' Drew remembered. 'And she never asked.'

'Anyway, it seems that Desmond was bothered by the fact that you'd lied to him, and decided to wait a bit longer. He sensed something must be up. Didn't want to be accused of rushing things afterwards. There's nothing so final as a cremation, as he knows all too well.'

'So now there'll be a postmortem. He *was* poisoned, you know. We've got evidence.'

'If you think they'll find it after Sid's embalming, you might be disappointed,' she reminded him. 'He does a pretty thorough job.'

'We'll just have to see then, won't we,' said Drew. 'Just tell me – a few more things.'

'Go on then?'

'Have I still got a job?'

'Come on,' she laughed sarcastically. 'Our only hope is to make you the hero of the hour. I couldn't fire you now, even if I wanted to. The press would crucify me. Not to mention the good citizens of Bradbourne. What else can I tell you?'

'Did you know that Jack Merryfield was in love with you?'

He heard the deep sigh. 'Of course I did,' she said. 'After what happened last Easter, I could hardly be in any doubt.'

'Which was?' he prompted.

Her voice dropped; perhaps Olga was within earshot. 'Jack and Jim and I were all in the King's Head one evening, and Jim started trying it on with me. Nothing unusual in that, but Jack wasn't having it. He'd had a few drinks, and came up to us outside, spitting in Jim's face, calling him every filthy name you can think of. Said he wasn't fit to lick my shoes – stuff like that. Then he got all maudlin, saying I was the finest woman in Bradbourne, and nobody was going to lay a hand on me while he was around. I laughed it off, but I got the message clear enough. Scared me a bit, to be honest.'

'But he never took it any further.'

'Not till he applied for your job. No way was I going to have him around here every day. Far too complicated.'

'So it wasn't Jim's bad reference that decided you?'

She laughed. 'I barely even read it. Chucked it in the bin, I think.'

Where Sid happened to find it, and showed it to the wretched Jack, thereby tipping him over the edge from resentment to murder, Drew concluded. *Such is fate.* 'There is just one more question. Why did you visit Karen in hospital?'

'Julian asked me to. He suspected about Susie selling illegal Viagra, you see.'

'I see,' he lied weakly, too tired for any more. 'Thanks for telling me.'

'That's okay, Drew. See you tomorrow.'

Before he could warm up some soup for a much-needed supper, there was a knock on the door. When he opened it, there was nobody there: just an envelope on the doormat. He opened it cautiously.

Dear Drew (I hope I can call you that?)
I want to thank you for being such a friend to me and my family. If it hadn't been for you, Jim's murder would have gone unnoticed, and I would always wonder why he died when he did. I saw Jack's face this afternoon, as I think you did, and I knew it was his doing. That teabag came from him. He must have given it to Jim on Monday evening, telling him some story about it being good for his virility. I've taken it off the compost heap, and I'll give it to the police. I dare say there'll be others like it at Jack's place. I feel terribly sorry for Jack, of course. Jim behaved so badly towards him, if what he says is true. I just hope the courts will be sympathetic, too.

I didn't know Jack was David's father. When Julia developed MS, Jim wouldn't have any more children, in case they inherited it. He didn't know it wasn't hereditary until after he'd had his vasectomy. But he was good to the boy in the early years. Even David would admit to that.

I know Jim wasn't the ideal husband. I always knew about his women, but it didn't take anything away from me. I led my own life, as you probably realise. But I never wished him dead. It seems important that you should know that. David didn't, either. It was a terrible mistake on Jack's part to think we'd be better off without Jim. I won't ever forget him saying 'I thought you'd be pleased'. Even with the life insurance money, which I'm going to share between the boys, we'd all rather still have Jim alive. At least, I have to believe we would.

Jodie's going to drop this letter in for me. She's been such a tower of strength these past few days. She wasn't kept very long at the police station, and then came straight back here to me. I don't deserve such kindness, I know.

Well, I just wanted to say thank you. I wasn't always polite to you, and you must have been very worried about everything that happened. I hope the injury to your side will heal quickly.

With very best wishes,
Monica Lapsford
P.S. Think of me tomorrow –
it's my fiftieth birthday!!

Which more or less tied up all the loose ends, he thought, as he settled down next to Karen. She had slept all evening, and he hadn't heard her going to the bathroom: if a full-scale period had started, she'd have been woken up by it at least once. Perhaps they would be spared the heart-break after all.

He thought about Jack Merryfield, trying to get inside his head, to grasp the tangled reasons for doing what he did. To poison somebody, you needed a long slow drip-drip of resentment, building up day by day, year by year, to the idea; the careful planning; the secret nursing of a long-term campaign. The simple idea of supplying a doctored teabag was as impressive as it was unlikely. Jack must have known Jim's routines, known about his own personal teapot and Monica's preference for coffee. He must have hunted down the ideal bag design, with a single staple holding the thing together.

And who would have guessed Jack's quiet persistent passion for Daphne? Jim's betrayal over that; his imperfect parenting of David; his unsavoury sexual proclivities: it all added up to a powerful hatred. Combined with the knowledge of a handsome life-insurance payout, which Jack might have assumed would benefit David. No, Drew had no doubt that there had been ample motivation.

Daphne wasn't really angry with him; Monica Lapsford was positively grateful. There'd be evidence enough to convict Jack Merryfield of poisoning Jim Lapsford, even if it didn't amount to a capital murder charge. Jim's use of other substances might lead to trouble for Susie Hawkes and Roxanne Gibson, but the loss of young Craig might soften any judgments against them. Once they got it straight, the police and the courts might conclude that most people had suffered enough. Jack would get a mandatory sentence for murder, and David might even acknowledge the man as his father. Eventually.

The sounds of traffic and an overhead plane came through the open window. Drew thought about Bradbourne, and its people. *A town with no soul,* Roxanne had said. Searching for a pattern in the events of the past week, Drew could find little, other than a sense of lives frustrated and constrained by the urge for temporary thrills, and the avoidance of responsibility. Roxanne had dropped out of society. Monica had abandoned any effort to improve her marriage, turning instead to her boss for distraction. Decent people like Vince and Alicia seemed mere bystanders, doing no harm, but very little good, either. And then there was Daphne Plant, amoral scavenger, looking for the easy way out, fudging the rules, processing dead bodies efficiently and without emotion. She bore her own burden of responsibility. Where she could bring comfort, she brought only a cool politeness; where she could provide a check on the bending of regulations, she only colluded. Whatever might be going on in her personal life, it did not give her the right to exploit and manipulate her customers and her employees.

A soft snore from Karen brought him back to his own life. A lot had changed in recent days. The emotional switchback of potential fatherhood had already carried him away, even if this time it turned out to be a false alarm. The almost accidental blundering into a job as an undertaker would have to be seriously reconsidered. If he did choose to stay, he vowed to himself that he would approach his work with the integrity and commitment that he knew was necessary for his own peace of mind. He would stay in Bradbourne, and see what he could do, in his own small way, to lighten its lack of soul.

The publishers hope that this book has given you enjoyable reading. Large Print Books are especially designed to be as easy to see and hold as possible. If you wish a complete list of our books please ask at your local library or write directly to:

Magna Large Print Books
Magna House, Long Preston,
Skipton, North Yorkshire.
BD23 4ND